D0342537

SOUTHWEST BRANCH

THE LOVING WRATH OF ELDON QUINT

A NOVEL

CHASE PLETTS

This is a work of fiction. Names, characters, organizations, places, events, and incidents are either products of the author's imagination or are used fictitiously.

Copyright © 2021 Chase Pletts
All rights reserved.

No part of this book may be reproduced, or stored in a retrieval system, or transmitted in any form or by any means, electronic, mechanical, photocopying, recording, or otherwise, without express written permission of the publisher.

Published by Inkshares, Inc., Oakland, California
www.inkshares.com

Edited by Adam Gomolin, Matt Harry & Barnaby Conrad
Cover design by M.S. Corley
Interior design by Kevin G. Summers

ISBN: 9781942645948
e-ISBN: 9781947848047
LCCN: 2017955469

First edition

Printed in the United States of America

For Leo

LIKE OLD TIMES

ONE

ANOTHER SHOT SANG OUT OF THE WHORL. THE FARMER looked back, but the blizzard had swallowed everything—the forest, the river, the men shooting at him. As he cut through waist-high powder, he levered his Winchester. A spent shell ejected, the one he'd used trying to repay the man who'd shot his horse. It was blinding white in every direction. All he could do was let instinct point him away from his pursuers, and toward his boys.

As he struggled onward, the snow thinned underfoot. It was at his thighs, then his knees, then his ankles. The ground became slippery and groaned with each step. His left leg plunged suddenly, icy water gushing into his boot. He fell on his hands and yanked his leg from the jagged hole. Had he crossed onto the river? The Missouri rarely froze, but this winter had been ruthless.

He squinted back the way he'd come. Against a smudge of trees, a few small shapes, little more than gray blots, loped through the squall. He edged out farther from the bank, testing the ice. It winced but held his weight. When he looked back, the shapes were larger and more defined.

Wind had scraped off wide swaths of snow, exposing a slippery milk-blue surface. He struggled to keep his feet as he ran. The snow began to rise. It was up to his knees when something gangly swiped past his face.

He looked up at a copse of alders swaying in the wind. The branch that had fallen at his feet looked like a claw breaking out of the ice. He knew every bight and contour of that river. There was no way he'd crossed into Nebraska already, so what were the trees doing there? They sprouted from a little hump of land that looked like that island the boys liked to stop at for a nap. They'd caught a bushel of walleye there two summers past. It was smack in the middle of the river.

He climbed the hump. When he was in the middle of the trees, he crouched with his rifle and scanned his backtrack but couldn't see much past the end of the barrel. With his teeth he pulled off a glove and blew some life into his hand. When he dug into his ammo pouch, the cold casings stuck to his fingers. He loaded the carbine, then backed through the understory and braced his rifle against a thick tree trunk.

There was no sign of the shapes, no sign of anything but the blowing snow.

With the surprise of his position he could drop two, maybe three. But how many were there? He'd only just crested the ridge when they'd started shooting. Some son of a bitch had put a bullet in Delilah. There were five or six, maybe more. Not the most favorable odds, but it was that or keep running farther from his boys. If he didn't head back soon, the weather would get him. The weather or a bullet. The smarter scheme was to hide where he was, let them pass by, then double back toward home.

The butt end of the Winchester made a decent shovel. He scraped loose powder from around the base of the tree, then huddled against the trunk and buried himself until he was completely entombed. Raising the brim of his tattered silverbelly, he created a slit to see from. Seated in that cold sepulcher, he considered praying. He'd been saved years ago, but asking God for help still made him uneasy. So he prayed for the storm—that it would gain in potency and drive those no-account bushwhackers back into whatever hole they'd slithered from.

God wasted no time scorning the Farmer's prayers. They appeared in the storm, ghosts gradually collecting matter. He counted six. Armed with pistols and long rifles, they crossed the ice on big loping steeds, dry powder washing in broken waves over their gaskins. As they neared the island they fanned out across the ice. Either they were spreading the weight around, or they were about to surround him. Then one rider veered straight at the island and the Farmer's heart shot into his throat.

If he died there, it would be weeks before anyone discovered his body. And if the thaw came and broke up the river, they might never find him at all. He fought back the urge to go for his rifle. But he was still watching the rider come. Daddy used to say that you never look at a man unless you want him looking back. *So lower your damn head*, he told himself. *Shut your eyes, and don't breathe.*

In the darkness he sat completely still. Chunks of snow plunked across the top of his hat. The snow covering his face began to fall away. Wind burned his exposed cheeks, yet he kept his eyes shut.

The smell of a horse, then the scent of urine, came and went on the wind. Had the rider only stopped to take a piss?

When he opened his eyes again, the rider was roweling his horse across the river, the rest of his company already chewed away by the storm.

The Farmer waited a few minutes to see if they would double back. Then he pushed out of the snow and slogged toward the northern shore.

On solid ground again, he searched the bottom of the strath for his horse, but the snow had already erased her black body. Delilah had been his wife's mare, the only horse he'd ever named.

He climbed the steep face of the strath, careful not to leave any boot prints on the snowless rimrock. At the top of the ridge he jogged west across the albino foothills. The snow was up to his chest in places. By the time the hills had flattened out, he'd broken a sweat. The wind and snow picked up. He used the shoreline as a guide until a wide gray tongue appeared out of the frazzled white.

When he reached the inlet, he crouched at the shoreline, weighing his options. If he went straight across the ice, he'd be home in half an hour. However, if they had picked up his trail again, and caught him chancing across that coverless plain, he'd end up the turkey in the turkey shoot.

When he stood to relieve his cramped legs, something bit into his shoulder. Hoping he hadn't been winged, he reached over his back and groped a boney spear poking through his jacket. The bone belonged to one of the jackrabbits stuffed into his game bag. Breakfast for his boys. When he pictured their hungry faces, and thought of them all alone in that cabin, he hurtled across the ice.

On the far bank, he climbed a hill. At the crest he stopped, lungs on fire. Beyond the pain, another sensation stirred—a feeling of being watched. From the bluff he scanned the valley, but it was veiled by the storm.

He caught his breath, then jogged along the ridgeline. Gusts of wind threatened to blow him over the side. In his fatigue, he stepped on a cornice and the world dropped away.

For a happy moment he was weightless—until the cold powder exploded around him. He tumbled down a steep slope, flying headlong toward a tree. He covered his face with his arms just before plunging into a dark hole. Flailing in the loose snow, he sank deeper into the tree well.

Breathe, he thought. *Do that first.*

He drove a hand to his mouth, forming an air pocket. Then he began worming side to side until he could hear the storm howling in his ears. Soon he'd forged enough space to wriggle backward out of the hole. He was almost free when a pair of hands clamped on to his boots. He reached for the dagger on his hip as the hands yanked him out.

Flipping onto his back, he swashed the blade at a watery figure. The paired bores of a shotgun scowled down at him and he went still. Wiping the snow from his eyes, he looked up at a face he hadn't seen in years, a face just as rough and broken as his own.

TWO

RESTING THE SHOTGUN ON HIS SHOULDER, THE OUTLAW thumbed back his black bolero. From the Farmer's low vantage, the man looked like a giant with its head in the clouds. He was togged out in a buffalo coat that reached past his puttees. A blue silk mascada guarded his neck. A grin appeared, barely visible behind a thick, icy beard. The deep creases around his eyes hadn't been there the last time they'd seen each other. Too many wrinkles for a man still shy of forty.

"I'll be damned," said the Outlaw. His raspy singsong yielded to a sudden guffaw. "Ye was in there tight as a nun's cunny!" He offered a gloved hand.

The Farmer ignored the hand and pulled himself out of the tree well. From what he could see, they were at the bottom of a ravine. There was a big cottonwood nearby, a horse tied to it.

The Outlaw took off his hat. The flat black crown was flourished with a turquoise-beaded stampede string. As if to clear up any confusion, he presented his rocky profile. "I know you ain't forgotten this face."

The Farmer couldn't even look at him, hoping it was all some bad dream. Up the slope, he spotted his Winchester stuck in the snow like a fence post, his silverbelly imprinted in the powder next to it. He trudged uphill, collected his hat, knocked it clean, and squared it atop his head. Batting the snow out of his rifle, he looked up the ravine and considered going out of there at a dead run.

When he looked back, the Outlaw was down at the cottonwood, untying his horse. The Farmer started down the lumpy crevasse toward him. As he neared the tree, the Outlaw proudly presented his steed.

"Meet Artemus."

The lordly gray stallion had a bright white blaze between his eyes and high white stockings, and was fitted out in tooled leather and silver tapaderos.

The Winchester swung up. "Give me the reins," said the Farmer in a voice so sharp and clipped that it was all but lost to the wind.

"What?" said the Outlaw, not quite comprehending why the rifle was pointed at his chest. "What're ye doin?"

"I said give me the reins, Clayton."

Black kidskin gloves creaked as the Outlaw gripped his shotgun. But the barrel stayed against his shoulder. The Farmer switched the Winchester to his opposite hand, then took the reins from him. A frigid exhalation shot out of the valley and the Outlaw held his hat, the wind blowing him back a step.

"How long ye been out here?" he hollered.

It was a simple question, but the Farmer couldn't think of an answer. It was too much—the blizzard, the bushwhackers, now this.

"I said how far's yer diggings?" the Outlaw was crying over the wind.

The mention of home suddenly ignited the Farmer's senses. He shouldered the carbine, pointing the barrel just shy of the Outlaw's head.

"Clayton. You're not bringing this mess near my house."

"I go by Jack now," said the Outlaw, another icy gust blasting up the ravine. They turned from a wash of gritty particles. "They ain't gonna quit lookin fer ye!"

"They're looking for *you!*" shouted the Farmer.

When the wind calmed, the Outlaw lifted his head and spat into the air, then let his eyes sink back to the Farmer. "Why ye talkin like that?" he said. "Like a schoolboy."

"Why are you talking like Daddy?"

The Outlaw smiled, his mouth like a raw wound. He patted his horse. "Artemus here don't mind we ride double. Hop on back. Let's git on to yer diggings."

The Winchester was getting heavy in the Farmer's hand, but he held steady.

"All right," conceded the Outlaw. "If you wanna sit here arguing about it while they git there first, I guess that's yer business."

Every minute wasted was another minute he wasn't protecting his children. And truth be told, he wasn't sure he could pull the trigger if it came to that.

Eldon Quint lowered his Winchester and handed Jack Foss the reins.

The Outlaw climbed into the saddle, sheathed his shotgun, then offered Eldon a hand. "Like old times," he said. "Ain't it, brother."

They stayed off the main path, trotting a game trail along the ridge. Jack rode low in the saddle. Relegated to the skirt, Eldon had to press both hands into the horse's rump to keep from sliding off the back.

"Keep straight?" Jack asked as they neared a fork in the trail.

Eldon pointed him downhill. "This animal go any faster?"

Dredging a flask from a leather pannier, Jack offered it over his shoulder. It was sterling silver, embossed with a railroad spike. "That good gulch liquor."

Eldon refused the flask, which drew a look of disbelief from his brother. As they crossed a glade of basswoods, he kept repeating to himself that protecting his boys was all that mattered. And to do that, he needed to know exactly what he was up against.

"Who's after you?" he said. "Mannix Brothers? Big Tate and his gang?"

The Outlaw shrugged. "Reckon the list of potentially aggrieved to be quite lengthy." He tipped up his flask and drank, then screwed on the top. "I kilt the Mannix Brothers five years ago."

"So who is it then?"

Breath swirled from the Outlaw's mouth as he shook his head. "Well, I don't know, Eldon. Maybe some fiddlehead called me a cheat and I shot him in the toe. Turns out he's got six big brothers who're all real sore about it."

The dagger was digging into Eldon's hip, but he couldn't adjust it without sliding off the back of the horse.

"Good God!" hollered the Outlaw, another gust pelting their faces with ice. "I don't know how ye do it. I was quite happy to be passing right through this icebox. But then that sundries seller called me 'Mr. Quint,' askin how things is up at the farm."

It used to be that Eldon could tell in half a second that his brother was lying to him. But he couldn't tell a thing about the man at the helm of that horse. In fact, he wasn't even convinced Jack Foss was real. A little voice told him to take out that dagger and make sure there was blood running through his veins.

"Can't tell ye how many stories I come up with," Jack said. "Thinkin ye mighta got swallowed up by the earth, or met one of them painted ladies what likes to poison men fer their bankroll. Yeah, I had me more theories than a Jesuit. But not a one of em included you livin back out here."

Eldon kept quiet as they rode through snow-blown forest. When they came to a path of unsullied powder, he directed them west and they rode against the wind until two cobble-stone pillars appeared out of the squall. Beyond the pillars, the forest broke into a vast snow-swept field halted on all four sides by walls of trees.

A pitched-roof cabin of tarred logs and yellowed chink-ing stood pale in the distance, thrashed by wimpled sheets of white. Near the cabin stood two vacant corrals, an outhouse, a springhouse, and an unpainted barn that Eldon and the boys built three summers past, just before Hattie got sick.

On the Farmer's order they rode the purlieu, searching the rim of the tree line for tracks. When they found nothing, Jack wheeled the steed across the snowfield.

"Goddamn," he said as the log cabin came into view. "That it?"

"We don't take the Lord's name in vain in my house."

"Brother, I ain't even sure ye can call that a house."

The barn had four horse stalls, two of them occupied, a dirt-floored animal pen with no animals to speak of, and a sour-smelling hayloft. As Jack boarded his gray in Delilah's vacant stall, the swaybacked mare clapped her teeth while a black-and-white paint stamped nervously. Jack greeted the two horses. "What's their names?"

"I don't name my animals," Eldon said. He was standing in the bay, staring out the open barn doors, the tree line just a faint bruise a hundred yards off. "On fresh mounts, we could make Yankton in a few hours."

The Outlaw crossed his arms atop the swing gate and looked at him. "Ye don't think they got people watchin the road to Yankton?"

Eldon turned and kicked the gate, sending Jack back onto his heels. "Who's *they*, Clayton?"

"I told ye," the Outlaw hissed. "I go by Jack now."

"I don't give a damn what you go by. Who's out there?"

"Jest Tricky Bender and his gang," he said with casual pride. "Yeah, I got his big brother bout four o'clock this mornin. Shot him right through the left eye."

The news went through Eldon like a cold claw. All at once, the aggression guttered out of him and his palms started to sweat.

"You killed Sonny?" he muttered, trying to stop the picture of that snarling lout from forming in his mind. That porcelain skin and congealed black hair. He could almost smell the creams and tonics. Never was there a killer as vain or dangerous as Sonny Bender. Except for his brother, Tricky.

He scooped up his Winchester and slung the game bag over his shoulder. "I can't believe you brought them sick critters to my door."

Jack was smiling at his horse. "They was comin of their own accord."

"The hell does that mean?"

The Outlaw only shrugged, like it was all a game to him. But it didn't matter what he meant, did it. Not if Tricky Bender was coming. They would need to reinforce the windows, build firing ports, secure the front door.

"We better pray this storm don't let up anytime soon," Eldon said, the words wincing out of his dry throat.

"I'll leave the praying to you, brother."

Eldon faced the barn doors, the cabin just a shadow in the distance. What would he tell his boys? He hadn't even thought about it.

"Stay here," he told Jack. "I'll come back, we'll haul those planks down from the loft and use em to reinforce the shutters."

"Back from what?" said Jack. "I got the chilblains already. I need me a warm-up."

"I need to talk to my boys." Eldon said it quickly, as if the revelation that he had two children might just fly over his brother's head.

But the surprise stuck on Jack's face even as he loosed a chuckle. "Ye got kids? How many? Boys or girls?"

Eldon stopped at the doors and looked at him. "Ian turns seven in the spring. Shane just made twelve."

Jack nuzzled his stallion. "Hear that, Artemus? Jack Foss is an uncle."

Watching the Outlaw caress that horse, it was like they were six years old again and Clayton was stealing off with a shoat bigger than he was, britches around his knees as he ran for the hills. Every spring during the slaughter, that boy would do his damndest to free as many piglets as he could. But Daddy would always catch him and whip him good. Then he'd pick out the cutest piggy of all and make Clayton drink its blood for supper.

"I was in jail," Eldon said, the words slipping under his teeth.

Jack lifted his eyes. "Ye was what?"

"You wanted to know what happened to me. They put me in jail. For almost two years. In Philadelphia." He swallowed, fighting a gluey dryness on his tongue. "When I went to see about those investments back east. You were still in the hollers."

Jack's eyes squeezed into two dark slices, leering like an angry reflection.

Despite a parched throat, Eldon continued. "They told me I owed a debt to a man I'd never laid eyes on in my life. Must've seen I had some capital, figured me an easy mark. When I got out, I didn't know where you were. I looked for you. But Jack Foss is a hard man to find."

"You'd know," said Jack. "I'm guessin yer boys don't know nothin bout me then."

Eldon stopped in the doors, the wind making his eyes water.

"They know I got a brother."

"And yer missus, what's she know?"

"She passed on."

The Outlaw removed his hat. "Well, I'd have sent condolences," he said coldly. "Had I known ye was married."

THREE

THE CABIN WAS CHILLY AND DARK, THE EARTHEN AIR RIPE with the odor of unwashed socks and unwashed boys. Eldon set his Winchester in the corner by the window, hung his coat on a peg, then slung the game bag over his shoulder and walked up the narrow keeping room.

It was a cold, murky room, split down the middle by a flimsy pine-board wall that separated two small bedrooms. The two sash windows at either end never let in enough light. The furnishings were an odd mix. A cheap table and two rickety chairs sat before the roundstone hearth at the far end across from the kitchen. The tiled credenza by the front door was from a previous life, as were the hutch in the kitchen that once stored his mother-in-law's china and the four-poster bed his wife had sent out from Springfield. He couldn't shake the feeling that he was living in the mouth of his failures. All he saw was cracked chinking, a leaky roof, a cobwebbed kitchen window where an owl had killed itself last spring.

According to his neighbor Dick Cottersman, the death of an owl was bad medicine. He'd dismissed the warning as Indian nonsense, but now wondered if he should've paid heed.

On his way to the kitchen he stopped to add another log to the hearth fire. The adamantine clock on the mantel ticked sharply. It was almost eight in the morning, though in the dimness of the storm it felt more like dusk.

Across from the hearth, an archway of thick round logs opened into the small kitchen. Eldon had wanted the house to be a simple square. It was his wife who'd demanded the L-shape. She'd always been a private person, and wanted at the very least to have the illusion of different rooms.

Pale light fell from the broken window onto the boys. They were sitting side by side at the kitchen table, sharing a tattered wool blanket, so engrossed in their work that they scarcely lifted an eye to greet their father.

The weather had kept them out of school all week, but they'd been good about keeping up with their studies. However, today was the Sabbath and they'd traded their schoolbooks for more enjoyable activities. Shane scribbled in his frayed journal while Ian sketched in his foolscap tablet with bits of charcoal. They had been working together on their first book, Ian the quiet illustrator, Shane the boisterous recontour.

The kitchen window rattled under a hard gust. Eldon walked up and closed the slatted pine shutters, locked them into place with a flimsy casement fastener.

"Hey," Shane protested, the room all but thrown into darkness. The boy was sharp-boned and scratchy-voiced with thick chestnut hair and long, gawky legs. Eyes too big for his face. A face that might one day arrange itself handsomely.

Eldon opened the shutter slats. Thin strips of light fell across the boys' faces. "I don't want the wind blowing the window in," he said, placing an oil lamp on the table.

With a box of matches from the shelf, he lit the lantern that hung over the kitchen table and adjusted the wick.

There were two beeswax candles in the hutch that Hattie had purchased during their last trip to Yankton. What was he saving them for? He couldn't recall, and he set them on the table and lit them.

"What'd you get, Pa?" Ian said, eyeing the game bag.

The younger boy had inherited his mother's fair complexion, thin blond hair, brilliant green eyes, and freckled cheeks, along with her sensitive disposition. He was the type to ferry grasshoppers and spiders out of the house in the summertime, and give all the livestock funny names—back when they had livestock, before they sold the hogs to pay down the chattel mortgage and the doctor bills.

Eldon scooped three jackrabbits from the game bag, set them on the countertop next to the basin, then turned to the boys. He had to tell them something.

"Delilah's dead," he said.

Shane looked up. "What?"

"Now listen to me, both of you. There's something—"

The sound of the front door kicking open cut him short. Wind shot up the keeping room and blew through the kitchen, flattening the candle flames.

The door slammed. Boots stomped up the hardwood floor. The boys stared into the fire-shadowed archway, waiting with frozen expressions to see what would come out of the dark. One of the candles blew out suddenly.

Smoke ribboned through the bars of light dividing the figure of Jack Foss into thick slices. He stepped into the kitchen, pulled off his black bolero, and ran a hand through his scraggly brown hair.

A gust of wind twisted the house.

Eldon tried to speak but had no saliva left. He went to the water pail and drank. "Boys," he said a little too loudly. "This is . . . this is Clayton."

"I go by Jack Foss," said the Outlaw, setting his hat and gloves on the table. He latched his thumbs to his gun belt, displaying his bone-handled Colt Peacemakers for the boys to see. "You all can call me Uncle Jack."

Shane's eyes swelled in disbelief. "You mean *the* Jack Foss? But, Pa, he looks just like you."

"He's my brother," said Eldon.

"Twin brother," added Jack. He matted his beard, showing the boys his profile. "But as ye can see, I got all the good looks."

It was true that they were twins, but Eldon no longer saw much resemblance, other than the fact that they were both six feet tall and had brown hair and rough features. Jack Foss—with his untamed beard, outsized peltry coat, and grandiloquent disposition—was a larger-than-life personality, while Eldon Quint moved quietly through the world, leaving as faint an impression as possible.

"I thought he was dead," Shane said to his father.

Not even wanting to see how that registered on his brother's face, Eldon kept his eyes on his son. "I said I didn't know where he was, not that he was dead."

Shane shook his head. "No, you said your brother was dead. I'm sure of it."

Draping his buffalo coat over the bench, Jack smiled suddenly at Shane. "Ain't a man alive can kill Jack Foss."

The boy was in awe, as if he couldn't believe that the man from all those *Fireside Stories* he kept hidden under his bed—the ones he didn't think Eldon knew about, covered over with church weeklies and copies of the *Chicago Inter-Ocean*—was standing right there in front of him.

"You do look like President Garfield," Shane murmured.

It had been affirmed in a number of periodicals and lurid dime stories that the infamous Minnesota Jack bore an uncanny resemblance to the recently murdered president, James Garfield. Eldon, too, was as fine-looking as the deceased head of state, though he did not wear jewelry or a beard and his clothes were homespun.

"So where you been all this time, Uncle Jack?" Shane asked nervously.

Eldon put his hand on the boy's shoulder. "You can ask your uncle all the questions you want later. But right now I need you both to listen. We're gonna go out and gather up some planks from the barn, and I want you two to—"

"Planks for what?" said Shane.

"So we can keep the storm from blowing in the windows. I want you both to stay here, all right? Ian, help your brother get started on those hares. Let's get breakfast on."

Both boys just stared at him, Ian already getting scared, Shane trying not to be. He wanted to tell them that it was all right, but maybe a dose of fear wasn't a bad thing.

He walked up to the shutters and closed the blinds. The bars of light vanished, and it felt not like dusk but night. When he turned up the lantern, the tarred walls glowed dull orange. He relit the candles extinguished by his brother's entrance, then turned to Jack, who stood in the corner, the shadows carving away parts of his face. He was looking around the kitchen.

"This place is tidy as an Alsatian furrow," he said, tossing Shane another grin. "Bet he keeps you busy."

"Yessir," said the boy.

"Yer daddy likes bein the boss."

"All right," Eldon said, waving his brother out.

"Pa," said Ian. "You never told us what happened to Delilah."

Eldon walked back to the child and squatted to his level. "She broke her leg," he said. "I had to put her down."

"She was hurting?"

He nodded. "Lucky for me, your uncle, who I haven't seen in . . ." He tried to smile at his brother. "How long's it been?"

"Thirteen years," said the Outlaw.

"Thirteen years, and here he comes riding out of the storm just when I need a hand. Now, isn't that something special?"

Ian studied his uncle, then nodded. "It is, Pa," he said. "It's very special."

The brothers gripped their hats as they trudged through blowing snow. Inside the barn, Eldon climbed up to the hayloft and started handing down stacks of four-foot planks. "We should get word to Dick," he said.

Jack heaved the boards into a pile by the barn doors. "Dick?"

"Cottersman."

The Outlaw stood squinting up at him. "Ye mean old Iron Sights? That half-breed lives out here too?"

"About a mile up the trail. Be nice to have another rifle. I'd go myself if not for the boys."

"He got to be seventy years old by now."

Eldon offered another stack of planks. "Three on six, that's odds I can live with."

"I git caught on the road," Jack said, taking the boards, "it's gonna be *one* on six."

You get caught, thought Eldon, *there won't be anything more to worry about.*

They carried the planks and a sling of tools back to the cabin. Eldon checked on the boys. Ian was watching Shane struggle to peel the skin off a frozen hare. Eldon reminded them both to stay in the kitchen, then ushered Jack into his bedroom.

It was cramped, that ridiculous four-poster bed taking up most of the space. A lone window looked west. Jack ambled around the room, studying what there was to study: a nightstand, a brass lamp, a pewter picture frame, a cross hanging above the bed in an oblong area of discoloration once home to a silver platter. There were other signs of a life, though just about everything Hattie had dragged out here from Springfield had been sold long ago.

Eldon opened the top drawer of his dresser. A wooden panel divided it in half—his underclothes on one side, Hattie's on the other. The delicate scent of her French perfume seeped from a cut-glass flacon nestled among the undergarments. He dug out a pair of socks, shut the drawer, then sat on the bed and pulled off his boots.

"This yer missus?" said Jack.

As he peeled off his wet socks, he glanced at the tintype. "Yeah. Hattie."

Young and honey-dipped, she stood with her hands clasped around her pregnant belly, a guileless expression across her comely features. She was on the porch of a handsome clapboard home.

"Where's this?" Jack said, pointing at the house.

"Here," Eldon said. "Before the fire."

There'd been many fires, but that one had taken their home just a few months after he'd finished building it. The only good luck was that half the furniture had been late to arrive from Springfield and was spared incineration. But now the credenza, the hutch, and the four-poster bed that seemed far too vast without his wife's warm body to fill it only reminded him of what he'd lost. He took the tintype from his brother's hand and returned it to the nightstand. Then he went to the chest at the foot of the bed, opened the lid, and started pulling out stacks of braided mats, heaving them toward the door.

"What's them?" said Jack.

"Fire mats."

"What ye got so many fer?"

"I sell em. Ten cent per. You can build a fire on snow or grass so it doesn't burn."

Jack looked repulsed. "Yer sellin fire mats?"

Eldon held one up to show the warp and woof of tightly woven metal. "You couldn't poke a knife through one if you tried. Put a couple together and they'll stop just about any-thing, save—"

The sound of a muted sneeze cut him short. He walked over and swung open the door. Shane stepped back, sneez-ing again into cupped hands.

"You come to say those hares are dressed and on the spit?"

"What's going on, Pa? Ian's scared."

Eldon waved him into the room, glancing up the keep toward the kitchen. He shut the door. "Listen to me, Shane. There might be some men on their way here."

"Men?" Shane said, glancing at his uncle.

"Bad men," said the Outlaw.

"I need you to keep an eye on your brother," Eldon told the boy. "And get breakfast on the table, all right? Can I depend on you for that?"

"Yeah," Shane said, disappointed. He looked up. "Can I hold a pistol at least?"

"Go mind your brother."

"But we got—"

"You're saying *but* when it ought to be *yes, sir.*"

"Fine—*yessir.* I just aimed to tell Uncle Jack we got two nickel-plated S&W Model 3s and a mess of cartridges for the Winchester."

"And now you've told him. So aim to finish those hares."

"Can I at least load em?"

"Don't go scaring your brother, all right? Tell him we're guarding against the storm and keep the rest between us men."

The boy nodded. "Yessir."

Eldon held open the door and watched him shuffle through the dark toward the kitchen.

Jack plucked a cigar from behind his ear. "Can the boy shoot?"

On a high shelf sat a round maroon hatbox. Eldon took it down and stood holding it, feeling the weight of what was inside.

"Only ones doing any shooting," he said, "is you and me."

The Outlaw struck a match against the wall and held it to his cigar. The flame flared in a swirl of milky smoke. "So ye told em I was dead?"

Eldon went to the window, closed the shutters and locked them. "I'd heard you got killed over some plundered flasks of quicksilver." He picked up a hammer and some nails and started hammering a plank across the window.

"That before or after they put ye in jail fer no reason?" asked Jack.

Wind screamed between strikes of the hammer. The Outlaw sucked his cigar, the cherry burning red-hot. For a moment the muscles around his eyes and mouth seemed to come loose, as if there were some softer layer of flesh rippling behind them.

Tucking the hatbox underarm, Eldon headed for the door. He knew he had to get the cabin secure, but the only sure way to do that was to get his brother out of it.

FOUR

AFTER THEIR CLAPBOARD HOME HAD BURNED, ELDON BUILT A humble log cabin on top of the old foundations. The Indian attacks had ceased, so there was no need for reinforced shutters with rifle ports. But now that they needed such protections, Eldon decided they would sandwich the fire mats between two-inch-thick planks and nail them to the shutters.

To speed things along, Jack headed to the kitchen with Shane as his apprentice, while Eldon and Ian started at the north end of the keep by the front door. When Eldon closed the shutters, the only source of light became the hearth fire at the other end. Ian had become scared of the dark since his mother passed and had begun to suck his thumb. Eldon assured him they were just being cautious, but the child seemed to know that trouble was on the way. When he went to his bedroom to gather oil for the lantern, he realized there was no sawing or hammering from the kitchen, just his brother's chattering voice.

Marching up to the archway, Ian trailing behind, he stood looking into the kitchen. Lamplight quivered against the black walls. The planks and fire mats sat unused on the table, the skinned hares swaying on a ceiling hook, watery blood plunking into the basin.

Settled into Hattie's blue press-back rocker—yet another item from their previous life—Jack was spinning a yarn while Shane sprawled at his feet, wrapped in a blanket, scribbling like mad in his journal.

"That was back when me and Sonny was partnered up rustlin beeves," Jack was saying, "before we had us that disagreement regarding the disbursement of wages."

Still scribbling, Shane looked up. "Is it true you hauled off a whole safe full of gold from the Aurora?"

"Twice," said Jack. "Took off the Aurora twice. Same with the Rock Island and the Union Pacific. Ye raid somethin once, they ain't expectin you to hit it again the follerin day."

Eldon cleared his throat. "How's breakfast coming?"

Shane jumped up like a bangtail and got to work cutting down the hares. "Pa, how come if you're brothers you got different last names?"

"His name's made-up," Eldon said. With a glance at the shutters, he asked Jack, "You gonna keep beating the devil around the stump or get to work?"

The Outlaw leaned back in the rocker. "My nephew's shown a keen interest in penning a breathtaking biographical account based on my exploits. We been gettin acquainted."

"Get acquainted with that shutter. I'm already near finished in the keep."

The jackrabbits made a wet slapping sound as Shane tossed them onto the countertop. He slit one up the belly, exposing the shiny white membrane.

"Uncle Jack, is it true you killed Sheriff Don McGill with a crossbow?"

Eldon walked up and touched the boy on the shoulder. "We can trade stories later. Ian, come on, let's finish up."

"Can I stay with Shane?" Ian said.

Eldon gave his eldest a look. "Shane?"

The boy snorted. "Yeah, I'll watch him."

Jack turned from the shutter. "And I'll watch em both," he said, a smile bright enough to send a chill up Eldon's spine.

Turning out of the archway, the Farmer stood looking down the keep. It was thirty paces end to end, but seemed boundless in the dark. He dragged one of the chairs from the hearth down to the end of the room and set it before the window. At his feet he set a lantern, lit it, then hung it from the peg next to the front door. Then he sat before the boarded-up shutter and measured a square portion the size of a fist that he wanted to cut out from the bottom of the frame. The wood cracked easily. As he worked, he heard Shane and Jack carrying on in the kitchen.

"Seems like you got all the good stories," Shane was saying. "Pa don't hardly say two words about his past adventures."

"Yer daddy got plenty of tales," Jack replied. "But he wanted to be a farmer and I wanted to be an outlaw, so I got all the good ones."

"If you're twins, does that mean Pa got the same miraculous powers of bilocation like them books claim you got?"

"I ain't allowed to talk about it. But ye know what they say. Jack Foss can be in two places at once."

"Gol dangit," Shane shrieked. "Wait till I tell Molly."

"That yer sweetheart?"

"Molly Wachiwi? My sweetheart? Heck no. We're just best friends, is all."

"She Santee?"

"Her momma's Sisseton, I think. Her spirit name means *dancing girl.*"

"Yer daddy don't mind ye cavortin with an Indian?"

"He says they never done nothing to us we ain't done to them ten times worse."

Eldon's chisel bit off a big hunk of dry pine. A rod of dusty light shot down the keep, piercing the darkness.

Crouching down to see through the notch, Eldon squinted until his eyes adjusted to the brightness. The tree line, just a vague notion twenty minutes ago, now appeared brown as chert. Maybe it was just a lull, or maybe the storm was letting up.

"Don't forget," the Outlaw was saying, "what's in me is also in yer daddy. And what's in yer daddy is in you. In that sense, I'm jest as much yer paterfamilias as he is."

Hearing more prattle than work, Eldon stomped back to the archway and glared into the kitchen.

The Outlaw was back in Hattie's rocking chair, with little progress made on the shutter. Shane was gutting the hares while Ian sat at the table, sketching by candlelight.

"Does that mean I got magical powers too?" Shane said, watery blood painting little streams down his arms.

"Nobody has any magical powers . . ." Eldon trailed off when he noticed the stoppered bottle of whiskey in Jack's hand. "Where'd you get that?"

"I got it for him," Shane said with a pluck of defiance. "I know you keep it in the hutch for when Mr. Cottersman stops by."

The stopper made a squeaky pop. Jack stared at his brother, eyes rimmed in red. He took a long pull. The last thing Eldon needed was him getting drunk before a gunfight.

He was about to say as much when a thud shook the kitchen wall.

Ian and Shane looked up, startled. Eldon went to the shutter, motioning for them to get back. He turned the casement latch and slowly swung open one of the panels. Gray light poured into the kitchen. He pressed his face to the cracked glass and looked out. Another avalanche of snow slid off the roof. He locked the shutter, casting them back to the darkness. Jack sat watching, taking big punishing gulps of liquor.

"Why don't you set an example for your nephews," said Eldon, "and get this shutter secured."

"Well, I would," said the Outlaw, "but this here rocker's mighty comfortable." He cast a roguish smirk at Shane. "And I am reluctant to vacate it."

Jack rocked back, a finger caressing the butt of his pistol. "I ain't scared no more, Eldon. Not even a little." His eyes were as hard and cold as his rocky features, but something desperate stirred behind them, something the Outlaw wanted to keep hidden.

"It was our mother's chair," Ian said without looking up from his tablet.

"That's right," said Shane. "She spent about all her days in it, knitting that same sweater. Pa don't like anyone sitting in it. Not even us."

Jack banged the cork into the whiskey bottle with his palm. Then he pushed out of the rocker, brushed past his brother, and settled at the kitchen table across from Ian. Tobacco crackled as he lit a fresh cigar and blew rings of thick smoke that expanded in the orange light of the lantern. Ian sat drawing, glancing between the Outlaw and his tablet. Finally he tore out a page and handed it across the table.

Jack received the charcoal sketch and held it to the candle-light. Eldon glanced over his shoulder. It was a portrait of Jack Foss from the neck up, but unlike the dashing figures that appeared on the dime story covers, this was a somber rendering. The nub of a cigar slouched from his mouth and his eyes were downcast, desultory. Jack tried to hand the portrait back.

"That ain't me," he said. "Ye drawed yer daddy and scribbled a beard on him."

Ian shook his head. "No, it's you," he said, already on to a new sketch.

"No, see, Jack Foss always got a smile on his face, and a smile is all in the eyes." He pointed at the smudged portals. "Do them eyes look like they're smilin to you?"

When Eldon chuckled at how easily a six-year-old had gotten under his brother's skin, Jack's head snapped around. The Outlaw's eyes looked wilted and forlorn, just as Ian had drawn them, yet his mouth twisted into a wicked smile as he leaned over the table to examine Ian's new sketch.

"What's that?" he snorted. "A ring or somethin?"

"Momma's carnelian ring," Ian said. "Shane would've got it if he was born a girl. Fire got it instead."

Eldon eyed the sketch, then looked at his brother. "He likes drawing her things."

"Ian," Jack said, turning to the boy. "Ye ever heard of Big Don McGill?"

"If you're not planning to do any work," Eldon broke in, "you can keep an eye out that loophole around the corner. Nice and warm by the fire."

Smiling at Shane, Jack ignored him. "Big Don McGill was the most feared sheriff in all the hollers of south-ern Arkansas," he told the boy. "Had a dozen toadeaters orbiting his person at all times, but I knew he kept hisself a blue-haired squaw down Desha County. Or maybe she was half greaser, I don't know . . . she spoke no Spanish to me. Anyhow, she took me up to her room and—say, what do you boys know bout the smell of a woman's quim?"

"Clayton," Eldon snapped. "Enough. Why don't you just park yourself at that loophole and let's all take a break."

The whiskey had glazed Jack's eyes. "Cause this one in particular smelled so bad, I almost couldn't go through with it." He laughed. A sick, ragged chortle. "But ye shoulda seen this gal, brother. Her top half was first-rate, but she had legs like a churn dasher, ankles three feet thick." He drank, then wiped his mouth and smiled at the boys. "Y'all ain't old enough to know it yet, but passion befuddles a man's mind. Must also dampen his sense of smell."

Eldon spoke through clenched teeth. "Get up and park yourself at that window."

But Jack didn't seem to hear him, his gaze stolen by some inward darkness. "I told her not to pick up that knife. But a man has to defend hisself."

Ian looked up with a frown. "You hurt her?"

Jack shook his head vaguely, something vile and dark screwing into his eyes. Eldon glanced at the maroon hatbox on the table, the one containing his revolvers.

"Ian," he said sharply enough that he startled the child. "Go stoke the hearth fire. Shane, get the spit set up, get those hares on. Now. Let's go."

He watched the boys hurry through the archway to the hearth across the keep, their forms shadowed against the firelight. Then he stood glaring at his brother. "This is my family you're fooling with," he said quietly.

The Outlaw's cigar released a last gasp of smoke as he stubbed it out on the tabletop. He looked up with eyes that did not move yet appeared to be in perpetual motion, like stones at the bottom of a river. "What's that make me then?"

The crust had shaken loose from his face, a raw, moist tissue beneath like the backside of an eyelid. He gritted his teeth and pulled his hat down as if to restore whatever layer of protection he'd lost.

"We got an hour," Eldon said, "maybe two till the storm dies out. I am asking you, Clayton. Get on that loophole."

Jack pulled the stopper, drained the bottle, then set it on the table. He pushed unsteadily to his feet, the muscles of his face twitchy and taut.

Shane appeared in the archway holding two iron Y-shaped spit forks. "Pa, I can't find the spit rod. It might be in the springhouse. I could make sofky instead."

"Sofky?" Jack said, throwing a disgusted look at Eldon. "Well, I woulda thought yer soldiering days had cured yer desire fer that foul concoction."

"Soldiering?" Shane questioned his father.

Jack looked at him in disbelief. "He ain't told you boys bout the war?"

Shane's eyes blasted even wider. "Pa, you fought the Rebs?"

"Not the Rebs," Jack said before Eldon could get a word in. "We was up against somethin ten times as scary. Them Santee. Whipped up on em too, ain't we, brother?"

Shane gaped, begging his father for confirmation.

"Your uncle's exaggerating," Eldon said. "We were like every other settler trying to prove up his land. Got caught up in it is all. We weren't soldiers; we were kids."

"Not officially," said Jack. "But when yer facing down a bloody tomahawk, ye don't tend to make—"

"All right," Eldon said. "Get those hares on the spit."

Laughing to himself, Jack picked up the whiskey bottle again. There were a few drops left and as he tipped it back he stumbled into the glass doors of the hutch, shaking it.

Shane pointed at the top of the tall china cabinet. "There it is!"

The long spit rod hung over the edge. As Eldon pulled it down, he struck a tin can of Argonaut tomatoes sitting up there next to it. The can hit the floor with a heavy clank. The top was wrapped with cloth and bound with twine. Eldon reached for it, but Jack got there first and stood rattling the contents, grinning crookedly.

"Give it," Eldon said, holding out his hand.

Jack held up the can for the boys to see. "Yer pa was always squirreling away capital. A satchel here, a wad there. Had more stashes than a prairie dog got holes." He shook it, the rattle of coins playing like sweet music on his face. "Been workin hard on this one, I see. Tell ye what, brother. How bout you tell me what yer savin up fer and we'll see if I can't think up a better use fer it."

"Just gimme the damn can," said Eldon.

Jack feigned offense. "I thought ye didn't use no gamy language in this house."

"Hand it over."

"Or what?"

Their eyes locked together like brazed metal.

"You know what," said Eldon.

The kitchen was silent, save the tick of the mantel clock and the crackle of the hearth fire. Even the wind had settled in as a spectator.

Jack held up the can, goading his brother with a little tug on the knotted twine. "Best tell me what yer savin up fer."

"It's to take them to visit their mother in Springfield," Eldon said through his teeth.

Shane looked up, his face twisting through confusion and then anger. "You had that money all along and we haven't even been to see her?"

The house shuddered with the return of the wind. The lantern hanging over the table swayed, ruddy chunks of light scampering about the tar-colored walls.

"I've been saving for a trip come spring," Eldon said, turning to look his brother in the eye. "You got a better use for it than that, *Jack*?"

"Shucks, brother," said the Outlaw. He set the can on the table. "Ye ain't no fun."

Eldon picked up the can and went into the keeping room, which seemed even darker now despite the trembling glow of the lamps and candles.

As he stowed the can in the tiled credenza by the door, he had to steady himself against the wall. He thought he was done with that kind of grief, but there it was, running over him like a storm.

After a few deep breaths, he walked over to the loophole. Squatting under the boarded-up shutter, he set his forearms across the sill and peered through the crude opening. The snow had stopped completely. The little square of gray light shimmered against his eyes. Wiping the wetness from them, he reached for his rifle.

FIVE

THEY'D BEEN HOLED UP THREE HOURS IN THAT DARK CABIN
and Eldon couldn't stop moving. Winchester over his shoulder, ammo pouch on his hip, he went like a soldier on
parade, checking the kitchen loophole, then the loophole by
the hearth, then down to the loophole by the front door,
then to his bedroom to peer through the boarded-up shutters, and back again to the kitchen.

Meanwhile, Jack had taken up residence before the
hearth fire. He sat watching the boys turn the spit, breathing in the aroma of those roasting hares as drops of grease
rained across the coals, hissing on impact.

"Those smell done," Eldon said, pausing his rounds to
inspect the skewered game.

"Few minutes longer," said Jack, the whiskey snagging at
his words. To the boys he said, "In olden times, men roasted
the king's meat. All day long in front of a fire turnin that
spit. Then some fancy pants come up with a system so a dog
could do it. And dogs started roastin the king's meat. Put
all them spit jacks outta work. And there's a lesson in that.
Don't never choose a profession that can be performed by
what walks on four legs."

Shane laughed and looked at his little brother, but Ian
didn't get the joke.

Jack winked at the nervous child. "My little turnspit dog." He patted the pocket containing the portrait. "Quite the artist you shall make, Turnspit. Though ye need to work on the capturing of the eyes. Cause them warn't my eyes. Say, did yer daddy tell ye to draw me like that?" His eyes slid to Eldon. "With that stupid look on my face?"

Sweat beaded on Jack's forehead, his eyes all stirred up by the whiskey.

Eldon walked into the kitchen and looked through the loophole at the eastern pasture. The clouds had curdled, showing bits of blue. In the distance, noonday sun mottled the colorless foothills.

He heard Jack's unsteady steps behind him and turned around.

Jack leaned a hand on the kitchen table and exhaled, as if it had been some great exertion to walk ten steps. He flipped open the maroon hatbox and looked inside. He stared at the revolvers for a long moment. He was suddenly very still. Then he looked up.

"These them Model 3s ye took off Harlan Scrim?"

He picked one up and looked at the underside of the butt. Eldon watched his eyes cloud over.

Jack sniffed the nickel-plated barrel. "Look like they ain't never been fired."

"They haven't," Eldon said, reaching for the other gun.

He turned the top-break revolver over in his hands then looked at the butt. His thumb ran automatically over the small railroad spike imprinted in the strip of metal dividing the tight-grained cherry grips.

"Ye ain't taught yer boys how to shoot a pistol?"

Shane called from the hearth. "I can shoot," he said. "Got two deer last summer with the Winchester."

Jack clapped the cylinder shut and let the barrel drift in his brother's direction. "I bet yer a crack shot, son."

"Point that elsewhere," said Eldon.

The hammer clicked to the first position—the safety position—then to the second, the firing position.

Jack looked down the sights. "First pistol I ever shot was Daddy's Model 1. I believe Daddy lost them guns at Birch Coulee." He chuckled at the memory. "Some Injun probably shot hisself in the foot with one."

"What's Birch Coulee, Uncle Jack?" Shane called from the hearth.

"Now there's a tale to tell," Jack said, throwing a grin at his brother.

Eldon looked at the box of shells sitting next to the hatbox. Then he set the pistol on the table and went through the archway to the hearth to look at the hares.

"Let's get those off," he told Shane. "They're done."

When he turned around, Jack was behind him, painted in the quivering firelight. Holding the Model 3 down at his side, he stared, expressionless, then settled in a chair before the fire and took out his kerchief. As he began to polish the revolver, he addressed the boys, though his eyes lingered on Eldon.

"Birch Coulee's where yer granddaddy met his demise. September the second, eighteen and sixty-two. Go on, Eldon. Tell em the story."

No longer did Eldon have the luxury of hoping this was all a bad dream. As he stood before the fire, he crossed his arms, fingers searching out the raised scars on his flanks. Beyond the thick wads of tissue, a lead ball floated behind his ribs like a forgotten moon. It ached still, before a rain or late at night, when the pain visited his dreams, when it had a painted face and big black eyes and a shrieking voice. When it donned its buffalo horns and ribbons and colored buckskin tied in knots. Its weasel tails, its tomahawks and knives. Its plundered watches, breastpins, earrings, and bonnets. The white crepe shawls it wrapped around its black head that still smelled of slaughter.

"Get those hares off," he said suddenly.

The Outlaw looked up, a threat in his eyes: *I'll tell them if you don't.*

Eldon sat in the other chair and leaned in close to the boys, the heat from the fire stinging his chapped cheeks. "Remember I told you I was raised in Minnesota? That your granddaddy was a trader at the Agency there, and sold provisions to Indians?"

"By provisions, he means whiskey and rum," said Jack.

"No," Eldon said. "He sold all sorts of things. Anyhow, one day there was a disagreement with the Indian agent and some of the Dakota chiefs. The government was late with the annuity payment and the Indian agent wouldn't—"

Jack interrupted. "That fuckin Indian agent wouldn't give em no food even though they was starvin half to death."

"We don't use that language in this house," Eldon said calmly.

The Outlaw belched into the fire, then smiled at the boys. "That Indian agent was a real sick bastard. Loved messin with them red devils. Said he wouldn't give em no food till the payment arrived, which, mind ye, was already two months late comin from the government."

"Wait," said Shane. "But isn't the government the one giving them the food?"

"Exactly," said Jack. "It's no wonder them Indians started raising hell, slaughterin settlers by the bushel. And that's when—"

Eldon broke in. "That's when me, Clayton, and your granddaddy had to leave—"

"It's *Jack*," the Outlaw said, tense and sweaty. "How many times I gotta say it, brother?"

Eldon looked at him, then carried on with the story, figuring that if he stopped talking, he'd never get another word in.

"The Indians were raising hell," he told the boys. "Not all of em, but enough that we had to get to Fort Ridgely to be safe. Few days later, the people in charge gathered a burial party and we joined up to help."

"Burial party?" Ian asked.

"It's a group of men who go out and bury the dead. We joined up with about a hundred soldiers and about fifty settlers and . . ."

Ian mumbled something, a thumb in his mouth.

"I can't understand you with your thumb in your mouth," said Eldon.

"Were the dead people your friends?"

"Some. That's why we wanted to bury em quick and proper. After that, we camped in a field between a stream and the woods. And that field came to be called Birch Coulee. Now, the men in charge told us there wasn't an Indian for fifty miles, so we went to bed feeling safe. Just before dawn, one of the picket guards came running into camp and—"

Jack shot to his feet, eyes trembling. "Ye could already hear them war whoops and them tom-toms and them guns crackling like the Fourth of July. Little Crow had us outnumbered three to one. We had no trenches, no breastworks—they ain't even give us the proper ammunition. Damn ordinance officers gave us sixty two-caliber shot for our fifty eight-caliber muskets. We had to whittle down each and every ball to fit the barrel. Thirty-six hours under bombardment. Twenty-two men dead. Twice that wounded."

The firelight glistened against Jack's face, his eyes raw around the edges. For the first time in three hours, he didn't say a word for a good minute.

"What happened to Granddad?" Shane said.

Eldon cleared his throat, the dryness returning. "We'd packed the wagons around the camp the night before, and I found him under one of the buckboards. He'd been trying to dig a trench with his bayonet."

"Was he dead?" Shane asked.

"Yes, he was."

"Was he all bloody?"

"No, he just . . . he had a funny expression on his face. Like he'd been told a joke."

"Why?"

Jack screeched his chair closer to the boys. "Did you know that yer granddaddy used to make us lug around this giant footlocker packed with books? And not skinny books neither. Heavy tomes. Every night, he'd pick out a book and we'd take turns readin to him while he drank his rum. There was this one I remember, bout these ancient peoples who believed there warn't no such thing as good or evil in the world. They believed that things jest happened, and it's up to us to decide if what happened was good or bad or somewhere in between. I can see yer both wonderin how this circles back to yer granddaddy. First thing to know is that yer pa left out a crucial detail of his demise."

Shane stared in anticipation. Ian chewed his thumb. Eldon implored his brother with a look, but there was no mercy in the Outlaw's eyes.

"Yer granddaddy was scalped."

Shane gasped at his little brother. Ian looked shrunken and unnerved.

Eldon set his rifle against the wall then knelt before his youngest boy and took him by the arms. "Your uncle's just trying to scare you."

"I ain't tryna scare him," Jack said. "I'm tryna educate him."

Eldon's eyes snapped to him. "Like how Daddy used to educate us? You know, you're starting to sound just like him."

A smile seethed across the Outlaw's face as he turned back at the boys. "See, the brave what done the scalpin, he must of got interrupted halfway through, cause that flap of skin and hair was still attached to the back of Daddy's skull. It was all dried out in the sun, rolled up like a scroll. Now, I guarantee there ain't a brave alive woulda left that scalp behind and missed out on adding a new eagle feather to his headdress. So I knew somethin funny'd happened. Listen up now, cause here's where it all comes together. See, I reckon that while Daddy was bein scalped, he recalled that book I read to him bout how there's no good or bad unless we think it so. And he decided that havin his hair peeled warn't so bad after all. And went and had hisself a good chuckle over it. Now imagine yer peelin a man's scalp and he jest up and laughs at ye. I reckon you'd be scared half to death. And that's why that brave ain't finished the job. Thinkin this here white man is some *baaaaad* medicine. But Eldon didn't see it that way, did ye, brother? You was ragin like a river. How many of them sombitches you kilt?"

Two thunderstruck faces pointed at the Farmer.

"I never killed anyone," he said, eyes on Jack. "Tell em you meant the horses."

The Outlaw stayed quiet just long enough to make Eldon's stomach turn.

"Course I did," he said with a grin. "All them horses picketed out before the coulee, bout ninety of em, they was all shot up with arrows, lyin there suffering in the sun. Yer daddy, animal lover that he is, went around puttin each one outta its misery."

The hearth coals hissed and popped, little black craters opening where the grease struck them.

"And that's the story," said Eldon. "Now let's get those hares on a plate. Who's hungry?"

"Pa, my tummy hurts," Ian said. "I need to use the privy."

Eldon looked at Shane. "Help your brother with the pot."

"Why? He can do it himself."

"Shane. Help him, please."

The boy dragged his little brother down the dark hall and they vanished into the bedroom.

Eldon sat in the chair across from his brother, folded his hands across his lap, and stared at him. "After we eat," he said quietly, "we're riding to Dick's. All of us. Then you can be on your way. I'm done listening to your crap."

As Jack took out a fresh cigar, a beam of sunlight shot through the loophole in the kitchen and bleached his stony features. He jerked his chair out of the ray and sat in shadow, rolling the cigar between his thumb and forefinger. He had set the Model 3 at his feet and Eldon leaned to pick up the revolver, then went into the kitchen and sat in front of the box of cartridges. He broke the top then opened the box of shells. When he looked up, Jack stood in the archway, the finger of sunlight exploding against his chest.

"I know ye still think yer stud duck," said the Outlaw. "But a lot changes in thirteen years. Though yer still a liar, ain't ye. Ye warn't in no jail. And ye knew I wasn't kilt over no quicksilver."

"It's not that simple," Eldon said, his voice small and faraway.

Jack spoke through his teeth. "Tell ye what then. I got me an emergency bottle of combustible in my pannier. We can git us into the cups, and you can explain what's not so simple about you vanishing on me like smoke in the wind."

"You wanna get to it?" said Eldon, his throat hot and dry. "How about telling me what the hell you're doing here? And don't feed me some half-cocked story about some sundries seller mistaking you for me. You come here for a reason."

The Outlaw stepped through the archway like something had reached into his chest and dragged him forward by the heart.

Eldon stood up, the revolver cocked in his hand, the trigger cold against his finger. As their eyes tangled, Shane emerged from the darkness holding the soiled chamber pot at arm's length. Ian wandered up next to him, tucking his shirt into his pants.

"It's a ripe one," Shane said, pushing the pot toward his father.

"Lord is that ever the effluvial odor," said Jack, breaking the heated spell. "What'd you eat, Turnspit?"

"He gets it bad when his nerves clench up," Shane said.

Eldon took the pot and walked down the candlelit keep. At the front door, he set the pot down and pulled on his boots. With the Winchester slung over his shoulder, he lifted the pot and opened the door.

Light blasted his eyes, a dry arctic wind blowing him back on his heels.

He stepped outside, wading into the high snow, then shut the door and stood studying the sun-bleached tree line a hundred yards across the field. He took the pot around to the side of the cabin and heaved the turd into the snow.

As he was coming back around, eyes watering from the wind, an owl lurched from the barn roof. He watched it swoop low across the field and veer skyward at the pasture line, where three distant figures huddled in the trees.

SIX

SLUGS POPPED AGAINST THE TARRED LOGS, WHISTLING aslant into the atmosphere. Eldon was belly down in the snow, ears full with his own panting.

Move, he told himself.

In a flail of chunky snow he sprang toward the door. Distant rifles barked as he shouldered into the house and kicked the door shut. Bullets snapped through the chinking as he charged up the keeping room, rods of light shooting past, diffusing against the two chairs overturned before the hearth.

He banked through the archway into the kitchen, then seized the boys by their shirt backs and thrust them into the corner between the cookstove and the hutch, curling his body around them. Their eyes squeezed shut as another swarm blew pale geysers in the chinking and clanged off the hanging pots. They looked up at him, eyes knocked wide open, cheeks flushed, their breath hot and moist against his collar.

Jack crouched under the window, looking through the loophole. "Where they at?"

"North pasture line," Eldon said.

"How many?"

"Three. About eighty yards north. In the trees."

At an untroubled pace, Jack crawled to the opposite corner of the kitchen, where his shotgun sat propped against the archway. He flung the bandolier over his head, as if this were all just part of his day. He broke the shotgun, selected a pair of shells from his bandolier, seating them one by one in the tubes.

Eldon felt for his rifle. Realizing he'd lost it in the scramble, he crawled to the edge of the archway and peered down the keep. His Winchester lay on the floor in front of the bullet-pocked door.

"Pa," Ian said. "Will they get us?"

Eldon scuttled back to the boys. "Nothing's gonna get you, I promise."

"Where's your rifle?" Shane screeched. "You have to shoot back!"

"We're just gonna stay here a minute," he told them as another volley of fire raked the cabin.

The boys coughed, choking on the pulverized chinking and saltpeter. Eldon went for the water pail on the other side of the cookstove, but a slug spanked a frying pan from a ceiling hook and it whomped him on the head. Both hands went to his skull. Shane tried to slip past, but Eldon snagged the boy around the belly and flung him into the corner.

"What are you doing?" he barked.

The boy was on the verge of tears. "Someone's gotta shoot back!"

He was trying to be like the dime novel outlaws that hid under his bed, trying to conquer his fear with swaggering banditry, but all that bluster only tugged twice as hard at the terror in his eyes.

"It's all right to be afraid," Eldon told him. "But you gotta be smart at the same time. Right now we're letting them spend their energy and ammunition. And just when they think we're beat down, we'll show em how far we are from it."

The boy wiped his eyes, then gathered his hands between his knees and sucked snot. "All right," he whispered.

Jack was back at the kitchen window, looking through the loophole. "We can't let em git too close to the house. I do believe they got dynamite."

"Dynamite?" Eldon said. "Well, isn't that nice. Anything else you wanna share, Clayton? They got a six-pound cannon you forgot to mention?"

A voice boomed from the north side of the property. *"Foss, ya back-shootin son of a bitch! We got ya on all sides!"* Though it belonged to a man, the anger had ground it down to a throaty, feminine shriek.

The Outlaw sucked his teeth. "I hate that son of a bitch."

"If I got to start countin, Imma a sever a finger for every minute ya make me wait, and a toe for every bullet ya put in my brother's back!"

Jack ran to the other end of the keeping room and shouted through the loophole. "Tricky, I ain't never shot no man in the back, up to and includin yer peckerwooded brother!"

"That's Tricky Bender?" Shane squealed.

Another hail of gunfire punched through the walls and Eldon shouted for the boys to get down. When the shooting stopped, he inched around the archway to check on them. They were hugging each other behind the stove, unharmed.

The plink of brass caught his attention and he squinted down the keep. Under the windowsill, Jack was on his knees, collecting some scattered ammunition he must have dropped. His hands trembled, just like they did when Daddy would toss a handful of knucklebones across the supper table. The lay of the bones would decide his fate. Either he would eat, or suffer a lashing for whatever slight had instigated the game. What Eldon saw wasn't an outlaw collecting bullets, but a cursed child who could not alter his fate.

"Clayton," he said.

His brother's head snapped up.

"You all right?"

With a dismissive snort, Jack Foss was restored. He scooped up the bullets and grunted that he was fine, then turned and squinted through the loophole. "They're comin round," he said. "Three of them ham-shitters on shaggy mounts."

Eldon charged down to meet him and picked up his rifle. "Three I saw were afoot," he said, crouching behind him. "You saw three more on horses?"

"They're on the move," Jack said, stepping aside so Eldon could see for himself.

Eldon raised his eyes to the loophole. Hugging the tree line, three riders galloped around toward the back side of the cabin.

"I got em," he said, running up the keep to the southerly loophole.

"Whip up on em!" shouted Jack.

The boys watched their father through the archway, eyes like signal fires. All Eldon had to do was keep those fires lit. He set the barrel on the sill and slid it through the narrow square, stopping when it butted against the pane. The glass was frosted over. He drew the rifle back then punched the barrel through the glass. After clearing the shards, he adjusted the stock against his shoulder. Looking down the sights, he raked his eyes across the snowfield, waiting for the riders to come around. As the seconds ticked on, he became aware of the wind and cold, the sun, the stink of burning hares, the tang of tobacco, whiskey, and gunpowder. Every sense pricked.

Three riders appeared on his left flank a hundred yards across the field, whipping their horses. The lead man bounced up and down in the notch of Eldon's rifle sight, hugging a brick-colored cylinder to his chest. It was a little larger than a coffee can. The air drained from Eldon's chest. The butt plate kicked into his shoulder. The rider flailed, dropping the brick-colored roll into the snow. He wheeled his horse. Eldon shot at him again. Gripping his guts, the rider vanished behind the springhouse thirty yards away.

Eldon levered another round into the receiver and put the second rider in his sights. The man held a small shotgun in one hand. Eldon breathed. The Winchester bucked. The rider flew sideways and his boot twisted in the stirrup. The pinto dragged him in a big swooping circle then lit out for the trees.

The last rider was coming at a mad gallop, fifty yards and closing. He wore a blazing red-and-yellow bandanna around his neck, and might as well have pinned a bull's-eye to his chest. The rider grew in the sights. Eldon touched the trigger. Aimed at his chest. But hesitated. He was just a kid, maybe a few years older than Shane. A cheap hat flopped over his eyes as he tried to keep his rusty six-shooter aimed.

Eldon settled his sights on that red-and-yellow scarf. He imagined Shane aboard that horse.

The shot hit its mark, all but severing the kid's shooting arm. The six-shooter dropped from his dangling appendage and he fell from his nag, swallowed by the powder.

Eldon put his mouth by the loophole. "I winged you on purpose! You don't leave out right now, I'll be forced to send you up."

The kid was flapping in the snow like an injured bird.

When Eldon turned from the loophole to reload, his brother was standing behind him, staring down with a look of disgust.

"Winged?" said Jack. "Are you stupid?"

"He's a kid."

"Foss," cried Tricky Bender. *"Who else ya got in there with ya? Whoever you is, do us all a favor and kill that back-shooter! I'll personally reward ya one thousand dollars!"*

Jack charged back to his loophole and emptied his Colts at the tree line. "You ain't got no thousand dollars, ye low-born, lily-livered, scrofulous, poxy bastard!"

"Quit wasting rounds we don't got to waste!" Eldon hollered.

With a murderous look, the Outlaw marched back up the keep. "Reload," he said, his two smoldering Peacemakers sailing through the air toward Shane.

The boy scrambled from behind the cookstove, caught the guns, and dashed back to the corner, where Ian waited with a box of ammunition.

"Stay behind that stove!" Eldon warned. The boy hardly looked up, busy loading the guns. He went back to his loophole, but Jack was already there, crouched under the window, looking through.

"That what I think it is?" he muttered. His hand reached toward Eldon. "Lemme hold that carbine."

"What is it?" Eldon said.

Jack turned. Eldon held on to the rifle.

"Ye want yer boys outta this?" said the Outlaw. "Then we need to start doin things how we used to."

Eldon exhaled. Then he handed over the Winchester.

Jack set the barrel on the sill and aimed through the loophole. "We're boring with a big auger now, boys."

Eldon looked over his shoulder through the loophole. The rifle was pointed at a brick-colored roll the rider had dropped thirty yards away. It was half submerged in snow a few paces from the springhouse. It hadn't registered before, but now it was obvious what it was.

"It's too close," he said.

Jack grunted. "No it ain't."

"Clayton. Give me the rifle. It's too damn close."

"No, it ain't."

Eldon lunged. As his fingers grasped the barrel, the firing pin set in motion all that had stacked up before it. But he kept reaching. Not for the rifle. For his brother.

He felt pressure in his ears. Then heat. It was like getting kicked by a horse. Still, he held his brother, shrouding him from the blast, just as he had all those years ago when nothing could tear them apart, not even twenty pounds of dynamite.

SEVEN

LIGHT BURNED THROUGH CLOSED LIDS. A THIN RINGING filled his ears. He was choking on dust. With shaky hands he brushed the debris from his face and opened his eyes. A lustrous diamond of light tore into the blackness. He blinked and rubbed his face. There was a gaping hole where the boarded-up window had been just moments ago. And then some big snorting beast rushed past, batting the diamond like a reptilian eye, and Eldon rolled away in fright. Pain was everywhere, though he couldn't perceive any specific injury besides the feeling of being kicked in every part of his body.

The big snorting thing blinked past again, stamping and whinnying, a bitter exhaust in its wake. This time he didn't flinch. As he moved closer, a blast of wind burned his cheeks. The window was gone.

The hoofbeats were coming around again. He rubbed his eyes until the blur of sun-bleached images resolved into recognizable shapes. Cutting through high powder, the horse thundered past, dirt-speckled, muscles rippling, a smear of orange and black trailing out behind it. The mare circled a scorched crater, flames and smoke streaming from her mane. As she came around again, a scream startled her and she fled for the trees, a thread of black smoke left to dissipate over the field.

Squinting, Eldon searched for the source of the scream. Amid the whitewashed wreckage of the springhouse, one of the Bender boys lay cupping his slippery entrails with both hands, begging for his mother.

Eldon groped for his rifle to put him out of his misery. Chunks of wood and glass rained off his chest. The trail of ruin ran down the length of the keeping room, as if a cannonball had blown straight through the cabin.

The Bender boy had gone silent. When Eldon looked out, he was slumped over next to a pair of black boots that stood upright in the snow. Their owner was speckled across the field, big gobbets of flesh melting scarlet pits into the snow.

The Farmer lurched to his feet and steadied himself on the archway. The boys were huddled behind the cookstove where he'd left them, hugging each other once again. Shane started to get up, but Eldon waved him down.

Gunshots dragged the Farmer's attention back to the diamond in the wall.

Jack seemed to float in the glare, pistols blazing as he advanced through expanding wreaths of gun smoke, locked in a deadly cotillion with the kid in the red-and-yellow bandanna.

Belly down in the crater, one bloody arm packed against his chest, the kid tried to shoot left-handed. Ignoring the wild shots, Jack dropped to a knee, two hands on his Colt. The kid poked up from behind the berm and fired another clumsy shot. Jack fired a single round. The kid's head snapped back. His hat spun straight up in the sky and hung against a patch of blue, flipping like a coin.

The Outlaw scampered back through the hole in the wall and turned past Eldon into the kitchen. He grabbed the ammo pouch from Shane, then hunched against the cookstove and fed cartridges into his guns. "That's three down," he said, wildness in his eyes. "Three more ham-shitters to go."

Eldon slapped himself to break up the shock. The Winchester lay on the floor at his feet. He picked it up and levered it. A spent cartridge plunked across the floor.

Suddenly Jack was in his face. "I'm goin round front to draw em out," he growled. "Git on that front door and watch my back!"

"Hold on," said Eldon. "We got shelter, plenty of ammo. They know there's more than one of us but got no idea how many. We got the advantage here."

A vein blasted out of Jack's forehead. "I ain't one to be *done to*, brother. I'm the one who does the *doin*." He put a finger in Eldon's face. "You fuckin shoot to kill." He shouldered past, heading out through the tear in the wall.

Eldon ran down the keep toward the front of the house. The front door was all but gone, but the boarded-up window was intact. Eldon crouched at the loophole and searched the tree line, but the glare off the snow streaked away any details.

A whistle sounded from the corner of the cabin, a few feet away. Balancing his rifle on the sill, Eldon whistled back. Jack trudged into view from his right, sawing through belly-high powder. At the left of his periphery, he could see about half the barn. Twenty paces dead ahead was the outhouse, the tree line a hundred yards beyond that. He searched for that scabby lacebark where he'd first spotted them, but they were gone.

As the wind kicked up, waves of ice snaked across the pastureland.

"Three o'clock!" Jack hollered.

Eldon swung his rifle eastward and picked up a rider cutting out of the trees. At the same time, a mountain of a man stepped out from the corner of the barn with a big-bore rifle. The rider was bait, and Jack had taken it.

A pandemonium of shots cursed the air. The Outlaw ran for the outhouse, vines of snow sprouting all around him. Eldon turned from the rider and shot at the big man, forcing him back behind the barn. Then back to the rider. He fired once and wiped the man off his horse.

He looked to see if his brother had made it to the outhouse, and the shutter exploded overhead. He dropped, glass and wood raining down. The shots kept coming. They sounded distant. There was a third rifleman in the trees. Tricky Bender.

Eldon bellied over to what was left of the front door and tried to get eyes on the man in the trees. The shooting had stopped.

Ten paces ahead, Jack turned, huddled against the outhouse.

"Hold out your hat," said Eldon.

"Huh? Hell no. I like this hat."

"I need to see where he's holed up."

"Hold out your own damn hat then."

"You're the one who wanted to *do the doing*, remember?"

A long breath steamed out of Jack. Muttering and shaking his head, he balanced his bolero on the barrel of his Colt. He removed the beaded stampede string and stuffed it into his pocket. Then, crouched low, he inched the hat around the side of the outhouse.

Eldon watched the trees. A flash preceded the small clap. The bullet chomped at the wood inches from Jack's hand. A hundred yards north, beneath a sprawling oak, lay the infamous bushwhacker, Tricky Bender. At that range he was just a flyspeck, yet the Farmer spent the whole tube on him, forcing Tricky to retreat into the forest.

With Tricky lost in the trees, Eldon turned his attention to the man hiding behind the barn. As he reloaded, he called low across the yard at Jack. "When I say so, stand up and draw that big bastard out from behind the barn."

Jack shook his head. "Goddammit, the hat's one thing."

Eldon levered the rifle, then crouched out of sight behind the doorway. "Come on, *Jack*. Raise up and give him a wave. Don't be shy."

The Outlaw hesitated. In fact, he seemed outright shaken, and was looking at Eldon as if he didn't trust him. He'd never looked at Eldon that way before.

"Go on," said Eldon. "I got you."

"Do not fuckin miss."

"You know I won't."

Slowly, the Outlaw peeked his head around the side of the outhouse. When the big man failed to appear, he stepped his whole body out. Then he started waving his arms and dispensing any malediction that came to his tongue.

A shadow panned from the side of the barn. Eldon watched it grow, then kicked through what was left of the front door and charged into the barnyard.

The big man raised his rifle at the Outlaw. Eldon whistled and the man turned. His first shot sent him stumbling back, the second flung him into the arms of the Lord.

He heard the horse before he saw it.

"Behind ye!" Jack barked, raising his pistol.

Eldon turned.

Tricky rode high in the saddle, a six-shooter in each hand, charging around from the back of the house. He was just as squat and mean as Sonny, though he'd never outgrown his boyishness. Sallow and pruned, he looked like a child who had spent too much time in the bathtub. But that didn't change the fact that he had Eldon dead to rights.

The bark of a pistol cut the Farmer's prayers short.

The horse reared up in front of him. Tricky slid off the back, landing half on his feet. His guns jerked up toward Eldon, but he couldn't muster the strength to raise them higher than his waist. He fired a shot into the snow then stumbled to a knee.

Jack put another hole in his gut. Hot air burst from Tricky's mouth and he sat hard in the snow. Circling around behind him, Jack holstered his revolver and drew his knife.

Eldon looked back at the house. In the ruined doorway, Shane and Ian stood watching, their hoary faces frozen in anticipation. He waved them back. "Go on!" he snapped. "Get back in the house!"

Ian obeyed, but Shane didn't budge, his pale face frozen in the destroyed window.

Standing behind Tricky, Jack showed him the knife, bolsters and rivets flashing in the sun.

With a look, Eldon begged him to finish the job. But the Outlaw seemed intent on relishing the kill. He yanked Tricky's head back, exposing the pale white of his throat. Then he looked up, matching eyes with Eldon. His face rumbled as he plunged the blade into the side of Tricky's neck and jerked outward.

A steaming blossom erupted from the throat, strangling the man's cries to a swinish gurgle. The kind of sound that haunts the mind forever.

Eldon prayed that his son had vacated the window, but there Shane stood, the disturbance settling across his face like a curse.

EIGHT

JACK LINGERED IN THE RUINED DOORWAY, WIPING HIS HANDS on a rag. Blood covered his pants, drenched his shirt, and speckled his face. "Yeah," he said, wiping himself down. "A seventy-thirty split is more than generous, given I done five-sixths of the killin."

At the other end of the keep, Eldon stood hugging his boys, their bony arms locked around him, staring at his brother like he was a monster.

Jack ambled up and stood before the dwindling hearth fire. "Hope they ain't ruined my hares," he said, appraising the bullet-splattered jackrabbits. What edible meat remained had gained a healthy char. He peeled off a nub then offered it to Shane. "Git ye some."

The boy didn't take it, nor did he return the Outlaw's roguish smirk.

Jack's eyes slithered to Eldon. "So how ye plan to settle me up?"

"Settle you up?"

He nodded at the hole in the wall, the dead men beyond. "Each one of them sombitches got a bounty on his head. A full thousand fer Tricky Bender. Dell Grimmwood and Lester Spivey, that's five hundred apiece. Them other three I ain't sure of, but count on at least three bushels of beans per carcass. Fer now I reckon you can settle me up with what ye got in that rusty can of tomatoes. I'll come back fer the rest later."

Wind moaned through the walls, turning the cabin into a sad, tuneless instrument.

"I'd collect from the marshal myself," Jack added. "But then I'd have to play a God-fearing granger named Eldon Quint."

This had to be some kind of jape. But the Outlaw's eyes were grim and serious.

"Tell me this wasn't your plan all along," Eldon said.

The storm brewing on the Outlaw's face looked ready to spend its force as he spoke through his teeth. "Yer boys don't need to be witnessin my mean streak."

Eldon walked into the kitchen, scooped one of the Model 3s off the table, and held it at his side. "Get out of my house."

"That gun don't got no bullets in it."

"Shane."

The boy retrieved the ammo pouch and handed it to his father. Eldon stared at Jack as he loaded the revolver, each cartridge seating with a hollow plunk. Jack was the first to break the gaze. He smiled and tipped his hat at the boys.

"Shane, ye look me up when yer ready to compose my magnum opus. Turnspit, you keep practicing on them eyes. Windows to the soul. Remember that." He turned for the ruined door but stopped in the entranceway. Sunlight crowned him as he smirked at the credenza. "Well, here I go," he muttered, "never to return."

"Jack," warned Eldon. "Don't even think about it."

"Think about what?" said the Outlaw as he reached into the credenza and took out the tomato can full of money. The money Eldon had earned going door-to-door, selling off his pride one fire mat at a time. Jack ripped off the cloth and dumped the bills and coins across the tiles. He shuffled the bills then stuffed them into his pocket. "Ye made all this sellin them dinky mats? Lord gives you a decade of fire and plague, and a burnt-up wife to boot, and you prosper."

Eldon set the Model 3 on the kitchen table and marched toward his brother. Without breaking stride, he struck him across the mouth. Jack staggered, a hand going to his lip. Spitting blood, he unbuckled his guns and tossed them across the credenza and put up his fists. It had been a long time since Eldon had beat his brother senseless, and now it was a long time coming.

Feinting high, he lunged low, slamming Jack across the floor. Swooping in behind, he threaded an arm around Jack's neck and cranked.

Punish him, he thought. *For being weak. For being a blight on your reputation. For costing you more opportunities than you can count on two hands.*

Gasping for air, Jack rolled to all fours and pressed up to his feet. Eldon clung to his back. Jack heaved his body backward. The edge of the credenza bit into the back of Eldon's skull. Pain swarmed his sinuses. Then he was on his back, body to body with his brother, sweat in his eyes, blood in his mouth. Jack's forearm crushed into his throat. As he began to lose consciousness, he looked at the vein bulging across his brother's forehead and imagined the same blood running through him, the same rage, the same hate. For a moment it was like it used to be, back when they shared everything, even the pain. But his limbs were fading, the darkness taking his mind.

A voice cried in the distance. His eyes flicked up. Shane stood in the archway, raising the Model 3, struggling to draw the hammer back. He was screaming at Jack. The sight of him charged Eldon with a last burst of energy. Wedging his wrist under Jack's forearm, he turned his head, muscled the pressure off his neck, and ordered Shane to put the gun down.

Jack tried to reposition the choke, but his forearm, slick with sweat and saliva, slipped to one side. Eldon scuttled out from underneath, swooped behind him, and coiled an arm around his neck, wrapped his legs over Jack's hips, rolled to his back, and arched his body like some medieval torture device. Blood from Jack's chin ran hot across his forearm.

A snort, a clipped retch, a shiver—the sound of life sputtering away.

Thirty-five years of looking after a brother who did nothing but drag him down, who forced him to return to the frontier to raise a family.

A hand pinched his knee. It was his brother letting him know that he was giving up, just like when Daddy used to make them fight each other for their supper and Eldon would whip up on him. Eldon kept his arm tight. Then Jack wasn't moving, eyes rolled back, capillaries exploding in the sclera. His tongue sat between his teeth like a worm. A second longer and his face would stay locked in that grotesque repose forever. Yet he could feel his resolve fading, and tried to talk it back into his arm.

You're close, he said, *you're almost there.*

The muscles loosened. He felt breath return to his brother's chest.

A shadow crossed over them just then. Eldon looked toward the glowing tear in the wall where a crooked figure stood surrounded by light, far too tall to be Shane. The figure walked into the keep. A raw stripe ran along his hairline where Jack's bullet had skimmed the top of his head. His body was black as creosote from the explosion, and the red-and-yellow neckerchief that before had looked like a bull's-eye now resembled a ring of fire. He stood by the hearth, a pistol in his left hand, his right arm all but severed at the elbow. Shane spun around, the Model 3 still raised in his hand.

The Bender boy's left arm swiped up.

Eldon tried to yell, but all that came out was a scratchy burst of air.

Shane squeezed the trigger. The half-cocked hammer clicked harmlessly, though that small sound was lost in the explosion of the opposing weapon.

The shot punched the boy in the gut, piercing the journal in his jacket pocket. A murmuration of shredded paper burst up around him like a thousand tiny birds.

Having passed through the boy and his journal, the bullet shattered the oil lamp on the kitchen table behind him. Shane fell back into a rain of coal oil and broken glass, scraps of paper floating down, settling on his chest like flakes of snow, each piece scribbled with dreams, fears, desires. Fanciful stories about gunslingers and cowboys; saccharine verses he never had the courage to say to Molly Wachiwi; loving things he wished he'd told his mother before she died; angry things he wished he'd said to his father's face.

Eldon sat in shock, the chapters of his son's life dancing in the wind and smoke. When the Bender boy panned his weapon to find a new target, Eldon lunged for Jack's gun belt on the credenza. Squinting at the sun coming through the front door, the kid fired. There was a rush of air as the slug just missed Eldon's head, though he hardly noticed as he dug out the iron and blew as many holes in the kid as the weapon allowed.

He ran to the kitchen. Shane's legs were bent underneath him as if while kneeling in prayer he'd been kicked in the forehead. His jaw moved slowly. Eldon sat and dragged him into his lap. Gently, he brushed the glass and flakes of paper off his face. The boy's skin was pale. His mouth stopped reaching for air.

"No, keep breathing," Eldon said. "Shane. Breathe. Open your eyes."

With a powder-burned finger, he pushed up his son's lids. Put an ear to his mouth, then readjusted the body to encourage a breath. He did this again and again, then looked around the kitchen for help.

In the archway stood Ian, his freckled cheeks wet and ruddy and slack with shock, his mouth frozen in a soundless cry. Eldon wanted to hold him, to hold them both, but he couldn't let Shane go. If he let him go, it was over. The boy would grow cold, his muscles would stiffen, his skin would shrivel, his heart would disintegrate. He had to keep him warm. He pressed the body to his chest and hugged him.

When he looked up again, Jack stood in the archway, his mouth flat and grim as a hatchet mark. He was holding Ian against his shoulder, covering the child's eyes.

Eldon's rage condensed into a single molten point between his eyes.

"Put him down," he said.

In his mind he'd screamed the order, but it had come out as a whisper. Even so, the Outlaw set the child down.

The Model 3 sat in a puddle of coal oil. Holding Shane with one arm, Eldon picked it up and raised it at his brother. Jack stared down the barrel, his body posing no argument to such a fate. The Farmer might have done it had Ian not thrown his arms around him. The hurt crashed down all at once. He held on to both of his sons. When he opened his eyes, Jack Foss was gone.

NINE

HE LAID THE BODY ON THE BUNK. FOLDED THE ARMS ACROSS the chest. Licked his thumb and cleaned blood that had crusted the upper lip. He rested his hand on the unmoving chest. Dull pupils half concealed under warped lids. The finality of it—that those black circles would never dilate or constrict or behold something new or beautiful. He drew the lids down with his fingers and stood there.

One of Shane's boots had fallen on the floor. He reached for it and saw books piled under the bed. *Fireside Stories*, *Beadle's*, *Frank Starr's* dime novels. Encomiums to Jack Foss buried under old newspaper. One cover peeked out, a sensational illustration of *Minnesota Jack*, the Outlaw spitting fire from his twin pistols, a damsel wrapped around his waist as his steed made an impossible leap over a speeding locomotive.

Last night, when he'd put Shane to bed, he could've read him a book. Instead he shut the door with hardly a good night.

He slid the boot back on to Shane's foot and tightened the laces. Ian watched from the corner, big malachite eyes carefully tracking his father.

"Come say goodbye," Eldon told him.

The child didn't move.

"He's on his way to heaven, but he'll hear you."

Ian climbed onto the bunk and touched Shane's chest. He threw his arms around him and promised to talk with him every day, to never forget him. Eldon watched, pushing down what that book cover had dredged up. These were the last moments with his son—Jack Foss wouldn't take them, too.

He told Ian to stay put. Then he went into the kitchen and found Shane's blanket, the gray one that belonged to Hattie. Back then it had been dotted with green circles. But the green had been chewed away by locusts, leaving perfectly round holes in the prickly wool.

The feel of the thick blanket left him panic-stricken. Should he wrap Shane in calico instead? They had plenty of that, a whole bolt, but they only had a few good blankets. What would keep Ian warm? The calico was so thin. It would let the last of the warmth escape Shane's body. He couldn't abide that, and he brought the wool blanket to the bedroom and wrapped his son while Ian watched. There was something else to take care of and he told Ian to stay put until he called him.

From his bedroom he took the bolt of calico from the closet then returned to the keep, the air thick with saltpeter and blood. As he covered the dead Bender boy in the brittle fabric, the wind slipped into the house. He could hear it. The empty tomato can rolling back and forth on the floor, its contents gone with the Outlaw.

The Farmer crossed the barnyard, Ian in his arms, the child's face buried in the nape of his neck, hidden from the death spoiling their land. Eldon's legs moved unsteadily beneath him, as if pulled by strings, but his mind had congealed to a single burning focus.

In the barn he stood before the empty stall where they'd boarded Jack's steed. The gate creaked in the wind. He turned to the doors and looked across the field. His brother's tracks went in a straight line through the gates.

The old swayback gave him guff when he saddled her. It took all he had not to whip her. He set the child atop her sagged frame.

"Ride straight to Dick's. Take the game trail, stay off the road."

"You aren't coming?"

"I'll meet you there."

The child started to weep. "I want to stay with you."

"I bet Laura will make you a batch of her famous corn cakes if you ask. I'll be there by the time they come out of the oven."

He led the mare to the barn doors and scanned the fields. The shredded outhouse, the big man encased in snow, the rider with his head crowned in blood, Tricky with his head nearly sawed off. "Don't look anywhere but straight ahead."

The child wiped his eyes. "Are you gonna kill Uncle Jack?"

Eldon slapped the horse and stood watching the child shrink into the distance.

When he had loaded his Winchester, he boarded the paint and rode east. His brother's tracks led down a darkening trail, heavy powder sucking at the horse's hooves. The land was still and gray. That dull quiet a new snow brings.

Darkness closed over the sky, the last of the daylight punching out of a fire-stewed horizon. Soon the Outlaw's tracks turned short and lazy. Eldon had been riding thoughtlessly for a time and when he looked up, he didn't immediately recognize where he was. The road would eventually merge with a trafficked thoroughfare used by the express mail run, passing through Yankton, Vermillion, and Sioux City. That was where Jack would go, where he could spend that money the fastest.

The trees ahead opened to black sky and a hazy moon. The tracks veered into a snowfield dotted with junipers. Eldon turned his horse into the field and found Jack's gray roped to a branch. He rode past the animal, pursuing sluggish boot tracks. Encircled by dark walls of fir and birch, the field came to resemble a coliseum floor. Cloud shadows swept past, wind picking up, the moon glazing everything in pale turquoise.

Among the stubby junipers, Jack sat in the powder. He faced away from the trail, drinking from a calfskin canteen. Eldon sat his horse ten yards away. The air was cold and pure. Dropping from the horse, Eldon dragged the Winchester from its scabbard.

Muttering to himself, Jack was in some kind of deranged state. He turned as Eldon trudged up, then pushed to his feet, poised in a half stance like a startled animal. Eldon brought the rifle up. Jack stared, drunk and blubbering. Eldon asked God to forgive him, then fired.

The Outlaw spun in a half circle, dropping his calfskin bladder. With an almost comic ignorance of the fact that he'd just been shot, he began searching for the lost canteen. Closing the distance, Eldon levered his rifle. The metallic toll of the ejected cartridge caused the Outlaw to abandon his search. He hobbled on, packing one leg like a hipshot deer. Eldon stalked him as he circled back toward his horse, smelling the reek of whiskey. The Outlaw limped up to his animal and reached for the tether.

Eldon stopped a few paces away. "Turn around."

Wedging his boot into the tapadero, the Outlaw attempted to swing onto the horse but winced and sunk back into the snow. He touched his hip, found blood on his glove, and looked up in amazement.

"Ye shot me?"

Eldon raised his rifle. "Grazed. But I aim to make it tell with the next one."

The Outlaw flopped his body clumsily over his mount and tried to get a leg over. As the horse stamped and whinnied, he reached for his pannier, then pulled out a small metallic object and swung it toward his brother. Eldon fired a shot just as the horse reared. The bullet meant for Jack struck the gray in the center of its brilliant white blaze and the animal fell onto its side. Jack howled, his lower body trapped under fifteen hundred pounds of horse.

"Lickspittle fucker . . ." His voice broke. "You killed Artemus . . . killed my horse."

Icy breath swept over the field, struck the trees, and released an avalanche from the branches. Boulders of snow thudded down around them, though Eldon took little notice of the excitement in the landscape as he stood over his brother. In his mind he'd already written the death sentence; all it needed was a period.

The two-shot pistol Jack had secreted from his pannier sat atop the snow, so small that it hardly dented the powder. Eldon picked it up, put it into his pocket. He held the rifle across his chest and looked down.

The Outlaw sucked snot and spat. "There ye go," he said, "killin horses again." The words seemed to heat the air between them.

Eldon leaned the Winchester against a tree, untethered a gripsack from the dead horse, and dumped out the contents: two empty whiskey bottles and three handbills for members of the Sonny Bender gang. He pocketed the handbills, then went through Jack's pannier. When he didn't find the money there, he went into Jack's pocket and pulled out the roll of greenbacks.

Jack looked surprised.

Eldon shook the money at him. "You brought this on yourself."

The Outlaw tried to smile and said, "Murder me, brother, you can kiss the God-fearing granger Eldon Quint goodbye."

"You cost me a son."

The Farmer pointed his rifle.

"At least tell me why ye left," begged the Outlaw. A desperate smile crossed his lips. "Daddy said never die curious of what killed you. Remember?"

For a split second Eldon saw his brother, six years old, running for the hills, a shoat squealing in his arms, Daddy hot on his heels.

He shook off the memory, then looked down at a face just as rough and broken as his own. The shot rattled against the trees.

Snow plumed next to the Outlaw's face. His eyes blew open and he sucked air under his teeth, grabbing his ear.

Eldon took his Colts, left him under the dead horse, and boarded his paint.

"Don't leave me like this," he heard his brother say. "Eldon, don't leave me like this."

He wheeled his paint onto the road, blocking out Clayton's voice.

The indigo strip churned out of the void as he kicked the horse faster, hoping the night would swallow him whole.

TEN

THROUGH STONE PILLARS HE RODE, OVER ICE-BLUE FIELDS blotted with dark spots of carnage. The dead—ruined and contorted and encased in snow—reached up to grab him, but he rode too fast.

He stood in the shattered mouth of his cabin. Walked the dark throat of the keeping room to the archway. Lingered over the kid who'd killed his son.

No, shot him. It was the past that had killed his son.

The wind had blown the thin calico sheet off the kid's head. Crinkled eyeballs. A demented face that seemed to be caught in a warped mirror.

Something danced out of the moonlit kitchen. He watched the scrap of paper float out through the hole in the wall, carried off by the wind.

In the kitchen he found more pulpy fragments trapped in a wine-dark stain on the floor; others flitted in the gusts that whistled through the injured walls. He collected bits of Shane's journal, wiping off the blood, stuffing shreds of crooked script into his breast pocket.

In the bedroom, Shane's body lay on the bottom bunk. Eldon drew back the wool blanket. Then he pulled off his own undershirt and lay down next to his son's body, clutching the cool, waxy flesh. Shane's stiff joints resisted his embrace. His back was dark in color where the blood had settled. Eldon held him tighter, desperate to make that fluid chirr, to return the color to his cheeks, to lift the corners of his mouth, to compel one last smile.

Hattie rocked in her chair, cradling baby Shane. Eldon smiled when the baby's eyes found him. Sunlight shone through the window, so thick you could scoop it out of the air. He reached for the cooing tot, but Hattie stopped rocking and tightened her grip. But Eldon wanted to hold his son and yanked the baby from her arms. Shane wailed, frail limbs jerking convulsively, his mouth shuddering. Eldon tried all he could to calm him, but the baby wouldn't stop screaming. The smell of smoke caused him to look up. Flames raged against the windows. The fields were on fire. Hattie reached desperately for the child. Eldon didn't want to let him go, but the flames had reached their door.

He woke in darkness, face raked and twisted, hugging his firstborn so tightly that if Shane weren't already dead, he would have been suffocated. He could feel his wife pulling on the body, and was too afraid to let go. If not for Ian, he would be at Shane's side. But he was here, and the boy was alone, stuck between this world and the next. Alone. The word echoed around in his mind. He couldn't let him be alone.

He needed to be with his mother.

A musky scent in the air drew his eyes to the foot of the bed, to a hulking shadow. A flame hissed to life in the shadow's hand and streaked upward. The match revealed a hard face with the sharp angles and the deep-cut lines of a primitive carving.

"Nephew."

It was the voice of an old man, of a friend and neighbor.

Dick Cottersman's eyes sank as they traced Shane's pale body. He removed his hat and ran crooked fingers through his cropped hair.

"Nephew," he said again, the word dragging plaintively out of his mouth.

In the kitchen Dick lit one of the beeswax candles. Eldon stared at the flame, watching it dance in the wind as he told his neighbor about the Bender boys, about Shane and the gun he didn't know how to use, about leaving his brother for dead.

"Pray with me," Dick said.

It sounded like he was speaking through six feet of bedrock.

As the silence unreeled, Eldon began to calculate how long it would take to get to Springfield. The steamers wouldn't be running yet. Maybe three, four days by train?

He must've been thinking out loud because Dick said, "The trains is snowed out. Have been the last two weeks."

He couldn't let Shane wait two weeks aboveground. Two months probably, given this winter.

"We should pray," Dick said.

"I don't want to pray," Eldon said.

He blew out the candle, then paced the kitchen, shaking the numbness from his limbs. There was only one other option.

"I'll take my wagon," he said.

The old man lifted his heavy brow. "The snow is up to the hubs. It's up to the telegraph wires in Yankton."

Eldon dug the handbills out of his coat and stuffed them into Dick's hand. "Half that bounty's yours if you collect for me. Send me my half on the road. I should have enough to get there. Which is good, cause we need to be leaving at first light."

"First light?" Dick blinked, a sure sign of distress. "Hold it, nephew."

Eldon didn't want to hear it, and started through the archway. Dick stood in his way, lifting his palm. His beaded bracelets reminded Eldon of the stampede string that wrapped his brother's hat. He wondered if Clayton's lungs had exploded from the cold, if he was drowning in his own blood.

Dick was talking again. Eldon barely listened. Something about how waiting for the train would be safer, that there were dangerous men on the road.

"He needs to be with his mother," Eldon heard himself say. "Needs to be buried by his family, not some sheriff seven hundred miles away."

"You still blame yourself but you begged her not to go."

"Get out of my way, Dick."

The old man pointed a long, gnarled finger. "You're free, nephew, free to do as you please. But so am I. Try to leave here with Ian in some buckboard, no tent, no provisions, no preparation, I tear that wagon apart with my hands. Then you go nowhere."

Eldon looked past Dick. His rifle was leaned against the hearth. "You think we're free?" he said. "After what we done, you think we're free men?"

The old man's face closed up, as if a forbidden thing had been spoken.

"You know what freedom is, Dick? It's the distance between a man and what's coming for him."

He lay next to Ian in the living room of Dick's commodious brick farmhouse, watching the shadows from the fire dance on the ceiling. In the morning, Dick brought him outside to show off the work he'd done to his buckboard. He'd installed a driver's bench, raised the sideboards, and wrapped the bed with an oilcloth tent that had cinch flaps at either end to seal it against the cold. What was before little more than a mud wagon now resembled a modest prairie schooner.

Dick's wife, Laura, came out and announced breakfast, but Eldon wasn't hungry. The full-bodied schoolteacher, with her tightly pulled raven hair, held no truck with a man's empty stomach and forced him to come in and eat.

Ian was already at the table, swollen-eyed, mashing a stack of griddle cakes with his fork. Eldon stared into his coffee. The surface swirled black and oily.

When he raised his eyes, Laura gave him a look, waving her eyes at Ian.

Eldon sipped the lukewarm coffee and cleared his throat. "We're leaving today," he told Ian. "We're going to bury Shane next to Momma. The trains aren't running and we don't know when they'll run again. Which means we have to go by wagon. Uncle Dick is gonna lend us Patsy and Little Joe. Good horses. They'll get us there safe."

The child mashed griddle cakes and would not look up.

Eldon looked at Laura.

She wiped her hands on her apron, then hurried up and smothered Ian in her wobbly arms. "There's nothing to be afraid of. Your pa knows how to keep you safe."

Ian stopped mashing the cakes. "But I don't want to go."

Laura looked at Eldon. It was an offer. *He'd be safer here.*

"Don't you want to see your brother buried?" he asked his son.

Gritting his teeth, Ian shook his head. "I don't want him to be dead."

"I know you don't," he said. "But he is. And he needs to be with Momma. Needs to be buried next to her. So he has someone he knows up there. Can show him around."

Ian sat thinking very hard, then nodded to himself. "So he's not alone, right?"

"Right. So he's not alone."

After breakfast Dick and Ian went out to pack the wagon while Eldon readied Shane in the barn. The boy's skin was about the color of the moon. Flecks of ice clumped his lashes, hair, the insides of his nostrils. Clayton probably looked the same about now.

After wrapping the body in more blankets and tying them with twine, Eldon carried Shane out to the wagon. As he loaded him into the boot, Laura had the idea of installing a partition down the center so they wouldn't lose all that space for their stores.

When they'd packed all the provisions and had gotten the last of their gatherings together, they collected on the porch to say farewell. The day was bright and windless but bitterly cold, the sky a thin shell of bone blue.

Laura handed Eldon a supper basket. "Corn cakes and stewed pork." She smiled down at Ian, though when she raised her eyes to Eldon, they were drained of all but worry.

Having just greased the axles, Dick rubbed his hands on his shirtfront, leaving a dark smear of pine tar. "I'll collect on those bounties," he said in his rumbling monotone. "By the time you pass through Kansas City, I think. Should be waiting at the Western Union there. I'll keep what I need to repair your home."

"Dick," said Eldon. "You don't have to do that."

"I'm an old man now who can't even hunt in winter. I need something to do."

They boarded the wagon, father and son settling side by side on the cold driver's bench. The old man held his wife. His proud, quavering voice rang over the deadened landscape as he sang his song of mourning.

With a sharp command, Eldon started the team, heading for the icy road that would return him to a world he'd spent the last thirteen years running from.

THE ROAD

ELEVEN

IAN LEANED OVER THE BUCKBOARD, POINTING BEYOND the plodding horses. "Two hundred and ninety-nine," he announced, looking up at his father.

Eldon followed his gesture across the same gray desolation that had filled his eyes for the last week and a half. As they drew nearer, his leg bobbed, the heel of his boot tapping on the footrest. Two whitewashed planks, rotted at the edges, formed a cross. It looked like all the others—three feet tall, with the same begrimed complexion as the aging snow that crusted the prairie.

Desolation and white crosses. That about summed up the journey so far. Monotony was a slow killer, chipping away at a man's vigilance. There were times he imagined that they'd made no progress at all, that the same stretch of frozen prairie had revolved endlessly beneath their wheels since Dakota.

It was lack of sleep, he told himself. And that damn nightmare. He'd be scrambling up the keep, trying to get to Shane before the Bender boy's bullet. Never could beat fate, but he tried, night after night. It drove Ian out of his mind. It would be the middle of the night and he'd have to tell his father to quit kicking his feet. But Eldon couldn't stop running, not even in his dreams.

The child pointed at the other side of the road. "Three hundred!" he said.

Eldon bristled at the shrill pronouncement. He'd become so sensitive to loud noises that even the snort of a horse set him off. Ian had learned to comport himself circumspectly—no clanging of pots at suppertime, no coughing too loudly, no shouting. He didn't always succeed, but Eldon preferred the occasional clang or cough to the glassy-eyed silence the child presented during the opening leg of the trip.

They passed the three hundredth cross, marking the three hundredth dead traveler. Eldon tried to stop his thoughts from swirling. If he'd never gone hunting, if he'd just stayed home, maybe his son would be alive.

Maybe if you never abandoned yer brother in the first place.

The voice came from beside him, but the driver's bench was empty.

That's twice now ye abandoned him.

It was behind him, seeping from the dark mouth of the tent.

It ain't him ye should be pointin a finger at.

Now it was between his ears.

"Shut up," he muttered.

Ian looked up from the buckboard. "Huh?"

Eldon cleared his throat, trying to evict Jack's voice.

"Nothing," he said.

From Dakota they'd followed the Missouri east, the river like a strip of iron burned into the moon-white ground. He'd kept to the inland trail despite the comparative ease of the lowland route. Something had told him to steer clear of water. Maybe seeing his own reflection would remind him of his brother, frozen under a horse. Or maybe it was the temptation to sink his own body beneath the ice.

"Stop it," he muttered.

Ian looked up. "Huh?"

Eldon spat. "I said stop counting crosses."

Eventually, the upper trail merged with the lowland route. At a bend in the river a settlement of dugout homes pushed like boils out of the earth. Eldon figured they'd better stop to trade. Last night, Ian hadn't properly restored the tailgate and an animal had gotten into the boot. Thankfully, Shane's body was untouched, but they'd lost their salt pork.

He parked the wagon in a fir grove thirty yards from the settlement. After tucking one of the Model 3s into his waistband, he lifted Ian out of the wagon and handed him a stack of fire mats.

"Stay right behind me," he said.

As they stomped through the snow, Eldon felt a presence behind him. It touched the back of his neck. Hard calluses and ropy fingers. A hand that didn't know sympathy or reassurance. He shook loose of it. Daddy didn't have a say anymore.

They wandered a maze of dugouts and sod hovels topped with slabs of snow painted black by the peat fires. A slushy makeshift town square, crowded with rain-rotted mules and homicidal roosters, was populated by a dozen gaunt women scraping laundry. They lifted their hollow faces as Eldon and Ian crossed the muddy terrain. Eldon announced his purpose to trade. A round-faced man in a scratched leather apron toddled immediately from one of the rude little dwellings. He had flaxen hair and spoke a globular language that reminded Eldon of the Norwegians in Minnesota. He gestured and one of the women went into a home and returned with a cake of tobacco. The aproned man cut a quid and held it up, indicating his willingness to trade. They sat on two damp logs and spoke in pantomime. After some back-and-forth, they settled on two fire mats for a dozen biscuits and a jar of calf's-foot jelly. When Eldon turned to hand Ian the supplies, the child was gone.

He shot up. "Ian?"

The women were staring at his feet. He looked down. The Model 3 had fallen from his waistband. The aproned man spoke sharply and the women fled for their black doorways, shooing curious children inside. The man gestured at Eldon to leave at once.

He hurried through a warren of mud-walled alleyways, calling his son's name. By chance he emerged at the same place he'd entered. A set of tracks led to the fir trees he'd parked his wagon behind.

When he reached the wagon, he found a slat-ribbed dog licking bits of pemmican from Ian's palm. He caught his breath, trudged over, scooped up the animal, and launched it back toward the settlement. The mutt hit the snow, cartwheeled, then bounded away.

"But he's hungry," Ian protested.

Eldon seized him by the shoulders. "Don't ever run off like that again."

He's weak, said Jack.

Shut up.

Ye made him weak.

Eldon was fourteen again. The smell of burning houses wafted through the trees. Daddy was hustling the boys to the canoe, but a Dakota war party had beaten them to it, and he turned them back toward the house. When they came in, Teague barked joyously. Clayton begged Daddy to take their loyal setter to Fort Ridgely. Instead Daddy slipped off his belt and strangled the dog to keep him from alerting the Indians.

After they'd escaped, Daddy made sure to whip Clayton for making so much noise, then he whipped Eldon, too. The kindness Eldon showed his brother had made Clayton weak, and that weakness had almost gotten them killed.

Daddy's methods made for an unpleasant upbringing, but by the time Eldon was Ian's age, he could survive the frontier on his own. He hunted by starlight, tracked deer across flat rock, and could load and shoot almost any musket. Meanwhile, Ian knew only women's work. Thawing the pumps, emptying the bedside thundermugs, mending clothes, purging flies in summer. His favorite chore was making pumpkin leather and watermelon molasses with his mother. No wonder he was standing there now, weeping and sucking his fingers.

Eldon tugged the wet digits out of his son's mouth. "Don't do that," he said. "You feel nervous, you spit. Your brother teach you to spit?"

Ian spat. Saliva dribbled down his chin.

Daddy used to say that life on the frontier could never be lived on civilized terms. That it had to be lived savagely. The road was no different.

"There are no rules out here," he told Ian.

Tears spilled down his chapped cheeks. "Sorry," he said. "There's no place for kindness on the road. Understand?"

"Yessir."

He thought of Shane struggling to pull back the hammer of a pistol he'd never been taught to use. Ian had never even touched a pistol, but that would have to change. Like Daddy always said, there's no lesson in the second kick of a mule.

Daddy, who'd been more a force than a father. Brutal when sober, ruthless when drunk. Daddy, who would slaughter a calf come spring, but no meat would grace the boys' plates. Even now Eldon could taste the rank, curdled milk from the calf's stomach they were made to drink. And if he or Clayton aired their paunch before that stomach was empty, they'd both be hurled naked into a freezing lake, made to stay there until Daddy got drunk enough and fell asleep. Daddy, who made them fight for supper. Daddy, who only taught him to box, not Clayton. If Eldon didn't lose on occasion, his brother would have starved. Daddy, who said kindness was weakness, and weakness was to be exorcised with a lash.

When Eldon looked at his son, all he saw was kindness. Give him the lash and there would be nothing left.

TWELVE

They made camp in a glade by the river. Eldon put supper on, then dragged Shane's corpse from the boot and laid his body by the fire. Ian watched, longing to put his fingers in his mouth. Eldon told him to come say grace, but the child kept his distance.

"We don't want to forget about him," he said.

Resting a hand on the wrapped body, he showed Ian there was nothing to be afraid of. The child ambled around the fire, then hesitantly placed his hand next to his father's.

"Can we look at him?"

Eldon unwrapped some of the covering. Shane's waxy face shone blue in the firelight, his body hard as stone.

"Do you want to say grace?" Eldon asked. "Or should I?"

Ian looked at his brother. "We thank thee, Lord, for this food and may we ever serve Thy purposes."

They ate a quiet supper, then reclined by the fire, sipping hot water from their pannikins.

"Why can't we stay in a hotel?" Ian asked.

"Because it's safer out here."

"Cause of Uncle Jack?"

Eldon gave a faint nod.

"Because he was a bad man?"

He thought about that, then shook his head, unable to condemn his brother entirely. "He was a man who did bad things," he said. "There's a difference."

Ian poked the fire with a stick, sending a swarm of sparks into the night. "If you do bad things, can you still be good?"

Eldon watched the sparks die. "If you ask God's forgiveness."

"Can Uncle Jack be forgiven?"

"That's up to God."

"Because he's dead." It wasn't a question. "What if you died?"

"I'm not gonna die," he said. "Not for a long time."

"What if you did? What if you died tonight?"

"Then you'd have to gather some water, unhitch a horse, and make for that town yonder. You'd find the sheriff or whoever's in charge and they'd help you."

"What if we're not near a town?"

"Then you look for a road."

"I thought the road was bad."

"You'll have to take your chances. Find a farm. Sometimes there's still potatoes in the ground. Gotta watch out for dogs, though. I can't tell you how many times we went digging for potatoes and came back with nothing but teeth marks in our behinds."

"You and Uncle Jack?"

Eldon prodded the fire with his boot. In the sparks he saw Clayton running behind him, hands full of potatoes, a mangy hound on their heels. "That was back when we lost Daddy and the house and the store all at the same time."

"Where'd you live?"

"In the woods for a spell, before we . . ."

Ian stared at him. "Before what?"

He stood and beckoned the child.

In a stand of white pine he put the Model 3 in his hand. Ian held the weapon as if it were diseased.

"Cock the hammer. It'll click once. Keep going till it clicks again."

He tried to hand back the gun. "I don't want to."

"It has to click twice to work."

He struggled with the hammer. "I can't."

"Hold it like this, use your other hand to cock it."

"I don't want to."

Eldon squatted and looked at him. "The more prepared we are, the less we have to worry. Learning how to use this is part of being prepared."

"Prepared for what?"

For me not being here, he thought.

He pointed. "Aim at that tree, the white one there."

Ian raised the pistol. The shot startled him and he dropped the gun. The sound shook Eldon, too, even though he'd prepared himself. He picked up the gun and as he wiped off the snow he turned away so Ian wouldn't see his hands shake. When he offered it back, the child refused.

"Take it," he said.

"No."

He forced him to hold the gun. Ian shut his eyes and pulled the trigger. This time he held on to the weapon.

Eldon nodded. "Good. Now this time with your eyes open."

At dawn he woke the boy and took him into the woods. When they reached a patch of earth where the snow had melted, he pointed out the little disturbances where reeds bent, a rock was scuffed, a pebble had shaken from the earth. They came to a fast-running stream, a bit of leaves and sticks floating downriver past them.

Eldon pointed. "See that? Something just crossed upstream."

"What?"

"Deer maybe."

"A bear?"

"Maybe."

"I want to go back."

If he'd said something like that to Daddy, he wouldn't have been allowed back in camp until the beast was flung over his shoulder.

But Eldon wasn't his father. Everything he made Ian do, he'd do with him.

"Come on," he said, wading into the stream.

When the water was up to his waist, he sat down. The cold knocked the air from his lungs. He waved Ian forward. The child stepped in, shocked by the chill, then stepped back and stood on the shore.

"Come sit next to me," Eldon said.

"It's too cold."

"We'll make a fire on the bank. Come sit."

The boy went in up to his waist. His jaw trembled and he drew a sharp breath as it passed his chest. They sat, letting the cold dissolve their bodies. Daddy would make them do it for hours. He said it freed them of their flesh and opened their hearts to the spirit world.

Through shivering blue lips, Ian complained that he couldn't stand it a moment longer, that he had to get out, just had to.

"When your mind says you can't stand it even one second longer," Eldon told him, "it's lying to you. You're only halfway to what you can take."

The child didn't complain again. They closed their eyes. Some length of time passed. Then Ian looked up suddenly. Eldon had felt it too. Something had joined them. The water seemed to grow warmer. The sky brightened. Just for a moment, Eldon felt the presence of both of his sons.

They trudged up the bank, cut branches, built a fire, and sat naked sharing a blanket while they dried their clothes. On the way back to camp, Eldon stopped and pointed through a thick stand of hickory. Ian scanned a crisscross of dark branches. When the mighty thing lifted its head, he pointed.

"I see it."

"Shh. He hasn't caught our wind yet."

The buck was some forty yards away, nose in the air. A great crown of antlers lowered and he went back to lapping water from the stream.

Eldon offered Ian the rifle. With a look, then a big exhale, the boy took it. Eldon crouched behind him and oriented his body. Quickly, he showed him how to hold the rifle, then guided his finger to the trigger.

"Eyes open," he whispered. "Aim tight behind that front shoulder."

Recoil passed from the son to the father.

The buck staggered, went a few steps, then fell.

They butchered the animal, licking the salty blood from their hands, just as Eldon used to do as a boy. The only time Daddy smiled was after a good hunt. Now it was Eldon who smiled as his son sucked the redness from his thumb, proud of his first kill.

The coughing woke him before dawn. Ian moaned under a pile of blankets, burning with fever. Eldon would have let him rest, but a storm was gathering behind them and there was no time to spare. He had intended to make the river crossing before nightfall, but the graded road, rocky in spots but passable, had devolved by midday into two ice-clogged ruts. Ian groaned with each bump. The child needed bed rest.

A low sun pressed against their backs as they rolled up to a haggard collection of dark buildings set against a mud-flat. At the edge of a gangway, a flatboat drifted in the river. While Ian rested in the wagon tent, Eldon stood on the rocks that lined the shore and looked east across the river. There was no ferryman waiting at the boat. Down the shore was a sad little hut, smoke curling from its chimney.

Leaving Ian in the wagon tent, he walked down to the hut and knocked on the door. The Ferryman answered grumpily. He was an ugly man, a harelip locking his slab of a face in a permanent sneer.

"No crossing today," he declared. "Storm done stirred the currents."

To Eldon the river looked calm as could be. Figuring the Ferryman was just being lazy, he offered to sweeten the deal with a free fire mat—an offer the Ferryman dismissed with a snarl.

"Though if you is willing to pay a hazard fee of ten dollars," he said, his mouth hanging in a rubbery leer. "I might could chance a crossin."

"Ten dollars?" Eldon said, laughing incredulously. The Ferryman tried to slam the door in his face but he stopped it with his boot. "Now look," he said, turning serious. "My boy's running a fever. He needs bed rest and there's no hotel on this side of the river, so I need to get across tonight."

The misty flesh of the Ferryman's face tightened to near translucence. "Then you best cough up ten dollars."

"I can't afford that," he said.

And it was the truth. He hardly had enough to get to Springfield. If Dick didn't come through with that bounty money, he'd be in real trouble.

"Next crossing's in Omaha," said the Ferryman. He pointed upriver. "About seventy miles thataway. Might could see what your effrontery earns you there."

Git yer iron and show him what his effrontery earns right now.

Eldon returned to his wagon and opened the lockbox. It contained his traveling purse, the twin Model 3s, and Shane's journal, or what was left of it. The bullet hole at the center was a vortex of shredded paper and torn leather.

Imagine it, said Jack. *Watchin his chin wobble. Watchin that stain form around his crotch.*

He heard Ian coughing in the tent. "You all right in there?"

"Are we going on the raft?" asked the boy.

He looked down at the guns.

Go on, Jack commanded. *Show him who you are.*

"Soon," he told the boy.

He looked at the guns, then took five dollars from the purse and closed the box.

Across the river, the faint glow of a town pressed against the clouds. Big raindrops clattered as he roped the wagon to the ferry deck. It was a chain float that used the power of the river against a fixed tether. He sat with Ian on the driver's bench, watching the Ferryman kedge the chain along the gunwales. The man had accepted five dollars, but as a penalty was taking his sweet time getting them to the other side.

They left the ferry and rode up a wide dirt street, the shops and residences that lined it slowly going to seed. It was the kind of town still waiting for the railroad to arrive, which meant he should be able to secure a room at a cut rate.

The hotel had a mansard roof and tiered porches, and boasted a kind of gimcrack opulence. The lobby, with its cheap flourishes, imitated a more lavish establishment. Eldon had his son draped over his shoulder like a sandbag as he crossed the lobby, the check-in desk at the far end lit by two green lamps. Through a glass door he saw into the dining room. Only one couple was eating supper, the screech of their cutlery stinging his ears.

The room was on the second floor. Small and cold. A window that stared into a snarl of branches. After a bath, he tried to put Ian to bed and the child began sobbing inconsolably. Eldon sat on the bed and held him, singing the first song that came to mind, the one Daddy used to carry around on an old broadsheet:

The wind doth blow today, my love, with a few small drops of rain; I never had but one true love, and she in the cold grave has lain.

He used to imagine Daddy curled over Momma's grave, trying to dig her out for a last kiss. But when he got the coffin open, there were only bones and wisps of blond hair. All Eldon ever knew of his mother was that she was a blonde and could sing.

Ian had cried all the air out of his lungs and began coughing. He needed something to soothe his throat. With the boy over his shoulder, covered in a blanket, Eldon went down to the bar. It was bright and cluttered, like a drawing room. Mirrors and oil paintings fought for space above the wainscoting.

Three young men sat drinking beer quietly. Two older tradesmen chomped cigars in the back. Eldon pulled the blanket over Ian's head, then pulled down his own hat as he approached the bar. When he ordered brandy, the bartender filled half the snifter, but then, becoming aware of the child on his shoulder, topped him off.

Eldon ordered goat's milk, too, and as he waited, he caught his reflection in the backbar mirror. The beard he'd let fill in; the dark, clenched eyes; the cold expression. He looked more like Jack Foss than Eldon Quint.

Upstairs, he fed Ian a thimble of brandy mixed with goat's milk, then lay in the dark listening to him wheeze, thinking about the face he'd seen in the mirror.

A laugh jerked out of him—after all, how many men looked in the mirror and saw the brother they'd left for dead?

The laughter faded and his thoughts turned back to his sins.

They'd cost him a wife, a son, a brother. He placed a hand on Ian's chest and felt his heartbeat. It was the only thing left for them to take.

THIRTEEN

IAN HADN'T SEEN EVEN A PICTURE OF A CITY, SO WHEN IT first appeared on the horizon, just a greasy mirage, like something caught in a heat shimmer, Eldon waved him up front. The boy took up his usual position before the driver's bench, lying belly down against the footboard.

By the time the hazy image resolved into a sprawling burg of low-slung buildings and choking smoke, Eldon's stomach was tying itself in knots. He hadn't set foot in Kansas City—or any city—in thirteen years.

They carved through the outskirts, Ian hanging over the footboard like it was the prow of a ship. He inhaled the saline stink of the brining pits and marveled at the packinghouses and knotted train yards and fetid tanneries. But it was the heart of the city that truly impressed. His face lit up at the sight of the crowded ovate parks and long brick canyons. Eldon watched him, one boot tapping the footboard. The noise was unrelenting. He tried not to let it get to him, and spent his energy praying that Dick had come through with that money. At best they were a week from being broke, and Springfield was still ten days away.

According to the city directory, the Western Union was in West Bottoms, a tangled hub of factories and train depots at the confluence of the Kansas and Missouri Rivers. The route Eldon chose, the most direct according to the map, took them through a verminous slum of mudsill tenements.

As they rode, he tugged on his beard, hoping it had come in thick enough to keep him from being recognized. He dragged the reins, turning the horses down a dank street strewn with beggars. A corpse had been left to decay on the scoria. Ian suggested they stop to feed a few of the starving inhabitants.

"Remember what I told you about the road?" Eldon said.

Ian's eyes sagged. "No rules, no kindness."

"The city is no different."

The shantytown ended abruptly, and within a block they were on a busy commercial avenue that carried over a stone viaduct to West Bottoms. Traffic collected at the mouth of the bridge. Wagons, drays, sulkies; cattlemen on haughty steeds; granary boys stamping between the dramshops; fire-haired bosthoons yelling from the tenements; society women toting embroidered purses; bootblacks shining up businessmen, cigar smoke melting into the steely gloom. Eldon watched them all.

The circular logo of the Western Union Telegraph Company was stenciled in bright yellow letters on the storefront window of a squat brick shop at the corner of a flagstone square. Nearby stood a brewery, a packinghouse, and an elevated rail bridge.

A tribe of grackles had colonized the rooftop. Eldon parked down from the store to keep the birds from sullying his wagon. The air smelled of soot and hops, and you could taste slaughterhouse blood on the tongue. He stood studying the telegraph shop, considering all that might go wrong inside. While Ian was busy watering the horses, he buckled into his guns.

When he stepped into the shop, the chime of the doorbell was lost to the insectile clicks and whirs. He told himself, *It's only noise, it can't hurt you.* Behind a polished counter sat three young women tapping on strange contraptions that resembled small upright pianos topped with sewing machines. One of the women pointed at the service bell. When he rang it, a turkey-necked old-timer lifted his head off a bookkeeper's desk and yawned. He found his spectacles and hobbled up to the counter. "Afternoon," he said, adjusting his green eyeshade. "What can I do you for, sir?"

"Name's Quint. Should have a wire from Yankton. Sender is Dick Cottersman."

"Got a code?"

"Yellow medicine."

The clerk picked up a clipboard. Resting his liver-spotted forearms on the counter, he started to say something, but as he looked at Eldon his face slackened into a gape.

"I'll be proud as a peafowl with two tails," he muttered. "That really you?"

Eldon's throat dried up and he tried to swallow. "Pardon?"

"How many does this make?"

"How many does what make?"

"Well, what number am I?"

"I don't have the first idea what you mean."

"You must've robbed at least twenty of these here shops. I only imagine you keep count. I've read the criminal mind prides itself on its illicit achievements. So here I am wondering, what number am I?" He lowered his voice. "I know you're Minnesota Jack."

Shock spiraled in Eldon's chest. He wanted to explain that Jack Foss was dead under a thousand pounds of horse-flesh three hundred miles away. Instead he said, "You have me confused. I'm just here to pick up some money."

Keeping his hand visible, the clerk reached down and took a folded circular from a drawer. He pressed it flat on the counter so Eldon could see. "If you're not that racken-sack paw-pawer, I'm a beetle-eyed fool."

The sketch of Jack Foss was a decade old, but the resemblance couldn't be denied.

Eldon was suddenly aware of the guns on his hips, the weight of them. "Like I said, you have me confused, old-timer. Here, I have my Grange card and a letter of identification signed by my guarantor."

He took out the papers and set them on the counter, covering the image of the infamous outlaw.

The clerk scanned the documents, then raised his eyes. His whole face seemed to wink. "People around here still talk about Harlan Scrim."

The Farmer couldn't stop his face from curling into something rude.

The clerk stammered an apology. "I just . . . well, they got his plaque still at the marshal's office. I pass it on the way here every day."

Tell him if he don't shut his trap, you'll split him balls to brows.

It was Jack again, giving his unwanted opinion.

"I never heard of any Harlan Scrim," Eldon said. "Now, would you check if there's a wire from Dick Cottersman for Eldon Quint?"

"Yes, sir, it's right here. *Cottersman*." He looked up from his clipboard.

"Would you bring it here?" said Eldon.

As if under the duress of a stickup, the clerk scurried to a stand-up safe against the wall, found an envelope, and brought it to the counter. He put the clipboard in front of Eldon and pointed. "Your signature, please."

Eldon tried to keep his hand steady as he signed. He glanced into the envelope, thick with twenty- and fifty-dollar notes. Two thousand six hundred in all, according to the telegram that came with the envelope, though Dick had kept a hundred dollars to repair Eldon's cabin.

Seeing all that money brought the Farmer a small measure of relief. It would get him to Springfield and then some. He pocketed five hundred dollars, then handed the clerk the remaining two thousand and said, "I want to send this to myself in Springfield, Missouri."

"Not a problem." The clerk winked. "Mr. *Quint*."

Eldon did his best not to run flat out of the shop. He crossed the darkening square, checking his pocket to make sure the money was real. The money got him thinking about Clayton. Before *Jack Foss*, his brother was a soft-spoken young man with dreams of busting broncs. Breaking horses was about the only thing he did better than Eldon, and he could ride a bronc longer than anyone. There was something in his nature that evened a mustang out. He could make a horse believe in the saddle on the first go. The only proud word Daddy ever spoke was when he told Clayton he could hang and rattle with the best. That was a long time ago.

Caught up in the memory, it took Eldon a moment to comprehend what was unfolding at the back of his wagon. A bulky man shaped like an upside-down triangle stood at the tailgate. Ian held the cinch straps closed as if guarding something precious inside the tent.

Hurrying, Eldon called to the stranger. "What's the problem, friend?"

The bulky man about-faced, two Colts barely clinging to his skinny hips. He wore a floppy dun-colored hat, a weasel coat, and filthy coveralls, his frowning brown mustache strung with mucus.

"This yar wagon?" he grumbled.

Eldon stood between the stranger and his son. "You all right?" he asked Ian.

"They're gonna hurt her," the boy said, freckled cheeks hot and ruddy.

A second man appeared standing on the footboard at the front of the wagon. "That ain't true," he said. His face was gaunt, his mouth a wreck of rotten teeth ground to black nubs. "We ain't put on her but what she done brought to herself," he said.

Eldon opened the tent flaps to see what his son was so diligently protecting. Inside was dark and rank. Gray light cut across a mud-caked face. Long dark hair, big dark eyes, maybe eighteen or twenty. Eldon leaned in for a better look but recoiled when he got a nose full of her rancid aroma.

"Ya git out here, girly," ordered the bulky man.

"Come on out," Eldon said, holding his nose.

She shook her head. "They mean to ravage me."

The bulky man guffawed. "We ain't gonter do no such thing—not with how you stink."

"Says the wastrel who plots my defilement as we speak." Her voice was powerful and cultured, completely at odds with her grimy appearance.

The bulky man wedged a hand into his hip pocket and struggled to pull something out. "It stip-o-fies here that we got to bring ya in unscraped."

The gaunt man leapt suddenly over the driver's bench, sprang through the front flaps, and snatched the girl from behind.

She thrashed and kicked and screamed bloody murder.

"Get up here'n help!" shouted the gaunt man.

The bulky man had just freed a handbill from his pocket and was now trying to stuff it back inside. He attempted to drag himself over the tailgate, but it proved too challenging. Instead he pulled a cudgel from his belt and stood at the gate.

Eldon saw Ian looking at him. The boy was scowling, as if he couldn't understand why his father hadn't already intervened. Pedestrians were beginning to circle the wagon. Eldon felt their eyes beetling over him. He put a hand on Ian's back. "This isn't our business," he said, guiding his son toward the front of the wagon.

But a shriek turned them back around. The girl had stabbed her bootheel into the gaunt man's foot and he was hopping on one leg.

The girl dodged the bulky man's cudgel and leapt over his head. He caught her ankle midair and slammed her down on the cold flagstones. Breath burst from her lungs in a throaty rasp. The gaunt man came around with a loop of rope to bind her hands. The bulky man straddled her, punishing her petite frame with his weight.

Eldon felt a tug and looked down.

Ian was pulling on his coat sleeve. "Remember what they tried to do to Momma?"

He was talking about the time Hattie was nearly ravaged in Yankton. It was the middle of the day and by chance a man coming out of the feedlot saw three vermin dragging her into the alley.

The hanging was front-page news. The death sentence had less to do with Hattie than with crimes the men had committed against more powerful entities. Even so, she had wanted to take the boys to watch. When Eldon refused, she said he was pigeonhearted for not pursuing the scoundrel who'd escaped. She attended the hanging by herself.

When Eldon reached into his coat, the bulky man went clumsily for his pistol.

"Fifty dollars to leave her be," Eldon said, showing the tender in a raised hand. "Fifty dollars, you walk away, no harm done."

The bounty hunters shared a glance. The bulky man seated his pistol and spat. "She's warth ten times that."

"Five hundred," added the gaunt man, speaking as much to Eldon as to the crowd, which now encircled the wagon.

The bulky man yanked the handbill from his pocket and displayed it for all to see. The girl's likeness was advertised along with a five-hundred-dollar reward for her capture. But no woman had ever claimed a bounty that high, not that Eldon knew of.

"It's fake," Eldon said. "You'll be lucky if her pimp gives you a free romp in recompense. That's what they do when one of the girls runs off."

The bulky man eyed his partner. "Jasper, I thank he tryna git us in the neck."

"Yep," fifed the gaunt man. He spat through black gums and set a hand on his pistol. "Feller, unless you got five hundred dollars in that envelope, you best collect your brat and git."

"Tell me this," said Eldon with an edge of impatience. "What'd she do to earn a five-hundred-dollar bounty?"

The bulky man scoffed. "The hell we care what she done."

Fer chrissake, said Jack. *Shoot em and be done with it.*

Just then, someone spoke up in the crowd. "You boys ought to take what you can get." It was the Western Union clerk. "That's Jack Foss you're parleying with."

The bounty hunters shared a look as the name rang out through the growing assembly. Even the shrill keening of the grackles that lined the rooftop seemed to echo the name forebodingly. Eldon, meanwhile, was too startled to move.

The clerk walked up, unfurled the circular, and passed it to the bulky man. "If he isn't that paw-pawer, I'm a ring-tailed tooter."

The bulky man showed it to his partner. "It do look like im."

"I'd take fifty bucks over being dead," said the clerk.

The crowd mumbled in agreement.

The gaunt man looked up from the circular and scoffed. "It ain't him."

Eldon's voice filled out in rakish singsong. "What good's five hundred dollars to a dead man?"

Besides the faint rumble of a freighter a mile off, it was dead quiet.

"But fifty bucks," he continued. "Hell, fifty bucks will keep a live man in whores and whiskey for a month straight."

The bulky man sputtered. "How-how we know you ain't just look like him?"

"You boys best quit while you're ahead," said the clerk. "We don't care to be mopping up your leakage on this cold evening."

The bulky man's eyes raked across the crowd. "Jasper, my mouth is gittin dry. Nothin good happens when my mouth gits dry."

Eldon wagged his chin at the rope binding the girl's wrists. "Set her loose."

The gaunt man hesitated.

Eldon walked up and looked him in the eye. "Set her loose."

Like a card player making a regrettable fold, the man bent down to untie the girl's wrists but paused to complain to the crowd. "If he's really Jack Foss, don't you all think he'd of just shot us by now?"

"I gotta get me a drink," the bulky man said. Then he turned and cut through the crowd.

Watching him go, the gaunt man straightened up, his smudged fingers hovering near his guns. Eldon's expression turned colder than the stones under their boots. The gaunt man snatched the fifty-dollar note like he was taking it from the jaws of a tiger. Eldon watched him carve a path through the square. Then he noticed the crowd was staring at him, silent.

"Ian," he said. "Get in the wagon."

Ian looked at the girl. She was on the ground, rubbing her wrists.

Don't be stupid, said Jack. *That ain't yer problem.*

Eldon nodded at her. "You. Get in if you want."

All three boarded the wagon. Eldon lifted the reins, his heart in his ears.

With a stiff command, the horses rambled over the cobblestones, heading for the viaduct. The river seemed miles away, the distant colonies of silos and smokestacks pale in the gloaming.

He felt sick. It wasn't the bounty hunters or the ease with which he'd slipped into that evil character, but how good he felt doing it.

FOURTEEN

"ARE YOU A REAL OUTLAW?" SHE ASKED BETWEEN GULPS from their canteen.

She was drinking as though she'd just crossed a desert. Breathing shallow and fast, she handed the empty bladder to Ian. As she sat back against the sideboard, her eyes curved up to meet Eldon's.

"No," he said from the bench. "I'm a farmer."

"Well, you had me convinced."

Eyes on the road, he breathed through his mouth to avoid her stench. It was almost dark and he lit a lantern, hung it on a hook attached to a metal arm, and swung the arm out to one side of the wagon. Ahead, a line of flatwagons tramped out of a coal depot, filing south toward the viaduct. The oily black rocks heaped in their beds discharged plumes of dust.

"What a terrible inconvenience to be mistaken for something you're not. Though it did benefit us back there."

The way she said "us" bothered Eldon more than her repugnant smell.

"What'd you do to earn a five-hundred-dollar bounty?" he asked, raising his voice over the road rattle.

"Nothing," she said.

"I doubt it."

She nodded, polite but cold. "And that is your privilege."

"Well, thanks for letting me know that," he said.

"No, thank you," she said, turning her great big eyes on Ian. "Thank you for raising such a brave boy."

The comment reddened Ian's cheeks.

In the lantern light, Eldon got a better look at her. She was small, swarthy, with a generously scooped physique. Grime spackled her almond face, her night-black dress, and her even darker hair. Though she wore a ratty burlap coat fit for a beggar, her cultured inflection told him she was no vagabond. There was something exotic about her, something beyond his experience, and yet there was something familiar about her too. She looked nothing like Hattie, who was gently angled and had fair skin and sun-kissed hair, yet he had a sense that they shared some quality he couldn't put his finger on.

Trouble, said Jack.

Trouble was the one thing he didn't need any more of.

Up ahead, the flatwagons slowed at the mouth of the viaduct, all but lost in the choking black dust. As Eldon idled the team, another foul odor struck his nose. The girl had crawled up behind him, her wild dark eyes so deliriously moony that they seemed to consume all of her other features.

"I apologize for my impertinence," she said. "I am grateful for your aid."

He nodded politely but wasn't fooled. He'd dealt with her kind before. Young and pretty. Playing her wiles to get what she wanted. Maybe that was why she reminded him of Hattie. Behind her comely lines and brash attitude dwelled something harder.

She leaned her elbows on the driver's bench and looked up at him. Her eyes, loomed with dark lashes, grew impossibly in size and splendor. "Might I inquire where you're traveling to?"

"Miss," he said, "sit back and let me concentrate on the road."

She retreated to the sideboard. "I apologize for my aroma." Her voice was stripped of everything now, even its pride. "I've been on the road a fortnight with nothing but the clothes on my back. Hardly anything to eat. Certainly I haven't had the pleasure of a bath."

She wasn't going to squeeze a drop of sympathy out of him. Ian, however, seemed so taken with her that he was immune to her odor.

"We can spare some food," he said. "Right, Pa?"

"Dear me," she said to Ian. "Your shirt is torn. We'll have to mend it." She buttoned his coat to cover the rip in his breast pocket. Then she brushed the hair off his forehead. "You're a handsome devil, aren't you. What's your name?"

The boy blushed and his lips pressed into a bashful grin. "Ian Quint," he said. "What's yours?"

"Nice to meet you, Ian. Minn Yancy." They shook, smiling, then she turned to Eldon. "And you are, sir?"

He could see how it would go. She had found in Ian something she could exploit and would do so at every opportunity to get whatever she wanted.

"I'll take you to the other side of the bridge and leave you off there."

Ian frowned. "But what if those bounty hunters come back? We can't leave her in the lurch, Pa. Not with what they had planned."

The worry on Ian's face sank Eldon's stomach below the hem of his trousers. Clearing dust from his throat, he told her, "We passed a train station. I can leave you off there."

"Thank you, but it would do me no good," she said.

They hit the cloud of coal dust and Eldon fell to coughing. He glanced back. "I can give you a few dollars for a train pass," he said. "But that's the best I—"

"Watch out!" she shrieked, pointing ahead.

He turned just in time to see an overturned donkey cart materialize out of the haze, a lumpy tongue of spilled coal blocking the road. He yanked the reins, veering the wagon into the swale that ran along the side of the road. They hit the slick depression at speed. The wagon sluiced. Eldon pulled the brake as they careened sideways. They hit a berm with a sharp crack. The wagon listed on two wheels, teetered a moment, then flumped back to earth. Eldon calmed the run-out horses, then called into the tent. What he assumed were cries of pain turned out to be laughter.

"We bumped heads," Minn explained.

Ian wiped black dust from his eyes. "I thought we'd tip for sure."

Eldon hopped down to check for damage. A lamplighter swooshed past on a penny-farthing, missing him by a hair. The man slowed, raised his wick pole toward a dark streetlamp, and ignited the yolky orb. A dampish glow cast over the line of wagons tottering across the bridge, their wagging carriage lamps cutting little orange smiles in the poison mist.

Eldon looked back the way they'd come. It was dark and dusty and hard to see much beyond big dark shapes and plodding animals.

"Ian," he said. "Get my rifle."

While the boy did as ordered, he plucked the lantern down from the hanger and used it to scan the undercarriage. The rear axle was splintered, though it might hold long enough to get them over the bridge. A cracked thimble skein on the left rear wheel also needed to be replaced. When he straightened up, he found Minn and his son standing by the tailgate, looking down the road. She was holding his Winchester.

"Hey," he said, raising the lantern to eye level. "What are you doing?"

She turned and squinted in the glare. "Watching our backtrack."

"Gimme that."

She handed over the rifle. "We need to keep moving," she said.

"Axle's cracked," he said.

"What?" she said.

"We got a cracked skein and a bum axle. If you're in such a hurry, maybe you ought to find another ride."

"Pa," Ian said. "We passed a wheelwright on the way here, just on the other side of the bridge. That big red building, remember?"

Eldon remembered but didn't say so. He told Minn, "I'll take you over the river and give you enough for a train pass. That's the best I can do."

Her eyes sank and she nodded.

They boarded the wagon. The axle groaned as they yawed over the rising span. Ian climbed up to the driver's bench.

"We should bring her to the next town," he whispered. "We can't let them get her."

Glancing over the side of the bridge, the eddied blackness sweeping underneath, Eldon said, "I'm sure Miss Yancy has her own plans."

"My plan is to be *anywhere but here*," she said, the comment coming disembodied from the dark tent. "The next town would certainly do." She inched into the light, looking at him. "I never did get your name. And I should know the name of the man who saved my life. How else might I include him in my prayers?"

He had to admire her tenacity, even though it wouldn't change his mind.

"Eldon Quint," he said, his voice skipping. He cleared the spur from his throat and said with as much certainty as he could muster, "My name is Eldon Quint."

FIFTEEN

By the time they found Deane & Company Wagon Repair, night had drawn a moonless shade. Eldon stood in the lamplit street looking up and down a canyon of brick and shadow. A buggy drawn by a single horse rounded into view. He set a hand on his revolver. Ian and Minn watched from the wagon as the buggy sped past, throwing up a curtain of slush. When the buggy disappeared, Eldon took his hand off his gun.

The stable and livery garage spanned the block, a brick monolith with a big sliding barn door and a row of arched windows carved into the upper story. At the far end of the building was a clapboard workshop, brightly lit, with a wheelwright working in the window. Eldon lifted Ian over the tailgate, then pointed down the block.

"See that man in there? Tell him we need repairs, tell him to come out here."

Minn heaved herself over the tailgate, splashing down in the slush.

"Can Miss Yancy come?" Ian asked.

"No," said Eldon. "Go on."

He watched the boy race up the street, then reached into his pocket. "We'll part ways here." There was a twenty-dollar bill in his hand, a generous offer he expected she would accept without argument.

"Can't you ride me out of the city?" she said.

He held out the bill. "You can hit the train station with a rock from here. You want out, that's your fastest route. We could be here for hours."

"Leave me off anywhere along the way. Please. I'll be no trouble at all."

"Take the money."

"Please," she said, her face on the verge of collapse.

He went into his pocket and added another twenty. "That should get you anywhere you want to go with enough left over for a hot bath."

"You could give me every penny you have," she fretted. "It wouldn't matter."

"I doubt that."

"What good is a train if his people are watching? Train, stage, steamship. He watches them all. Your money can't save me from that."

He.

That alone was reason enough to get rid of her.

Up the road, Ian skipped from the workshop, the wheel-wright trailing.

"Leave me in the middle of a forest. I don't care. Just anywhere but here."

She'll slit yer throat and rob ye blind, said Jack.

Ian scampered up. "That's Pa," he said. "And Miss Yancy."

The wheelwright was middle-aged and bespectacled. He shook Eldon's hand. Wood flakes stippled his frizzy hair and lumpy sweater. He seemed a queersome, twitchy fellow, but harmless. He introduced himself as Harold Deane.

"I was about to close for the evening," he said. "But this lad says you've got a busted axle and a cracked skein."

"Yessir," Eldon said. "I appreciate you taking a look given the hour."

The wheelwright caught a whiff of something and looked at Minn. He pushed up his specs, puckered. "Heavens, young lady, have you had a fall in a . . . a puddle?"

"You are being kind, sir," she said. "It was a cesspit. Luckily, I escaped. Thanks to these fine gentlemen."

The wheelwright pointed at his workshop. "The wash closet's in back. I just changed out the water. Help yourself."

She curtsied. "You are kind, sir."

"I'll go too," Ian said, taking her hand.

She smiled at him. Eldon watched them walk up to the shop.

She makin her honeypot, said Jack. *Yer jest too blind to see it.*

"Three dollars for the axle," the wheelwright was saying as he scanned the wagon with a lantern. "A dollar for the skein. Dollar and a half for labor. I can have her finished, oh, midmorning?"

"If I double your pay," said Eldon, "can you get it done tonight?"

"Well, let me see now. It's gonna take at least a few hours."

Eldon paid him triple and they drove the wagon through the sliding barn door. The garage was dark, but he made out rows of carts, buggies, and carriages in various states of disrepair. The young apprentice, who, given his specs and curly hair Eldon took for the wheelwright's son, began lowering a heavy chandelier from the vaulted ceiling.

"Can you work without that?" Eldon asked.

The wheelwright looked at him funny. "Without light?"

"You can use lanterns. Just don't light the chandelier."

"Why on earth would we do that?"

Eldon paid him another share to stop asking questions, then went through a red door at the end of the garage and entered the workshop.

The heat hit like a wall. He took off his coat. The shop had raftered ceilings and pine-board walls. A worktable and machines ran along one wall. Wagon wheel parts hung on another. Minn sat on a bench drying off in front of a coal stove. Ian skipped around the shop, kicking piles of sawdust, fiddling with spokes and felloes. He swiped a cup of cider off the top of a planer and offered it to his father.

"There's more on the stove," he said. "Mr. Deane said have as much as we want."

Eldon took the cup and drank. The sweetness stung at his stomach. "Getting hungry?" he asked.

"Yessir," Ian said. He glanced at Minn. "We both are."

"I'll find out what's nearby."

"I can ask," Ian said, already heading for the red door.

Eldon caught him by the arm and gave him some money. "Tell Mr. Deane to send his son to pick us up whatever's the fastest, then come right back."

When Ian had vanished through the red door, Eldon settled on the bench next to Minn. He took off his hat and rubbed his eyes.

"He's a sharp boy," she said.

She was scrubbed of her rind, though her clothes still stunk. Her face, chapped and windburned, was pleasantly angled. He set his hat in his lap and leaned back against the wall.

He pushed up the brim of his hat thinking he'd dozed only a few minutes, but as he looked around the shop he realized it had been longer. At a table across the room, under the dusty window, Minn sat reading aloud from a copy of *Les Misérables* while Ian sat on the floor next to her, tracing a finger in the sawdust.

The boy looked up. "They just arrested Valjean for stealing the Bishop's silver."

Eldon rubbed his eyes. A rich smell grabbed him. It was coming from a greasy brown bag sitting on the end of the bench.

"The repairs are nearly finished," Minn said.

Eldon stood and opened the bag, fishing out a drumstick. Warm salty juice spilled down his beard as he took a bite.

"You eat?"

"Not yet," said Ian.

"Your son made me promise to finish this chapter before we dine," Minn added.

Eldon brought the bag to the table, then tore it open and piled fried chicken, biscuits, and baked potatoes atop the stained paper.

"I want to get on the road as soon as the wagon's ready. So eat up."

While they ate, he went to the wash closet and rubbed the grime off the back of his neck. When he caught a whiff of himself, he splashed under his arms.

He returned to the table and ate another drumstick as he looked out the window. The street was dark and quiet. He went back to the bench. Across the room, Minn and Ian were still eating. Something about her posture caught his eye. She ate ravenously, both forearms planted on the table as if she were guarding a pile of gold.

So that was what she had in common with his wife.

The old habit would return when Hattie was especially peckish. Though she'd been adopted long before, she would still on occasion shield her food, as if to protect her plate from the rest of the hungry orphans. Minn must have seen him staring and relaxed her posture and ate at a normal pace.

He cleared his throat. "You know Lee's Summit?"

Still chewing, she covered her mouth and shook her head.

"It's where I expected to camp tonight. Not much of a town if I recall, but a freighter runs through pretty regular. I don't imagine he's got people watching the boxcars. I can drop you there."

She stood and curtsied. "God bless you, Mr. Quint," she said, brushing the long black hair out of her face.

Her left ear looked like an animal had chewed it up and spit it back onto her head. It was an old wound, unlike the pinkish scars on her forearms. And that dress was another curiosity. Hattie always kept up on the latest fashions and apprised Eldon of what was in mode. That was how he knew that Minn's dress, though tattered, was constructed of fine silk, the flouncing and embellishments in line with the latest trends. Were it not so fit and flattering, he would have assumed it pilfered.

She was about to sit when she froze, eyes on the window, then looked back at Eldon like a stunned animal.

He crossed the room toward the window as she stepped from it. The pane began to shake, dust falling. He wiped it clean, then looked out at the wet cobblestones shivering in the torchlight of what was coming up the road.

SIXTEEN

MINN WAS FROZEN, INCAPABLE OF SPEECH, BOTH HANDS crossed over her midsection as if she might be sick. Ian came up to look out the window but Eldon moved him back. The Farmer had counted six riders coming down the road, and there were more behind. They were Indian, and wore brightly colored dresses ornamented in gold and strings of pearls, as if they'd plundered their wardrobe from a dowager. They presented rifles and tomahawks, and had ash crosses thumbed into their kohl-streaked foreheads. Behind them, eight feathered headdresses appeared, then eight parade horses pulling a six-wheeled stagecoach, the biggest coach he'd ever seen. It must have been fifteen feet tall and twenty feet long. Canted torches were mounted to its sidewalls. Dozens of trophy heads studded its wintergreen exterior—wolves, bears, javelina, cougar—all manner of deranged beasts, their warped maws trembling in the torchlight. Eight more Indians trailed the stagecoach. And bringing up the rear, a pair of masked coronet players scored the infernal menagerie with stabbing notes.

The procession rumbled past the window and collected before the sliding door down the street. The coachman—an Indian in a vivid jade ball gown—stepped from the driver's bench and spread a small rug beneath the coach door. He kicked down the brass stepladder, then opened the door and stood at attention.

One enormous ostrich-skin boot, then the other, emerged from the door and squelched into the rug. The man unfurled from the carriage, a giant nearly seven feet tall. He was attired in a bright emerald tailcoat, a purple chintz vest, and grass-green slacks. After licking his palm, he ran long pink fingers through his orange gossamer mane, fashioning it into the shape of a dinner bell. Muttonchops ran like fire down his cheeks, and his neck was as thick as a man's thigh. The coachman presented a black Regent-style beaver hat. It was the tallest hat Eldon had ever seen. The giant set the hat atop his head, careful not to disturb his hair. He stepped into the light and grinned up at the big barn door like a huge, drunken baby.

Eldon stepped back from the window, not believing his eyes.

Impossible.

Was it *him*?

Of course it was. Who could ever mistake such a man?

It had been years—no, decades—but his mere presence dredged up nightmares in Eldon, and the visions swarmed his senses: bubbling, bloated flesh blackened by the sun; greasy grass heaped with limbs; thundering battle drums drowning the desperate cries of women and children.

When he turned from the window, Minn was staring at him. Perhaps he looked just as panicked as she did.

"You know him," she said, holding her stomach.

He nodded once. "What does he want with you?"

She didn't answer.

"Pa, we need to hide her quick," Ian said.

He was right. Eldon scanned the workshop for some-where to put her. There was the wash closet. A waste drum. A small space under the tool bench.

"I know," Ian said.

Taking Minn by the hand, he rushed her through the red door into the garage. Eldon followed through a maze of dilapidated buggies and chaises, oxcarts and school hacks. In a wide bay that smelled of pine tar sat his wagon. The apprentice lay on his back, greasing a fresh axle, while the wheelwright crouched at the back tire, polishing a new thimble skein. He smiled as Ian started to pull off the tailgate.

"Eager to get back on the road, I see?"

Eldon saw what his son was doing and began to help. As fast as they could, they moved the provisions from the right side of the boot into the wagon bed.

Minn stood holding herself, her face splotched red with hives.

The wheelwright wiped his hands on a rag, his easy smile befuddled by the frantic action. "We're just about through," he said.

Eldon pointed at the sliding door. "That locked?"

The wheelwright turned toward the big sliding door. Torchlight flickered in the undercut. "Yes," he said. "Is there someone outside?"

"I need a hammer and nails."

The wheelwright squinted. "What for?"

The apprentice climbed from under the wagon.

"You," Eldon said. He stuffed twenty dollars in the kid's hand. "Bring my horses around and get em harnessed. Quick."

The apprentice gawked at the money then sprinted toward the stables.

"Is something the matter?" said the wheelwright.

A hard rap shook the sliding door.

He spun toward the noise, a hand over his heart. "I don't want trouble," he said, already pleading.

"I'm trying to get you out of trouble," Eldon said. "Get a hammer and nails."

The wheelwright shot off to his tool bench.

They finished clearing the boot. Eldon waved Minn over. She peered into the slim compartment, then stepped back, covering her mouth, her eyes on the wrapped body.

"It's just my brother," Ian said.

"He's frozen solid," said Eldon.

As the wheelwright scampered up with a hammer and a pail of nails, another strike rattled the sliding door.

Minn startled, clutching her chest.

The voice outside commanded they open up at once.

Eldon snapped at Minn. "Get in."

She climbed headfirst into the dark space and shimmied on her belly until she reached the far end.

He picked up the tailgate. "It's gonna be dark. Try to close your eyes."

She hugged herself into a ball and buried her head.

He reaffixed the tailgate, then Ian handed him the hammer. The wagon shuddered as he drove in the first nail. He could hear her breathing harder with each strike.

The voice outside warned that in a matter of seconds the sliding door would be broken through.

"Go and open it," he told the wheelwright.

"I want no part in this," the man said.

Eldon could see the fear taking hold. In a state like that, a man was liable to do anything to save himself.

He pulled his coat aside so the wheelwright could see his pistols. "Do what I say and you'll be fine. Now open the door, tell em you're closed for the night."

The wheelwright pushed up his specs. Then he walked to the door and removed a heavy metal drawbar and set it in a sling bolted to the wall. With both hands he dragged on the heavy door, slowly drawing it open.

A wall of robed Indians stood blank-eyed, holding lanterns. Behind them, others stood passing earthenware jugs of alcohol, stomping their weapons on the ground and whooping. At the sound of the coachman's whistle the hellish minstrel show parted, making way for the giant's lumbering green form. Light played off his sweaty face, a diamond-studded Masonic pin glistering on his lapel. He stopped before the wheelwright and doffed his hat.

"Good evening," he said with a bellowing, syrupy drawl.

"We-we're closed," the man sputtered.

"Do pardon the late intrusion. Major Bertrand Sinchilla is my name. I am beset this cold evening on a desperate mission to rescue my lost daughter. Might I and my fellowship enter your premises?"

"There's no daughters here," the wheelwright said too quickly. "Just-just my son and our-our final customers of the evening."

The Major looked past the wheelwright.

Eldon turned to help Ian and the apprentice with the horses.

"You, sir!" the Major boomed, walking in past the wheelwright, followed by a detachment of six robed Indians.

Eldon kept his eyes on his work, swallowing the dryness in his throat.

The Major arrived before the wagon. "Good sir."

Eldon greeted him with hardly a glance. "Evening."

The Major furled his plump pink hands at his chest. He smiled, nests of broken blood vessels forming grotesque patterns on his cheeks. "Might I trouble you briefly?"

"We're fixing to rattle the hawks. If you don't mind moving your people out of the doorway . . ."

Beyond the Major, an impish white man marched into the garage, followed by a half dozen Indians. He had a pistol in one hand, a lantern in the other. He directed the Indians to spread out, and they began searching the dark maze of wagons.

The Major turned to his Indians. "He doesn't look like much of an outlaw to me. A lowly plow-chaser, perhaps?"

The Indians agreed with loud, sycophantic chortles.

"What is your name, sir?"

Eldon kept his eyes on his work, ignoring the question.

"Somethin wrong with ya tongue?" said a shrill voice.

It was the impish man, marching up, staring with hard little eyes as he holstered his pistol. He was jittery, couldn't seem to stop moving. He wore a long navy coat and a bright white bowler. A scar ran from his left eye to his neck. The skin on that side of his face sagged like melted wax.

"Speak up," he said, bloodhound nostrils belling over his black rake of a mustache. "Major, I can scent that garboon cunny from here."

"Rove," the Major reproved. "We are not in the business of jumping to conclusions."

The imp stood, rapidly caressing the pearl handle of the big knife on his belt. "She's fuckin here, sir."

"Excuse my second," the Major said to Eldon. "Mr. Brusco was a slave-catcher before the war, and this sort of pursuit revives his more excitable attributes."

"We need to be on our way now," said Eldon, tightening the hitch.

The Major's watery blue eyes fell to Ian. "And what is your name, lad?"

"Ian."

"Have you seen my daughter, Ian? Her name is Winifred, but she calls herself *Minn*. A vile truncation, surely, but poor judgment is a folly of youth."

Ian shook his head. "No, sir, I haven't seen her."

"But I haven't even told you what she looks like."

"Ian, get in the wagon," said Eldon. "Sir, if you don't mind clearing your people out of the door, please."

The Major stared at him. "My wife would say that our Winifred is the picture of pestilential perfection. Eyes dark as soil. Hair black as boiled molasses." He held his hand at the level of his thigh. "About yea tall."

"Her stank's all over this pig shitter," said the imp.

Eldon picked Ian up and gave him a look as he set him behind the driver's bench. He turned to the Major. "Yeah, she was here. But she left out a while back."

The Major's grin widened. "Left out to where?"

Eldon shrugged. "I gave her some coins for a train pass."

"Why would you do that?"

"She asked. Now, if you don't mind moving your people out of the way, we need to be getting along."

"Indeed," said the Major. "But you knew about the bounty. Those men showed you the handbill."

"I thought the bounty was a hoax," Eldon said.

"But why bring her here?"

"My son has a soft spot for the less fortunate."

"Adorable," said the Major. "Did you hear that, Rove? This man is a good father."

He looked at Eldon, smiling, a chuckle rolling up his throat, though it never touched his lips for a sudden paroxysm buckled his knees. His mouth sprang open, a tormented growl rattling the high windows. The robed Indians swooped around him, seizing his arms and legs, struggling with his massive bulk.

"Chair!" croaked the Major. "CHAIR."

A path cleared at the sliding door and the coachman emerged, green gown dragging in the muck. He unfurled a folding chair that he carried, and the Indians settled the Major into it. The coachman carried a foot pillow and used it to elevate the Major's boots. The Major's head lolled and he moaned in agony. The coachman cracked a glass vial under his nose. After a few ravenous inhales he seemed to find relief. The coachman pulled off his ostrich-skin boots and greasy socks, then began massaging the bulbous blue-veined joints below each big toe.

Breathing heavily, the Major beckoned Eldon closer. "Gout," he explained. Eldon began to speak, but he held up his big pink hand. "If you are withholding information because of something she told you, understand that her mind is gone. She is in grave danger and must be saved from herself. If your son cares at all about her well-being, then you must tell me everything."

"I told you what I know," said Eldon.

A wave of pain shook the Major and the coachman administered another vial.

"She has . . . has stolen from me," he stammered. "Something of great value. I make you this offer. Should you provide the information I need to rescue her, I shall double the promised remuneration to one thousand dollars."

Eldon's mouth burned. He couldn't believe it was him. What ugly jag of fate had landed him here?

When he could speak without contempt, he said, "If I were a betting man, I'd put my money on her heading for the train station. Now, I don't know if that's worth a thousand dollars to you and I don't care. All I want is for you to move your men out of that door and let us leave."

A hollow tapping sound stole Eldon's attention.

The imp was rapping the hilt of his bowie knife against the tailgate. "These nails is fresh. What you keep in here?"

Eldon walked up slowly. "Nothing to concern you, friend."

The imp's nostrils hissed. "Open it."

"I can't do that."

The imp stepped forth, tense and jerky, like he might haul off and crack him in the mouth. "Open the fuckin thing."

Eldon looked down at him. "You must be hard of hearing."

The imp stared at him, then turned to the Indians in the big doorway. "One of you devils bring me a jar of swill. I'm gonna burn this fuckin wagon to the ground. We'll see what's in it and what ain't."

Eldon moved his coat, showing his pistols. "Destroy my property, I'll have legal cause to stop you."

The Major howled from the chair. "Do you hear this?" he said to the robed Indians. "Maybe he's Jack Foss after all."

The imp spat and then pointed at the wheelwright, who had been standing quietly in the corner, an arm around the apprentice.

"Curlicue. Pry off this fuckin gate board."

The wheelwright stood boggled, then went to a tool bench along the back wall and commenced a halfhearted search for the proper tool.

Ian looked down from the wagon. Eldon walked up to where the Major sat. Two Indians stepped forward to halt his advance. Enjoying his foot massage, the Major casually flicked his hand, waving them off.

"Major," Eldon said, "in that compartment is the body of my murdered son. I'm taking him to be buried next to his mother. As a decorated leader of the Fifth Minnesota Regiment, I expect you to act as a man of honor and instruct your second to keep his hands off my wagon."

The Major took off his hat and cocked his giant orange head. Even sitting down he was nearly as tall as Eldon. "How do you know I led the Fifth?"

"I fought at Fort Ridgely and Birch Coulee."

"What is your name?"

"Quint. My father was Coble."

"Coble Quint was your father?"

There was a bang, then a squeal of wood. Eldon turned. The imp was wrenching a pry bar between the tailgate and the chassis.

"Why didn't you say so before?" The Major was preening. "Have I aged so terribly that you didn't recognize me?"

The Major ran his tongue along bone-colored dentures.

Suddenly Eldon could feel the boom of the howitzers in his chest. He could smell the rotting breastwork of black bodies and dead horses and hear the animal-like wails of mutilated soldiers. He could see the Major, younger, stronger, leading three hundred infantrymen, fifty cavalry, and two howitzers. He could see the desperate faces of the besieged soldiers when they saw the column snaking across the prairie, and heard the rumble of those big guns. They'd thought they were saved, but the Major held his men back and watched them die.

"I've spent a good deal of my life trying to forget the war," Eldon said. "It took me a moment to recall where I knew you from."

"We lost Coble at Birch Coulee, did we not?"

"That's right."

"I didn't know he had a son. I'll bet you were a handsome boy."

Another squeal as the imp jerked the tailgate a few inches off the chassis.

"And now you've lost a son of your own," the Major said, shaking his head.

No man could manufacture the grief on Eldon's face.

"Rove. Leave this man his peace."

The imp was positioning himself for a final heave. "I near got it."

"Leave it, I said."

Like a petulant child the imp hurled the pry bar into the air, just missing the wheelwright's head. "Fuck it then," he said, stomping out of the garage.

The Major looked amused. "As I said—excitable."

The tailgate was barely clinging to the chassis, left like a hangnail. Eldon prayed that Minn would hold on just a little bit longer.

"Be thankful you still have this handsome lad," said the Major, showing Ian a toothy grin. "Protect him above all else. Children are God's greatest gift."

He looked at the coachman. His boots were slid on and with the help of his Indians he rose from the folding chair and offered Eldon a bulbous hand.

It killed Eldon to touch the man, but for Ian he shook his hand.

"And where is it your wife is buried?" asked the Major.

"Jefferson City," Eldon said, trying to free himself from the Major's grip.

The Major clamped his other hand over Eldon's, consuming it in a fleshy bubble. "I see that you are no outlaw, Mr. Quint. You are a good man. I shall have my band play a dirge in your son's honor. Your father, too." He showed his big teeth. "I do frequent Jefferson City. Perhaps I shall pay a visit and we might get us into the cups. Are you a drinking man?"

"No, sir."

"Good," said the Major, something oozing black and tar-like around the edges of his hard blue eyes. "Good for you."

With a tip of his beaver hat, the Major turned and trundled out of the garage, the Indians pooled around him like courtesans, his stiff body yawing left and right, towering a foot above every other living creature, even the horses.

Eldon stood watch as the procession mounted up and then ventured down the road, the cornet players screeching out a mournful tune.

When he was sure they had gone, he spoke into the dark gap in the tailgate. "You all right in there?"

"Yes," came a whisper.

"You better stay in there till we're clear of the city and I can be sure they're not on our tail. I need to nail this gate back on, so you might want to cover your ears."

"All right."

"Just hold tight. You're safe now."

SEVENTEEN

HE POSITIONED THE CROWBAR IN THE GAP BETWEEN THE TAIL-gate and the chassis and gave it a hard yank. The screech of metal against wood echoed out of the dark forest, dissipating over the snowbound cropland beyond.

He paused to scan the brown strip of road cutting across the prairie a hundred yards from the edge of the woods where he'd hidden the wagon. He had watched for half an hour and in that time neither carriage nor rider had graced the road. There was no question in his mind that the Major would send scouts, but he couldn't keep her caged up with his son's corpse forever; it was already near midnight.

With one more heave the tailgate flopped into the snow. He kicked it aside and waved Ian up to the boot. Stopping before the black rectangular mouth, the boy struck a match. Light trembled down the stained wood, clearing the darkness. She was curled against the back of the compartment.

"Need help getting out?" said Eldon.

Big damp eyes flashed out of a tangle of hair. Thin streaks ran down her face, dry riverbeds cut by tears. When he reached in, offering a hand, her head snapped up, viperous, as if she didn't recognize him.

He backed off and let her worm her way down the slim compartment. Her elbow knocked the board that divided her side of the boot from Shane's, jostling the wrapped corpse on the opposite side. She halted, glancing down at him.

"It's all right," he said. "Hustle up, we need to move out."

She grabbed the frame and flung herself out. Pulling her black dress back over her knees, she stood in the snow shivering and scanning the dark forest. Her head tilted skyward. Through a mesh of branches came the light of a blank-eyed moon, bright enough to read by.

"Where are we?"

"About halfway to Lee's Summit," Eldon said, prying nails out of the tailgate. "Ian, show her where to sit."

The boy climbed into the wagon tent and pointed at an unoccupied space of sideboard near the back, walled in by feed bags.

"Right next to me," he said. "I have to keep my eyes skinned. Make sure nobody sneaks up behind us."

She nodded. "Smart idea."

"You can ride with us as long as you want. All the way to Springfield if you want. Pa said so."

She formed a look of gratitude, though when she faced Eldon, her eyes were sharp with suspicion.

Eldon lifted the tailgate. "We'll be on the road ten days or so. Get off where it suits you. We travel fast, eat and sleep outdoors."

She stood clutching herself, teeth chattering.

"Ian," he said. "Blanket."

The boy handed her a wool blanket from the back of the wagon and she wrapped herself in it. Wind shot through the trees, blowing her long black hair across her face. As she tied her hair back, moonlight varnished her mangled lobe.

"You need to keep out of sight," Eldon said. "For now, don't leave this tent unless I say. Keep your head and face covered. Don't speak to anyone. We don't need any reports traveling up the road of a dark-haired girl."

"Why are you helping me?" she said.

He climbed into the wagon and turned to offer her a hand. "The other part of this deal is you don't ask questions. Understood?"

He drove hard across the moonlit prairie, Winchester between his knees. Ian hung over the tailgate, yawning, eyes pinned to their backtrack. Against the sideboard, Minn sat surrounded by brown sacks of horse grain, wrapped and cowled, the only evidence of her presence the rank smell of her dress.

They followed a road of parallel grooves, gliding over gentle waves of land. The moon plunged toward the horizon, dragging a spray of stars out of dark blockades of forest. The emptiness of the plains slid over Eldon like cold water. He couldn't shake the notion that out of the dead landscape something awful would emerge. Every time he looked back, he expected to see the black shape of a rider against the horizon, but found only the thrum of Kansas City fading behind them.

After an hour, a jumble of dark buildings rose out of the white crust. Making it to Lee's Summit in no way delivered them beyond the Major's reach, but he was glad they had gained such a distance.

Just outside of town he found a thick grove of cedar and holly. A game trail allowed the wagon entry and led to a stream. They had fresh water, and the underbrush would cloak them from any distance.

The sky was big and crowded with stars. A cloudy night would have been preferable, yet he found comfort in the vast scintillation. It seemed to dampen the voice in his head urging him to abandon the girl, to run. But Ian had shown him that not only must he get Shane to Springfield, he must also arrive with his virtues intact.

As he fed and watered the horses, he overheard Minn in the tent quietly summarizing the rest of *Les Misérables* for Ian. Her voice was gentle yet assured, with a musicality to it. He looked into the tent. Ian lay against one of the feed bags, struggling to stay awake.

"Time to turn in," said Eldon.

Minn looked up.

"You two can take the tent. I'll sleep under the wagon."

He gathered a length of rope and some empty tin cans from the boot. He went up the snowy trail to the edge of the woods and strung a line hung with the tin cans low across two trees. An intruder would trip on the rope and rattle the cans. When he finished, he stood scanning the open country, then he returned to the wagon, hoisted the lockbox from the boot, and retrieved his pistols. He saw the envelope with his money and took that as well. With a blanket and a few fire mats he made a bed under the wagon, then looked into the tent. Minn was lying awake.

"You hear anything or get a funny feeling," he whispered, "wake me up. And no light, not even one match."

"I understand," she said. "Good night, Mr. Quint. Tomorrow will be a better day."

"Good night," he said, tying the tent flaps closed, thinking that it might just be the opposite.

The clank of tin woke him. It was so dark that he blinked, thinking his eyes were still closed. As he clamored from under the wagon the pistol fell from his chest. On hands and knees he groped the hard snow for it. He found his Winchester. There was another clank of cans and he swung the rifle in that direction. Twenty paces down the trail, a faint shape, all but indiscernible from the nocturnal aura surrounding it, appeared to be untangling a foot from the rope he'd tied between the trees. Cans clanged. He leaned against the nearest tree and took aim. His fingers numb, he couldn't feel the trigger. Afraid he might pull it accidently, he shook out his hand, trying to return some blood to his digits. Having freed itself from the rope, the shape trudged unwittingly toward him. As it approached, its contours became more defined and an unpleasant yet familiar odor fouled the air.

"Miss Yancy?" he whispered.

The shape halted. "Mr. Quint?"

He stepped into the trail. "What are you doing?"

"I had to . . ." She glanced back at the prairie.

"Oh," he said. "Next time, go in the trees, not where anyone can see you."

He looked past her. A foregleam on the horizon paled the eastern rim of the prairie. He imagined the Major's caravan rattling over the earth, coming for him.

"Be light soon," he said.

She spoke through a yawn. "Should I wake Ian?"

He looked at his wagon, the faint shapes of the horses beyond, four separate clouds rising above them. A question had been eating at him all night, and when he turned his eyes back on her, it slipped out.

"What'd you steal?" he said. "And don't tell me *nothing*. A man don't go through that kind of trouble for nothing."

"There's no buried treasure if that's what you think."

"I don't think anything, that's why I'm asking."

She pulled a blanket around her shoulders and stared at the ground, her face hardened by some angry recollection.

"I'm sticking my neck out here," he said. "How hard is he gonna come? Will he quit after a week? Or is he prepared to scour the earth for eternity?"

Her mouth pressed into a tight line.

"I won't be his property anymore," she said.

The words shook him.

His wife had told him the same thing before she left and never came back.

When morning came damp and mild, they decided over a cold breakfast that Minn would need new clothes should they hope to pass for a family. There was a mercantile shop in the center of town. Thinking it might draw attention if she were to go, Eldon took inventory of what was needed and went himself. He parked the wagon in an alley off the wide, treeless thoroughfare. Across the street he could see into the store. He left Ian in charge of the Winchester with the instruction to fire a shot in the air should there be any trouble. Tucking his revolver into his jacket pocket, he stood in the mouth of the alleyway, scanning the rickety shops, waiting for a group of schoolboys to pass before he crossed the street.

The shop had high ceilings and high shelves packed with farm implements, dry and canned goods, bolts of fabric, clothing—just about anything a person might need. At the early hour there were just two other shoppers. Eldon overheard the two young women gossiping in the clothing section. They were criticizing the store's elderly proprietor, who had chided them for the lewd act of dancing in church after the service had ended. Eldon looked across the store, where he could see the proprietor, a stiff old woman, her eyes like two blank walls of rectitude.

When the young women moved on, he ducked into the clothing section and hurriedly searched the meager assortment of dresses, blouses, frock coats, and boots.

He was never much of a shopper. But Minn would need a dress. Nothing so fancy as to make them seem monied, but appropriate to a family of their stature. He found a long cotton dress, cream-colored with a blue ruffled collar, and held it up, determining it to be about Minn's size. Draping it over his forearm, he moved on to a rack of coats. A burgundy frock coat with black lapels caught his eye. Hattie had owned one just like it. That was reason enough to choose a different color, something not so distinctive—the gray one, perhaps. Next, boots. Even though the bluestem ruined even the most robust of footwear, Hattie had preferred delicate shoes with brocade spats. It was her philosophy that one must always present good shoes, even if it meant skipping a meal. But there were no spats here, only bland jane boots. Hattie had been a hardheaded, demanding woman, but he missed her. He could hear her now, ordering him to stiffen his upper lip and get on with the job.

He marched up to the counter and laid the items before the crone in the high-collared gray dress. She picked through the items, then studied him closely.

"For my wife," he told her.

Her baggy face twitched. "Have I seen you somewhere before, sir?"

"No, ma'am, just passing through."

She began listing the items in her receipt pad but kept an eye on him. "You look very familiar," she said. "Where is it I know you from?"

Recalling the conversation of the two young women, he gambled. "The only place you might have seen me is taking sacrament at First Presbyterian. I used to frequent there in my days toiling for the railroad."

The tight white collar choking her neck seemed to relax. She reached for a basket of sweets on the counter and handed him one of the wrapped candies.

"Chocolate cures wanderlust and helps a woman bear a healthy brood."

He tried not to think of all those bloody pulps that had fallen out of his wife. "In that case," he said, straining to keep up the smile, "I'll gratefully take two for my wife."

He pushed the horses at a stiff gait, wanting to put as much distance between him and Lee's Summit as possible. Ian was quiet. In fact, he'd hardly spoken all morning. When Eldon asked if something was wrong, the boy shook his head.

Minn had been in the tent changing into her new clothes. She came out and sat behind them making funny faces at Ian until she pried a giggle out of him.

"How about a game?" she said. "We must keep our minds limber."

Ian lit up. "Can we play single hole?"

"You'll have to teach it to me."

He climbed into the tent. After rearranging their stores he set an empty tin can against the backboard then crawled up to the driver's bench and requested a coin.

Eldon dug into his pocket and handed one back.

"All you do is get it in the can," Ian told her. "First one to do it three times wins."

"But we're moving; won't it be difficult?"

Crouching behind the driver's bench, Ian lined up his shot. The coin arced across the tent and landed with a plunk in the can.

Minn clapped. "You're a ringer!"

"What's a ringer?"

"A professional posing as an amateur."

Ian thought about it, then went to collect the coin.

Eldon spoke up. "Where'd you learn to talk so properly?"

She was watching Ian reach into the can. "I was lucky when I was young," she said. "I had a good teacher, Mother Yancy."

"Your momma, you mean?" said Ian.

"She was very much like a mother to me. She used to say that any woman who wishes to be successful in life must speak clearly and competently; otherwise, no man will hear her."

"She sounds nice," Ian said as he crawled up with the coin. He sat looking at it for a moment. "Shane used to always beat me," he said. "Except one time when we pretended to play for Momma's ring. Her ring had magical powers. And a red stone big as a June bug. We were playing for who'd get it and I won."

Minn folded her arms. "So what you're telling me is . . . you're a gambling man."

He thought about it. "Yes," he said. "I believe I am."

"Well, let me have a try then," she said, holding her hand out.

Ian withheld the coin. "What are we playing for?"

"Ian," Eldon chided. "Just play for fun."

"But I'm a gambling man."

Minn laughed out loud, but Eldon hardly managed a smile. He looked at the rifle across his lap. Then around the side of the wagon tent. There was nothing behind them but empty road.

EIGHTEEN

By that afternoon the prairie had wrinkled up into wind-drawn hills scabbed with aging snow. Sun warmed their faces. The air steamed with a sodden perfume of decayed grass, and the drip of melting snow filled the valley. There were buds on the trees, streams rushing at full power, everything moss and mud and rebirth. Minn and Ian were happy to soak up the mild climes. But Eldon was gripped by anxiety. If Shane's body putrefied on the road, he would never forgive himself. When they came upon a patch of melting snow, he stopped and packed the right side of the boot with slush, hoping to keep the body frozen.

The temperature dropped as the sun sank, and they found themselves on a meandering trail of wooded foothills and mercury-colored lakes. While Ian napped, Minn sat behind the driver's bench, her eyes closed.

"Did you really fight with the Major?" she asked suddenly, breaking the silence that Eldon had sustained since lunchtime.

He coughed and spat. "Remember that thing I said about no questions?"

"Are we to pass the time in total silence?"

"Feel free to talk about anything you want."

"Except if you were the Major's lackey?"

He wouldn't give her the satisfaction of turning around. But he also knew she would keep pecking at him.

"I wouldn't say I fought with him. *Because* of him is more like it."

"What does that mean?"

"It means he started a war to get rich."

"So your helping me is some kind of revenge?"

"I didn't help you. My son did."

He coughed again, a rawness spreading down his throat.

They went silent, but he could feel her eyes on his back, probing.

"He's not really a major, you know."

She leaned over the bench to look at him. "Say what?"

"It's an honorary title. They give it to all the Indian agents."

She leaned even farther over the bench, intrigued. "For what purpose?"

"So they'll be respected, I guess. That's how the government operates. Thinking they can hand out something the rest of us got to earn."

"And what exactly does an Indian agent do?"

"Mainly they do what they can to swindle as much from the red man as they're swindling from the government."

She shook her head in disgust. "They call him a saint, you know. The newspapers. *Saint* Sinchilla. Because of all the orphan trains he's sponsored."

"I bet he owns the newspapers. Or at least drinks with the man who does."

They fell again into silence. A colder intermission, the specter of the Major hanging over both of them.

They entered a shadowed canyon. He scanned the darkening ridgeline with a heavy head. He was getting sick, he could feel it.

He'd been sick that day twenty years ago. A late summer cold. They were coming back from a hunt, him, Clayton, and Daddy. They found the McClures strewn across the barnyard, heads, hands, and feet stuffed inside their corpses. A pale newborn wailed among the lattice of appendages, struggling to latch on to its dead mother's breast.

They found Mary Finley after that. Down by the river where she used to sing and fiddle for them on sweltering nights. The skinny blonde with three dimples on each cheek. They'd both been sweet on her. She lay on the bank, riddled with greenbottle flies, a shoeless foot dragging in the current. The features had been beaten out of her face with her own fiddle.

There was a boom up on the ridge. Howitzers. He was squinting through smoke and bodies. The Major had parked his army half a mile from the men dying in battle—not as reinforcements but onlookers. He knew that every gallon of blood Birch Coulee soaked up made it easier to break treaty with the Dakota and snatch their land at the paltry cost of Mary's life and Daddy's life and the lives of a thousand others.

He was looking down at the sun-dried scalp rolled up like a scroll. All the lessons Daddy never got to teach him were written on the underside. Lessons he might have used to forge a different path, away from the death of his son and the ruination of his family. But that path had been snatched away at Birch Coulee, by a man the newspapers had since declared a saint.

A sheet of clouds rolled in with the evening. When it was too dark to differentiate between forest and lake, Eldon stopped to make camp. He hated the idea of camping in bottomland surrounded by steep slopes where even the clumsiest fopdoodle could sneak up on them unnoticed. But the horses were spent and so was he. According to his calculations, they'd traveled seventy miles from Kansas City—a commendable distance, though hardly enough to set his mind at ease. They hadn't lit so much as a match, but now, on an untrammeled trail far from any town, he decided it might be time for a hot meal.

He dug out a round pit about a foot deep. Inside he built a small cook fire, undetectable to anyone not directly above them. Suddenly he found himself wishing that Clayton were here like in the old days, when they'd take shifts on lookout, and he wouldn't have to be up all night, every creak of the forest quickening his heart. Yet the mere recollection of him conjured a dead son, and he returned his gaze to the fire.

Ian turned in after supper, leaving Eldon and Minn to sit in silence around the cook fire. She seemed uncomfortable with the starless dark beyond the ring of firelight. Her head would turn when a horse brayed or a fowl flapped into the air or something larger snapped around in the hardwood. Though her face was pleasing, it was hard to hold in the mind, as if it transformed with each viewing. Not so much a transformation, he thought, but a deepening of the features, as if it were gradually shedding a protective coating. In the feeble light her face had an enchanted quality, the sharp angles framed by waterfalls of black hair.

From the ridge above came a staccato symphony of yips that sent her jumping out of her skin.

Eldon reached for his rifle, smiling faintly at her reaction. "Coyotes," he said.

She hugged herself, eyes darting across the black hilltops. "Breeding season," he said. "They won't bother with us."

They sat back down. The fire had been reduced to delicate piles of ash. He added another log and returned to his seat. His head hurt, his nose was running, his throat was dry and scratchy, yet he felt a sense of calm sitting there with her.

"What are your aspirations, Miss Yancy?" he said, hoping to take her mind off the dark shapes lurking on the ridge.

She looked at him as if he were a statue who had just come to life. Then she held her eyes on the flames licking out of the pit.

"I'm going to be a schoolteacher," she said. "I taught most of the other girls to read and write—those who showed interest."

"Other girls?"

"Most of the girls he adopted had no education."

"The Major? How many girls did he adopt?"

"When I left, there was Tildy, Ciara, Regina, Abigail . . ." She continued, counting on her fingers, muttering the names under her breath. "Nine when I left." Her eyes dimmed for just a moment. "No," she said. "Eight. But there have been more."

"Eight girls at once?"

"He needs a staff to keep house." She looked at the fire, shaking her head. "'You're not here forever,' I'd tell the girls. 'He has you by law to the age of twenty-one, but then you're free. Use your time wisely.'"

"So they can leave?"

"The law says they can. But they don't. Unless he tells them to. Then they have no choice."

"But you did," he said. "And now you're off to be a schoolteacher."

She looked at him with smiling confidence. "Yes. In a big city like Chicago."

"Chicago?" he said. "Why of all places would you go there?"

"Well . . . I do admire it. The pace at which they've rebuilt after the fires? I find it enchanting that something so immense can be so decimated yet muster the strength to rebuild bigger and better."

"I'll give you that."

"You've been?"

"Long time ago."

She lit up. "Where did you stay?"

"Some big hotel. Had running water and hot baths and flush toilets."

"How luxurious!"

"Until you turned on the faucet and a bunch of little fishes come out."

Her face crumpled. "Fish?"

"Oh yeah. They come right outta the faucet. Live ones if the water's cold, dead if it's hot. They used to call the bathwater there *chowder* on account of all the cooked minnows that'd fill up your tub."

"You're pulling my leg."

"Cross my heart. Heck, I've seen it with my own two eyes."

She was silent a moment, then said, "I can live with fish in the faucet. I can live with that just fine."

They sat listening to the snappy crepitations of the fire.

"How old were you when he . . . ?"

"Nine or ten? Age is an estimation for an orphan."

"My wife used to say the same thing. Believe me, she used it to her advantage."

"Your wife was an orphan? Did she come out on the trains?"

"She was born in Missouri."

Minn yawned and stood up. "Time to turn in. Good night, Mr. Quint."

As she walked toward the wagon, he rose and pulled off his hat. "Miss Yancy?"

She turned, everything but her eyes swathed in darkness. There was something in them, something he recognized in his own gaze. Pain, fear, desolation, anger.

"I know what it feels like," he said.

"No," she said. "You don't have the first idea."

NINETEEN

No matter how fast he drove, the imp was on the horizon. Then he was upon them with his scar and his nostrils and his pearl-handled blade. Eldon went for his guns, but they'd turned into green serpents. The imp turned into a gallant sculpture of a man. It was Harlan Scrim. He rode a white stallion, a big silver star pinned to his chest. He looked at Eldon as they raced across a scorched prairie. Rivulets of blood dripped down his forehead, seeping from under his hat. "I want my guns back," he said.

The explosion rang from the center of Eldon's forehead out through his ears. He fell back into a soggy blanket and held his temples until the pain dulled. A pinkish glow seeped in under the wagon. There was a damp spot on the under-carriage where he must have just smashed his head. For a moment he thought he remembered the dream that had caused him to sit up so violently, but then it was gone.

"Mr. Quint?"

Her face came into focus. It had changed from last night, when it had loomed over the fire, shrouded in black. It looked like she'd just awakened.

"You look poorly," she said, studying him through squinted, sleepy eyes.

Ian's boots squelched into the mud and he crouched into view. He was yawning. "Pa, you were shouting."

Eldon crawled out from under the wagon and stood shivering in the dawn breeze. His shirt and pants were soaked. He had vague recollections of a storm lashing over the hills last night. Swallowing caused a dry, sharp pain in the back of his throat. He steadied himself against the wagon, feeling dizzy.

Minn put a hand to his head. "You're burning up."

"I'm fine," he said.

He fed the horses while Ian and Minn ate breakfast, and ten minutes later they were on the trail. Gloomy cloud cover had erased the sun. The reins felt sticky in his hands. He kept the horses at a moderate pace, which was all his pounding head could endure. To stay alert he calculated how many miles they might cover in a day, and how many more days to Springfield, and how long before he could bury his son.

At midday they stopped at a cobalt lake. Eldon forced himself to eat. By the time they got back on the road he was struggling to keep his eyes open. Minn was giving Ian elocution lessons in the tent and the sounds were driving him mad.

"*Daaa*," Ian was saying, over and over.

"Now put friction on your tongue so it doesn't punch out of your mouth," Minn instructed. "Listen: *thhh*. Hear the difference? It's gentler. Mou*thhhh*. Tee*thhhh*. *Thhh*is."

"*Thhhh*," said Ian. "Like that?"

"Say this three times fast: three free fleas flew three cheese trees."

"Three flee freeze—no wait . . ."

Eldon pulled a blanket over his ears to dampen the sound. The horses' hindquarters swayed rhythmically. At some point his head lolled, then snapped up. He wiped the drool from his mouth. Had he dozed off? He unwrapped the blanket from his head. Behind him, Ian and Minn were having an entirely different conversation in the tent.

"Was it just you?" Ian was asking.

"Oh no," she said. "There were at least thirty of us."

"Did you know where you were going?"

"We knew it had to be somewhere special. We never had new clothes before, but that day they daintied us up in new cotton dresses, stiff white pinafores, and perfectly pressed white gloves."

"You never even wore ready-mades?"

"All of our clothes were made of old bedsheets."

"Really? You must've been cold all the time."

"*All* the time. Though we had hot soup once a day to keep us warm."

"Is that all you got?"

"One ladle of vegetable soup, once a day. Nothing more."

"Not even some meat?"

"Once, I worked up the courage to ask the matron for a bit of her mutton and she bruised my arm with a wooden spoon."

"Did you cry?"

"Never. Orphans do not cry."

"Orphans do not cry," Ian repeated reverently.

Her eyes smirked. "Not where anyone can see you, at least."

He giggled.

Eldon turned, covering a cough. "You were on one of those trains, orphan trains? I heard about them. Man one time came out to the cabin asking if I needed extra labor. Said they're shipping children out by the trainload from the cities."

The tent flap opened and she looked out. "How are you feeling?"

He turned away, dismissing the question with a shrug.

"Was it nice?" Ian said, filling the silence. "The train?"

"Cold, noisy, everything covered in coal dust—it was magical."

He laughed.

"Truth be told, I was so pleased with my new white gloves that I hardly noticed anything else. I didn't even care when the nuns told us, 'Your past is not your past. Your life begins when you are chosen.' I was sure that with my perfect white gloves I would be the first one chosen."

"Were you?"

"Second to last. But only because I was small and dark and they thought I was a gypsy. Or a Mexican. The woman at Children's Aid had gotten me . . . oh—Mr. Quint? Mr. Quint?"

His head snapped up and he squinted. Two riders were coming down the slim trail toward them. He looked around for his rifle and realized it was on his lap. The riders wore big peltry coats and had rifles scabbarded to their horses. As they neared, he saw that one of them wore a white bowler. And had a scar down one side of his face.

The trail narrowed ahead, a ravine on one side, a steep hill on the other. He gripped his rifle. Something wasn't right. This was a damn bushwhack. He lifted the rifle but felt a gentle hand squeeze his shoulder.

"It's not him," she whispered.

Minn was behind him. She pulled her cowl up as the riders passed. They touched their brims and went on their way. Eldon looked at the man in the white bowler. He was taller than the imp and didn't have a scar—it was the string of his hat. He had nearly just killed an innocent man.

Wouldn't be the first time, said Jack, who was sitting on the driver's bench next to him, his blue face chipped and cracked, two balls of ice where his eyes belonged.

Just ask poor Missus Scrim, he said. *She'll be happy to remind ye.*

He thought he heard coronet music behind them and looked back expecting to see the feathered parade horses and the snarling trophy heads that studded the Major's stagecoach. His head felt heavy, but he rushed the horses. Stiff leather reins jerked in his hands and he raised his eyelids to a watery vision of four horses loping into the twilight.

Minn was behind him, shaking his shoulder.

"I'm fine," he said, then he fell from the bench.

The cold shocked him, dragged him from darkness, and wrapped his body in spikes of ice. Rough hands held him underwater and he fought, but they were too many. His lungs were scorched and desperate for air and he thought they had drowned him, but they lifted him from the cold lake and carried him naked and dripping into a strange building, up a strange stairway, into a strange room, and laid him on a strange bed. He struggled as they held him down. A halo of faces stared at him. He was kicking and clawing, fighting with all he had. Then a soft voice whispered in his ear. It promised that he would be well again if only he could stop running.

I'm dead, he thought. *I'm dead.*

He tried to wake up, but his eyes kept sinking into his head. Gauzy light bled through a curtained window at the foot of the bed. Birdsong. He was in a strange bed, in a strange room, wearing a strange pair of long underwear.

At his bedside his wife sat in a blue press-back rocker chair in a gray dress with green polka dots and her hair was braided down her back and beaded with turquoise. She was smiling pleasantly, eyes wide and green and unblinking.

"Would you like mint tea?" she asked, slapping the heels of her boots on the floor to stop herself rocking.

"Mint tea is fine," he said cordially.

Her face crinkled as if his words were patronizing or malodorous. "Mint tea? How dastardly, how positively dreadful. But the doctor says I must have it. Part of your little regimen to keep me 'even-keeled' like I am some drunkard."

He chuckled uneasily. "You and your exaggerations."

"And these doctors. Quacks, all of them. Quack quack quack. A gaggle of quacking ducks."

She screwed a cigarette into a jade holder then lit it, her silver lighter embedded with a red carnelian stone. She kicked back in her rocker, setting herself in motion. The smoke rose in the warm morning light.

"You have some message for me?" she said in her maudlin drawl.

"What message?" he said.

"Well, I have a message for you. You no longer exist. Like flatulence in the wind."

He sat up in bed. "Why do you say things like that?"

"You told me you wouldn't hurt a fly. *People*, on the other hand . . ."

"Dammit, Hattie. I told you ten times. I just look like him."

She tapped a long tube of ash on his bedcover, then planted her boots with a hard stomp and stood up. "Your arrogance astounds, even now."

"Where are you going?"

"I would like to take my son to see *The Pirates of Penzance*, but he is not here. He's never been to a theater. He's never been anywhere. Hurry up, won't you? I'm lonesome."

His chest fluttered, hands going clammy. "I'm going as fast as I can," he said, wondering how he might get out of there, though his legs seemed to fail him.

She broke into song. "*Oh, better far to live and die, under the brave black flag I fly, than play a sanctimonious part with a pirate head and a pirate heart!*"

"Stop," he said, wincing at her shrill vocalizations.

"Stop what—breathing? I've done that already."

"I can't think when you're like this."

She dragged her cigarette and exhaled and her spirit came out of her mouth and curled in the sunlight, mixing with grains of dust. "Do you remember when you hummed to me? The doctor said it would calm me down after the galvanization therapy. You sat at my bed, humming every tune you could think of. Do you remember?"

He remembered her screaming at him to stop, to leave, to die.

"How I must have made you feel," she said. "Trampled by horses. Run over by steel-rimmed wheels. Why ever did you marry me?"

"I wanted a family," he said. "So did you."

"I wanted what you told me to want."

"That's not true."

Her eyes thinned to little jade slits. "You don't deserve a family."

"A man can change," he said, though he didn't believe it.

She flicked the spent cigarette from its holder and screwed in a fresh one. "You haven't changed," she said, lighting up. "Now open your mouth."

"What?"

"I said open your mouth."

He blinked.

A doctor hovered over him, holding a spoon. He had big baby-like cheeks and wore thick specs that stretched his eyes to demonic saucers.

"I know it tastes awful," he said. "But it will help you sleep."

Eldon parted his lips to argue, but the doctor jammed a spoon down his throat.

"Son of a bitch," he sputtered.

The doctor packed his bottles of tinctures. "Bed rest, one more day." He was speaking to someone across the room. "But it looks like we're through the worst of it."

Eldon lifted his head off the sweat-stained pillow to look at his wife. But it was Minn rising from a small skirted chair next to his bed, the cords of her neck relaxing as if the doctor's prognosis had provided her some relief.

"Where am I?" he mumbled.

She glanced down at him as she rounded the bed. "The Jackson Mott Hotel in Clinton, Missouri."

She gave the doctor some money, then saw him out. After she locked the door, she walked back to her skirted chair, sat down, and watched him for a moment.

"How are you feeling?" she said.

"What?" he said, hoarse. "Fine."

"Fine?"

"Yes," he said. "Where am I?"

"I told you. Clinton, Missouri. Would you like some water?"

"No, I . . ."

She handed him a glass and he drank. The coolness felt good on his cracked throat. He finished the glass and handed it back. She sat looking at him.

"What?"

"Who is Harlan Scrim?"

He thought he'd misheard her, yet at the same time, knowing he hadn't, felt the powerful impulse, like a bug in his ear, to tell her everything. But that would ruin everything, just as it had with Hattie.

"Who's what?" he said, acting poorly.

"Harlan Scrim. You've been screaming his name for three days now."

The headache returned, screwing into his temples, and he rubbed his eyes. "I don't know," he said unconvincingly.

"You don't know."

He looked at her. "Three days?"

She folded her arms and looked at him.

"Well, I don't know," he said. "Stop asking questions. I don't know. I'm tired."

The sun must have emerged just then because the light was blaring through the curtains, stinging his eyes. He thought of Shane baking in the wagon, sat up, and struggled to free himself from the heavy blankets; he found out just what state he was in that a blanket could cement him so easily in place.

"Lie down," she commanded.

"My son will rot."

"I had the liveryman pack the chamber with ice. The temperature is barely above freezing. Now lie down."

"Need to get back on the road."

She took him by the shoulders and pushed him down. "I don't like being immobile any more than you do, but you must rest."

Three days he'd been out. She could have easily made off with his money, his horses, his guns, even his son.

"I'm fine," he said.

"You're far from fine. We could've fried an egg on your forehead. They had to throw you in a freezing lake. Ian was scared half to death."

"Where is he?"

"Sleeping in the next room. He refused to leave your bedside for three days. Wouldn't even bathe."

"But he's all right?"

"Yes, well . . ."

"What?" he said.

"We can discuss it later. You should rest."

"Tell me."

Straightening up in her chair, she cleared her throat, putting on the air of an interviewee. "Ian is a sharp boy, but he needs stimulation and schooling. As you know, I, too, have a journey to embark upon. And though I have this dress and this fine coat, which I greatly appreciate, I have no savings of my own, no horse, no prospects of any—"

"How much you want?"

"No . . . I'm not petitioning your charity."

"What are you petitioning?"

"I want to be employed. As Ian's governess."

The request took him by surprise. "But we're only a few days from—"

"From Springfield," she broke in. "I know. But I could stay until the burial. The ground is frozen and may be for some weeks. Ian shouldn't miss out on so much schooling. I beg you, do not deprive him. And if not me, please hire someone else."

He considered the offer. "A governess earns about five dollars a week?"

"Closer to ten, I believe."

He looked at her. Then offered his hand. "Deal."

She tempered a look of surprise, then grabbed his hand in both of hers and shook the blood right out of it.

"I won't let you down," she said.

The feel of her hand, warm and soft, reminded him of what he'd seen in her eyes a few nights back.

"The other night, when I said I know what it's like . . ."

"You don't have to explain," she said.

"I only meant I know what it's like to be running from something. When I saw the Major, it about set my skin on fire. What him and the war took from me . . . things I won't never get back. It's a hard thing to face."

Her eyes swelled. "What if you don't need it back? What if you're made stronger by what you've endured?"

He shook his head. "I don't think Harlan Scrim would agree with you there."

She folded her arms and looked down her nose. "Now you're just playing games."

"You really want to know?"

"After three days nonstop, yes, I'm curious."

"He was a marshal in Kansas City. Worked as a gun for hire for the railroads. The banks. Ranchers. Politicians. Indian agents."

She cocked her head.

"Did whatever they asked."

"Indian agents," she said. "You mean the Major."

"The men he worked for . . . they were not good men."

"What happened to him?"

He could almost feel it. The knife breaking the taut flesh of the scalp, scraping the bone underneath. He started to cough.

She adjusted his pillow, then sat in her chair and folded her legs.

He turned his head to look at her. "What's the worst thing you ever done?"

Her eyes fell. She seemed to know exactly what it was but was hesitant. She looked up and said, "I blinded the head matron."

"Head matron?" he said, eyes getting heavy.

"Of Mort. The Mortonson Orphanage."

"What was it like?"

"It was the second worst place I ever lived. I can still smell the slimy granite walls, the stink of lye. Every night, lulled to sleep by the shriek of starving children. My ward was nicknamed the Coop. Any show of weakness got you pecked to death like a chicken. The older children liked to tease me over my ear. The head matron thought I was smug because I knew how to read. She used to egg them on. She would tell me that a girl with one disfigured ear had no chance of being adopted in a home full of girls with both ears intact. A girl like me was destined for the industrial school, doomed to spend the rest of her life toiling behind a sewing machine, until her fingers bled and her heart shriveled like burnt paper. I made it my mission to prove her wrong. While the other children complained about the prayers or the endless hours of scraping dried shit from the edge of the latrine, I reveled in the discipline. That was the one thing they could never take away. But she tried, that witch. She tried. So one day I threw lye in her eyes."

Despite the words, her voice was calm, hopeful, and reassuring. Suddenly he wanted to tell her everything, but that doctor's potion was dragging him back to the darkness. He fought against it, then felt her hands on his chest.

"Rest now, Mr. Quint," she said. "That tincture is already sagging your lids."

HIM WITHOUT GUTS

TWENTY

"You could have saved me," she said.

Leaning over the rail of his iron bed, he reached for her hand.

She had beanpole arms. Sunny blonde hair, three dimples on each cheek. He smelled her hand. Syrup and apple blossom, just like he remembered. A welcome relief from the acrid, pustule sweetness that coated the pea-colored walls and filthy barred windows of the convalescent ward.

"I wanted to," he said, turning up his eyes.

"If you wanted to," she said coldly, "you would have."

She sat back on the bedside stool and locked her arms across her chest.

"Don't say that," he begged. "I'm not like he says."

She wore a sky-blue cotton dress, a cotton pinafore, and black leather shoes caked in reddish mud. Her skin was the color of butter, her bell-shaped haircut curled to mandible-like hooks just below her jawline. She was no more than twelve but had the dull blue eyes of a wearier soul.

"How many songs did I compose for you?" she said. "How many letters did I pour my heart into? How many fiddle strings did I snap on your account?"

He stared at the ceiling. There was a faint breeze. A cobweb flicked in a corner.

"I was a boy," he whispered.

"You saw the smoke on your way back from your hunt, before you tried to get to the canoe. You could have walked a hundred paces to my house to warn me. But you were angry. You *wanted* your brother to suffer. You've always been jealous of him."

He pushed up onto his elbows, shaking his head. "Have not."

"You must be a coward then. That is the only other explanation."

"I didn't know."

"You saw the smoke!"

"Daddy made us go to the canoe." He was breathing heavily. "I loved you."

"Then why let your brother ask my hand in marriage when it was for you I composed my brightest melodies?"

He was huffing air. She slid from the stool and gently laid him back down.

"They were all for you, Clayton."

"But ye chose him," he said, broken-voiced. "You said *yes.*"

"I said *yes* because he had the courage to ask. And because it's not real when you're twelve."

"I'm . . . I didn't know."

Her eyes sank. "Yes. Of course. All the songs and notes. How could you have?"

Her feet swirled in little circles, beads of red mud blotching the floor.

"Today would have been my thirty-second birthday," she said.

March the sixth. He knew it by heart. Said a prayer for her every year at midnight. It was the only time he prayed. And the one day a year he didn't get blind drunk.

"It's not enough," she said, as if she'd read his thoughts.

You're envious of him.

Had she just said that or was it in his mind?

"I ain't envious," he said.

"Then why cling to that evil character?"

"Jack Foss takes from the takers. Barons and tycoons. Government agents. Goddamn murderers."

"And what are you, Jack?"

He turned his face into the pillow. "I'm sorry, Mary. I'm sorry. I'm sorry."

When she didn't answer, he turned his head to look at her. The softness of her features had given over to sinew and struggle. Her skin shriveled and tightened. Her neck was lined and stubbled. Bruised pouches swelled under her eyes.

Late-born bastard. What've ye done now?

He looked in horror at the rough, pitted hands. The hard square face pulled tight to the bone. Daddy raised a fist.

"Daddy!" he said, hardly any voice left. "Please!"

With a gulp of air he sat up and opened his eyes.

Her hands were on him. Comforting him. She was a blonde too, though taller. And older. With a bit of an ungainly frame and an oblong face.

"It's all right," the woman said, easing him back into bed. "It was just a dream."

She wrung out a washcloth and dabbed his clammy forehead. It was cool and soothing. He lay there breathing, reality crushing in around him. She was his nurse. Nurse Daye. From Memphis. She smiled. Wet the cloth. Put it to his forehead.

"We just can't seem to shake this darn fever," she said.

He liked looking at her. Her thin nose and wild lemony brows. He liked her for reasons other men probably didn't.

She had the kind of face that shifted between homeliness and beauty depending on the vantage. She wore thin-soled shoes to reduce her height, even though her hair was always piled chaotically atop her head. He liked her sure-footed wit and lilting Southern drawl. He liked her carefree inelegance most of all.

She pressed the cool, damp towel to his forehead. "You were having a dream."

He didn't want to think about that. He wanted to think about her. He realized that he liked her because she reminded him of poor Mary Finley. A sick, overwarm sensation came over him as he tried to picture her face. She would slip droll little notes into his pocket when Eldon wasn't looking.

He rubbed his eyes, then smiled up at Nurse Daye. She had spent the better part of three weeks at his bedside, ever since that pair of bark-skins had found him under Artemus, on the brink of death.

"Ye look glorious as always, Nurse Daye," he said, his voice hoarse.

She folded the washcloth and draped it over the lip of a water pail. "You were screaming again."

He sat up. "I been meanin to ask ye somethin. Why in hell's creation does a glorious gal like you relocate to Indian territory?"

"We've talked about it at length."

"Have we?"

She had lost her parents to yellow fever. Wanted adventure. The West seemed exotic. She wanted freedom.

"Tell me again," he said.

She pressed a finger to her cheek in theatrical reflection, liking the suspense she was creating. "I suppose it was the circular they posted at school. An urgent call for nurses in the territories. And I—now, don't laugh—I always wanted to be part of something bigger than myself. And there is no bigger place than the West."

"So ye come to see an Injun."

"And here I am, stuck with the consolation prize: a farmer shot by an outlaw."

"Jack Foss ain't jest any outlaw. He's famous as Bill Bonney, Jesse Evans—"

"Dirty Dave?"

"Dirty Dave don't even rate."

"Well, it is quite an achievement getting shot. You should be proud."

He turned away. "Yer meaner than a snake."

"Oh stop, I know you're not that delicate."

"Here's somethin might surprise ye. I am one a the few white men ever shall you meet who does not desire to cast mud on the Indian so as to soothe my filthy conscience."

"And why, pray tell?"

"I know how they feel."

Her head dipped to one side. "How so?"

"Ain't jest them got ruined by the makin of this country."

"Well, yes, the Chinese—"

"Ain't talkin bout no Johnnies. I'm talkin bout the men what made this country."

Her eyes flicked up. "I'm not sure I follow."

"Daddy said this country was built on the backs of suckers, men conned into thinkin El Dorado lay jest over yonder. But the truth is, they was nothin but cannon fodder."

As she sat pondering his words, a little black cloud seemed to form over her head. "Do you truly believe that?"

He believed worse—that this country was built on the blood of suckers who laid down their lives not for family or country, but for the fat cats stealing land. He also believed that she hadn't come west for adventure. It was the sorrow of losing both parents that brought her. This land radiated sorrow so pungent he could taste it even now on the back of his tongue.

But he saw no reason to crush her fantasy. "No," he said. "I don't believe it."

The cloud over her head turned to sunshine. "Good," she said. "This is a beautiful country populated by good people seeking a moral and productive life."

She had good eyes, kind eyes, dull blue like Mary's.

"Darlin, what day is it?"

"You know what day it is."

He grinned. "Tuesday?"

She bathed him on Tuesdays.

A shudder of pain suddenly ruined his mood. She rose from her stool, drew down the sheet, and examined the discolored bandage covering his right hip.

"I need to change this," she said, turning.

He caught her hand. "Ye think what happens in life happens fer a reason?"

"Mr. Quint. You know I enjoy our daily peregrinations, but you also know I'm busiest in the morning. We'll talk after lunch."

"What if there ain't no meanin to any of it?" he said. "What if it's all jest dark as the inside of yer head?"

"And what if there is meaning in everything? After all, Mr. Quint, even you have come to mean something to me."

He drew her hand to his lips and inhaled the scent of pine water. They were alone in the ward, save the half dozen patients spread down the long hall, curtained and sedate in their iron beds.

"You are what they call a misanthrope," she said, holding back a smile.

"I'm what they call a pessimist, which means I see the world as it truly is."

"Then you should understand that I must see about my other—" Her eyes lifted abruptly and she retracted her hand and picked up the water pail.

He looked to see what had startled her.

In the entranceway stood a compact man in a baggy suit and a black bowler. Squinty and pin-eyed, he searched the ward; then, with a bobbling step, he crossed the hall, his hat bouncing against his floppy ears.

"Eldon Quint?" he questioned upon arrival, a thick mustache draping over his mouth.

"Mr. Quint," said Jack, showing his palms. "Ye got me."

"E. M. Kestrel," the man said. "I handle the collection of debt for this hospital." He looked at Nurse Daye and snorted. She took her pail and went down the hall.

"I ain't even mended yet and yer goin in my pocket?"

"My business does not concern your current condition." He took a folder from his black valise and scanned the documents within. "You owe a debt of two hundred and thirteen dollars to this hospital. I have a writ of attachment here." He showed the document. "Because you have chosen to ignore my repeated attempts to collect this debt, I must notify you—"

Jack waved a hand in his face. "I don't got no debt," he said. "Leave us be. It's time fer my bath."

"You owe this hospital a balance of two hundred and thirteen dollars for the care of your spouse, from April of eighty-one to May of eighty-two, when she received treatment for hysteria, melancholia, and bouts of catalepsy."

Jack's first thought was that of course Eldon would drive his wife mad. The Eldon he knew was controlling and selfish. The Eldon he knew had pretended to love Mary Finley so his brother couldn't have her. The Eldon he knew could do no wrong in Daddy's eyes. He tried to picture his brother at the altar, reciting a matrimonial vow with a straight face. It was so ridiculous that he laughed out loud, much to the disgust of Mr. Kestrel.

"What have you to say for yourself?" said the collector.

Jack's reply was cut short by a shock of pain.

That's what ye git fer delightin in yer brother's misery, said Daddy. *The misery of yer nephews. What kind of man dines on the sorrow of children?*

"Well?" snapped the collector.

Jack sat up and looked him in the eye. "If you wanna collect money from me, Kestrel, ye ought to grow a foot taller, git yerself a six-shooter and some lessons on how to use it. Then ye might come back and speak to me in that tone. And you know what I'd tell ye? That yer diggin a dry well."

The collector's bushy mouth puckered like a rectum, his face traveling through ever-darkening shades of red. "If you do not remit payment of—and I am being generous given your bereavement—of at least fifty percent of the principal by end of day, I will be forced to contact the U.S. marshal and commence proceedings to have you jailed as a bill jumper."

"Bill jumper? You blackguarding sombitch—I ain't no bill jumper. In fact, I will have the full sum this afternoon. Shan't even be a bother to me. Now git outta my sight. It's time fer my bath."

"If it is no bother," said Kestrel, "then why have you not settled the debt sooner?"

Jack thought of the can of tomatoes his brother had stuffed with nickels and dollar bills. Eldon Quint, reduced to selling fire mats door to door to save his mad wife. He never in a million years would have imagined it. And here was this officious, sniveling collector harassing him?

Big talk from the man who robbed him, said Daddy.

"My wife burned up in a fire," Jack said suddenly. "And I have been scraping and savin all winter to take my boys to visit her grave. I'm sure even a money-monger like you can imagine the dirge that has taken over my mind."

When the collector spoke again, it was with a tone of careful understanding. "Who will bring you the funds?"

"Dick Cottersman."

"He will come today?"

"I imagine he'll board his animal soon as ye get word to him."

The collector produced a steel-tipped quill and paper.

"Write his address and a note of explanation. I shall visit him this afternoon."

Jack did as requested, making up an address.

"Know this, Mr. Quint. If you leave this hospital before this debt is settled, I will be forced to engage the marshal."

Jack flung off the bedsheet and pulled up his muslin gown. A custardy purple bruise extended beyond the bandages wrapping his hip.

"As ye can see, Kestrel, I ain't goin nowhere."

Less than an hour later, with the help of Nurse Daye, Jack climbed out of a first-floor window in the chemist's lab.

He stood in the street in his buffalo coat, a pair of ironed slacks, and a pair of pilfered issue boots that belonged to a ranger who'd gone mad with syphilis and would never need boots again.

Nurse Daye looked worriedly from the window. She had initially refused to help him, assuming that he was only escaping a debt, but he swore there was more to it.

"There's men lookin fer me," he had told her. "That collector is gonna put my name out there. Won't take them long to connect the dots."

"But you're not healed," she had said.

It was snowing prettily, a vibrant spring snow, the last tease of winter turning the busy road into a collage of watery footprints.

Jack stood amid the morning traffic, eyes aching in the gray light, his body stiff and unwilling. Looking back at the window, he blew a kiss to his caretaker and promised that they would meet again.

Only after he said it did he realize how much he hoped it would come true.

When he turned from the infirmary, she called after him.

"Do write," she said. "But do your best to keep the letter brief."

He chuckled and crossed the road at a lurching gait, making for the first unattended horse that caught his eye.

TWENTY-ONE

IN THE HARD SUN THE CABIN LOOKED LIKE AN AGING SHIP-wreck on a plain of white. The bodies were gone, his brother was gone, but the reek of blood and gunpowder lingered. He stayed in the trees, where the snow had hardened to a hateful, sun-deprived crust, eager to slice up anything that punctured it. The roan he'd stolen in Yankton had thrown him twice already, and twice the tiny blades of ice sawed into his flesh, as if the land were punishing him all over again.

When he considered approaching the cabin, his stomach twisted and he could almost hear Mary Finley calling him a coward.

He stayed in the trees, at the edge of what happened, until the sky emptied of color and the night forced him to shelter in an abandoned milk house. Beneath the only corner with a bit of roof still intact he formed an itchy bed of cold straw. His thigh burned. Luckily he'd stolen some whiskey, and drank himself to sleep.

He woke in his childhood home. He was fourteen again. It was a dream, yet the soot stung his eyes and choked his throat. Still, he wanted to sleep in the burned-out shell, but Eldon wouldn't allow it. The Indians had just left. Soot got on his hands and in his eyes. He wanted to sleep in the burned-out shell, but Eldon wouldn't allow it. Too dangerous, he said. The sheep in the neighbor's barn were screaming. He wanted to set them free, but Eldon wouldn't allow that, either. He made him gut every last one so the Indians wouldn't come around and take them. Then he gave him Daddy's trunk of books to carry. It was all that had survived the fire.

At dawn he returned to Eldon's cabin. From the trees he saw a man aboard a brown mare trotting across the field, a mule tailed out behind hauling lumber stacked on two travois poles. Jack hadn't laid eyes on him in years, but even at three hundred paces he recognized the dark jagged frame wagging atop that horse.

When he reached the cabin, the old man laid out his tools. He replaced a lintel and installed a new door, then smeared chinking between the logs to patch the bullet holes.

Despite the improvements, the house still cried when the wind cut through it. The right thing to do was to tear it down. And the longer the old man worked in opposition of what was right, the angrier Jack became.

When the sun touched the treetops, the old man started to clean up.

A thought sat burning in Jack's throat. This was who his brother chose to spend his days with, this half-breed son of a bitch?

He followed Dick's tracks two miles up the trail to a comfortable brick farmhouse. He watched the old man through a window. Dick smoked his pipe and helped himself to a snack of jerky. After that, he took a few nips of something, then stashed the bottle behind a bag of sugar, hiding it before his wife came home.

As the sun set, Jack returned to his brother's cabin. He'd all but frozen to death last night and forced himself to go in and take what clothes Eldon had left behind.

In the bedroom he slipped off his damp shirt and put on one of his brother's. The fit was loose and irregular. They used to trade garments all the time, before they each carried a bullet. Eldon kept his behind the left rib. Jack's lived next to his kidney. Their bodies must have twisted around the wounds. Time had warped them differently.

He watched the old man again the next day, then followed him home and watched him enjoy his jerky and a nip from the bottle. After that, the old man went up to change in anticipation of his wife's return. Jack went into the barn to find a weapon and came out with a bent horseshoe.

The small brick kitchen was cold, yet it glowed with the sunset. Jack settled at the breakfast table. He helped himself to Dick's tobacco and his bottle of sweet rum. Daddy drank rum. A sinful habit he'd picked up from the Dakota chieftains, when he'd trade with them and smoke their pipes and wear their dank skins and examine their medicine bundles that smelled of toe rot. When that rum came out, the allegation that had trailed Clayton Quint since birth was sure to follow. He was a murderer, Daddy would say. His first murder committed the day he was born. For years, Jack would be sick at the mere waft of rum. But now he drank it heartily, with an eye toward hell, so Daddy would know how little he meant.

The stairs creaked.

Jack put down the bottle, then slid a hand into his buffalo coat as if to clutch for a gun, though all he held was that bent horseshoe.

Dick stopped in the entranceway. If he was surprised by the visitor, it did not read on the thick bark of his face.

"Ye know why I'm here," said Jack. He picked up the pipe and smoked, keeping the other hand in his coat. "So skip the wish-washin and maybe you'll live to see that fat wife a yers again." He nudged out the other chair with his boot. "Sit."

Dick stood in long red woolens, the knees worn out. *"Su-pe-hi-ye,"* he said in his hard baritone. "I wondered when you'd come."

Smoke mushroomed against a silvery-orange window. Jack set down the pipe. "Don't start with that *Soupy Hiya* horseshit," he said. "Siddown or I'll sit ye down."

The old man took his time settling into the chair. He glanced at the bottle of rum.

"I see ye still drink like a savage," Jack said.

Dick looked up from the bottle. "And you, *Su-pe-hi-ye.* You still act like a child who never learned his manners."

Jack swigged the rum then pushed the bottle across the table.

The old man ignored it.

"I seen my brother's cabin. I know ye collected them bounties."

Dick set his palms on his knees. "You know why Dakota people have three names?"

"Quit stalling."

"Each name must be earned."

Jack snorted. "What'd they give you? One and a half names?"

"I was *Anunkasan*, swift and powerful like the eagle. Then *Iron Sights*, who does not blink at Death. Now I live in a house, I go to church, I farm. My name is Dick Cottersman. But you are still *Su-pe-hi-ye*. Him Without Guts."

"I should kill ye fer givin me that name."

The old man shook his head. "I would never give a child that name. I said as much to your father. He felt differently."

Given all that Daddy had put him through, it shouldn't have come as a shock. Yet it felt like a knife twisting in his guts.

Jack drained the rum and smacked the empty bottle on the table. "I ain't bout to sit here takin shit from no cut-hair turncoat."

"You know nothing of my struggles, *Su-pe-hi-ye*."

Jack swiped his eyes around the kitchen. "I know the government don't build these brick shitboxes fer any old breechclout."

Slowly, powerfully, Dick stood up.

Jack reached into his coat. "Siddown."

The old man's long arm ventured into the hall and came back with a stained cattleman's hat. He sat and stared at the hat, turning it over in his hands.

"When your father gave me this hat, my father said it was a white man's hat. If I put it on, I was making a choice. My father said he would never make such a choice. Yet he died with short hair, and was buried with a Bible in his hand."

He held up the hat for Jack to see.

"I keep it now as a reminder of how to treat my own children." He put on the hat. "It makes me sad to think how you've changed. That you would value a bounty above your kin."

Fists crashed on the tabletop. "Warn't about no bounty," Jack said.

The bottle shattered across the floor, shards burning with the last gasp of the sun.

"Then why do you want the money?" asked Dick.

The anger shook off Jack's face. He was tired. His hip was starting to throb. "Jest give it to me," he said.

Dick leaned in. "Make amends with your brother. Take responsibility for what you've done. There's time still."

Jack pushed unsteadily to his feet. "Gimme the money."

"Earn back your name."

"I will shoot yer squaw in the face the minute she walks in that fuckin door!"

Dick looked on placidly. "I sent the money to your brother. Only kept a small sum to make repairs on his cabin."

"Sent it where?"

"Philadelphia."

Jack stared at him. "Lie to me again, Iron Sights, yer gonna see what happens."

The old man turned his head and nodded at a rolltop desk in the sitting room. "The receipt is in there."

"Git it. Slow. Keep yer hands where I can see em."

The old man stood and shuffled into the room. Something about his eager stride bothered Jack. Despite the scream of his hip, he staggered after him. Dick was reaching into one of the drawers when the cold punch of iron knocked off his hat.

"Turn around, put yer hands on that wall."

When the old man failed to move, Jack ground the horseshoe into the back of his head like it was a revolver.

Dick put his hands on the wall, mortar squeezing from between the bricks.

Jack looked into the drawer. He set the horseshoe on the desk, then lifted out his Peacemakers. "He gave you my Colts?"

"Traded," said Dick. "For provisions."

Eldon was twisting the knife.

Jack made sure the gun was loaded, then drew the hammer. "Where's the money you kept?"

Dick nodded at a different drawer. Jack dumped it out. Wrapped herbs, decorative boxes, a fist-sized medicine bundle wrapped in pigskin.

"Where?"

"Cigar box," Dick said. "With the pretty squaw on it."

Jack was counting the bills when he saw a folded yellow paper tucked into the envelope slot of the desk. It was a receipt from Western Union for two thousand five hundred dollars, wired four days ago to Kansas City.

There was a charcoal drawing pinned to the wall in front of him of a sad woman in a rocking chair knitting a sweater. It looked like something Ian had done. Perhaps it was a picture of his mother.

Suddenly a question that had been lingering at the rim of his mind came to the fore, and it struck him that Dick might have the answer.

"What did Eldon do to his wife?"

Dick looked back, hands on the wall. "Not your business. Not mine, either. "

Jack looked at the drawing. At her sad, downturned eyes—much like the ones Ian had bestowed upon him. He looked at the back of the old man's head. A deep scar formed a canyon across the top of his scalp where a Chippewa's tomahawk had tried to split him like a melon.

"Where was she from?"

"Hattie?" Dick shrugged. "What do I know."

"Back east?"

"She never said."

Jack stuffed the money and the receipt into his jacket. Through the window he saw a distant rider loping up the road, holding a lantern.

"Here comes yer wife," he said. "Ridin up on an ugly mare fatter'n she is."

He nudged the old man with the gun.

"Be honest. What'd my brother do to her?"

"He loved her with all his heart."

"Ah-huh. And what else?"

Dick lowered his head. "Some people are . . . delicate. They feel too much."

"Ye mean his wife?"

Dick was silent.

"Then why'd he bring her out here?"

He must have lied to her. The lie all men told their wives when they were out of options. That she'd have her own glittering garden. That great riches were just around the bend. That she'd spend her mornings gathering dog eye and columbine, and her afternoons nursing on the gallery, a cool summer breeze rattling the bluestem.

As boys, they used to tell each other a similar lie about their mother. That before she died, she'd spent her days dancing in the jimsonweed smoke, flowers in her hair, her feet floating above the tangled grass, turning the anguish of the prairie into song. He could hear her even now:

The wind doth blow today, my love, with a few small drops of rain; I never had but one true love, and he in the cold grave has lain.

Jack was staring at the cattleman's hat.

He picked it off the ground and reseated it on Dick's head. The crown was tied with the same beaded string that decorated his own bolero.

The same string Daddy wore.

"Here's the problem," he told the old man. "I let you live, yer gonna tell my brother I'm comin, and I really wanna see the look on his face."

"Get on with it then," Dick grumbled. "Just don't let my missus see."

"Turn around then. Ain't gonna shoot you in the back."

When Dick wouldn't turn, Jack pressed the barrel between his shoulders. The knurled hammer felt rough against his thumb as he drew it back.

"But I will if I have to."

Dick turned from the wall, eyes like tree burls. "Make amends."

Jack spat between his teeth. "You want them to be yer last words?"

"There's still time. Admit what you did."

Jack's arm had started to quake. "All right, shut up."

Dick seemed to grow larger before his eyes. He donned eagle feathers and war paint. "Earn back your name," he thundered.

The Outlaw tried to raise the gun but couldn't, not with his mother and all the other people he'd killed hanging off the barrel.

TWENTY-TWO

HE LAY IN THE SOD CABIN OF HIS YOUTH, DADDY AT THE foot of his bed, light glistening off his wet skull. His scalp was peeled back, the flap of flesh and hair rolled into a scroll and tied with beads that coiled in a pool of black blood on the floor. He begged for Daddy's opinion. Did he still think him evil just for being born? The light behind Daddy brightened, until all was blistered white. When the light faded, Shane stood in Daddy's stead, holding a dinner plate. A white owl was perched on his shoulder. It dipped its head from side to side as it eyed a skinned hare on the plate. Shane lifted the plate and the owl plucked a string of meat with his beak. The hare screeched, half alive, and the screech became the skirl of a steam whistle.

He felt the train buck and rattle. Spring brakes took hold, countersteam valves chuffed. They were slowing down. Jack sat up in a sun-warmed seat, gaunt and disheveled, still shaking loose of the nightmare. He looked out, the factories and ocher warehouses haunted by a sunburned mist. His reflection in the dust-glared window—a beard down to the middle of his chest. Greasy hair curled over his shoulders.

The locomotive jostled up to the platform, coming to a sudden stop. He looked out at the people racing by. Hardly ever did he worry about being recognized, but Kansas City was where Jack Foss was forged. That was twenty years ago, and besides, not a soul on earth would mistake the ragged creature in the window for Minnesota Jack.

His body crept with sweat as he sat waiting for the car to empty out. He reached into his coat for his flask and felt a creased piece of paper. He pulled it out and unfolded it in the light. The charcoal had smudged, creating a dark ring around the rendering of his face. But the eyes were intact. The sad gaze raised his hackles even more than the first time he'd seen it.

A spot of blood in the lower right corner of the drawing unnerved him. Whose blood? He scraped it clean with his thumbnail. It reminded him of Eldon somehow. The image of a thumb dipped in water came to his mind. In the wavy reflection, two boys circled with raised fists while Daddy reclined, drinking rum, watching them scrap for the privilege of supper. And Daddy would hoot when the brutal strike came, felling one of the boys. The victor would stand over the vanquished, fists balled, sun tracing him in flame, ready to kill.

It was an act.

Put on for an audience of one. The moment Daddy succumbed to his drink, Eldon would rush his brother down to the river and clean his wounds. Wetting his thumb in the cool water, he would scrub the blood from his mouth and the inside of his nostrils.

That was their routine. A beating, and then kindness. Beating then kindness. Beating, kindness. Until he could no longer distinguish one from the other.

When he looked up, the train car had emptied out. Stuffing the sketch into his coat, he limped down the aisle, leaning on seats, the pain in his hip barking with each step.

Sun warmed his face as he hobbled onto the platform. He stood inhaling the cold sooty air, then pushed through a pair of tall brass-fixtured doors. As he entered the cavernous station, an enormous clock chimed three times to mark the hour. He stopped to gaze up at the cathedral ceilings, the air vibrating with the hum of travelers. Suddenly he was engulfed by a raucous wedding party that seemed late for their train, drunk and carousing harmlessly. He was awe-struck by the rosy maidens in the highest of fashions, the confused father wiping his pink forehead, the mother shrill and fat, the drunken uncle singing to the flower girls who in turn teased the porters struggling under mountains of luggage. The bride and groom appeared. The bride wore a blue ribbon in her hair and for a moment Jack thought it was one of Harlan Scrim's daughters. But the bride didn't have dimples like he remembered, and she was probably too old. Still, just the thought of her shook his bones, and for a long time after, he stood like a rock in a river, the bustle of the station splitting around him.

When he could bear it no longer, he carved through the crowd and purchased a razor. In the washroom he hacked off his beard and cut his greasy hair.

He didn't care if they recognized him, didn't care about anything anymore.

The doorbell chimed as he pushed into the Western Union. He took one look at the old clerk and knew that his brother had been there already.

"Mr. Quint!" said the clerk. "Have you changed your mind then? Will you do us the honor today?"

Jack thumbed back his hat and rested his arms on the counter.

"This might sound peculiar, but when did ye last see me?"

The clerk's brows went up. "This a test, sir?"

"No, sir."

"Well. Today's Friday . . ." He picked up a frayed notebook and thumbed through. "You paid us a visit last Thursday, I believe. Yes, here it is. Last Thursday. Well, I thought you'd be in Springfield by now."

Jack leaned over the counter. "What makes you think I'm goin to Springfield?"

The clerk stammered. "I–I just figured cause that's where you sent that money." His lips wobbled into a nervous smile. "Oh, and I should tell you, since you're here . . . I told the missus of our last meeting, because, see, she used to be friendly with Harlan's widow and the two girls there, and Missus Scrim had once—"

"What?" said Jack. He looked around confused, wondering if his thoughts had started to leak into the air for all to see.

"I was just-just saying that Missus Scrim had once told my wife Tilly that the man who killed her husband was the devil incarnate. But I told my Tilly that it couldn't have been you. You're a father, not some violent animal. I believe it was probably someone else that did it and used your name. In fact I'm sure of it. And I wanted to let Missus Scrim know that, but she is no longer listed in the city directory."

Jack nodded at the clerk's logbook. "Might I see that?"

The clerk handed it over the counter. Jack ripped out the pertinent pages. "I wasn't here Thursday, I wasn't here ever. Got it?"

"Yessir," the clerk said, nodding vigorously. "I don't remember anybody named Jack Foss or Eldon Quint or whoever coming in here at all."

Jack put on his hat and smiled the way Eldon might—polite, but without much of anything behind it, like it was a chore.

"Thank you kindly," he said. "And have a pleasant afternoon."

He turned for the door then turned back. "You ever see Miss Scrim or her daughters, tell them I'm sorry bout what happened to Harlan. Whoever done it to him."

The next train to Springfield wouldn't leave until morning. Under the blue twilight he wandered the city until he came to a corner saloon, Stack's Tavern printed on a crude sandwich board in big gold letters, the blacked-out windows crooked and warped. The kind of place that could swallow a man.

When he entered, three ragged whores looked up from a booth. It was catacombic. Candelabras flickered. Muzzleloaders and oxidized percussion pistols decorated the garlanded walls. At a resin-topped bar, two old-timers sat drinking beer, their boots resting on a bone footrail. Four men sat in a corner playing faro, the pother from their cheroots swirling orange in the light of the paper chandelier. More booths fanned out in back, occupied with drinkers, the only evidence of their existence the glowing cherries of their cigars swiping up and down in the airless gloom.

Jack sat at one of the stools. He picked up his aching leg and set his boot on the footrail. A fire-bearded barkeep stood, hands on his hips, looking at him. Jack set his palms on the waxy bar top and smacked his lips.

"Friend, I am lookin to drink myself into an early grave."

The barkeep set a cloudy tumbler before him. "You come to the right place, friend. How big a shovel you want?"

When a fiddler started up, one of the whores walked over and invited Jack to dance. He paid her no mind and sat drinking from an unlabeled jug. To entice him, she pulled out her breast and licked her nipple. Good manners demanded that he applaud the trick, but he declined further intimacy.

The bar filled. He drank through another jug, convinced that he'd become impervious to alcohol. At best, the combustible took the edge off that infernal fiddle music. He caught his reflection in the backbar mirror and sat maligning his stone-chipped face. The jagged cheekbones, the bulky, crooked nose, the lopsided brow—every feature shaped by a wound.

He'd missed Eldon by a week and a day. He could get to Springfield by train tomorrow if he wanted. He tried to imagine the shock on his brother's face. But Eldon was never particularly expressive. Always kept part of himself hidden.

Jack finished off the second jug. He could put a real hurt to him if he wanted. But now that seemed like too much of a chore. Around him, the whores, stripped of their outer shells, danced in underclothes surrounded by seamy, corroded mouths, hands searching pockets for change.

Without Nurse Daye, his hip had become polluted. He poked at it until a curdled purulence seeped through his trousers. He dumped the dregs from the jug onto it and laughed and fell off the stool.

And then he was outside of the establishment with little recollection of leaving, swaying and gulping the frosty air. There was a hitch rail in the alley. Three horses serried before a trough. One of them, a corvine-eyed Arabian white as the clouds, caught his attention, its concave nose and broad chest the picture of nobility.

He stumbled closer and stood like a man trying to balance on the edge of a sword. Harlan Scrim used to ride a horse just like it. The white knight on his white stallion. The horse could be a gift for his girls.

He saw the blue ribbons in their hair and something broke loose in his stomach. His retching startled the horse and it kicked him dead in the thigh.

Knocked across the trash-strewn stones, he laughed because it hurt so damn bad, and because he deserved so much worse.

The Lodo stood crooked and bawdy against the black warehouses. A peeling sign above the entrance advertised first-class accommodations, though even the dimmest of travelers could see it was a fandango with rooms to rent by the hour.

Dragging one leg, Jack hobbled up the porch steps past whores half clothed despite the snow, caressing their men, whispering into their ears.

The saloon room was sweaty and packed with late-hour clientele twirling to the jumpy tune of a bolero band. Men drank in ragged banquettes, groping whores like they were selecting heifers at auction.

Jack went to a bar. It was sunk into the back wall, beneath a catwalk writhing with whores in negligees and colorful boas.

The tall, cave-chested barman saw Jack coming and grew a smile. "Yooper!" he screeched. "That Mr. Buzzwig I see?"

Jack steadied himself against the bar. "Bob."

"Where ya been at, Mr. Buzzwig? Ain't seen you since the fodder-pullin days."

"On my travels, Bob."

The barman waved around the saloon. "I got in a heap of new inventory. You got a fixin for exotic types? I got greaser mixed with Eye-talian, Chink crossed with Mick, even got me a—"

"She here?"

"Oh, what you keep foolin with that peg-legged trollop for? I told you, I got ones with half the age and twice the truckle just waiting—"

Jack leaned over the bar. "Ye got a soozy lip on you, Bob."

"I'm just tellin you what's what."

"She in back or not?"

"Where else I'd put her?"

He grabbed the spindly barman by his suspenders and jerked him closer. "Take that tone out yer goozle when ye speak her name."

The barman nodded. "Yessir, you're right, Mr. Buzzwig, I do apologize. She's just right in back there."

Jack gimped down a murky hall wallpapered in vine-like coils. He passed many doors, an impossible number of doors given the limited space. Some stood open, still sharp with the scent of what occurred inside. Others were closed, blunting the grunts and shrill theatrics of their occupants.

At the end of the hall was a lacquered black door, a brass knocker in the shape of a magician's wand at the center. A paper lantern glowed blood orange above the door. Jack preened quickly, then rapped the knocker.

Mattress springs groaned. The scrape and clack of wood on wood.

The door swung open. A broad-chested woman with a wide cameo face leaned against the frame. Stuffed into a tasseled blue corset, buttered in cosmetics, she was evading middle age with every tool at her disposal.

"Magpie," said Jack. "Fit fer a visitor?"

"Mr. Buzzwig," she said with only the promise of a smile. "Don't you look like what scraped off the bottom of a boot."

"Yes, ma'am. I reckon."

She turned into the room. The wooden peg supporting her left leg from the knee down scraped along the floor. She opened the door wider. "In with you, then," she said, releasing the strings of her corset, pulling out her hair pin, a mountain of amber curls falling around her shoulders.

His hip was a swirling puddle of violet and pustule yellow. He lay on his side, britches pulled below the knee while she sat with a bowl of warm water and a rag cleaning the wound. The bed was stripped of all but the bottom sheet.

"Leave it like this," she cautioned, "you'll end up on a stump like me."

He was staring into the dimness of the room and didn't answer.

She leaned over to see his face. "Well, I never heard less words come out of your mouth. I'd wager you might actually have something to get off your chest."

"No, ma'am. Jest tired is all."

"Tired? You look like a bee fixin a swarm."

"Ye know that ain't my style."

Grinning to herself, she dipped the rag, wrung it out, and dabbed the pus oozing from the bullet hole. "It's nice to see you, Clayton."

"Yes, ma'am. Nice to see you."

She cleaned and dressed the wound with dry rags, then presented him with the option of pulling up his britches or removing them entirely. Choosing to remove them, he lay on his back while she emptied the bowl of rose-colored water, then returned to the bed. Her mess of tawny locks filled the crook of his arm. She lay with her chin resting on his chest, looking at him with a questioning smile.

"You just gonna set there lettin it eat you up?"

He was quiet for a moment, then said, "Did you know there's a caldera three hundred miles northwest of here that at one time erupted and covered the whole of this continent in ash?"

She twisted his chest hair.

"Hey," he said.

"This character you like to play. It ain't you. And I never liked it."

"All I'm sayin is, a man got more to worry about than his own troubles."

"Like what, geology?"

He leaned in and kissed the top of her head. Her skin glistened, unctuous in the light of the tallow lamp. Her hair smelled like after a rain. Her clothes like rosewater and orange peel. She wrapped him in her arms. He let the air out of his lungs, feeling at ease. He ran a hand through her hair and looked at the ceiling. It was stenciled in vines and black roses.

"Ye think goodness is somethin can be learned?"

She nuzzled him, purring. "I think if your aim is to learn it, you'd already be in some kind of trouble."

"Either ye got it or you don't."

She propped her head on her hand, ruby hair crowning her face. "I'd say there's little to be done to make a man into somethin he's not. But whatever he is, you can surely destroy that. Just be mean and cruel and you can destroy the best in anyone."

His hip was starting to bark. He rolled onto his side. "Yeah," he said.

She ran a finger up his spine and massaged his neck. "What's wrong?"

He shook his head. "Jest went all upside down."

"Is it something can be rectified?"

He twisted to look at her. "You got a trick that resurrects the dead?"

She spooned up behind him. Warm, scented breasts against his back. "No," she whispered, pecking his earlobe. "But I got tricks."

"Do ye."

"Ready for your ticket?"

His jaw loosed toward a smile. "Believe I am," he said, feeling half alive again. "In fact, that's jest what I'm hankerin fer. A ticket to the show."

"Which has improved since your last visit. Got me a new coup de grâce."

He reached over the side of the bed for his britches, went in a pocket, and produced a silver coin.

She frowned. "Do I look like one of them *jolies putains*?"

He produced a second coin. "I like it when ye talk that dirty French to me." Then dropped them each into a brass slot cut into the top of the nightstand.

There was a hand crank on the side. She turned it until a purple raffle ticket spit out from the slot. On it, printed in swooping script:

Magdalena's Magical Show
of Charm and Wonderment—25¢

He sat with his ticket as she went around the room turning up a kaleidoscope of colored lamps, banishing enough of the murk to reveal a Victorian parlor of pale yellow wallpapering, tumescent furnishings, and thick velvet drapes that produced the effect of something warm oozing in from all sides.

She fixed a drink from the bar cart and brought it to him. Then, offering a sultry smile—this little tease not for him, but marking the start of the show—she vanished behind a dressing screen painted with red and yellow dragon scales.

The disappearance of a peeping greenfinch was how the show began. She draped a silk napkin over the top of its cage, waved her hands, intoning some made-up words, and when she lifted the veil, the bird was gone. Yet its singsong continued, muffled, disembodied—a ghost bird. She pretended not to know where it was coming from. Then, with the practiced realization of a mime, she reached under her hoopskirt and extricated the little creature from her crotch.

The Outlaw drank and clapped madly.

Magdalena performed more tricks with playing cards, red balls, metal rings—all of them made to disappear, only to emerge from some unmentionable crevice.

For the grand finale, she stripped down to her ruffled undergarments. With a flourish, she collapsed the dragon-scaled dressing screen, revealing a sleek black coup de grâce box sitting on the floor, surrounded by candelabras, red boas, and dark drapery. It was about the size of a coffin, though it seemed more intriguing than ominous, and Jack perched at the foot of the bed, slurping whiskey with great anticipation.

The hinged top creaked open. She waved a hand over the velvet interior and tapped the side of the box with her peg leg to demonstrate its durability. Her leg swiped into the air and the prosthetic came gently to rest on the rim of the box. It was painted with colorful imps, angels, dragons—all manner of fairy-tale creatures. She traced a finger from its tapered tip, up the inside of her thigh.

She stepped one leg into the box, then the other. Bending over, she gripped the sides of the box and dipped her head, dogging up on all fours. Her fanny wagged in the air, then she slid her buxom frame into the soft velvet and turned onto her back. Her hand danced out of the box like a trained cobra. She gave a playful wave, then reached for the braided strap attached to the lid and slowly drew it closed. When the lid clapped shut, the box collapsed, all four sides flattening across the floor.

Poised at the edge of the bed, Jack stared in awe.

There was a faint scuffling beneath the floorboards. Then a latch clicked across the room. He turned toward the closet and stared at the slatted doors, shifting the weight off his hip.

Candle flames popped in the silence.

The closet slapped open and she twirled into the room, nude save a strategically placed marabou boa. He clapped uproariously and whistled as she kicked off her prosthetic and fell across the bed, taking him down with her.

She never kissed her clients, but she kissed Jack.

He closed his eyes as she lay next to him, stroking his hair. "Will ye jest set there a spell?" he said, too tired to lift his head. "He won't leave me be. Jest sit, so I can rest."

She kissed him. "I ain't goin nowhere."

Then she began to sing, and the song followed him into a dream.

"The wind doth blow today, my love, with a few small drops of rain; I never had but one true love, and she in the cold grave has lain."

TWENTY-THREE

A SQUARE OF ACRID LIGHT CREPT UP HIS STUBBLED CHEEK AND knifed under his lids. Street noise clattered in from a barred window carved into the sooty gray stone above. Against a hammering pain he sat up and clutched his skull. His hat was gone, his stringy hair matted with blood. His guns were gone too. He squinted through the corroded bars. It was a dim basement jail. Other than the pair of boots crossed atop a desk, there didn't seem to be anybody else there.

Something warm dripped from his nose and splotched the concrete. He touched his nostril and licked the blood from his fingers. He tried to remember what had happened when he'd left Magdalena. His hands hurt. Bruised knuckles split like overripe fruit. He had a vague recollection and saw himself raging against three leering figures.

He searched his pockets. They'd taken everything except for that damn portrait. He outspread it in the concentration of light. The sad, pathetic gaze Ian had given him.

Ian, who no longer had a brother.

The drawing was smudged and streaked, more than before, his features warped and demented, monstrous, even. And his eyes, once sad and doleful, were screaming. It was a truer representation of Jack Foss than Jack would ever admit.

A gate clanked.

He stuffed away the portrait as two arguing voices spilled into the jailhouse. The boots dropped from the desk and a goliath of a jailer loafed into view. He waited at the mouth of a stairwell as the two men descended.

The first man to emerge was a thin gray constable with an avalanche of beard. "And what should I tell Mayor Kinney? I can't just turn him over on your word."

The man trailing was impish and nervy. "Ain't my word," he said. "It's the Major." His skin was as white as his spotless bowler. "The Major's a personal friend of Mayor Kinney's father."

That quieted the constable, but only for a moment. "Mr. Brusco, you are proposing I release Jack Foss—*the* Jack Foss."

The imp turned from him and walked up to the bars.

Jack watched him approach. A deep scar ruined one side of his face.

Leaning against the bars, the imp studied him, nostrils twitching. Then he looked back at the constable. "Ya gotta be dumb as a tree frog to think that heap is Jack Foss."

"Well, who is he then?"

"Granger outta Indian territory named Quint." He kicked the bars. "Ain't that right, boy?"

The constable chortled. "Granger? Mr. Brusco, do you think a granger would have the sand to all but obliterate three able-bodied men over some harmless comments to a crippled whore?"

"I know you ain't asked it," said the imp, "but it goes without sayin that the Major will compensate you handsome for your troubles."

"How handsome?"

"Handsome as a stakerope on a fifty-dollar pony."

The constable thought about it, then looked at the jailer and nodded. The jailer unlocked the cell and stepped aside.

The imp walked right up to Jack and stared at him, flexing his hands. "I knew you was a fuckin liar."

Jack shot a comet of blood from his nose, then ran a finger down one side of his face. "What happened there? Cut yerself with Daddy's shavin razor?"

The constable turned, hands on hips. "Does he sound like a granger to you?"

The imp stood pawing his crotch. "He got a mouth on him. But the Major gonna straighten that. Major can straighten a man faster than Scripture unbends a soul."

Through the loose fibers of the flour sack he could make out a columned building, like a courthouse but bigger. He'd been in transit twenty minutes, riding horse's ass behind the imp, his mouth gagged with burlap so dry, it was like chewing sand. He'd been all but ready to curl up and die back in that jailhouse. Now all he wanted to do was feed that shifty midget his white hat.

They had stopped before the columned building. Someone yanked the rope binding Jack's hands, and the ground punched him. Some men dragged him to his feet. They smelled of musk and rum. Indians. Four of them from what he could discern. They hustled him up a set of chalky steps, through a heavy door, into an anteroom rich with the aroma of tobacco, leather, and brandy.

Through the mesh he could see the outline of a man in a Scottish Rite cap opening a set of double doors. The musky hands dragged him down a long, dark hallway, then another hallway, to a set of pillared doors at the end. When they parted, he was hurled inside. He slid across the floor on his belly. His hip burned as they dragged him to his feet and yanked the flour sack from his head.

It was a dim, vaulted space the scale of a ballroom. Against the far wall, a gold throne sat below a huge coiled uraeus, the hissing viper flanked by two towering pharaohs that reached three stories to a coffered ceiling leafed in bullion. On the walls, colorful frescoes depicted scenes from The Contendings of Horus and Seth, a text Jack had lugged around for years in Daddy's heavy trunk of books.

Despite the enchanting Egyptian theme, his attention was on a gargantuan silhouette amid the golden columns. At first he thought it was the jailer, but this man was big, much bigger. Seizing him by the arms, the Indians scuttled him up to an octagonal table and sat him in one of eight high-backed chairs.

The giant stepped up to the table, shadows peeling from his face.

Jack went cold at the sight of him. The huge swampy grin. The fiery muttonchops. The vulgar boil of a nose. The limply protruding tongue. Bone-white dentures.

It was the only face on earth Jack despised more than his father's.

The Indians sat two on either side of him. They were dressed in gowns, ornamented in pearls and gold, and wore the makeup of society women, yet they spoke gruffly in their mother tongue, packed pipes, and passed earthen jugs of rum.

The Major stood in his pea-green suit and purple bow tie, shaking his head. "I expected more from a man of the Fifth, Mr. Quint."

His pink, wormy fingers gripped the table and he leaned over the Eye of Ra inlaid in mother-of-pearl and ebony.

The Indians were chuckling, but he silenced them with a glance.

"Do you know why I keep these devils in my outfit?" he said. "Why I provide them with food, shelter, the finest squaws? Dependence, Mr. Quint. Without me, they are lost. That's what the spittoon kickers in Washington never understood. The savage is not our enemy, but a vast, untapped source of labor. Give him a house, a plow, our Lord and Savior—give him purpose—and he is loyal as that red setter of your father's."

Jack's face twitched at the mention of that loyal pup, who Daddy had strangled to keep from alerting the Indians.

"You lied to us, Mr. Quint," said the Major.

"Well, golly," said Jack. "I am but a God-fearing granger who has never told a lie to anyone. So I don't know how that's possible."

The imp's nostrils bubbled. He reached for his blade.

The Major put up a hand. "Enough."

The imp stomped over to an empty chair and slammed himself down in it and crossed his arms like a livid child. "He's a fuckin liar, Major. I hate fuckin liars."

Ignoring him, the Major clasped his hands behind his back. "You were shrewd to stay here in Kansas City," he told Jack. "My people have been scouring all four corners of the earth, and here you are, right under my nose the whole time. Was that her idea?"

Her.

Of course there was a *her.*

Always was with Eldon.

"Why, yes, it was," said Jack. "She's smart as a whip, that one."

The Major's pinched blue eyes slid to the imp. "Is it me, or has this farmer developed a curious accent? Have you a brick in your hat, Mr. Quint?"

"Wish I had a brick in my hat," Jack said. "You all are boring me to death."

The Major exhaled. Then looked at his second.

The imp placed his white bowler on a chair. He rounded the table, grabbed a fistful of Jack's hair in each hand, then smashed his face into the tabletop until blood blotted out the Eye of Ra.

"Rove, don't pop him too much," said the Major.

The imp slammed him one more time, then stood breathing heavily and wiped his hands on the chest of one of the Indians.

Jack picked up his head and sneezed. Blood and mucus splattered across the table. The Major leapt back in disgust. One of the Indians came with a cloth and cleaned the front of his green suit.

The Major circled the table, chin tilted up in contemplation.

"Either she has put you under her spell, or there is some other skullduggery afoot. Which is it, Mr. Quint? Are you in love with her?"

Jack eyed a revolver on one of the Indians' hips. He looked at the Major. "What's that you said?"

"It's nothing to be ashamed of. We have all tasted her witchcraft and it is potent. No one worse than my wife." He shook his head plaintively. "Yes, you heard that right. My own wife nearly perished on her account. And for what? She only wished to run our household in the proper fashion.

Yes, she may have used her peach tree switch a little too fervently, but a healthy dose of pain is good for little girls. Certainly she did not deserve that vile moniker Winifred had them using behind her back. *Horseface?* What does that even mean? She looks nothing like a horse. More like an angel. Despite the cruelty, my poor Penelope desired only the best for our girls." He let go a wobbly breath. "What Winifred did to her . . . it was simply inhuman. What kind of vile mind does it take to convince a perfectly healthy soul to commit herself to eternal damnation? Only a witch could possess such black magic."

Whoever this Winifred was, Jack was keen to meet her.

The Major halted behind him and draped his big pink hands over his shoulders. "I thank my Heavenly Father every day for guiding me to her in time. The question I ask myself now, Mr. Quint, is have I found you in time—or has she doomed you, too?"

Thick fingers slithered up the back of Jack's neck and through his hair. Jack tried to shake him off. He'd once watched the Major pinch Mary Finley's cheek. He was inviting her to his mansion in Saint Paul. He invited all the pretty girls for a visit.

Suddenly the Major seized Jack's head with both hands and pressed it down against the tiles. He put more and more weight into his hands, until Jack thought his eyes would pop out of his skull and brains would spray from his sockets.

"Fight her influence," growled the Major. "Fight it with everything you have."

At once, the Major released him and continued to circle the table.

"Reveal her motives to me," he said. "And I shall forget this Sturm und Drang, and allow you to walk from these premises with all your parts intact."

"Same goes for ya son," said the imp. He was cleaning his fingernails with his knife. "He's with her, ain't he? At that whorehouse ya visited last night? Hell, that's where I'd keep em if I was you. The Major don't like no whorehouses."

"Is that right, Mr. Quint?" said the Major. "Is my daughter sequestered in that rancid fandango?"

Jack's instinct was to go for the revolver on that Indian's hip. But that wasn't what Eldon would do. Eldon would factor the odds and devise a smarter scheme. And what exactly would that be?

He used to pretend to be his brother. He'd use the mirror in the filigreed powder compact that once belonged to Momma. It was the only keepsake they had of hers. He'd practice copying his brother's expressions, his laugh, the way he moved. These were subtle differences, and it didn't always work. But the times he got it right, he was even thinking like Eldon.

"Yer right," he told the Major, head hung in shame. "I see it now. She put me under her spell. I apologize for my mendacity. That is not who I am."

The Major walked up, shooed away the Indians, and sat in a chair next to Jack. "There, there," he said, rubbing his back. "Tell me everything."

"She put me under such duress. I am a pious man, but she has led me to drink. I lied to you earlier—I do have a brick in my hat, but only because I am under her spell. She keeps my mind cloudy. And you are right, sir: I did have her at the whorehouse, but she's been gone since yesterday. I think she's abandoned me."

"He's lyin like a rug," hissed the imp.

The Major sat studying Jack, then, snapping his fingers, he told one of the Indians, "Bring the jar."

The Indian scurried across the room in his blue gown and from a closet he hefted a five-gallon jar packed with shriveled chunks of what looked like pickled roots. He set the jar on the table before the Major and unscrewed the lid. It had a pungent, musty odor.

"If I recall," said the Major, "your father came from hill folk. Thus I presume you have passed the toe at least once in your life?"

"Can't say I've had the pleasure," said Jack.

"I see. Well, the ritual is simple enough, though we practice a slightly different variation."

With both hands he lifted the jar. Shriveled things floated in murky liquid, each about the size of a small sausage.

"Take the jar like so," he said. "And have yourself a healthy sip—but . . . but!—you must drink until one of the thumbs touches your lips, or the ceremony loses its potency."

Hefting the jar to his mouth, the Major drank, tipping his head back until one of the shriveled bits touched his lips. He released a vaporous exhale and plunked the jar on the table, then dabbed his mouth with a kerchief provided by one of the Indians.

"I have been adding to this jar for more than three decades. When you take a man's thumb, you take his humanity. He becomes less than an ape." His smile grew perverse. "Were you to ask my Indian friends, they would tell you that what a man loses in this world is not returned in the next. Thumbless for eternity. But that is savage bunkum, and we are not savages. We are not liars, either, are we."

Jack nodded at the jar. "What're they soakin in?"

Buffed fingernails drummed against the side of the jar. "Only the finest combustible this side of the Mississippi."

He slid the jar across the table. Jack breathed the sharp aroma. Amid the stew, a gold ring bit into one of the shrunken knobs.

"Why's that one got a ring on it?"

The Major became wistful. "It is the first thumb I ever took. Call me sentimental, but I like to remember which it is." He smiled thinly. "Now drink up."

Jack brought the rim to his lips and tipped it back. The pungent spirit spread through him like steam. He couldn't help but want more. With the next sip his gullet opened so wide that the ringed thumb vanished like a swallowed goldfish.

The Major staggered to his feet. "God, man! What have you done?"

The Indians stood frozen with anticipation while the imp rapidly stroked the pearl handle of his knife.

A righteous belch exploded from Jack's inner reaches. He wiped his mouth, then looked at the eyes glaring at him. "Pardon me."

The imp shot to his feet. "I don't got to stop at ya thumbs, granger. I'll take your feet, your eyes, ya fuckin manhood—till you ain't nothin but your hard parts."

There was a silence, then all of a sudden the Major clapped and roared with laughter. "He drank the thumb! Glorious!"

The Indians joined in his mirth, chuckles building to riotous guffaws.

When Jack turned around, the Major was behind him, still chuckling, but there was madness in his eyes.

"Shall we go now and rescue my daughter from that house of ill repute?" said the Major.

Jack shook his head. "She's been gone since yesterday, Major."

"You'd better hope not," he said with a gaping smile. "If you defile my tabernacle one more time, Mr. Quint, you'll be swallowing your own two thumbs."

TWENTY-FOUR

THEY RODE UNDER THE DEAD CHARTREUSE EYE OF A LOW WIN-
ter sun, following the Major's hulking stagecoach through a
muddy brick canyon. Jack bobbed like a worthless sack on
the back of the imp's horse.

Worthless since the day he was born.

He'd never seen even a picture of his mother, though
he could see her now, emerald-eyed, strong-jawed, and
fair-skinned, blond hair tangled and sweaty, a face racked in
agony as she struggled to push out her late-born son.

The subject of her untimely death was a popular one,
bandied about in the back of Daddy's store, prompted by
a card game and copious helpings of ale and whiskey. He
would sense it coming, run to the house, hide under the bed,
and hold her filigreed powder compact to his chest while he
told her he was sorry through gushing snotty tears. Those
were the longest nights, when he'd wet himself but would
be too afraid to get up and change because Daddy might
wake up.

Daddy spoke his name in one of four ways: a bark, a bay,
a growl, or a gale of boorish laughter. What did he have to
give his late-born son but disappointment and contempt. He
would let it be known what he thought of Clayton, whether
speaking to a church circle or a circle of men glowering

with drink, the late-born's name chewing out of his hateful mouth.

"The first one," he'd say, "no trouble at all. But that other. Twenty hours he tore her to shreds. She ain't had a chance."

Momma was a beloved woman. A celebrated woman. A leader, even among the most stubborn homesteaders. Daddy beat him every night, or made Eldon do it, because he wanted to remind him of what he'd taken from them. The beauty he'd stolen.

But what hurt him more than the beatings was the sympathy heaped onto his brother. Poor Eldon, they'd say, robbed of your mother by that filthy afterbirth.

What did Daddy have for Eldon? Adulation, discipline, and hard shots of wisdom.

If only Eldon had despised him as much as the rest. It would have been so much easier to give over to oblivion. But Eldon protected him, defended him, loved him. And how did he repay him but with the murder of his son.

Outside the Lodo, a cowled hag hunched over a steaming lard bucket, serving bowls of black beans and sorghum to the stockmen stumbling out of the bordello, still plastered in the afterglow of their exchanges.

The Indians parked their animals at the hitch rail. The imp cut Jack loose, and he landed facedown in the horse flop.

In the street, the Major unfolded from his ludicrous stagecoach and stood looking at the three-decker fandango. Repulsed, he summoned one of his Indians and was given a silk kerchief. Covering his nose, he waved his troupe onward.

The Indians dragged Jack to his feet and compelled him up the creaky porch steps. He was swaying and belching like a wastrel, Rove Brusco's hard little hands knuckling into his back. He imagined cutting them off and chuckled at the thought of beating a man to death with his own severed hands.

The imp shoved him through the door. "Laugh it up. While you still got a mouth."

In the saloon, smatterings of lowborn clientele sat drinking in the banquettes, watching an indecent puppet show on a candlelit stage.

As the Major and his troupe approached the bar, they were taken by the show, depicting a young maiden caught by a farmer-puppet in the act of coitus with a multitude of farm animals. When the farmer put a stop to her fun, the audience booed and hissed.

"Let er fuck the horse!" someone howled.

The Major's repulsion twisted deeper into his face. "Despicable," he grumbled.

"Mr. Buzzwig!"

The spindly barman waved.

Jack stumbled up to the bar, followed by the Major and his men.

Taking account of the steely ensemble, the barman added, "Mr. Buzzwig and associates!" Then he sighed at the Indians. "Oh, I'm sorry, Mr. Buzzwig, but we don't serve no Injuns up in here. They got to go."

Jack looked at him. "They ain't here fer that."

The barman's eyes flitted from the giant, to the imp, then back to Jack. The Major pressed his hands on the bar top and leaned slowly toward him.

"You are the owner of this establishment?"

"I am," he said, offering his hand. "Robert Dallas. My regulars call me Bob."

The Major glowered at Jack. "Where is she?"

"Where's who?" the barman interrupted.

The Major hissed through his teeth. "My daughter."

The barman squinted, not hearing him. "Who's Dottie?" He turned to Jack. "Mr. Buzzwig, if you done screwed her in my place of business, you know I'm entitled to a piece of the earnings."

The Major's eyes burned, but the barman seemed unaware of his situation.

"She in?" Jack asked.

The barman frowned. "Hold on now, you gonna waste these fellas on *that*? I mean, not that there's anything wrong with her, but I got a gaggle with half the age and twice the truckle. I can even do you fellas a group rate."

Ignoring the offer, Jack waved the Major and his retinue down the hall, toward the orange lantern at the end. As they reached the lacquered door, the lantern painted them in devilish colors. He lifted the magic wand and knocked. As hard as he'd tried to think of one, he still had no plan beyond showing up.

Magdalena appeared in the doorway, a frenzy of red curls, her shawl glowing purple in the light. She looked from Jack to the men crowding behind him, then back to Jack with a look that said she understood he was in distress.

With a smile, she opened the door wider, waving them into her parlor. The Major had to duck under the door frame. "Tall fella, aren't ya," she said cheerfully.

They gathered around the bed while Magdalena pulled on a pair of red satin gloves that reached up past her elbows, then hobbled around the room, her peg leg dragging and clopping as she turned up her colored lamps.

"Where is my daughter?" demanded the Major.

"Magpie," said Jack, "these men are kin to the maiden I brought to bunk. I already told em she left out the day past and—" He belched several times. "Sorry, them thumbs is ruining up my innards. I told em I don't know where she's gone to. Ye have any ideas?"

Magdalena shook her head in apology. "All I know is, she said she needed to flee to more upscale accommodations. Over across the river."

Jack pounded the indigestion out of his chest with a closed fist then turned to the Major. "Well, there ye have it. She's gone, like I said."

The Major was staring at Magdalena. "Describe her," he said.

She glanced at Jack.

"Don't look at him, look at me. Describe her."

"Magpie don't see too well," Jack broke in. "In fact, she—"

"Shut up." The Major pointed a shaky finger at her. "Describe my daughter, whore."

"Well . . . well, she's very pretty, of course. Fair skinned. Long hair . . . I believe blond or auburn?"

"Rove," the Major said to the imp. "We'll need a bigger jar."

"She's blind as a mole," Jack argued.

"I'm not going to take your thumbs, Mr. Quint; I'm going to cut off your head and mount it on the side of my coach right next to your son."

Magdalena tittered nervously. "Well, before you go and do all that, why don't you boys let me show you a trick." She strutted up to them. "Gentlemen," she said, letting the straps of her dress fall down her shoulders. "Your attention please."

She turned and collapsed the dragon-scaled dressing screen, revealing the black coffin-sized coup de grâce box behind it. She glanced faintly at Jack, then opened the lid and waved a hand over its velvet interior.

The imp had his pistol out and was looking between Magdalena and the Major, itching for an order to raise hell. But Magdalena's bosom had stolen the giant's attention. He was even smiling at her.

Meanwhile, Jack swayed a little closer to the black box. He imagined that it dropped into a space under the building. He would grab her by the waist and fling them both into the box and swing the lid shut and they would escape together.

As he turned to signal Magdalena of the plan, two hands punched into his chest. He looked up as he fell back. It was Magdalena. She had just shoved him. He reached for her wrist but only got a red satin glove. Velvet swallowed him as he fell backward into the box. The last thing he saw was her peg leg kicking the lid shut.

It was dark for a split second, then the floor opened beneath him and he dropped onto a dusty bedroll. Rolling to his stomach, he scanned the wide dirt-floored space. He was under the building. A few yards away, a rope hung down. The trapdoor to the closet. If he had a pistol, he could—

There was a muffled pop. A shriek. Then something heavy rattled across the floorboards. Trickles of dust fell into his eyes. He wiped his forehead and felt something sticky. Another drop struck the floor, blowing a small crater in the dust. He looked up as the drops became a thick cord of red pouring from between the boards. He heard shots but did not move. He felt the bullets thudding the ground, the floor-boards exploding overhead. Hot slices of metal cutting past his face. He didn't care about any of it. Only when a bullet grazed his elbow did it shock him enough to realize his situation, and he rolled out of harm's way.

As the bullets thundered around him he scanned the low, wide space. It was walled in. But directly across there was a square of barred light, blinking as something passed before it. That vent was the way out.

He crawled on all fours to the other end of the building, then swung around and kicked out the vent with both boots and hauled himself up by the hitch post. He stood between three horses, dripping wet, scanning the backside of the whorehouse for the fastest way to get back in there and kill them all.

You go back there and you die, said a voice.

Startled, he looked around.

"Daddy?"

The three horses on either side of him stamped and nickered.

Be smart, they said.

Steal me.

Sell me.

Buy a gun.

Then kill them all.

The whores stood clustered in the evenfall. They had made a little camp in front of the porch and were huddled under sheets and blankets and men's coats. The Lodo had been cleared by the constables an hour ago and the stretcher-bearers were already inside but had yet to bring out any bodies.

Across the street, in an alley between two warehouses, Jack peered over a mound of metal scrap, watching the front door of the Lodo. He'd sold the horse to an unscrupulous livery owner and used the money to buy a clean shirt, a new bolero, a rimfire Colt, and four boxes of forty four-caliber cartridges.

The front door kicked open. The stretcher-bearers appeared. They wore pale coveralls and hauled a blanketed corpse. The whores cleared a path and the men went up the lawn toward the street. An arm fell over the side of the stretcher, the short-fingered hand frozen in clawlike torpor.

Jack recognized the appendage. So did the whores, who knew it belonged to Bob the barman. Some smiled grimly. A few chuckled with a cold satisfaction at the murder of their pimp. The stretcher-bearers carelessly dumped the remains into the bed of a buckboard, then hurried back inside. Jack didn't take a breath the whole time they were gone. When the next body emerged, only one dainty boot peeking from the blanket, there was an uproar. Whores sobbed and held each other. Some fell to their knees, shrieking with grief. The blanket covering her body was soaked through with blood, but a lock of tawny hair hung over the back of the stretcher, unsullied, like a coil of fire.

Jack took off his hat and held it over his chest. She was the last person on earth to love him. He didn't deserve to mourn her. Not yet. Not until they were all dead.

The whores gathered around the back of the buckboard as the stretcher-bearers gently slid Magdalena's remains into the bed, treating her more kindly than the barman. A gust of wind came up the street and the blanket covering her body flipped open. Not only had she been shot, but her nose, ears, lips, and thumbs had been crudely severed.

Don't ye look away, said Daddy.

Her stump was showing. Just below the knee, where the skin pinwheeled in on itself. It had been his favorite place to kiss her.

The buckboard lurched and pulled away. Jack climbed from the scrap heap and went to the mouth of the alley and watched it ramble down the road.

It might as well have been carting rubble.

He went back through the vent under the hitch rail and bellied across the dirt to the trapdoor. When he pulled the string, a hatch dropped open. He raised himself into a cube of darkness and groped for the closet door. His hand brushed the garments crowding around him. Ruffled cotton, cracked leather, soft feathers, ribbed shapes. The smell of rosewater and orange peel filled the air.

He pushed open the slatted doors and limped into the parlor. The colored lanterns were like dying stars, struggling to hold the darkness at bay. Her smell was everywhere. He could taste her, just as he could taste the gunpowder that killed her.

The floorboards were riddled, bullet holes clogged with blood. Blood everywhere. Smeared and splattered over the bed, the ticket box, the bar cart, the cluttered mix of scientific gadgets, magical implements, and conjurer's trifles.

On the other side of the bed, the black box sat flat across the floor, its velvet guts stoven from the edges.

He rounded the bed and sat on the edge of the mattress. He placed his hat on the bed and sat a good while with the Colt in his lap. His head sagged forward and slowly he lifted the barrel to meet his temple.

Something was sticking out from under the bed.

He set the gun next to his hat and lifted the prosthetic by its leather straps. Blood spackled the painted wood. With his sleeve he wiped it clean, then held the peg leg in his palms, studying the monsters that populated its conical realm.

Every selfish act, every reckless venture, every vicious murder—he felt them all swirling darkly in his heart. He hugged the prosthetic, squeezing his eyes against the tears, and lay down on the bed. Fingers moving softly up his neck. Through his hair. That mossy smell. Her breath warm on the back of his ears.

Everyone who ever cared about him, who showed him affection, who loved him—they were dead. All but Eldon, though the Major seemed eager to fix that.

He sat up, still clutching the peg. A bolt shot through him and suddenly everything was clear. He had to find his brother. Warn him of what was coming.

He reached into his pocket and took out the drawing. It was smudged and distorted. And yet its meaning was suddenly clear.

Ian hadn't drawn Jack Foss, but what was beneath him.

That boy was the only innocent thing in his world, the only thing he could still protect.

He stood up wielding the peg leg like a club.

Magdalena's spirit coursed through him, bestowing him with one last gift, something he'd lacked for far too long.

Purpose.

FLOWERS FOR THE GRAVE OF LORD DORIAN HICCUP

TWENTY-FIVE

It was high noon when they arrived in Springfield, Missouri, Queen City of the Ozarks. A fine rain dimmed the atmosphere, yet spirits were high. The journey from Clinton had been short and uneventful. Productive, even, thought Eldon. He and Minn had managed to carry on a cordial discourse, never once mentioning the Major. He was doing his best to look at the bright side of things.

And yet he couldn't help but compare Minn to Hattie. They were both orphans, both comely and strong-willed. But where Hattie had used the distress of her early years to excuse her ever-maddening behavior, Minn used her past to propel herself toward something better.

Two days ago, while settling a bill at a feed store, he caught sight of her through the window. She was just sitting in a rocking chair, sharing a laugh with Ian. The image shook him so deeply that he almost dropped the bag of grain he'd been holding. It was all he'd ever hoped for.

There was a moment when he caught her gazing across the fire, studying him the way he studied her. One night when she was washing up, he glimpsed her bare collarbone, mighty as the prow of a Viking ship.

He pushed the image aside and focused on why he was there. What would he say at the grave of his wife, gone eight months to the earth already? He would have to explain, as best he could, why their firstborn would be buried beside her.

The reins trembled in his hands. He turned the wagon through a towering gap in a wall of brick buildings and entered a large plaza. Trailing a butcher cart piled with dead calves, they maneuvered through a crush of wagons while sack-coated tradesmen and garish maidens seemed to float effortlessly above the slurry of mud and waste.

Eldon was awestruck. The city had sprung from adolescence into adulthood. Once surrounded by tented shops, by impermanence and uncertainty, the Public Square now counted among its sturdy facades a dry goods store, a bank, a jewelry shop, a columned courthouse, and a bookstore that Ian excitedly pointed out to Minn.

While his passengers tracked the scenery, Eldon's ears began to ring. It was so loud. Too many people. Too many memories. Too much of everything in too small a place. Pulling down his hat, he touched his face to make sure his beard was still there. Already he wanted to flee back to the wilderness, to the wild places, where a man was alone, where he could be replenished by the unfenced lands, the burned cliffs, the icy lakes of fir and spruce country, the cold nights where distant dots of fire spoke into the black outback of space. He had told himself it was Jack Foss he was running from. But all along it was this place that scared him most.

Down the road from the square was Springfield's newest hotel, the Beekman. It was six stories tall and carved from Chicago stone. It boasted one hundred luxurious rooms and stretched the entire block. Eldon reckoned they deserved an indulgence, but the nightly rate was too preposterous to overcome his frugality and they went in search of something slightly more modest.

A block south they came upon the Wellman, a small red-brick hotel that abutted a dank canal and boasted thirty-six unadorned rooms, a billiard table, a grungy saloon, and the Half Dime Lunchroom, where every dish cost five cents. The lobby was dark wood, dark brick, dark leather furnishings, and the dark atmosphere was perpetually smoky, though no one appeared to be smoking. A tiered chandelier hung above a row of pentagonal windows carved into the wall high above the reception desk. Thick fingers of pasty light poured between twin staircases carpeted in ghastly maroon.

They took two adjoining rooms on the second floor, at the end of a peeling burgundy hallway. While Minn excused herself to the washroom, Eldon and Ian returned to the square to purchase new suits for the burial and to pay their respects to Hattie. Within the hour they were back with four garment boxes. In the first three were new suits that differed only in size. In the fourth, a blue bustle dress with pristine white gloves that Ian had picked out especially for Minn.

They knocked on the door that adjoined their room to hers, and the moment she answered, Ian thrust the rectangular box into her hands. When she opened it, her mouth slackened inexplicably and then snapped shut as if to stop the rising vomit. When she tried to speak, the words caught in her throat and she simply shook her head in refusal.

"You don't like the color?" Eldon questioned with a glance at Ian, hoping the boy might be able to decipher such a bemusing response.

She lifted the dress and admired it, yet could not stand to hold it with more than the very tips of her fingers, as though it were coated in poison.

Eldon explained, "My wife was a fashionable woman. She'd want us all looking our best."

Minn folded the dress and with a polite wag of the head declined to accept it. Then she saw the luminous white gloves. Emotion trembled through her. She picked them up gently, handling them like precious artifacts from the past.

"Might I keep just these?" she said softly.

"Of course," he said, about as mystified as he could be. "Ian picked those out special." He grinned at the boy. "Guess he knows you better than me."

Regaining her practiced smile, she set the gloves aside and gave Eldon a once-over. "If your wife would want us looking our best, I suggest you have a wash and a shave. We don't want her mistaking you for a soggy hillman."

She turned him to face the mirror.

He took off his hat and inspected himself. Coiled whiskers had overtaken his face. She was right: his head looked like an abandoned home after a long, rainy summer. Still, his first instinct was to prevaricate. The beard protected him, masked him, it was essential, it was—

"Disgusting," she declared. "It must go."

They dressed and collected in the hallway. Combed and clean-shaven, Eldon's skin crawled in the new suit. He kept fussing with his hair until Minn's smile threatened to break free of its boundaries. Her hair was pinned in a black bun and she wore her cream-colored dress with the ruffled blue collar, a gray coat, and her brand-new white gloves. She seemed to be having problems with the left cuff and requested Eldon's help. Taking hold of her wrist, he worked the button through the brass grommet. Their eyes lingered. They broke the gaze simultaneously and marched down the hall, Ian shuffling behind, new boots clacking on the floor.

As they made their way out through the lobby, a young spot-faced desk clerk shuffled up waving a yellow envelope at Eldon.

"Mr. Quint, this came a few days ago."

Eldon walked over. "Few days ago? How's that possible? We just got here."

The desk clerk pointed at the red stamp marking the envelope *urgent*. "I'd wager whoever sent it had it delivered to every hotel in the city. I got a whole box full of ones just like it. My apologies for not bringing it to your attention when you checked in earlier. I just now recollected seeing your name and sure enough."

Thanking the desk clerk, he wandered into the lounge, unsealed the envelope, and pulled out the delicate yellow paper. The communication was brief:

> *Watch out. Su-pe-hi-ye is coming. Left March 8.*
> *Careful, nephew.*
> *   –Dick*

A group of rowdy businessmen had just entered the hotel and were collecting in the lounge, batting off the rain, sparking cigars, racing to the saloon to order drinks. Eldon studied each soggy, bearded, windburned face as if his brother were already among them. He read the message again. The brother in him was relieved that Clayton had survived; the father in him was scared.

When he caught Minn's quizzical look, it struck him that there was another matter he needed to attend to at haste: his money, which he could only assume Jack knew about, and would be chomping at the bit to collect.

"Pa, what's it say?" Ian asked, as if he'd asked twice already.

"Just Uncle Dick checking up on us." He fished some coins out of his pocket and pointed at the lunchroom. "Get you and Miss Yancy something sweet."

The boy snatched the coins and bolted for the lunch counter.

Slumped against the back of a leather couch, Eldon took a moment to collect his thoughts.

"What is it?" she said.

"We got to make a stop before the mortician."

Her eyes grazed the yellow paper.

He considered lying, but determined it irresponsible. "I got a brother," he said in a low voice. "Goes by the name of Jack Foss."

"Yes, the man they took you for in Kansas City." She was nodding as if she'd already pieced it all together. "He's coming here?"

"Yes."

"With what intention?"

"A score to settle."

A score ye shoulda settled back in Dakota, said Jack.

Her face was hard and expressionless. "So we're in danger."

"You and Ian have nothing to worry about."

Her eyes searched the men as they crossed the lobby, gloved hands pressing across her abdomen. "Sounds as if I have plenty to worry about."

He nodded, understanding. "I'll give you what you need to get set up in Chicago. We'll pick up a schedule; I'll get you on the first train."

Her fists clenched so tightly that the troublesome button on the cuff of her left glove popped loose.

She looked down at it. So did he. They laughed.

"Finally," she said. "A sign!"

He offered his hand. "May I?"

She exhaled, the worry just behind her smile. She gave him her wrist. "Please."

TWENTY-SIX

THE CLERK NERVOUSLY COLLECTED THE BILLS, THEN StUFFED the pile into an envelope. "There you go, Mr. Quint—two thousand dollars, minus two dollars for the transfer fee." He was an uncanny facsimile of the old man in Kansas City, though about thirty years younger. "Western Union thanks you for your business."

Eldon received the envelope and tucked it into his jacket, all while looking at the man. "By any chance, does your father work at a Western Union?"

"Oh . . . well, yessir."

"Does he work in Kansas City?"

"He's fixing to retire, sir."

"You ever seen me before?"

"No, sir."

"Anyone looks like me been poking around the last few days?

"No, sir."

"You sure?"

"Been here all week, sir."

Eldon laid a fifty-dollar bill on the counter and slid it to the clerk. "If someone who looks like me—beard, no beard, whatever—comes in asking about this money, you stall em for a few hours and get a message to the Wellman Hotel."

The clerk looked at the note, then at Eldon. "That all I gotta do?"

"That. And tell your father I said hello."

The musty brick mortuary sat like an outcast in its treeless plot. The building had windows and a front entrance, but to Eldon they looked oddly placed. The world had been playing tricks on him ever since he'd read that telegram. He helped Minn and Ian out of the wagon. Then he went around back and took out his lockbox, opened it, and removed Shane's journal. He knew the boy was with him, but he liked the feel of it in his pocket.

They climbed the crooked steps. Eldon knocked on the big black door until a walrus of a man appeared, wiping scraps of food from his peppery Vandyke. The mortician was heavily perfumed, a sweet and sour scent like rotten strawberries. They had interrupted his lunch, though he wasn't vexed. With a smile that seemed to fluctuate between jovial and doleful, he ushered them in through the door and took their coats.

"I'm looking for a coffin. For a boy. Just made twelve."

"Dear me," intoned the mortician. "You are the father?"

"Yessir."

The mortician nodded, then commenced a tour of his brightly lit showroom, moving with a bandy-legged shuffle between open coffins, each canted upward on a velvet stand. When Eldon described what he wanted, the mortician nudged him subtly toward such luxurious additions as cherrywood veneer or French fold interiors or a double-thick mattress and matching silk pillows.

"Just give me a box," said Eldon. "One that won't get dirt in it."

"Well, yes," said the mortician. "Yes, of course. But as the earth is still quite frozen, I must assume you will be storing the remains with us for a matter of weeks—if this infernal winter ever quits, that is. Thus, I might reasonably suppose that you will require a Bateson?"

"A what?" said Eldon.

"A popular device of proven efficacy that promotes peace of mind for the bereaved. I mount a bell on the lid of the coffin and connect it with a cord to the allegedly deceased's hand. Should—"

"Allegedly? What the hell are you saying?"

"Should this be a case of premature burial, the faintest tremor would sound the alarm."

Eldon sucked air under his teeth, the voice of Jack Foss burning in his ears. Minn looked over. He tried not to look back but couldn't help it.

Her eyes were calm and sweet.

He looked at the mortician. "No such device will be necessary. But thank you."

"So you believe him to be sufficiently deceased?"

Why don't ye make him *sufficiently deceased,* Jack said.

"Sir," said Eldon. "I believe him to be frozen solid. And if you ask me one more goddamn question about it, you might as well give me two coffins."

"Understood," said the mortician. He turned for his receipt pad but paused. "Yet to err on the side of caution, shan't we at least leave your son with a crowbar and a shovel? I have both available for a reasonable sum."

They transferred Shane's body to the basement, where he would stay until the ground softened enough to accept him. Abandoning the boy left Eldon feeling as though he'd lost a limb. As they walked over the gravel road toward the cemetery, he began to question if he was awake or asleep, dead or alive, himself or someone else. He looked up at the sky, the cold pressing down on his shoulders. The drizzle had turned to snow flurries.

They passed through the scabby lych-gates. He stood looking over a stretch of sallow land bound by stone walls.

Be straight with her, he told himself.

For once in your life be straight.

They arrived at a central plaza surrounding a Gothic chapel. Ian ran ahead, stomping the frozen puddles.

"Mind keeping him occupied for a few minutes?" asked Eldon.

Minn nodded somberly. "Of course."

He ventured down a gravel path, dodging swirls of ice. The letter from the sheriff had included a plot number—124—and though he wasn't sure of its location, the cemetery looked new enough that much of the land was still pasture.

A sign sent him through a grove of dogwoods—Hattie's favorite tree. He braced himself as a white placard with a plot number came into view: it read 126.

He went down the path toward a shabby patch of grass that contained a single headstone. The placard read 124. His heart was in his throat. He wasn't prepared. But how does one prepare to speak the words that in twelve years of marriage he'd never found the courage to disclose?

A stone bench along the path was etched with the words *O rest beside the weary road and hear the angels sing*. He sat down and practiced what he might say. The headstone was different than he'd pictured. It was shaped like a heart on a pedestal, its base carved with the thorns of the acanthus. He had requested a simple stone. It was all he could afford, yet this one was intricate. He got up and walked farther along the path until he could read the inscription:

Lord Dorian Hiccup, 1809–1881

He checked the placard again, then looked around in dismay. At the top of the hill stood a small cathedral. A sign on the pitched roof read Office.

The cemetery warden sat behind an ornate wooden desk, scanning a large record book. Thin and clammy, he had one glass eye that moved badly, while his good eye dispensed compassion as if it came out of a jar. After closing the book, he took off his reading specs, squeezed the bridge of his nose, and exhaled heavily. "I'm afraid there is no record of your wife being interred here, Mr. Quint."

Eldon was gripping the arms of his chair as if they were the gunwales of a lifeboat. "You checked her maiden name?" he said. "Wilder?"

"Yes, both names. And the date of the committal was . . . ?"

"August the twenty-eighth of last year."

The director shook his head, his glass eye moving slower than his real one. "No, you see, that's not possible. Not a soul was laid to rest here in late August or September. Problems with the groundwater." He paused, then folded his hands across the desk and leaned in. "Is it possible Sheriff La Grange committed her elsewhere and you failed to receive the notice?"

Eldon calmly repeated what he'd said three times already.

"I got a letter from the Greene County Sheriff saying my wife was buried here, at this cemetery, on August the twenty-eighth. I received a bill for her headstone and for the ecclesiastical fee, and was given a plot number—124—but there's some other fellow called Hiccup buried where my wife should be and I want to know why."

"I'm terribly sorry, Mr. Quint, but I don't know what else I can do to help you."

When Eldon failed to respond, the man tapped his fingers on his record book.

"The name of every soul laid to rest in these grounds is recorded here in this book. Every single one. Your wife is not among them." He leaned over the desk. "Talk to Sheriff La Grange."

He emerged from the office, bloodless and beaten. Wind and snow burned his face. The clouds pressed down. As he wandered back to the plaza, a thought took shape that was so vile, so unspeakable that he had to strangle it off.

In the middle distance, Ian sat on a bench, sketching, while Minn perused the gravestones, hands behind her back. When she looked up, she must have read something in his gait, and began to walk toward him.

That thought was clawing up his throat, trying to get to his tongue. He sank to his haunches, both hands pressed to his mouth to stop it from forming into words.

He looked up. Ian was jogging toward him, passing Minn.

"Can I see her yet?" he hollered.

Did he know? Did he know why his mother wasn't buried here? Why she couldn't be buried here? The answer rattled around his throat like a moth in a jar.

Don't say it.

If you say it, then it's real.

And if it's real, then it's your fault.

Jack Foss laughed. *But ye already know that it is.*

TWENTY-SEVEN

THE SHERIFF'S STATION GREW LIKE A MALIGNANCY OUT OF the igneous blocks and barred windows of the jailhouse. Eldon gave Minn the reins, then walked up to the heavy iron gate and heaved it open. The anteroom was stale and cold. A saggy-eared deputy looked up. He seemed to twist like a tree out of his desk.

"I need to see Sheriff La Grange," Eldon said.

The deputy spoke in a slow, tremulous voice. "Sheriff's travelin back from Saint Louis. Will not return till late in the night if not by tomorrow."

Eldon left a name and where he was staying and told the old deputy three times that the matter was urgent.

Back at the Wellman Hotel, he sent Minn and Ian to eat supper, then he went up to the room and sat at the edge of his bed for five minutes, staring at the wall. Then he stood and pulled on his heavy coat and hat, and went down to the livery. They fetched his wagon and he pulled away from the hotel at a fast trot. He sat hunched, shivering in the cold rain, driving his team hard with the whip. In a few minutes the dense canyons of the city settled into tidy rows of simple residences.

He crossed the train tracks and turned down Commercial Avenue. Twelve years ago this neighborhood had been prairie and a few trees. He swung a hard turn down a dead-end dirt road. There were new houses on Peach Alley Place, but he found the old house at the end of the road. It was a two-story house with a pitched roof that flattened into a widow's walk. The scallop-pattern shingles had once been painted blue. Now they were dull gray. Weeds had overtaken the front yard. There was ice on the roofed galleries that ran along the front and back of the house. Some people called them porches now, but Myrna had always called them "my galleries."

He parked in the rutted drive beside the house and set the brake. Then he climbed down and walked past the scuffed porch posts into the backyard. The property sloped down to a tree-lined stream. Beyond lay a brown field and an old orchard of leafless trees that ended at a dense blockade of forest.

He stopped walking as if someone had grabbed him from behind.

The skeletal remains sat at the edge of the downslope. The frame of blackened support beams, scaly and abraded, barely held the outline of a small barn. In that burned and brittle structure, his wife had drawn her last breath.

Beyond the barn, under a leafless willow tree, two granite stones pushed out of the earth. Wind burned his face as he stumbled forward. He clamped a hand over his hat. He stood under the willow. A black stain crept up the trunk where the fire had licked it. He heard himself mumble the names etched into the polished gravestones, then the numbers dating their deaths the same day. He looked down at the frozen mud where his wife had been laid to rest beside her mother. The smell of her flesh burning greased his nostrils suddenly and he looked toward the heavens and tried to breathe. The snow looked like falling ash.

It had been the last week of July, just as the harvest was coming in, when the letter arrived. Myrna Wilder, near death, desired to see her adopted daughter one final time. Even though Hattie had visited her mother all of three times in a decade, she became so hopelessly distraught that she insisted on making the seven-hundred-mile journey immediately. But it was the first decent harvest in years, and Eldon couldn't even spare one of his sons to accompany her.

Because of a crippling fear of trains and steamships, Hattie boarded a stagecoach in Yankton. For three weeks Eldon and the boys waited for some form of correspondence. A few days before Hattie was set to arrive in Springfield, a letter came from Fort Scott, where her stage had stopped to change horses. He remembered the words:

> *The air is pleasant, the country bountiful. The lowland green casts all the way up the serrated hills, and the soil is black and better than any in Dakota. It is light country. The answer to why we toil in the dark wilderness, even when the comforts of civility are within reach, still eludes me, husband. But, alas, the hour has tolled and these questions no longer burn holes in my mind.*

She never passed up an opportunity to scorn the territories, though this letter, even for her, was disturbing enough to send a shiver up Eldon's spine, and only when a second letter arrived, postmarked from Springfield, did he breathe a sigh of relief.

The boys had made him promise that if they were at school when a letter arrived, he would wait for them to open it. So he waited until the three of them were seated around the table. As he began to read, he found himself trying to swallow the words out of existence. The letter was from the Greene County Sheriff. Hattie had died in a barn fire, the blaze so intense that not even a bone survived.

Included with the letter was a copy of her death certificate, along with an estimate of burial fees. Eldon wired the Greene County Clerk's Office to make sure the information was correct, and received a prompt confirmation—her death certificate was valid. That was the word they used. *Valid.* As if it was something he deserved.

TWENTY-EIGHT

"We have positively no record of you staying here," sniffed the hotel manager, glaring over his pedestal at the rough-looking man.

"Check again," Jack said with a growl.

The soaring lobby buzzed with a convention of dignitaries in stovepipe hats. Their cigar smoke all but obscured the dark oil paintings that hung on the walls. Jack hated places like this. It took an act of will to keep from pulling a pistol and robbing every plutocratic fool in sight.

Riffling perfunctorily through his ledger, the desk clerk shook his head. "No, Mr. Quint, I assure you, you are not a registered guest at this hotel."

The Outlaw lit a cigar. "And you never seen me before?"

"Not ever in my life."

On the sidewalk in front of the hotel he smoked and studied two Indians as they passed. Picking flecks of tobacco off his tongue, he watched their reflections in a storefront window across the street, making sure they didn't belong to the Major. They weren't wearing dresses or robes and seemed sober, which was evidence enough. He was about to turn from the reflection when he caught sight of a white man in a chestnut suit. The man returned his gaze, lighting a cheroot that pushed through his thick mustache, then ambled down the street.

The snow had turned to a fine drizzle, the horizon dark with a coming storm. After flicking his cigar into the road, Jack lifted a heavy carpetbag, which contained a pair of socks, a change of drawers, his .44 Colt rimfire, and Magdalena's wooden leg. It was approaching noon. He'd been to four hotels already. With the six he'd visited the night before, that was ten in all. There were two more listed in the city directory. If Eldon wasn't at either one, Jack would have to expand his search to the flops and boarding houses. By his estimation, he had seventy-two hours before the Major showed up.

Hotel number eleven, a banal brick structure, spoke to Jack as he studied it from across the street. Bland, shabby, and unremarkable were its compliments. If his brother occupied the city, this forgettable pile of bricks was where he would lay his head.

In the lobby, Jack stood confused by the dull amalgamation of maroon carpeting, stained wood, and tobacco-colored upholstery. A young clerk was behind his desk, his pimpled face like a diseased flower—though as Jack closed the distance between them, the flower wilted into a pose of shock.

"Mr. Quint," he gasped. "Golly, what happened?"

Jack smiled in spite of the black eye and busted nose he'd received from the imp. "Bandits," he said with a strained exhale.

"Mother Mary—did you file a complaint? The sheriff's station is just north of the square."

Jack set his hands on the polished cherrywood of the reception desk. "Son, I am weary like you wouldn't believe.

I'd like nothing more than to retire to my room and not be disturbed."

"Of course," said the desk clerk. "Do you need assistance getting upstairs?"

"Jest a new key. They made off with even that."

He took the key and limped up to the second floor, to a door at the end of the burgundy hall. After making sure that he was alone, he took the rimfire Colt from his carpetbag, not because he wished to hurt his brother, but because he suspected that Eldon might regret putting that bullet in the snow instead of in his head, and would attempt to correct the mistake.

With his ear to the door, he slid the key into the lock and pushed inside. In the entranceway he stood listening to the mild rain, then shut the door. The bed hadn't been slept in. The dresser drawers were empty, as were the pockets of the trousers heaped on the bedcover. There was a knock on the adjoining door in the wall next to him.

"Mr. Quint?" inquired a female voice.

He took off his bolero, ran a hand through his tangled brown hair, then reseated the hat and unlocked the door. A swarthy girl stood, her hands on her hips.

"Where have you been all night?" she demanded. "We've been worried sick. Good god, what happened to your face?"

He could see her rapidly cataloging his features—his big, nicked knuckles, his waistband lumped with the shape of a pistol, his dirty buffalo coat, his off-kilter stance from leaning on his good leg. Her face slackened and she backed into the other room.

"Winifred, I presume?" he said, touching the brim of his hat. "I'm J—"

"I'll scream," she announced.

"Hold on now."

"Stay back," she warned. "I know what you've come for. Ian told me everything."

"Jest listen to me now—"

She tried to slam the door, but he stopped her. A small creature scampered through. Jack turned his head. Ian seethed, showing his teeth, then darted to the bed, dug under the pillow, and with both hands dragged up his father's Model 3.

Jack showed his palms. "Easy now, Turnspit."

The boy's angelic face was transformed, the innocence scuffed from his bright green eyes. "You come to hurt us?" he demanded.

"I come to talk," said Jack.

The girl spoke calmly. "Ian, bring me the gun."

"Try to hurt us," said Ian, "I'll teach you a lesson. Pa taught me to shoot."

Using both thumbs, the child cocked the hammer to the first, then second position.

"I see that." Jack stepped toward him. "But listen to me—"

"Get back!" he screeched.

Jack's hands inched higher. "You can point that thing at me, but keep the flailin to a minimum. That gun got a hair trigger."

"Ian," the girl urged, "come to me."

"Get out or I'll shoot you in the knee," Ian snarled.

Backing toward the exit, Jack said, "I guess I'll be on my way then."

He reached and opened the door, backed into the hall, then drew the door closed. As the latch clicked, he put his ear to the door panel. When footfalls neared, he swung the door open again, striking the girl in the chest. As she stumbled back, he lunged inside, snatched a clump of her hair, spun her forward, and wrapped an arm around her waist. She flailed, hot as a bronco.

Ian swung up the gun. "Let her go!"

Jack walked the thrashing girl toward him. Once he'd forced Ian into a corner, he slapped the gun from the boy's hands. The Model 3 slid across the floor, vanishing under the bed. When the girl dove for it, he seized her by the hair and launched her through the adjoining door. "Me and Turnspit need to talk," he said, then he slammed the door and bolted it shut.

When he turned around, Ian was sprinting for the hallway. Catching him by the shirt back, Jack kicked the door shut and twisted the lock. Then he reached under the bed, picked up the Model 3, and stuffed it into his coat. Ian was thrashing so wildly that he had to pin him down on the bed.

"Quit fightin me," he snarled. "Or I'll wrap you up in these bedsheets. Wanna be wrapped up so tight that ye can't move?"

Ian gasped. "Get off me!"

"If I let you up, you gonna listen to what I got to say? And don't say yes unless ye mean it."

Ian stared up at him, panting.

Beneath the patter of rain was a faint rumble of thunder, so low and distant that it was more felt than heard.

The boy spoke through his teeth. "I'll kill you."

"Ye got heart, Turnspit," said Jack. He settled his weight on the boy. "But I need me an answer."

"Yes," he grunted.

"Yes what?"

"I'll listen."

He seated Ian on the edge of the bed, then sat next to him. "Where's yer daddy?"

The boy wiped his eyes on his shirtsleeve. "Don't know."

"I ain't come to hurt him."

"How do I know?"

He shifted, his hip burning. "Yer gonna have to take me at my word."

Ian looked at him. "You're hurt," he said. "Cause Pa shot you?"

"Ain't you supposed to be listenin?"

"He could've killed you. But he's not like you."

A deep boom of thunder shook the room.

"Yer pa is a good man," Jack said, grimacing through the pain. "And yer right. Him and me might look the same, but we ain't. Surprise ye though it may, there was a time he was a heck of a lot meaner than I ever was."

"No," said Ian. "You're lying."

Rain clattered against the windows, cold wind whistling around the seams.

"Believe me," Jack said. "He done his share of villainy. During the war and after."

Ian shook the words out of his ears. "He only killed horses. He said so."

The cold air shuffling through the room turned warm and carried with it the smell of all that horse blood drowning the grasses at Birch Coulee. There had been at least ninety of them scattered around the field, rotting in the sun or huffing in agony. Nobody seemed to give a tinker's damn, so Clayton got a rifle and went around putting each one out of its misery until that corporal yelled at him to stop wasting bullets.

He ran a hand through the boy's blond hair and held him tenderly by the back of the neck as he whispered the truth. "Those warn't horses he kilt."

A key rasped. The hall door swung open and a bald, flimsy man in a dark suit held open the door as the girl bolted inside and swept Ian off the bed and into her arms.

"Get out," she snarled at Jack, holding the boy to her chest.

"Sir," said the bald man, pausing a moment to inhale some courage. "I am the manager of this hotel. If you would please follow me downstairs."

Ignoring him, Jack told the girl, "Git packed. Yer movin to another hotel."

"We are not," she fumed.

"Yes, ye are, now git packed. It's fer yer own good."

The manager cleared his throat. "Sir, you need to leave this room at once."

Jack's eyes slid to meet his. "Friend," he said, "this is a family matter and I would appreciate it if ye would give us some privacy."

The manager looked at the girl, unsure of what to do.

Jack patted him on the shoulder. "Why not help the lady gather up her things."

The girl set Ian down and pointed at the open door. "Leave at once."

"Fine," said Jack. "You wanna wait here fer the Major to show up? That's on you. But the boy's comin with me. Turnspit, git yer gatherings."

The girl was staring at him, her face twisting through shock, fright, and finally disbelief. She asked in hardly a whisper, "How do you know that?"

"No time to explain," Jack said. He fished a coin from his pocket and stuffed it in the manager's hand. "See that their things is packed and downstairs in five minutes." Then he looked back at the girl. "Where's my brother?"

She pressed her lips closed as a gust of rain slapped off the window.

"He left last night," Ian said. "And he didn't come back."

Jack felt his throat getting dry. He headed for the door, then turned and looked at the three of them. "What're ye all standin around fer? Downstairs in five minutes."

TWENTY-NINE

THE SPOT-FACED DESK CLERK WAVED AS JACK LIMPED PAST the front desk. "Mr. Quint . . . Mr. Quint, Sheriff La Grange is waiting for you."

He pointed at the lounge, to an older fellow seated on a leather couch reading a newspaper, bobbing one leg. Hearing his name, the sheriff looked up from his periodical. Jack's prevailing instinct was to dig out that Model 3 and open fire. But the sheriff appeared to be alone. After folding his paper, he stood up and approached Jack with a doleful expression, like a man bearing grave news.

"I got your message, Mr. Quint. Should we speak in the saloon?"

Jack looked at him a moment, and then nodded. "Lead the way."

They settled on two rawhide stools at the empty bar.

"I know it's early," the sheriff said, "but you might be needing yourself a sip."

A gaunt, hawkeyed man of middle age, La Grange seemed to carry the troubles of his profession in the crevices of his face. A tan hat covered hair the same shade of iron as the star pinned to his vest. Like most lawmen he sported a mustache, but his was extravagant, extending two inches from each side of his face, waxed into hypnotizing spirals.

Jack ordered rye, the sheriff black coffee. They sat silent for a moment.

"I have to admit," said the sheriff, "I have been dreading this day for eight months now. Figured if you never came, then you'd be better off not knowing. But here you are." He blew steam from the surface of his coffee but refused a sip. "As you've reckoned by now, that letter I sent neglected certain details of your wife's passing."

Jack gave a grave, close-lipped nod.

The sheriff blew on his coffee again, then nudged it aside as if ordering it was a mistake. "I went back and forth on whether or not it was the Christian thing to do and . . ." He removed his hat and placed it on the bar. "The reason you couldn't find your wife's grave is cause she's not buried out at Hazelwood. She's not buried out there cause the county saw fit to rule her death a suicide." He took a sudden slurp of coffee and burned his mouth. "As I imagine you're aware, suicide cases can't be accorded the same service of the dead as peace-parted souls."

Jack downed the whiskey and held the glass to his forehead. Given what he knew of Hattie, it shouldn't have sent such a hard jolt through him, but it did. "Mothers don't do that," he muttered. "Do they?"

"In this line of work, you come to see that people do all manner of things, whether there's a lick of sense to em or not."

La Grange ordered Jack another whiskey.

Jack accepted the refill, but for the first time in memory he didn't feel like having a drink. "How did you come to know it was that?"

"I don't know if you want to hear the details."

Jack stared into the amber glass and turned it with his fingers.

It was true that he and Eldon had broken apart somewhere along the line, but they were still two halves of a whole. And he'd come to understand that you go and split something like that up, something that's meant to be one, those two halves keep chasing each other, whether they know it or not. He'd also come to reckon that he and Eldon were locked in the same downward spiral, and the only way to get free of it was to come together again. And to do that, he needed to know his brother's pain, and his brother needed to know his.

The sheriff let go a long, weary exhale and took another mouth-burning gulp of coffee. "Your wife . . . we believe she arrived at your mother-in-law's the morning of August the twenty-seventh around eleven o'clock. She would've discovered then that her mother had passed on. The folks that'd been tending to Mrs. Wilder had stopped by that morning around ten and found her expired. She went in the night—peaceful, from what they said. They left to make the arrangements. Had no idea your wife was set to arrive." He paused. "Now, I don't make a habit of assumptions, but I can only imagine that finding her mother like that, well, that just might be what pushed her over the edge. Mr. Quint, you sure you wanna hear all this?"

Jack nodded, imagining what it must have been like for Hattie to discover her poor dead mother, the dark thoughts closing in from all sides, crushing what little hope remained.

"I imagine it was a hard thing to witness," the sheriff continued. "Especially if her mind was already in a state. Again, that is only my assumption. What we know for a fact is, around noon, your wife went out to the barn, piled up some hay bales, and doused em in coal oil. Then she got a rope and climbed up to the loft and tied one end round the rafter and the other around her neck and . . .''

Jack was damn near grinding his teeth to the roots. He slammed the whiskey to put a damper on it. The sheriff ordered him another. Jack downed that one as well.

"Wait," he said. "But if she done that, what was the bales fer?"

"I troubled over that myself," said the sheriff. "Till we found the torch. Now, I couldn't for the life of me draw up what she was doing with a torch. Had she wanted to burn the place down, a book of matches would've sufficed. But what I come to estimate is she lit that torch and was holding on to it when she stepped off the edge of that loft. I think she was hoping the rope would do its job on her and the torch would fall into those bales, light a blaze, and burn away any trace of what she'd done. To spare you and your children. Would've worked, too, had all of Mrs. Wilder's animals not gone stampeding up Peach Alley Place, alerting the neighbors. I imagine your wife didn't want to burn up the critters, and set em free just before she went through with it. Neighbors saw the shoats cutting loose and went to check on the property. By then the fire'd overtaken the barn. They tried to get in and cut her down, but it was just too fierce."

"She had two boys," Jack said, drawing air under his teeth to stop his voice from breaking. When he tried to picture it, he saw Nurse Daye swinging by the neck. Then she became Mary Finley, writhing against the rope. Then Magdalena, her face mangled and dripping blood.

He felt a hand clasp his shoulder, the sheriff's voice distant, telling him not to blame himself, telling him that she was buried now at his mother-in-law's place. There was a crinkle of paper and he looked over. The sheriff had taken a fold of butcher paper from his pocket, opened it, and set it on the bar top. A big carnelian ring stared up at Jack, the oval stone crusted with soot.

"I thought it might stir your suspicions if I sent it to you," said the sheriff.

He took something else from his pocket and laid it on the bar. A sealed envelope, the words *For Eldon* scrawled across the front.

"This was in the house."

Jack saw her, her rigid body swaying in a mouth of flames.

He thanked the sheriff, and the man lifted his hat off the bar top, left some money, and went out of the hotel.

The envelope was sealed. He thought about not opening it, but curiosity got the better of him. The letter was a single page, written in sweeping script.

Husband,

I expect you shall rejoice upon reading this, as I was but a source of vexation and misery for you. Why then should I drag on in this shameful existence, not one ray of hope, save our children. Though even they were not enough.

I remember when you were kind. But that memory has been snuffed out by an avalanche of broken promises. Had you not kept me prisoner in that dreadful wilderness, we might have lived a long, happy existence. Instead, with each unborn misery, you rushed me to my doom.

The children mustn't know. For them, I shall, in my method of ascent, remove any question of sin. They should not think my soul walks in the tule swamps but in the wavering green of heaven.

There, Husband. Now we both have our lies.

As my final hour tolls, I will do my best to forgive you. Though all I can say now is, may God watch over our children. Be kind to them. I was unworthy of their love. Be happy, all of you. So shall my spirit find solace in that.

H–

He folded the letter and returned it to the envelope. The only thing to do was burn it. As he searched for his match-book, Ian and the girl came down the stairs, a porter trailing with two pieces of luggage. He slipped the letter into his pocket and stood.

As the girl approached, Jack noticed a grotesque snarl of flesh peeking through her black hair. She must have sensed his gaze and pulled her hair over the mangled ear. He reached into his coat and held out the Model 3.

"I'm not tryna dragoon ye," he said. "I'm tryna help."

She stared at the pistol and then took it. She checked that it was loaded, then hid it inside her gray coat. "We should go," she said, taking Ian by the hand.

They went swiftly out of the Wellman, Jack toting their luggage. With the rain, all the cabs were filled, though they only had to go a few blocks.

"Get a room under Buzzwig," he told the girl. "Tell em yer husband is joining later. Here . . ." He reached into his pocket for some money.

Across the street the man in the chestnut suit pushed off the side of the building, tossed his cheroot, and blew smoke out the side of his mouth. Jack saw him slip his right hand into his pocket. He began to walk north through the rain, shadowing them.

On the sidewalk ahead was a meat vendor. A carving knife sat on a bloody cutting board. As they passed the stall, Jack swiped the knife. "This way," he said, veering Ian and the girl down a narrow alley that cut between granite buildings.

Taking Ian by the hand, the girl hurried up next to Jack. She glanced over her shoulder. "He's coming," she whispered.

Ian looked up. "Who?"

"Jest keep looking ahead," said Jack.

They were about halfway to the next block when he began to slow his pace. Minn hurried Ian along. When they were a dozen steps ahead of him, Jack set down the luggage and crouched as if to tie his boots. The clack of the man's shoes grew louder on the pavement. Jack stood quickly and turned.

There was a dull pop as the carving knife pierced the chestnut suit and split the man's sternum. Wrenching downward, the blade unveiled the man's entrails in a wash of blood. Jack took him by the arms and gently seated him against a stack of crates. A small caliber revolver was clenched in his right hand. Jack tossed the carving knife, then wiped his bloody hands on the man's jacket. After pulling the man's bowler over his face, he rifled his pockets and found a handbill that advertised a ten-thousand-dollar reward for the capture of Jack Foss, alias Eldon Quint.

He turned suddenly. The girl had crept up behind him and was looking over his shoulder, holding Ian behind her. He showed her the handbill.

"Believe me now, Winifred?"

Her eyes hung on it, then she looked at him. "My name is Minn."

She pulled the hair out of her face, exposing her ruined ear, the shock in her eyes replaced by a white-hot rage. It was suddenly obvious to him why Eldon had taken her on. She was one of them.

THIRTY

WHEREVER HE WAS, IT WAS PITCH-BLACK. *DEAD*, HE THOUGHT. But would hell be so dark and cold? Maybe he was in jail. He reached for his silverbelly, but it was gone. Where he lay was cool and slightly concave, and made of smooth stone. It had a faint smell, acrid and sweet. When he shifted, something rolled off the side of the slab. The shrill clatter of glass bouncing across tile caused a terrible pain between his eyes. His sides ached like someone had packed his kidneys with buckshot.

What had fallen from the perch sat on the floor in a slash of dull light coming from the top of the stairs. The bottle of rye was drained of all but the dregs. The residue on the back of his tongue almost made him sick. He lay back across the slab. A round metal drain dug into the small of his back. He wondered how much blood it had swallowed. Suddenly he knew where he was. But how did he end up there? He recalled an intense desire to be with his son, to be next to him, to hold him one last time. He rolled to look at what was on the next slab. Mercifully, Shane's corpse was still wrapped in white sheets. He smelled faintly of curdled milk.

The door at the top of the stairs shrieked open and he held his head. Stormy air blew into the basement. A rectangle of drab light fell across the tiles, a well-girthed shadow wobbling at its center, growing larger until it blotted out the light completely. The mortician's sweet and sour perfume filled the basement.

"Mr. Quint?" he said, holding up a lantern.

Eldon covered his eyes.

The mortician held the lantern at his waist and circled it around the room, pausing on the empty bottle first, then Shane's corpse on the slab. Neither object seemed to arouse much surprise or interest.

"You must be feeling poorly," he said, setting the lantern on the edge of the slab.

Eldon grunted in affirmation.

"I am in possession of a remedy for that infernal pounding in your head, if so you desire."

Again he grunted.

"If you'll follow me upstairs . . ."

He shook his head.

"Right. Well, sit tight and I'll go fetch it."

While the mortician was upstairs, Eldon tried to recall more of the night before. He remembered sitting on Myrna's back porch drinking from a bottle he'd found in the cabinet. He had put a pistol to his head, the cold muzzle pressing against his temple, his rage condensing in the tip of his finger. He had to point that finger at someone. All he had to do was pull that metal switch and that would show Hattie how sorry he was.

What crossed his mind in the split second before he crossed himself out with a bullet was a face, Minn's face, fixing him with one of her down-the-nose looks. She had withstood a brute for how many years and had been made stronger for it, and therefore she had every right to pillory him, to call him a louse and a clod. A silly granger so caught up in feeling sorry for himself that he was willing to turn his son into an orphan.

Daddy used to say *no rules,* but he never told them that one day they'd have to join the world of rules, and hide the savage soul the frontier had forged in them. The soul he had hidden from his wife, his children, even himself. He had made up a whole new history, but they still paid for the old one. The lie wasn't through with him.

By the time the mortician returned, swiping rainwater off his cloth coat, Eldon had succumbed to his throbbing head and was lying across the slab.

"Rise up, Mr. Quint," urged the mortician. "Life is an ascendant force, always reaching upward like a seedling breaking free of the soil. Rise! Rise! Rise!"

He showed a jar full of a sludgy purgative he called May-Apple Ooze.

"Take this cure and your sickness will melt away like snow in the rain."

Eldon peeled himself off the slab and reached for the goopy concoction.

The mortician held the jar just out of reach. "There is a small fee. A mere fifty cents per dose."

Eldon stared at him.

The mortician glanced at the gun on Eldon's hip and chuckled. "But, of course, for a returning customer, one dose free of charge."

"I need that coffin."

"Coffin? For yourself?" He broke into a nervous titter. "A bit premature, don't you think?"

Eldon pointed at the jar. "Gimme that."

The mortician handed it over.

Eldon drank then wiped his mouth. "I'm taking my son with me."

"Taking him where? It's raining cats and dogs."

He drank more, then handed back the empty jar.

The mortician gaped at it. "But that was ten doses."

The rain beat the roads to mud and he had to lean into the horses to keep the wagon from getting stuck. As he turned onto Commercial Avenue, shopkeepers were scuttling in and out of storefronts, laying duckboards to keep their customers above the runny earth. Everything seemed to be melting, everything except the sense that he was falling toward the end of a very short rope. He turned down Peach Alley Place. At the end of the road stood Myrna's fading blue house, a house that, with his wife's passing, now belonged to him. He drove into the backyard. Just past the scorched barn he reined in the horses, halting under the willow where the gravestones pushed out of the mud.

In the wagon bed, under the oilcloth tent, lay the coffin that held his son. The only thing left to do was put six feet between him and the father who had destroyed his life.

In the shed off the back of the house he collected a shovel, a pickax, and a rusty wheelbarrow. All his old tools, abandoned when he shuffled his bride and new baby off to meet their doom.

As he exited the shed he felt the disparaging gaze of the washroom window on the second floor. Shane was born there in the bathtub. They could have stayed here. Could have made a life here. But he was too afraid. Always afraid.

He tossed the pickax and shovel into the wheelbarrow and pushed it across the muddy hillside to the gravesite.

Under the willow, next to his wife's remains, he measured the dimensions of the grave using stones as markers. With the shovel, he scraped away the top layer of mud, but the earth a foot below was hard as stone.

With a mighty slash of the pickax he tried to open the frozen ground. The dull tool bounced back at him. He kept at it, feeling neither rain nor cold, as if the act of swinging drew a shield around him.

Calluses ripped from his hands, his palms stung by splinters—the tool was taking its revenge on its neglectful owner. He swung and swung, liberating a clump here, sending up a spark there, but the ground rejected his plea.

When it became a chore to even lift the tool over his shoulder, all he had to show for his efforts were bloody hands and burning lungs. He dropped to his knees and clawed the hard soil like a man trying to dig out of prison. Before long he was beating the earth with his fists, and would have smashed them to a pulp had something not seized him by the back of his jacket. The Devil had finally come for him. He collapsed on his side like a dog, waiting to be punished. When his punishment failed to arrive, he opened his eyes. A man stood over him, transformed by the rain into a runny specter.

The man took him by the lapels and tried to drag him to his feet. There was a distant voice shouting, "Get up, get up!" He struggled—until an open hand crashed across his jaw. The slap stopped him from moving. The man hooked him under the arms and Eldon let himself be drawn up. On his feet again, he stood facing the man and the man was him. The dripping body just like his—warped and twisted by its wounds. He had expected to meet some burning malice in Jack's gaze, but there was only pain.

Whatever poison had run between them drained away. Eldon wiped his hands on his shirtfront, leaving dark smears. His fingernails hung by threads. Closing his broken hands, he spoke to his brother. "Can't get through it," was all he could muster.

Jack brought him under the willow and sat him against the black trunk, then stood looking over the terrain. He reached for the pickax. Eldon watched him wheel the ax over his shoulder again and again. After a while, he got up, got a shovel, and they picked and shoveled together, until a dark rectangle opened in the earth. Neither man stopped to rest and no words passed between them. Just the sharp *chuk-chuk-chuk* of metal against dirt.

They dug until the dead grass was at their shoulders. The rain had let up. Under the willow they sat on the edge of the grave, breathing heavy, boots dangling in the pit. Eldon tried to keep from sobbing. His brother's dirty hand tightened on the back of his neck. But when Jack tried to pull him close, he resisted. Anger flared and he seized the Outlaw, but his hands and arms were too tired to hurt him.

JACK FOSS

THIRTY-ONE

ELDON'S HEAD WAS IN HIS LAP. STEAM CURLING OFF THEIR clothes, heavy clouds scudding overhead, swallowing the treetops. He felt like a child, yet their roles had been reversed. It used to be his head in Eldon's lap. Now he shouldered their pain.

When Eldon sat up, Clayton told him, "I didn't come fer no bounty money. I came cause I heard Sonny Bender got it in his head that Jack Foss was hidin out in Dakota. I'd been in Arkansas fer six months, so I started wondering if maybe you warn't dead."

Eldon looked past him, toward Shane's coffin in the wagon bed.

"I got to Sonny in Yankton. I jest wanted answers. Didn't go as planned. I know I should've killed the rest of em then and there but . . . but I followed em. What's the chance they'd run into you? A million to one?" His head was in his hands. "I know I should've killed em all before, but I jest . . . I had to know why you disappeared on me."

The mist closed in around them like swamp gas. Eldon stared into the pit. "Harlan Scrim," he said. "You wanna know why, that's why."

The name rattled around Clayton's chest, but he couldn't understand what it had to do with anything.

"Man had a family," said Eldon.

"I know," Clayton snapped. "But you said he worked for them, you said that made him just as bad."

Eldon was silent for a long time. His head began shaking slowly. "Made him greedy," he said. He spat over his shoulder. "But killing him the way I did made me something worse."

Clayton saw blue ribbons. Two scared little girls listening to their father die in the next room. He'd tried to cover their ears.

"If I didn't change," said Eldon. "If I didn't change then and there, I never would have."

Clayton laughed out loud even though the words went like ice through his veins. The idea just seemed like such an affront, such a lie.

"You think you can change?" he said. "After what we done?"

Eldon didn't answer, but the truth was in his eyes.

How come he got to do the changing when it was him who started it all, him who created Minnesota Jack after that judge wanted to see him hang for stealing bread, him who convinced his brother that they could be as one and get back what was took?

"If ye really meant to change," said Clayton, "you wouldn't have jest up and vanished into thin air like it was nothin to you."

Eldon pulled off his silverbelly and turned it in his dirty, blistered hands. He squinted up at the rain starting to fall again, then looked at the hat in his lap. "You'd have ruined it for me," he said. "You'd have ruined my lie."

"Yer a selfish son of a bitch, Eldon."

"I know."

Clayton looked over. Eldon looked about as beaten down as any man ever had.

"You never told yer wife?" he said.

"No," said Eldon, his eyes drifting. "But she knew."

Remembering what the sheriff had given him, Clayton reached into his jacket and took out the fold of butcher paper. He loosed the blackened ring and held it out in his palm. Eldon stared at it for a moment, then picked it up with two fingers. The sight of it seemed to break him in half.

The last thing Clayton wanted to do was feel sorry for him, but he couldn't help it. He was just as broken, just as beaten down, just as ruined.

"Sheriff said it was jest one of them things. Spilled coal oil. She must've dropped her lantern. Got confused behind the flames. I'm sorry."

Wetting his thumb, Eldon rubbed away the soot. It was a deep red carnelian stone shot through with veins of black. His mouth curled up, his jaw shivering.

"Hattie used to tell Shane that if we never made him a sister, he'd get to pawn it for a pony."

He looked at Clayton and they both laughed, and there was such a concentration of hurt rising up between them, rising with the steam from their mouths, that the rain seemed to bounce off it.

Clayton pushed up from the edge of the grave and offered his brother a muddy hand. "We need to go," he said.

THIRTY-TWO

Lightning flashed across the sky, giving shape to the heavy clouds. Eldon held the reins tight and kept the team steady. He never wanted to get somewhere more in his life than he wanted to get to that fancy hotel, but the trip across town was fraught with blocked roads, drowned livestock, and washed-out crossings.

Clayton sat beside him on the driver's bench, filling him in on the rest of his escapades with the Major. When he fled Kansas City, the imp followed, so he led the former slave-catcher on a wild-goose chase to Saint Louis. After losing him in the bricks, he scattered enough clues to keep the bloodhound occupied at least another day. Even so, with ten thousand dollars on their head, and every bounty hunter in five states coming their way to collect, in a day all bets would be off.

So they had a choice: prepare for war, or run. They'd been running twenty years, and reckoned that was about long enough. Eldon had his son to think about, of course, though according to Clayton, the Major had threatened Ian, too. Said he was going to mount his head on the side of his stagecoach. Well, that about decided it. The only way to keep them all safe was to put the Major in a pine box six feet underground.

The sky opened as they rattled along the cobblestone roundabout in front of the Beekman Hotel. Eldon paid the livery boy to hold the wagon out front. Then they dashed through the downpour, checking every face for threat.

They went up to room 308 and found Minn and Ian safe and sound in the elaborately decorated suite. A table was littered with playing cards and dinner plates brought by room service. When Clayton and Ian left to take down the bags, Minn held Eldon back.

"Are you sure we can trust him?"

"Clayton hates Sinchilla as much as either one of us."

"You were quite assured of his villainy yesterday."

Thunder shook the windowpanes and rattled a porcelain tea service atop the credenza. It was the storm punctuating her doubt.

"We need to go," he said. "Just trust me on this."

She took the Model 3 from the dresser drawer and put it in her coat pocket. Then she turned to Eldon. "Why should I?"

"Because I know."

"But how do you know?"

It was an uncanny ability she possessed, to make him feel small and transparent. He found himself grasping for a way to appease her. Not with the truth, because the truth was they couldn't trust Jack Foss—not the Jack Foss who tried to steal off with the money from that tomato can. But he had to believe they could trust Clayton Quint, who would steal off with shoats in the springtime to save them from the slaughter, who went around putting all those injured horses out of their misery at Birch Coulee while Eldon tore off looking to butcher as many braves as he could get his hands on.

"He's trying to climb out of where he's been," he said. "I'm the only one who can help."

"You haven't seen him in a decade; how can you help?"

He strained to drag up the words. It was all so tangled—the man he was, the man he wanted to be, the lies, the truth.

"Because he's my brother," he said.

She stood staring at him.

"I know," he said. "Because I'm the one who put him down there."

On the ride back to Myrna's blue house, he did what he could to keep the horses above the mud—his thoughts, too. But the two quarrelling voices at his back weren't helping. He looked into the tent. Minn sat facing Clayton, poised like a cobra, badgering him with questions about his evasion of the imp, Rove Brusco, in Saint Louis.

"Do you know how he earned that scar on his face?" she was saying. "A mother and daughter escaping New Orleans . . . they had a week's head start, plenty of help, and three hundred miles between them. And do you know how long it took that wretched bastard to track them down? Four days. I will say it again. Four days."

"Which is more time than we need," said Clayton.

She sat back against the sideboard and folded her arms. "I imagine Rove Brusco was the last thing that poor woman expected to find in her churchyard." Her eyes went to Ian. "Cover your ears."

"Why?" argued the boy.

"Please just do it."

The boy pressed a palm to each ear.

Minn's eyes returned to Clayton. "Do you know what she did next? That woman? She killed her own daughter. And would have done the same to herself had he not tried to grab her. She had a broken piece of shovel in her hand. She missed his artery by a quarter of an inch, which is just far enough to make you doubt that God has a say in any of it."

Nobody said a word as they turned down Commercial Avenue, then onto Peach Alley Place. Eldon reined the horses. The homes at the top of the street had flooded. Some neighbors were out filling grain bags with sand and dumping old bales of hay to divert the water. Clayton climbed up front with the Winchester as the blue house appeared through the precipitation. Perched on a rise, it was still free of the brown soup that lapped around it.

As Eldon pulled into the drive alongside the house, he had a moment of sheer panic. Would it be better to get out of town? Rent a room? It would put them in the public eye. But at the house at least they could defend themselves. And he could get Shane in the ground next to his mother. As long as they stayed vigilant overnight, he could bury Shane, then in the morning get Minn and Ian somewhere safe.

But where was safe?

He hopped down from the wagon and looked at the house, hoping he hadn't left it in some kind of sordid mess the night before. While Clayton kept watch, he clambered up the porch steps and pushed inside.

Wind and rain blasted the tall curtained windows in the whitewashed sitting room. Everything looked to be in order. He remembered not having the courage to look around much last night, and had chosen to drink out on the porch. He'd known that if he went inside and walked those small closed rooms—rooms that once had him clawing for a way out—the memories would come crashing back. But now he stood in the kitchen. Looking at the buckled floor he'd always intended to fix. The wall of ledged, uneven brickwork where Myrna used to stash her half-smoked cigarettes. She never cared much about being a lady.

Up the crooked stairs he went, rounding the half landing into a crooked hallway. The house had settled at some point and there wasn't a right angle to be found. As he went down the hall he glanced into the three small bedrooms. When he reached the end, he looked into the washroom. A claw-foot tub sat on cracked terra-cotta. Shane was born right there, right in that tub. The first pregnancy had been stillborn, and there was no sweeter sound than the sound of his baby crying for the very first time.

He went back up the hall and turned at the stairs. There was a round stained glass window carved into the wall above the half landing. Thirteen years ago he was standing right there when he decided to kill off his old life. He hadn't felt much remorse at the time. It was every man for himself, just like Daddy had taught him.

THIRTY-THREE

WHILE HIS BROTHER WAS IN THE HOUSE GETTING IAN AND Minn situated, Clayton got all four horses out of the traces and led them one by one down to the stream where he'd strung a picket line. He was bringing down the last horse, a brown mare, when Eldon came out and stood by the wagon, looking up at the sky. The rain had gentled some. Though something black and heavy was rolling down from the north. Clayton went back up the hill to meet him. Eldon had his head tilted back, eyes clamped shut.

"He givin ye any good advice?" asked Clayton.

Eldon opened his eyes. "This is the second time I'm praying for a storm to get worse."

"Maybe I'll join ye then."

They stood there a moment looking back toward the road. Eldon blew air through his teeth. "Just gotta make it till dawn."

Clayton looked north toward what was coming. "I don't think we're goin anywhere tonight, even if we want to."

"Yep."

He spat. "I'd whip a baby fer some tobacco."

"Might be in the kitchen."

"Yeah?"

"I'll dig it up."

Clayton nodded appreciatively. "Once this passes, you all need to hit the trail."

"You getting yourself killed for no good reason won't do anybody any good."

Clayton closed his eyes. There was Shane on the floor, staring up in shock, his mouth opening and closing, reaching for air. Clayton looked down the hill, past the stream and the fields and the snarled orchard. There was a strange brightness to it all. He spat, then turned around and nodded at the black clouds gathering strength on the horizon.

"Now would be the time to get him buried," he said.

Eldon pointed at his hip. "You're bleeding," he said.

A dark stain spread down Clayton's trousers.

"There's a bottle of rye in the pantry. Just don't go finishing it." He nodded at the widow's walk on the roof. "Once you get fixed up, we need to take shifts, at least till morning."

"Come morning," said Clayton, "you all is leavin here and never comin back."

He went in the front door, stomped the mud off his boots, and swatted his hat dry. To his left, Minn stood at the kitchen window, looking out at the road, and Ian was drawing at the dining room table.

"Eldon says it's time to lay Shane to rest."

Ian scowled at him. "But it's raining."

"Not right now it isn't. Git yer coat. Yer daddy's waitin."

The boy slid off the chair, grabbed his coat, and marched out the back door.

Clayton limped up to the pantry and searched for the bottle of rye. When he turned with it, she was standing in the doorway.

"You're tracking blood across the floor."

He looked down at his hip. "I'm sorry, I didn't realize—"

She waved him out. "Don't just stand there; let's have a look."

They settled at the dining room table. He sat on the bench seat and slowly brought down his trousers. She peeled away the crusty cloth Magdalena had used to cover the wound. She found a pile of clean rags and doused a few with rye and began to clean around the fetid purple opening. When she tied the first bandage, he flinched.

"Too tight?"

He shook his head.

"You remind me of my friend Tom. He was a stable boy. He helped me to escape. On Penelope's horse, no less. He was good with horses."

Clayton grunted as she wrapped his thigh. "That might be a little too tight."

She loosened the bandage, then grinned to herself. "I wished I could've seen her face when she realized I'd stolen off on her prized stallion. It almost made the suppers of fish bones and the weeks spent locked in the basement seem worth it. We used to call her Horseface, but now that I think about it, I realize it's an insult to horses."

He smiled.

Her eyes ran over him. "You know, you and Eldon do look very much alike. And yet there's something very different about you."

He looked away. "The years'll do that, I guess."

When he looked back, she seemed to be cataloging the broken parts of his face. His thick, crooked nose. Lumps of bone around his eyes. It was after a bout one night, when Eldon was cleaning his wounds down by the river, that he first noticed his face changing. They'd built a fire on the bank and sat there while Daddy slept, and he saw his reflection in the dark waters. It used to be that he looked at Eldon and saw himself, but after that, he looked at Eldon and saw what was meant to be, while his face became a record of weakness and sorrow, pathetic and unworthy of life. The afterbirth, the late-born. A monster that never should've seen the light of day.

She finished wrapping the bandage, and he stood and pulled up his pants and thanked her. She smiled kindly and the smile hurt him. It twisted his stomach and he tried and failed to stop picturing her hanging there along with the others—Magpie, Mary, Momma—all the women who cared about him and were cursed for it.

He nodded at the back door. "They're waitin fer ye."

She stood looking at him with compassion, which he wanted nothing to do with.

"Hurry up," he said. "Rain's gonna start up again."

"Remember to change your bandages every day."

"Yes, ma'am," he said, refusing to look back at her, to curse her like the others.

When she'd gone, he took the Winchester and went up to the second floor. At the far end of the hall, a rope dangled from the ceiling. He dragged it, unfurling a pull-down ladder. After slinging the rifle over his shoulder, he climbed the rungs, pushed open the hatch, and dragged himself up to the widow's walk.

The four-by-six-foot perch was wrapped in a white-washed fence and provided an unobstructed view up Peach Alley Place to the wagons slugging along Commercial Avenue. Storefronts were being boarded up. Turning south, he looked over the backyard.

Eldon, Minn, and Ian were walking across the dead grass. They gathered under the willow tree. The wind gusted, willow branches thrashing over their heads. Eldon stood at the head of the grave. It had started to rain again. They huddled in quiet mourning and looked like a family.

A family with no place for a busted, broken, time-stained son of a bitch like him. Magdalena would say the monsters of iniquity and duplicity were everywhere, but there were just as many monsters of goodness. Maybe that was what he'd been all along.

THIRTY-FOUR

Eldon stood at the head of the grave, muddling through a prayer in a voice so brittle that the wind all but carried it off. At some point he stopped talking altogether, his heart caught between too many things he didn't have the courage to speak out loud.

Heavy raindrops fell around him. He stared into the black hole. He wanted to jump down, tear off the lid of the coffin, and beg his son's forgiveness. He gripped his hat in his hands. Ian's face was buried in Minn's dress.

What else could he say? That losing his son had warped his soul in some terrible way? That any hope he had in goodness, in the world, in himself, was gone? There was no getting around it. He would punish himself every minute of every day that was left to him. When he looked up, his brother stood watching from the rooftop, a small dark shape against the blackening sky. Clayton turned back toward the road, but Eldon knew he'd been staring into that dark hole thinking the same thing.

He picked up a shovel and stabbed it into a pile of dirt, plowing the dark substance into the grave. Rocky earth rattled off the top of the casket as the rain fell harder. The thunder rumbled like cannon fire. A streak of white split the sky in two. Then it was done.

A wan droplet of fire danced atop the stubby tube of wax, capturing Eldon's attention. He'd allowed only one candle to be lit, to illuminate the windowless dining room where Ian had settled in to draw while he waited for supper. The boy hadn't said a word since the burial. Eldon wanted to console him, but the endless clatter of precipitation, which might have soothed under other circumstances, wouldn't allow him to summon a clear thought. He heard footsteps and looked up from the flame. Borne in from the dark, Minn carried two bowls of beans. She gave one to Ian and the other to Eldon.

He took the bowl and looked at it. Despite the argument of his stomach, food was the last thing he wanted. "I'll bring it up to Clayton," he said.

Her eyes searched him, calm but intense. He ignored a sudden need to be held by her, and took the bowl up to the second floor. He pulled down the ladder, and knocked on the hatch. When it opened, cold rain fell through the square, spattering his face. Through squinted eyes he saw Clayton looming against the blackness. Balancing the bowl in one hand, he dragged himself up to the small patch of roof.

Clayton pulled him up, then crouched down under his buffalo coat. Eldon closed the hatch and scanned the road. The only signs of life were the few dim windows in the neighboring houses. On a clear night you could see past the train station to North Springfield, but the rain had washed away everything beyond the storefronts of Commercial Avenue. He squatted next to his brother and offered the beans.

Clayton refused. He set the bowl aside, then dug into his coat pocket.

"Found this in the kitchen," he said, handing over a crinkled pouch of tobacco and smoking papers. "Probably older than the stars but better than nothing."

Clayton received the gift thankfully.

While he rolled a smoke, Eldon scanned the darkness, big drops of rain pelting the brim of his hat, some loud enough to sting his ears. "How you reckon he'll come?"

"Right down that road."

"Not the type to use the back door."

The wind blew and they held their hats down. When it settled, Eldon stuck his hand in his jacket pocket and felt the rough edge of Shane's journal and began to imagine some alternate life where they weren't stuck on a freezing rooftop waiting for another group of killers, where he could give his son a proper funeral, with all his friends in attendance, with Dick and Laura and his sweetheart, Molly. Thinking of Molly, he chuckled. Clayton looked over, smoke shooting from the corner of his mouth.

"I come in the house one afternoon and Shane's bedroom door is closed. I went and knocked and I hear rustling inside, like I'd caught him up to something. When he opens the door, he's got nothing on but a breechcloth made out of a sheet, and on the bunk there, also wearing little more than a few strategically placed strips of fabric, is Molly Wachiwi. I asked what was going on and he says, 'We're having us a soldier's lodge, and I'd kindly appreciate it if you didn't interrupt us again.' So I asked who they were planning to go to war against, and he says Faulkner Macklin and his posse. Then Molly—who's not the shy type, mind you—she says, 'Faulkner is our mortal enemy, worse even than a Chippewa.

We have strategic discussions to carry, Mr. Quint, if you'd kindly leave us be.' I said, 'All right, but at least put some clothes on.' She says, 'Do we look like cut-hairs to you? We live by the old ways.' I didn't even know what to say to that."

He looked over, expecting Clayton to be amused, but found him bundled under his coat, a fist pressed to his mouth, eyes crumpled in despair.

It put a hard knot in the back of Eldon's throat. He stood and swung open the hatch. "I'll be back up to relieve you after I put Ian down. Don't fall asleep."

Clayton looked up, his face hardening over. "Not on yer life."

He went back downstairs. Minn was reading to Ian in the dining room, the lone candle flickering off the boy's captivated face.

He stood in the dark, watching them. The boy's head resting on her shoulder, her arm around him. When he walked up, Ian raised his head, red-eyed, yawning.

"But I'm not tired," the boy whined as Eldon picked him up.

Minn stood and handed him the candle as thunder rumbled. There was a question on her lips, but she withheld it and kissed Ian good night.

He carried the boy up to what was once Shane's nursery, set the candle on the night table, and tucked him into a sleigh bed that stood against an angled wall.

"Why's Momma buried here and not in the cemetery?" Ian asked.

"She wanted to be buried here," he said. "Next to her mother."

Turning on his side, Ian stared at a white crib that sat under dusty netting in the corner. "How long did you live here?"

"About two years."

He yawned. "Why'd you leave? I like it here."

"There was more opportunity out west."

"Did Momma wanna go?"

That was the last thing she wanted. A cosmopolitan gal like her reckoned life would be chockablock with lavish excitement and exotic experiences. Instead she got fire, drought, and panic in the economy.

"She thought it'd be an adventure," he said. He kissed Ian's forehead, then rose from the bed, picked up the candle, and blew out the flame, casting the room in darkness.

"But she must've liked it here if it's where she wanted to be buried."

"She liked it plenty."

The boy spoke through another yawn. "Then why did you leave?"

He stood in the darkness, hoping the child might just fall asleep, and yet he could feel those big green eyes pressing him for an answer.

"I never lived in a settled place," he said. "Never got used to being around so many people."

"Were you afraid?"

"Yeah," he said. "Guess I was."

"Of what?"

"That I wasn't . . . I wasn't good enough for a place like this. That people would see I didn't belong."

"Do I belong here?"

"You belong wherever you want. Now go to sleep." He pulled up the covers, picked up the dead candle, and crossed toward the half-open door.

"Pa?"

He turned back, the boy's face just a vague outline in the darkness.

"Were you a bad man once?"

The rain, which had finally receded into the background of his mind, now pounded in his ears like a tidal roar.

"Yes," he whispered.

"Did you ask God's forgiveness?"

He nodded.

"What did He say?"

Eldon fought a tremble in his throat. "He gave me you."

As he closed the door, there came a hard knock on the ceiling overhead. Quietly, he dragged down the ladder. The hatch was already open and he pulled himself into the rain.

Clayton was crouched at the railing, Winchester aimed down the road, a halo of hard precipitation outlining his bulk.

"What is it?" Eldon said, huddling beside him.

Clayton nodded toward the top of the road. A little orange dot hovered in darkness. Eldon wiped rain from his eyes. The light was just bright enough to give the vaguest shape to a pair of black horses and the carriage they were hitched to.

"They turned down a minute ago, then jest been set there."

They sat watching another minute.

Eldon turned for the hatch. "I'm going down. Keep that rifle ready."

"Hold it," said Clayton. "Look."

He turned back. The light had begun to move. The wagon was turning. It continued up the road then vanished down Commercial Avenue.

"Maybe they was jest lost," said Clayton.

Eldon's heart was banging in his ears. "Maybe," he said.

He went downstairs to make sure the house was secure, and nearly ran over Minn in the kitchen. She was clutching the Model 3. "Is it all right?" she said breathlessly.

"It's fine."

They stood at the dark window and looked up the road, silent for a while.

"Tomorrow," she said. "What happens tomorrow?"

He'd considered every possibility available to him and still didn't have an answer. Staying in Missouri wasn't an option, and Minnesota was out, along with the rest of his former stomping grounds: Arkansas, Kansas, Oklahoma, and Iowa. He'd always wanted to see the Pacific, but that just seemed fanciful. The only question he should be asking himself was where would be best for Ian. Where would he be safe?

Far away from me, he thought.

When he looked at Minn, she was holding an old newspaper, pointing at the timetable. "It's six months old, but they don't change so often. It says there's an early train that changes in Saint Louis. We could be in Chicago this time tomorrow."

He faced the window. Their shapes reflected in the glass, dark and vague, like a painting scraped of its color and life.

She must have sensed his hesitation, because, quite bluntly, she said, "You can't keep blaming yourself. Point your eyes forward."

She set the newspaper on the kitchen table and looked at him.

"When you were sick, you asked me about the worst thing I'd ever done. I told you I'd blinded a matron. But that's not the worst."

"I don't care what you did," he said.

He just wanted to close his eyes, just for a minute.

But she wasn't going to let him.

"A few weeks before I escaped," she said, "a new girl came to live with us. Young, fresh from the trains. Regina was her name. Long red hair down past her knees. The Major liked her right off. I told her that the only way to survive in that place was to make the Major love you. He must love you above all others. That way, none of the other men are allowed to bother with you."

"I don't want to hear this," he said.

"The first night she got wildly drunk. Dancing, making a show of herself. After cigars, the Major took her up to the playroom above the barn. A room he uses. The next morning, Tom found her in the . . . she was in the stall, hanging from a leather strap."

His head sagged in anger. How many lives had he ruined? A hundred? A thousand? And how many thousands more would those ruined lives destroy?

"I was lying to myself," said Minn. "Telling myself I was helping her. But the truth was, I used her to keep the Major distracted so I could escape."

Rain and wind rattled the windowpanes.

"You can't blame yourself for that," he whispered.

When she finally looked at him, her eyes were cold.

"I've made terrible mistakes," she said. "But I will not give over to despair. Neither will you. Not while you have a son."

He stood in the darkness long after she'd gone to bed. As he climbed the stairs to relieve his brother, the house seemed to sway under him, like a ship yawing through some dark passage. Moving absentmindedly, he found himself in the bedroom he'd shared with Hattie. The hard bed, the slab of a dresser topped with baubles, everything with a cake of dust on it. All those keepsakes from a life he hadn't had the courage to embrace.

Running away. Wasn't that the defining characteristic of Eldon Quint? Thirteen years ago, he'd been so desperate to escape that he traveled all the way to Philadelphia. But, finding it too foreign and uncomfortable, he made his way to Springfield, a city ripened by the arrival of the railroad. He staked a considerable chunk of his capital despite knowing nothing of business, and was expertly swindled.

What did he do then but wallow in pity and drink? That was when he met her, the ravishing saloon singer whose expertise at resisting his charm was unparalleled. He smiled at the thought of her back then, how the sweet sting of her French perfume had wiped clean the aftertaste of his former existence.

That dusty bedroom was filled with her scent, and he walked into the hall and stood listening to the rain. It was a marriage of convenience. She got financial stability, he got a woman of cosmopolitan grace to impress the business set he desperately wished to infiltrate. There might have been a time when he wanted to love her as his father had loved their mother, to the farthest boundaries permissible by the heart, but their union was fleeting at best. Perhaps she'd never even loved him at all.

Floorboards creaked as he traveled toward the pull-down ladder. The washroom door was open. In a fall of pale light sat the claw-foot tub where Shane was born. When she was pregnant, he'd promised they would stay in the city. Another lie. To live in the rubble of the past had become so much easier than to persist against his dread of the present. He'd convinced her that prosperity could only be found in the West, that it would take less than five years to prove up a farm, that when the railroad reached them, they would sell their land at maximum profit and relocate wherever she pleased.

As he stared into that stained tub, rain beating against the window, a flash lit the washroom. Fields of bluestem waved at him like a million open arms, welcoming him back to his homeland, where rye grew high as a house and five cuts of a sickle made a sheaf. Soon those fields were dead carpets. The worst drought in a generation, they said. But he wouldn't be discouraged. He desired more land, more sons. A desire that died inside of his wife, again and again. He had told her so many times that when the railroad came, he would make good on his promise—so many that his lie caught fire. Great belts of flame washed over the land, taking their home, their crops, their livelihood.

Yet that was a mild test compared to what would come.

The sound of the rain slamming into the washroom window—it almost sounded like that day the locusts had arrived. He'd been in the field when the horizon flickered. A little black cloud, like a distant whiff of smoke, grew and mussed, roaring out of the lowland like a demonic visitation. The sound was something out of a nightmare. A million tiny shears chewing up everything but the chattel mortgage. They settled a foot thick, like a black-green snow. Ate through everything, even the green fabric of Hattie's favorite blanket, the one destined to become their son's death shroud.

The clatter of the rain was starting to make him dizzy. He climbed into the tub and lay with his knees in his chest and tried to get beyond the sick feeling.

That plague had done to his farm what he had done to his wife. Every little death was a stain on their chances. Then a miracle, Ian was born. Yet Hattie was more desperate than ever to return to Springfield. That was when the catatonia started. She wouldn't speak or move for hours. Whole days sometimes. He found her one evening bathing naked in an icy pond. She claimed to be cooling off even though the temperature was near freezing. There were small cuts running up her right arm.

A week later she was in the infirmary, accusing her husband of holding her captive so she couldn't tell the world the truth—that he was a murderous outlaw posing as a farmer named Eldon Quint. She claimed to have written proof, things he'd told her when drunk. She tried to explain it all to the doctors, starting from the beginning. She said his father died, then when he was fifteen, a judge wanted to hang him for stealing bread. As he stood trial, a name appeared in his mind like a burst of sunlight. Jack Foss would strike fear into the hearts of tycoons and cattle barons, solicitors and judges, and the crooked lawmen they used like their own private army.

No one believed a word she'd said. In fact, the doctors thought her mad and wanted to cut out her womb. Eldon refused. He still hoped for more children.

After that, Hattie spent her days in a rocking chair, knitting a sweater she never intended to finish. All the while, Eldon, like every other farmer, was drowning in debt thanks to the railroads, and had to apply for government aid. They expected him to sell his livestock first—not that he had any left. And what did that son of a bitch government agent tell him when he asked for more than three dollars?

If you're so damn hungry, eat those damn locusts.

He lay gripping the edges of the cold, empty tub. It flashed before his eyes—his son's first breath, his brother tearing off with a shoat, his wife singing in the sunshine.

Before the war, the Major told the Indian chiefs that if their people were starving, they could eat grass or their own shit. What the Dakota must have felt after that, the fire it must have stoked in their bellies. The fire that burned in him still.

THIRTY-FIVE

NEITHER CARRIAGE NOR RIDER HAD TURNED DOWN PEACH Alley Place since that black coach. Sopped and wind-battered under a lump of buffalo fur, Clayton could be sure of that, having kept his eyes pasted to the road every second of every minute of every hour.

The neighboring houses were dark and he'd smoked through most of the dry-as-dust tobacco. To ward off fatigue he decided to play a game and tried to recount the name of every man he'd ever sent up. It was a grim task, but would keep him awake.

First in line were the two braves he'd spent a few ill-timed musket balls on at Birch Coulee. But he'd been a hundred yards off and wasn't sure that he'd even hit anyone. He saw one of the braves later. The boy had been stepped on by a horse. His head was crushed so badly, it looked like beef stew.

The first man he was sure that he killed—a gambler and outlaw by the name of Flash Autry—had accused him of stealing a gold piece during a game of stud and had given him quite the tarring. As he lay on that floor, blood choking down the back of his throat—all for a coin he didn't even steal—he saw Daddy looming over him, wiping his knuckles, sneering at the *late-born*, the *afterbirth*. He couldn't remember taking out his gun, though it was suddenly in his hand. Flash had laughed at him, until a slug tore into his thigh. The image was still vivid in the Outlaw's mind, Flash's hands waving in entreating little circles, his lips pleading for mercy. The real moment of triumph, however, was the dark stain that spread across his crotch.

Recalling the sight of that son of a bitch groveling at his feet made him smile. It had marked a turning point. He'd never experienced anything close to the absolute power of taking a life. The effects had been immediate and intoxicating. His hand had steadied, the pistol all but melting away, so effortless to wield that when he squeezed the trigger a second time, he felt nothing but the recoil and a sense of contempt for the caricature at his feet. He stood watching remorselessly as blood trickled from the dark nickel-sized hole between the gunslinger's eyes, and he knew his life would never be the same.

And who was next? He searched his memory. It was that train robbery, wasn't it? He could see her still face, clear as day, that poor old dame who got her head punctured. It was an accident, of course—he'd been gunning for her husband when she jumped in front of the bullet—but nonetheless, it made him sick to recall it. He'd been so angry at the man for losing that woman her life, he shot him five times in the chest, reloaded his pistol and shot him twice more in the head.

There was a reason he never went rummaging through his memory. He would have to admit that the old dame wasn't the last pure soul to perish on his account. At the time, he'd reckoned it the price of doing business. About then he started drinking as much as he could stomach, until he could stomach enough to forget. Though he never did. That boozy haze blotted out everything but their faces.

That was the beginning of the end for Jack Foss. Just a few years later, Clayton would receive an unmarked bundle from Philadelphia containing his half of the capital Eldon had taken east to invest. He didn't question its return at the time, thinking that his brother must have had a change of plans. Yet after a few weeks, when no further explanation arrived, he began to worry and had boarded a train to Philadelphia to make sure Eldon was all right.

Thirteen years of searching followed. It had been worse not to know. Hope cannot die on its own. It needs something to kill it, or it becomes its own form of pain. Meanwhile, his brother had been in the very house he was presently freezing his ass off to protect, playing family man with a cuckoo blonde.

The thought made him sick and he lifted the flask.

There was a knock under his bottom. Startled, he nearly dropped his flask, though it was already empty. He opened the hatch and helped his brother up.

"Go on down," Eldon said. "Get yourself dry."

"I'm all right. Go back to yer lady."

"She's not my lady. And don't go talking like that in front of her. You'll scare her half to death."

"I doubt I could scare her half to anything."

"Go on down and get warm."

He *was* out of whiskey. "Want my coat?" he asked.

"I brought up a tarp." Eldon looked around. "Shit. I think I left it by the stairs. Mind handing it up when you go down?"

He gave him the rifle and began to lower himself through the hatch. His boot soles were wet and he slipped.

Eldon caught his arm. "Got it?"

"I'm good."

"Careful."

"I'll pass up that tarp."

He crept down to the kitchen, hoping there'd be something left in that bottle of rye. Lighting a match, he searched the pantry and found only a sticky green bottle. The gluey label read *Crème de Menthe*. All hope drained out of him. There was still a bit of tobacco in his pouch. Reasoning the sweet liqueur would go down easier with a smoke, and feeling suddenly overheated, he ventured out to the back porch.

Naked trees shivered against the rain's metallic clatter. He sat and rolled a cigarette, slimed it, and lit up. When the stale smoke singed the back of his throat, he cooled it with the sugary spirit. A stutter of lightning illuminated the twin gravestones. He plodded down the porch steps, past the black bones of the barn. Under the heaving branches of the willow tree he crouched before the graves and put the cigarette to his lips but found only a mushy nub of paper stuck between his knuckles.

"Hattie Quint," he said, tipping his hat, the storm raging overhead like an angry ocean. "Hello to you. I'm yer brother-in-law, Clayton. How is the temperature of the River Styx? Guess I'll find out soon enough. Or is it all jest black as night and I'm out here like a caboose talkin to myself? Surely I hope not."

He drank and held the cooling confection on his tongue. A hard gust sent dead leaves and sticks blasting past him like a swarm of bats, plastering her headstone. He wiped the gravestone clean.

"There. Good as new." He took another pull and coughed. "I drink any more of this, I'm liable to turn green. Here, you might like it."

The green spirit he poured out swirled oily and rank in the mud puddle.

"I always could beat the nation when it come to drinkin. Yer husband, though. He could drink a band of pee-drinkin Indians into the carpeting. He done jest about everything better than me. But I reckon . . . I reckon I woulda treated you better than him. I don't mean to cast no mud, I'm sure he meant well, but . . ."

He looked up as a flash gave shape to the clouds. With numb fingers, he set the bottle on the ground and stuck his hands into his pockets to warm them. Feeling something, he took it out. Raindrops splotched the white face of the envelope. He thought he'd burned it back at the hotel. He turned it over in his hands. The letter. He had to shake away the picture of Hattie's body swaying in that fiery mouth.

"Whatever we was meant to be got all twisted after the war. Maybe before it too." He picked up the bottle and drank, hacking at the sugary sting. "Every settler enters into a bet with the government: one hundred and sixty acres against five years of starvation, fire, plague, drought, and gettin your limbs hacked off."

He ran his fingers across her name carved into the headstone and imagined tracing the soft lines of her face. The sharp, damp crevices became supple and warm. He could feel the curve of her bottom lip, the sudden angle of her jawline, the softness of her earlobe, the exotic scent released when his fingers dragged through her hair.

"They tell you to go out and prove up yer land. Be a farmer. Do God's work. But that ain't what they really want from ye. Yer jest out there clearin a path fer the damn railroad."

He saw them all standing in the darkness, hundreds of them with big blank eyeballs. Mary Finley was there. So was Harlan Scrim. And Momma.

"They told us we were gonna be farmers. Fuckin lie that was."

The distant slam of the porch door turned him back toward the house. He squinted through the rain at a shapely silhouette.

"Eldon?" she hollered.

There was a pistol in her hand.

He turned, showing his palms. "Nope, it's the other one."

She held open the porch door.

He walked up the porch, nodding thanks, and shook off his coat before he entered.

They settled at the dining room table. There was only one candle lit, and the edges of the room were dark. He sat rubbing some feeling back into his hands.

"Hungry?" she asked. "I saw a can of peaches in the pantry."

He nodded and then watched her vanish into the darkness of the kitchen.

"Can't sleep?"

"I get hungry in the middle of the night," she said.

The windows flashed. He saw her pouring peach slices into two bowls.

She brought the bowls to the table and they sat eating in silence.

"Was it you that killed Harlan Scrim?" she asked suddenly.

The sweet sting of the peaches made him cough. "Harlan Scrim?"

She stared at him.

He cleared his throat. "Yeah. Yeah, it was me. Busted down his door, shot out his knees. Took his scalp right there at his kitchen table. Pinned it to the door of the U.S. marshal's office. As a warning."

"Was Eldon with you when you did all that?"

He shook his head vaguely, but she kept looking at him until he couldn't stand it any longer.

"Yeah," he said. "He was there. He, uh . . . he was there to keep the two girls outside. So they didn't have to hear their daddy screaming. That kind of thing takes a toll on a young mind. And he didn't wish no future harm on them girls."

Minn tilted her head to one side. "How nice of him."

Her mangled ear was exposed. It reminded Clayton of the pinwheeled flesh that capped Magdalena's severed leg.

When she caught him staring, she covered the gnarled lobe with hair.

"Don't mean to be rude," he said. "I'm curious how it happened."

She stared into her bowl.

"A body wears its history," he said. "Might as well wear it proud."

Her eyes swung up. "It's a habit. Deformities tend to put people off."

"Not me," he said. "Best lady I ever knew lost her leg at the knee. Pair of cocksuckin Frenchmen—pardon my language—but these sombitches took advantage of her when she was jest a youngern. Middle of winter, they left her in the woods with a torn shawl and one shoe. Anyone else woulda gave up and froze. By the time she got back to camp, her foot had turned black." He choked down the hard sting that thinking of Magdalena produced. "But she warn't ever ashamed of it. Used to tell me that God don't judge you on yer merits. He judges you on yer scars."

Her eyes softened at the edges, her head falling forward as she nodded. "I like that."

He cleared his throat. "Tell me the story."

"It would bore you to sleep."

"Perfect."

She set down her fork and dabbed her mouth with the back of her hand. "I had just run away from St. Anne's Home for Destitute Children—"

"Don't blame ye with a name like that."

"We took up residence in a yard of decommissioned omnibus cars. I became a pickpocket."

"You was an outlaw too? I like that. How old were ye?"

"I don't know—five or six?"

His smile grew. "Got the jump on me then."

"Yes, well, my career was short-lived. A man caught me lifting his wallet and beat me righteously. Somehow I made it back to the yard. It was winter and we slept on the steam grates for warmth. When I woke, a rat had come up through the lattice and was chewing on my ear."

He reared back in horror. "Goddamn."

"No, I thank that vermin every day of my life. Had it not caused me to scream so terribly, that charitable soul, whoever he was, never would have carried me to a foundling hospital. They fed me, nursed me back to health, then put me on a train to be placed out. I don't think I knew it then, but I was very lucky. I was adopted by a wonderful family. Mother Yancy taught me to read and run a household.

Father Yancy spoiled me at every opportunity. But he was once a dredger on the Erie Canal . . ." The twinkle drained from her eyes. "He'd contracted a terrible illness. He fought as hard as he could. Two days after he passed on, Mother Yancy was thrown from her horse. She perished later in the night."

It wasn't the outcome he'd expected, and found it quite upsetting to imagine, though he didn't want her to know that and, scarfing down the last of his peaches, he licked his fingers nonchalantly. "What happened then?"

"I was sent to Mortonson, up in Jackson County. I was eight or nine by then, and the head matron told me I was too old to ever be adopted. Yet the very next day, I was 'selected.' The church was filled with young girls. We were instructed to stand on the stage and make ourselves appealing. We were used to being little actresses by then. Some danced or sang hymns. I recited the alphabet, front to back then back to front. He made a grand entrance. I believe he recited Scripture. Then he went around lifting the girls' skirts to make sure their legs were straight. I tried my very best to impress him. But I was dark-skinned and small, and my hair was cut like a boy. When I was chosen, the matrons told me how lucky I was to be selected by the most powerful man in the state." Her expression curdled. "How *lucky*."

It surprised Clayton how easy it was to relate to what burned in her eyes—so easy, in fact, that he became even more uncomfortable. "That is a turn of rotten luck. But you done held yer mud despite that damn son of a gun. And that's somethin."

She didn't seem to be listening. "I *was* lucky," she announced suddenly, the rage washed from her face by a wave of steely resilience. "I was lucky to have experienced love and kindness. To know those things existed. That they are attainable."

Nodding quickly, as if he had the slightest idea of what she was talking about, he attempted to clear the discomfort from his throat. "Well—uh—them Yancys sure sounded like decent folk. I am real sorry for what happened to em."

She sat looking at him, really looking at him, like she had earlier. But this seemed even more intense, as if the full power of the sun were shooting from her eyes. It startled him, yet he was unable to look away, as if she'd captured him in some kind of invisible net. Sadness dragged across her face. "But you weren't, were you."

"What?" he muttered.

"Lucky."

He couldn't speak.

"No," she said. "You weren't lucky at all. Yet here you are, same as me."

There was compassion in her eyes, yet the words made him sick. Her touch startled him. He looked down and found her warm hands covering his. Yanking his hand away, he screeched back from the table.

He could see them in Chicago, in a fine town house enjoying supper together. "Tomorrow, you all is gettin on that train," he said.

She opened her mouth to argue.

He beat his fist on the table. "Yer goin. I'm stayin. You all can be lucky again."

THIRTY-SIX

ELDON WOKE WITH A START, FLIPPING THE TARP BACK FROM his head. The rainwater it had collected splashed down the roof. He pulled himself up by the small white railing. It had been dark only a moment ago; now it was early morning. A cottony fog crept over the neighboring houses. He couldn't even see Commercial Avenue.

Lifting his Winchester, he opened the hatch and clambered down to the second-floor hallway. Ian was sound asleep in his bed. Eldon watched him a moment, then went down to the kitchen and checked that the windows and doors were all still locked. A mantel clock said it was just after six. Stairs creaked. He spun, swinging up the rifle. Minn halted just below the half landing, a hand on her chest as she gasped.

"Sorry," he said, lowering the weapon.

She came into the kitchen and stood at the window. Storm light painted her smooth, weary face.

Seeing her there, he was struck by the possibility of it all. A whole new life. Another try. All he had to do was reach out and grab it. After all, hadn't he a duty to live for Ian? To be a father?

"The station's about a mile from here," he told her.

She stood looking at him, pale light falling across her back. "Then you've decided."

"Roads might still be flooded. We should give ourselves plenty of time. Twelve hours from now, you'll be looking out a window at Chicago while a fish swims out of the faucet."

A smile broke through the exhaustion. "Are you sure they'll be running?"

"Fingers crossed," he said, trying to match her enthusiasm. "Keep an eye out while I wake the boys."

"Eldon," she said with a mix of excitement and trepidation.

He turned at the base of the stairs.

"We'll make it," she said. It was a statement as much as a question, as if she needed him to patch the cracks in her certitude.

He pointed his eyes at the front window, reminding her to keep watch, then turned for the stairs.

He woke Ian, ordering the boy to gather his belongings. Down the hall he knocked on his brother's door. There was no answer and he pushed inside. Clayton was somewhere under his shaggy buffalo coat, one socked foot jutting from the mass of dirty fur. Coughing at the sharp menthol odor, Eldon shook him to little effect. He yanked off the buffalo coat and something fluttered from the pocket and fell at his feet. The envelope was warped and rain-splotched, though he could still make out his name scrawled across the front in Hattie's script. He picked it up and looked at it for a long moment.

"Eldon . . ."

He looked up.

Propped up on an elbow, Clayton squinted from the bed. "Don't," he said.

Eldon looked at the letter and saw his wife's face, raw, tear-streaked, shaking with contempt. It was the night they'd buried the stillborn behind the springhouse. She had wanted to call it Alice if it was a girl. It was. When he promised they would try again, she snorted in disgust. Snot shot from her nostril. When he tried to wipe it clean, she bit the side of his hand.

He opened the letter and read.

The rain was as loud as rifle fire, so loud that it seemed the storm had migrated between his ears. As he emerged from the bedroom, Ian shot past, lugging his bag. At the top of the stairs the boy looked back. "We can't miss the train. Hurry!"

"Be down in a minute," he muttered.

"Where's Uncle Clayton?"

"He'll meet us later."

"Why later?"

"Go help Miss Yancy while I get the horses hitched."

The boy looked at him with big, probing eyes.

Eldon feared that he'd been seen through, but Ian turned suddenly and rattled down the stairs, calling gleefully for Miss Yancy.

The Farmer leaned against the wall, closed his eyes, and thanked his wife. She reminded him that he'd never had a choice, that there was only ever one way to protect his son.

In the crashing rain he hitched the horses then went in through the back door and changed into dry clothes, the wet ones laid out on the floor like a corpse.

He heard Minn and Ian talking as he went down the stairs. He stopped on the landing to listen.

"What will Pa do?" Ian was saying.

"Whatever he chooses," Minn replied. "Open a hard-ware store?"

"Then I can work there."

"You'll be far too busy with school."

"Will we live in a house?"

"Well—"

"You'll live there, right?"

There was a pause. "I was thinking of an apartment. Something with a view."

"Me too! What's the tallest building in Chicago?"

"We'll have to see."

"Can we go to the top of it?"

"The very top."

Eldon went down and handed Minn a bonnet he'd dug out of Myrna's room. She looked at him curiously as she pulled it on. Plum-colored and two sizes too big, it slumped atop her head like rotting fruit.

"Where's Clayton?" she asked.

"He's staying."

Her eyes fell. "Maybe I should speak to him."

"No time," he said, heading for the door. "I'll bring the wagon around to the porch."

She stopped him in the doorway. "Are you all right?"

He nodded and hurried through the door before she could see what was breaking across his face.

The North Springfield passenger station—redbrick, pitched roof, sinewy white trim—rose out of the tinny clatter. The gravel lot was packed with coaches, travelers scampering under the gushing eaves, knocking shoulders as they crammed into the small station house.

Eldon halted his team, jumped down, and dragged their bags out of the wagon bed. As thunder pealed across the sky he scanned the passing faces, every man with his hat pulled low, every woman using a cowl to hide her face.

He hastened Minn and Ian under the gushing eaves, hardly feeling the cold water soak through his clothes, hardly feeling anything at all.

"What about the horses?" said Minn.

He ushered her and Ian inside. "Clayton will pick them up."

Cutting through the pandemonium, he went straight for the ticket line. As he paid for the tickets, he felt her looking at him, and knew that if he looked back, he would give himself away.

They waited in silence by the platform doors until a bell rang and a porter called out the arrival of the seventy-thirty to Chicago.

Rain clattered like buckshot off the ruddled tin roof that sheltered the platform. They stood amid a crowd of soggy voyagers under the gabled overhang as the gun-black locomotive quaked past, screeching to a halt in a squall of black smoke. Porters shuffled from boarding doors, placing footstools on the platform.

Eldon rushed them toward the line for the Pullman car.

"Sparing no expense," Minn commented.

He waved them up the steps, into the car.

The Pullman was luxurious. Plush seating, carpeted flooring, stained wood, polished brass fixtures, a domed roof. After handing Ian their bags, he pointed to their berth. While the boy got situated, Eldon took Minn by the arm into the tight space between cars. He already had the envelope out and placed it in her palm, closing her hand over it. As she looked at the thick wedge of bills peeking from it, her face cracked. When she tried to give the money back, he shoved her hand away. "Take care of my son."

"Wait," she pleaded.

Calls of *all aboard* rang out. A steam whistle screamed. He put a folded note in her hand. "If I don't make it, give it to him."

She looked at the note, mouth agape, then raised her eyes.

He whispered into her good ear. "Buy a wedding band. Never tell anyone you're alone or where you're going. Never use your real name. You're Mrs. Buzzwig. Have the name listed in the city directory. I'll find you if I can." He turned to go.

She grabbed his arm. "Wait," she snapped.

He pressed her against the wall. Her eyes, big and wet, searched his face, just as Shane's had during the gunfight, wanting to believe he was a good man.

He saw himself in a comfortable Chicago home, sitting at a supper table, saying grace with Ian and Minn. He saw the door burst open, two men charging through it. The first man dragged his family into the next room, the second grabbed him by the hair and yanked back his head. A blade scraped across his hairline. Hot blood in his eyes. He looked up at the man peeling back his scalp and saw Jack Foss smiling down at him.

Minn's fingers tightened on his arm.

He couldn't look at her, and cut through a crush of boarding passengers, refusing the awful urge to turn back. His boots hit gravel. He marched up the platform, keeping his eyes down. If he saw Ian in the window, he wouldn't be able to go through with it.

He veered into the station house and elbowed through the crowd. As he passed the washrooms, a hand clamped onto his shoulder, and for a brief moment it felt sympathetic, like some provident force come to guide him. He didn't see the two other men pushing off the wall until they'd already surrounded him. When he tried to twist free of the man who'd grabbed him, the other two seized his arms. They flung him toward the washroom, knocking the door open with his head.

He slumped, knocked for a loop, as they ejected a gawker and locked the door. They wore rumpled overcoats, collars over their ears, hats pulled over their eyes, flashes of metal on their waists. Two were around his age, the third was younger.

One of the older men, hard-nosed and pockmarked, twisted Eldon's arm and slammed his face into the tiled wall, knocking off his hat.

"Where's the girl?" he demanded.

When he didn't answer, the other man, pudgy with a beard the color of the sun, stuck a pistol in his ear. "Speak up."

Eldon spat on his boot. The butt of a pistol crashed into the back of his skull. He slid to his knees, touched his bloodied head. "Mercy," he pleaded. "Have mercy."

His accosters shared a dubious look.

"You sure he's Jack Foss?" said the youngster. "He don't—" The kid gasped and doubled over, clutching his testicles with both hands.

Another fist shot like a piston into the crotch of the bearded one, who joined the youngster in hunched agony.

Eldon jumped to his feet, unlocked the door, and threw it open, smashing the hard-nosed man in the face.

As he stepped out, a dagger pricked his gut. He looked up at the wily dark eyes of a towering old-timer with a gray horseshoe mustache.

"Gentle down or I'll poke you," he said, not even a tickle of malice in his voice, as though he were only giving directions.

A blur of motion and sound passed the platform doors—the train pulling out of the station. Relieved, Eldon raised his palms. "I'm gentle as a one-horned steer."

The old-timer eyed his wounded associates disdainfully. "You all searched him?"

"Ain't got a chance," the hard-nosed man honked, both hands clamped over his gushing nose. The other two stood spraddle-legged, clutching their damaged manhood, and shook their heads.

The old-timer patted Eldon down, took his pistol. "The heck you smiling at?"

Eldon wiped blood from his mouth. "Nothing," he said, shooting a smirk at the old shit-heeler's associates. "Good help is hard to find, is all."

Pulling out a pair of iron fetters, the old-timer grunted a laugh. "You're telling me, sonny." He turned Eldon around, dragged his wrists together.

Feeling strangely at ease, the Farmer let his eyes drift around the station, past the ticket booth, the lunch counter, the platform doors where Minn and Ian stood clutching their chattel. The grin dropped off his face and he flapped his eyelids, trying to wipe the trick out of his eyes. The old-timer's hands were rough on his forearms as he clamped one of the cold metal shackles on to his wrist. Eldon stomped his heel into the old man's boot, spun, and kneed him in the groin.

The youngster lunged, caught an elbow to the throat, and flailed backward into the crowd. Eldon hurled a series of mad haymakers at the other two, striking them with the fetters that hung from his wrist.

Something bit into the back of his head. He fell to his knees. Someone kicked him in the ribs and he fell onto his side, his cheek scraping the gritty tiled floor.

They were hooking his limbs, dragging him to his feet, warning him to be still. When he caught his breath, he started up again, weaker now, but fighting with all he had—anything to keep their attention on him instead of those platform doors.

A boot collided with his temple. His face was on the dirty tiles again. He squinted through a haze of grit and blood. The old-timer stood over him, waving some kind of badge at gaping passengers, ordering them to mind their business.

They dragged him up, his head lolling. One of them tried to pull a sack over his head. He evaded long enough to look at the platform doors. Minn and Ian were gone.

THIRTY-SEVEN

IN THE BEDROOM HE DRESSED IN HIS LEATHERS AND HIS peltry coat, then looked out the silvery window. He saw the
reflection of his rubbled face, streaked and distorted by the
rain, transformed into something rough and scowling and
hateful.

Ye ain't no good, Daddy said. *Afterbirth like you, made of his
brother's leftovers–ain't nothin but useless.*

"Yer wrong," Clayton said, standing his ground.

*Ye think you got the strength to rise up in righteousness and
sacrifice? Ye think you got the manishness to die right?*

He stood, chest heaving. "You don't know what I got."

Nothin that wouldn't cower at the snap of a wet fart.

"Ye don't know what I got, you never did, you never
bothered to look."

*What do I need to know about the goddamn afterbirth? Weak
and useless.*

"I am afterbirth!" he roared, the pane vibrating under
the explosion of his voice. "But that don't make me useless!
That don't make me weak! I can do somethin yet, you'll see.
You'll see."

The only response was the prattle of rain beating against
the hazy ghost of his face. He wiped steam from the glass
and looked down upon the flooded road. A sea of white was

blowing in from the north, from Commercial Avenue, swallowing everything beyond the roundabout in a swirling gulp.

Before Eldon left to take them to the station, he'd said two words—*get ready*—and Clayton knew just what that meant. Thirteen years he'd dreamt of renewing their covenant. The first time they rode together as the Outlaw, they were fifteen years old. They'd camped on a stretch of woodland train tracks that curved around a limestone quarry filled with rainwater. Blackflies were out in force, chewing them to bits, buzzing so furiously that they almost couldn't hear the train. Eldon had put his ear to the track, calm as a windless lake, while Clayton was sick with nerves as he piled quarry stones across the ties. It had all seemed so exciting when they were buying matching getups and matching guns with money from the judge's silver. When it came time for the raid, he couldn't stop his hands from shaking. The actual robbery was a blur. Days later, Eldon showed him the clippings. The newspapers spoke of an outlaw, young, handsome, and vicious, called Jack Foss, scourge of the railroads, who witnesses claimed had the uncanny power to be in two places at once.

It would be their claim to infamy and their curse of ruination, though at the time it never seemed like they had any choice but an outlaw life. They were taking back what was took. No rules. But he had a choice now. And he chose to do right for his descendants, to leave evil behind.

Nurse Daye had been right all along, hadn't she. There was meaning to everything. In the rain, in a rifle, in a wooden leg. It was a shame he hadn't seen it before now. But getting to the end of something was often the only way to understand what brought you there in the first place.

Eldon had been gone most of an hour already, but the station was only a mile away. Maybe he was lost in the fog. Or maybe he got on that train after all. Maybe he was on it right now, watching it all blow past. Just twelve hours from the granite and marble towers of Chicago. Knowing Eldon, they'd have a place to live by the end of the week. A supper table where they could tell each other about their day, about what made them sad or happy. Ian would grow up far from the land that had only sorrow to give him. He would go to a good school. Minn would teach there and be headmistress in no time. Eldon would open a livery stable. Now, wouldn't that be something? Wasting the days feeding horses and weeding out their tails and raking out their stalls.

He turned from the window, hoping that was how it would go. On the bed lay his brother's Winchester. He had already cleaned and loaded it, asking God to bless each cartridge as it snapped into the tube. He dragged the carpetbag from under the bed, then lifted out Magdalena's peg leg and set it on the bed next to the rifle. It brought a smile to his lips as he thought about seeing her again, getting a ticket to the show.

There were loose cartridges in the bag and he scrounged them up and stuffed them into a leather pouch. He tied the pouch to his belt loop, then shoved what remained into the pockets of his trousers. When he was done, he went back to the window and looked up the road and saw nothing but seething white.

When he turned again, Magdalena's leg was staring at him, judging him, wondering if he was strong enough to do what was needed. With shaky fingers he traced the colorful designs: manticores, centaurs, griffins—*monsters of goodness*, as she had once called them. Wrapping both hands around the tapered end, he lifted the peg leg into the iron light and swung it through the air. He felt her power coursing through him.

Something out the window caught his eye. He traded the leg for the Winchester. A dark shape was racing toward the house. He flung open the window and took aim. The four horses pulling the tented wagon came fast into the round-about, throwing curtains of mud. Minn held the reins, long black hair swishing side to side, Ian's freckled face veering up to the second-floor window.

Clayton slung the rifle over his shoulder, shuffled down-stairs. He stepped out onto the front porch as the wagon sluiced alongside the house.

Minn set the brake, then she and Ian hopped down, their mud-splattered faces tied in knots. "They took him," she said breathlessly.

He brought them inside. While Ian dried off, she filled Clayton in on the details. After they had accosted Eldon, she'd followed the bounty hunters to the Public Square and had watched them drag him into a dark saloon.

"I want to go with you," said Ian.

Clayton took him by the shoulder. "Not this time, Turnspit. Yer job's to stay here and protect Miss Yancy." He said to Minn, "You got that Model 3 and that money?"

She patted her dress pocket.

He gave her a handful of extra shells, asking God to bless them, too. "Take two horses from the wagon. Ride one, tail the other behind. Yer taking a straight shot over the creek and across the fields. You'll pass through the orchards, and just before ye hit that line of forest you'll see a road. Take it south. First town you come to is Spartanville. There's an inn run by a man called Dobney. If it ain't him, it'll be his son, also called Dobney. Tell em yer with Mr. Buzzwig. They will give you a room. Eldon will meet you there tonight. Understand me? Tonight."

Ian was staring up at him. He ran a hand through the boy's feathery blond hair, then took his face between his palms.

"You will see your father tonight," he promised.

Aboard his brother's paint, he rode all out against the earth-battering rains, from the outskirts of the city, through three feet of mud and drowning earthworms, over downed telegraph wires and floating livestock, to the canyons of downtown, where the only people braving the elements were trying to save their homes or businesses from the flood.

The Public Square had been reduced to a brown lake, the surrounding buildings hardly a shadow in the thrashed atmosphere. The saloon Minn spoke of stood cater cornered to a dry goods store. There wasn't a soul out on the plaza, not that he could see. The wind was cold and his hands shook. His stomach churned just as it had before that first train robbery twenty years ago. He felt like a tyro about to air his paunch.

He tied the paint under the eaves of the store and stood at the corner of the covered boardwalk. Dun-colored water lapped at his knees as he surveyed the saloon. The big window at the front was washed over with steam and he couldn't see through it. He ducked into a side alley, thinking there would be a back door.

At the back of the building he peered around the corner into a fenced lot littered with bags of refuse and old chairs. A small square portico hung over a heavy back door lined with metal strapping. Sheets of rainwater poured over the sides of the portico and Clayton didn't notice the man standing under the roof until he heard him cough. A cherry brightened and a puff of smoke emerged. There was another cough, like it was the man's first time smoking.

From the corner he crept along wet brick toward the smoking man. Then he reached through the falling water, grabbed his collar, and flung him into the trash heap. He put his pistol in his face. It wasn't a man, just a terrified kid of fifteen or sixteen.

"P-please," the kid sputtered, palms covering his face, rain drowning his eyes. "Don't shoot!"

"Shut up," said Clayton.

He reached down and relieved the kid of a rusty dragoon revolver. The kid looked familiar to him, though maybe it was only the terror in his gaze that he recognized, the terror he'd seen in Shane's eyes just after he'd been shot, the terror he'd seen a hundred times over.

"How many more's inside?"

Blinking and wiping his eyes, the kid looked up, awe-struck by the face staring down at him. "But you . . . you was just inside. You was shackled to the—"

"How many more?"

"T-two," he stammered.

"Which one's the leader?"

"Big Ricky. Well, Janko pretends he is, but it's Big Ricky."

He dragged the kid to his feet and pointed at the back door. "Go yell fer Big Ricky to get his big ass out here."

"You ain't gonna shoot me?"

"Long as ye don't do nothin dumb."

The kid trudged over to the door, opened it, and shouted down a dark hallway. "Big Rick! Hey, Big Rick, you best get out here!"

Clayton hurled him toward the alleyway. "Now git," he said, and the boy splashed off around the corner.

Flattened against the wet bricks near the back door, he heard slow, heavy footsteps approaching. The door opened. When an old-timer with a horseshoe mustache poked his head out, his nose bumped into the muzzle of the .44 rimfire.

"Hands where I can see," said Clayton. "Turn around."

The man stared, dumbstruck. "What in the Sam Hill."

"Turn around," Clayton said, pressing the barrel to the old man's head. This time he obeyed. Clayton took possession of his twin Schofields, then nudged the old-timer through the door with his gun.

He trailed the man down a dark, paneled hallway, past a water closet and a galley kitchen, and stopped him at the entrance to a vaulted barroom bathed in gray from the big plate-glass window. The air smelled of burnt hair and seared flesh. Clayton shoved the man into the big room, a gun at his back.

Against the far wall, Eldon sat on the floor, naked from the waist up, both arms chained behind him to the leg of a roaring potbelly stove. A pockmarked man in a floppy brown hat was standing over him. He stomped his boot into Eldon's chest, pushing his back against the hot metal stove.

"Where's she at?" he demanded as Eldon howled and flailed.

"Hey," said Clayton.

The pockmarked man looked up and lost the top of his head.

"Son of a bitch," croaked the old-timer as his companion fell dead. Bits of the man's brains began to sizzle on the side of the potbelly stove.

Clayton scanned the saloon for other targets, looking over the six round tables stacked with upturned chairs. He checked behind the bar and in the wash closet. When he was satisfied that no one else was there, he went to tend to his brother. Slumped forward, Eldon's back was raw, the outline of the stove grate branded into his back. Blisters were forming, some as big as an apple, and he was moaning, half conscious.

Clayton shoved the old-timer at him. "Unchain me from that stove."

The man took a ring of keys from the shirt pocket of his dead companion and unlocked the fetters. Eldon collapsed sideways across the floor. He was covered in blood and for a second Clayton thought of the day he'd ridden into that Indian camp, just Eldon, his rifle, and a tomahawk he'd taken from a dead Indian at Birch Coulee. When he came back, it was as if he'd taken a bath in a stew of blood and chopped entrails.

"Now lock yerself up to that stove," said Clayton. "Today's yer lucky, old—"

The front door blew open, wind and rain shooting into the barroom. A bearded man stomped inside, turning to hold the door. The imp came in after, slapping rainwater off his white bowler. He was chuckling to himself and his demented eyes twinkled as if he'd just heard a cruel joke. Then he looked up and stopped abruptly, puzzled by the bloody corpse sprawled across the floor of the saloon. Only the hard drum of rain and the shriek of the wind persisted against the silence.

Clayton shot the old-timer in the neck, then turned both pistols on the imp and the bearded man and shot from the hip. The bearded man crashed across a tabletop, scattering chairs. When he stood up, he reached for his face. His chin was gone, his tongue hanging down like a short bloated necktie. Clayton emptied one pistol into him, then focused on the imp, who darted across the room, firing as he ducked behind an overturned table.

A bullet snagged Clayton's side, just under the right arm. He could hardly move, but he thought of Magdalena's face, carved to the bone, and stalked forward, blood sweating down his right flank as he blew holes in the top of the overturned table. One of his bullets shattered the huge, steamy plate-glass window. Glass fell like water, wind and rain exploding into the barroom.

The imp shot out from behind the overturned table and leapt through the window, vanishing into the storm. Limping across broken glass, Clayton shielded his eyes against the bedlam. There was nothing beyond the window. The maelstrom of wind and rain had swallowed the square. Standing before the dark, windy portal, he thought this must be what Death looks like when it comes.

THIRTY-EIGHT

To Eldon, the buildings lining the opposite side of the plaza looked like huge tombstones waiting to be carved. There wasn't a soul visible in the steely deluge, yet there might be a dozen rifles pointed his way and he wouldn't have a clue. His back burned intolerably under his shirt. He had to get beyond the pain, or it would sap what strength he had left.

He'd tried to listen to what Clayton was saying about his son and Minn getting on a horse, heading for Spartanville, to their old friend, a soldier turned innkeeper called Dobney, but the words were hardly squeezing past the pulse of pain in his ears. Such pain wasn't new to him. Daddy used to hold his feet to the fire when he did something bad, and he wouldn't be able to walk straight until the blisters dried out.

What he had to do was let Jack Foss ride out of that boiling plaza and leave Farmer Eldon Quint behind.

His paint waited under the eave across the alley, ears twitching. Clayton fetched the horse and helped Eldon swing into the wet saddle. They kept to the rim of the plaza, out of the boiling mud, then rode northeast. The roads were flooded and the only people they saw were two men and an old woman trying to free an overturned cart. Their donkey had already drowned and they were cutting him from the traces.

When finally they sloshed out of the boarded-up store-fronts of Commercial Avenue onto Peach Alley Place, the floodwater was to the horse's belly, the road a lapping brown waterway. In the distance they could hardly see Myrna's house.

As they went on, he scanned the neighboring houses. A dampish glow came from a few of the windows, smoke breaking from the chimney pots.

They forded the muddy roundabout and found that Myrna's house hadn't yet flooded. Eldon saw his wagon along the side of the house, three horses in their traces. Clayton had promised that Minn and Ian would be halfway to Spartanville by now, but it appeared they hadn't gone anywhere.

He slid off the horse, mud sucking at his boots as he crossed the yard. He bounded up the porch, pistol out, and pushed into the house. Muddy tracks ran down the hall to the back door. He followed them out to the porch, where they vanished in the backyard. When he slipped going down the steps, a hand caught him. Clayton held him by the jacket. He nodded that he was all right, then shambled into the yard.

Floodwater was starting to wash down the hill. He scanned the yard. At the bottom of the hill, among the wind-stripped trees, a small figure waded in the rushing stream. It was Minn. She was looking for something.

He realized Clayton was still holding on to his jacket. He tore free and started down the hill, hollering as he went, trying to keep his footing in the slick mud. Minn came out of the water. Lifting the sodden bell of her dress, she began running up the hill toward him. His feet were hardly moving, mud sucking at his boots, trying to stop him from finding his son. They met on the slope. She was gasping, soaked to the bone.

"He wouldn't leave without you," she said, her teeth chattering. "I turned my back for a second and . . ."

Clayton's voice turned their heads. He was down the creek a few paces, pointing at a coat splayed across the thin branches like a spatchcock fowl—Ian's coat.

Eldon ran full speed into the raging waters. Cold surged around him, water the color of drinking chocolate. He plunged his arms into the depths, grasping at stones and twigs and dead leaves, until the feeling left his hands, leaving them dead and rubbery. Suddenly he couldn't stand against the current and lost his footing. He went under, water shooting up his nose. His arms flailed but he couldn't find the surface.

Something tugged on his collar. His head broke out of the water. He wanted to scream for Ian, but there was only mud in his lungs. Clayton heaved him onto the shore. He lay on his stomach, coughing into the muck, then got his legs under him. Clayton tried to help him up but Eldon swatted him away.

Then, over the rain, he heard the boy's voice. He was back at the house, calling for him. He ran up the hill and shouldered through the back door.

In the hallway he called for Ian and heard him screaming out front.

He pushed out the front door, stepped onto the porch, and stood looking at the steaming passel staring back at him. The dead world hummed to life. Rain sizzled in his ears, and he felt every drop that hit him.

In the middle of the roundabout, six men in big hats and black dusters sat on shaggy horses, staring at him with the unscrupulous gaze of men who kill for money.

The middle horses parted and the imp shuffled out on foot, nostrils pulsing, his face locked in a snarl. His right arm was tight across Ian's neck. The boy's lips were pressed flat, holding in a cry. He was trying not to look afraid. But it was all right to be afraid, all right to be kind. He wouldn't have to wear that hard bark like they did. He could be sure of that.

Eldon crashed down the steps into the front yard, reaching for his guns.

The imp's knife wiggled across Ian's throat, just enough pressure to dent the skin. "Hold it," he said.

Eldon stopped at the edge of the roundabout, hands hovering over his guns.

"Send out that garboon cunny," snarled the imp. "Or I'll take off his fuckin head."

But Eldon hardly heard him. He was looking into his son's deep green eyes, like two signal fires that pleaded *don't let me end up like Shane.*

Then all at once the guns pointing at him swiped up, and from behind Eldon came the sound of a rifle being levered. He didn't have to turn around to know the sound of his own Winchester.

"Behind ye," he heard Clayton say.

The porch creaked as the Outlaw walked to the top of the steps. Eldon glanced over his shoulder, saw that the rifle was aimed at the imp's white bowler.

"Take that knife off his throat," Clayton demanded.

The imp's blade, rain-beaded and glistening in the drab light, stiffened against Ian's neck. "Bring her out," he said. "We trade. Straight up. Him for her."

The ground began to tremble. Eight heads turned at once.

Up the road something big was forming in the fog. But the Farmer kept his eyes on his son, so the boy knew that he was protected, despite what was lumbering out of the storm.

THIRTY-NINE

BIG SOGGY FEATHERS WAGGED OUT OF THE CLOUDBURST. Eight parade horses charged up the road, the green stage-coach throwing waves of brown, unhindered by the flood. Trailing the coach, a half dozen Indians in colorful dresses rode mules and carried rifles and torches. Eldon watched the bulky coach halt at the top of the roundabout, the Indians lining up in front of the animal heads decorating its exterior. Eldon counted seven hired guns, six Indians, one coachman, and the man himself inside that carriage.

Fifteen men to kill.

The coachman leapt down from his seat and slogged past the snarling trophy heads. When he reached the carriage door, he kicked down the brass stepladder and opened a huge purple umbrella that he struggled to hold upright in the wind.

A freshly severed human head graced the door of the coach. It belonged to one of the Major's trusted Indian guards. Perhaps he had defied an order. Now his long black hair hung down from his warped face, his braids dragged in the mud.

The sight of it shook Eldon as much as anything ever had, taking him back to that place of terror, before he'd seen the bloodied fields and severed limbs.

A thought crossed his mind. What if everything after Birch Coulee was a dream? What if he was just waiting to wake up back on that battlefield, his whole life ahead of him? He could do it right this time.

The door flung open, slapping the dead Indian's long black hair against a wagon wheel. The Major seemed to grow out of his transport. Three of the Indians wheeled their mules and formed a protective wall around him. Raindrops clattered off the big umbrella the coachman struggled to keep steady over his head. The Major stood looking from the Farmer to the Outlaw, then back to the Farmer.

"Well, that does explain it," he said. "Two brothers, one outlaw. Brilliant!" He turned and raised his big pink clapping hands and the Indians began to clap as well.

The hired guns looked on, eyes hidden under the brims of their hats, gloved fingers tapping on their triggers.

"They got her inside," the imp said, impatiently bobbing from side to side, his eyes, lips, and nostrils twitching in a strange pattern, while his knife hovered just below Ian's throat.

The boy cried softly. He was tired and cold, his lips blue.

Eldon's eyes slid from the Major, to the Indians, to the hired guns, and finally to the imp and his son. Just then a gush of floodwater flowed down from the top of the road. It sloshed into the roundabout, climbing around Ian's waist, forcing the imp to steady him. The wave slowed as it neared the house and lapped against Eldon's boots. He looked at his son, only thirty paces away though it seemed like miles. The boy was drawing jagged, choppy breaths, his mouth struggling to open and close just as Shane's had in his last moments, when he reached desperately for air before his lips went still.

"Think of the stream," he hollered to him. "When you think you're done, you're really only halfway there."

Ian's big unblinking eyes were locked on him. His jaw stopped rattling and his lips went flat and grim. The last of his innocence fell from his face like stone chiseled from a statue.

"Know what we have here, Mr. Brusco?" the Major was saying with his usual flare and bombast. "Romulus and Remus! Though I can assure you—these twins shall establish no great city such as Rome. Though I imagine we might bury them under one."

He waved his pink hand, parting the mounted Indians who guarded him. Taking a big step between the mules, he strode across the roundabout through rising water. He stopped ten paces short of the steps, where Eldon stood, a father with his hands hovering an inch from his pistols.

The Major smiled at him, showing his vulcanite dentures, big, ugly, bone-colored bricks. "I promise you, Farmer," he said. "No harm shall come to your child should you release my daughter this instant."

Eldon flicked his eyes at the imp. "Get that knife off my boy's throat."

"Afraid not," the Major said with a sigh. "I know we are men of the Fifth, but you and your simpleton of a brother have spent up the last of my patience. You have till the count of five to comply, and for every second you delay, Mr. Brusco will sever a portion of your son, starting with his thumbs." He began to count. "Five . . . four . . ."

The imp threw Ian facedown in the mud, twisted one of his arms back, forced the hand open, and pressed his blade to Ian's thumb joint.

". . . three . . ."

Eldon drew so fast, the guns might have been in his hands all along. One barrel pointed at the imp, the other at the Major, no choice but to leave it up to God and hope his bullets might wipe his sins clean.

The arithmetic of his violence was interrupted by the creak of the front door. Minn crossed the porch and walked down the stairs, past Clayton, into the pelting rain. She marched past Eldon, holding something he didn't get a good look at. At the edge of the roundabout, a few paces from the Major, she halted, long black hair slicked down her back, her chest heaving under her rain-soaked dress.

The giant's blue eyes oozed at her presence. He threw open his arms as if the promise of his embrace might reel her in. When it didn't, he capered forth, singing: "*A kiss forgives everything, a kiss makes us clean, a kiss for every room in the house . . .*"

Her hand swiped up holding what Eldon hadn't been able to see—but he saw it now, the rain-beaded nickel of his Model 3. But Minn wasn't pointing the gun at the Major like he'd expected.

"Don't!" the Major yawped suddenly, withering into his ostrich-skin boots.

With small, careful steps, Eldon edged up beside her, his guns still locked on the imp and the Major. She was pointing the pistol at her own belly, the barrel denting a small bump hardly visible through the wet rumpled cotton of her dress.

FORTY

THE MAJOR STAGGERED AT THE SIGHT OF THE GUN PRESSED to her belly and threw up his hands in such a ridiculous fashion that he seemed like a child who hadn't gotten his way. But his human guise of gawky ringmaster could not mask the venal beast that lusted for what grew in Minn's belly. He took a big, unsteady step toward her. She put her finger on the trigger and he shrieked. He began to shake all over, his eyes rolling back into his head.

The coachman dropped the umbrella as he tried to hold the giant upright. Three Indians slid off their mules and rushed through belly-high water to prop up the Major. The coachman cracked a glass vial under his nose. The giant huffed until his eyes opened and he was steady on his feet again. He straightened his tall black beaver hat, then faced Minn, hands clasped behind his back, trying to smile.

"Please," he said plaintively. "Put that silly instrument down."

"Let him go," she said, cocking the hammer.

Even over the rain, the click was heard by all.

The Major pointed at her. "Put it down this instant," he cried.

There was a wildness in her eyes. "It's your sin," she said, "but it's my baby."

The Major must have recognized her resolve, for his demeanor faltered. "Please just put it down!"

"Let him go!" she screamed. "Right now!"

The giant looked stunned, as if for the first time in his life he had no control.

She began to count. "Five . . . four . . ."

He screamed at the imp. "Let him go!"

". . . three . . ."

"Major!" the imp argued, his gouged, waxy face twitching madly.

". . . two . . ."

". . . one."

The imp shoved Ian face-first into the muck. The boy scrambled to his feet and charged through the purling flood-water. When he reached Eldon, he threw his arms around his waist and held on to him like he was bracing for a tornado. More than anything, Eldon wanted to hug him back, to have his head resting on his shoulder, to smell the grass in his hair—but he couldn't do it, couldn't lower the guns, not yet.

"Go into the house," he told the boy. "Get in the tub upstairs and stay there until I come get you."

Ian looked worriedly at Minn, but she didn't seem to see him.

"I'll come get you," said Eldon. "Me or your uncle. Now go."

The boy looked at her a moment longer. Then let go of his father, darted up the porch steps past Clayton, and vanished into the house.

Minn was still holding the gun to her belly. Though her body shook with cold, her eyes were steady on the Major. Eldon found himself staring at the gun in her hand, Harlan

Scrim's gun, wondering how it had ended up there. It seemed to make no sense, yet at the same time it felt preordained, as if that gun's true purpose was only now realized.

The Major looked at Minn, weeping softly, though the tears seemed only for show. As if to try something else, he became like a sickly old man trapped in the body of an oversized baby, hoping that might leach her sympathy. He opened his long, shaky arms to her and his jaw slackened. "I've done as you asked," he said. "Now please, put down that silly instrument and let me feel the touch of my son."

She spoke through a clenched jaw, but her words came sober and resolute. "It helps me to believe in God," she said, "knowing that after all these years, all those trips to that godforsaken playroom with all the unsuspecting girls, and still to this day He denies you a son. And if you do not leave here this instant, I shall do the same."

"Winifred!" he cried, stumbling at her. "Put it down, I beg you!"

Her arm flung outward suddenly, as if possessed, and the bullet slipped so easily from the gun, her face hardly blinking at the report as it rang off the raindrops. A comet punched into the Major's bloated green belly. He fell to one knee, clutching his gut. The blood pushed through his fingers as gun smoke fled her barrel like an excised ghost.

The Major's head flung back and he cried with the full force of his vocal cords. "DO NOT SHOOT!"

The order was obeyed despite the whoops of the Indians and the vaporings of the whites eyeing each other in dismay. The coachman and two Indians grabbed the Major while the rest of the men closed their mules around him.

The Major shouted a warning. "Any man shoots at my child, I will have your head nailed to the front of my coach!"

The hired guns were looking at the imp for an order while the Indians were getting the Major into his coach. Minn stepped in front of Eldon, spreading her body before his like a shield. Pressed against her back, he kept his pistols aimed over her shoulders. They backed up to the porch steps. He felt Clayton's hand on his shoulder, guiding him, and the three of them moved in unison up the steps and across the porch.

When they were all inside the hall, Eldon kicked the door shut and twisted the lock. The small click of the lock seemed like such insufficient protection against what would be coming. He had to get Minn and Ian to the back and on a horse. Clayton was already bounding up the stairs, calling for Ian. Eldon followed slowly. His wounds had made him weak. He steadied himself on the banister. When he looked up, his brother was coming around the half landing, holding Ian in one arm.

He lurched down the hall, waving them to the back door. He went through first and scanned the porch. He went to the edge of the steps, looked east, then west. Seeing no sign of Indians or hired guns, he signaled Clayton, who hustled Ian and Minn out the door. "Stay here," Eldon told him. "I'll get the horse."

He tramped to the eastern corner of the house and peeked around the corner at his wagon. The horses nickered and stamped. Beyond them, the Indians were on their mules watching the coachman furiously whip the horses. The Major's coach didn't budge, trapped by the high water and mud.

Chips of stone exploded in Eldon's face. Another bullet punched off the foundation. A man rode out of the trees firing at him from a shaggy horse. Eldon felt his side open up. He fired back, a single shot that opened a third eye in the rider's forehead. The man fell out of the saddle, but the horse kept charging toward Eldon. As he moved to catch the reins it was hard to lift his right arm, so he caught the reins with his left hand.

Blood slicked down his side as he jogged the animal through the rising water to the back porch, where Clayton stood guarding Minn and Ian with the rifle. Minn charged down the steps and helped Eldon steady the animal, Clayton and Ian following behind. Eldon gave Minn a leg up and she swung onto the horse and took control of the reins. He turned to lift Ian aboard, but a crippling pain ripped down the side of his body. Minn offered a hand and together they got the boy seated in front of her.

Eldon told his brother, "Get upstairs, get on that widow's walk."

Clayton slung the Winchester off his shoulder. "When I git up there, you board that other horse and foller after em."

Eldon nodded, even though he would do no such thing.

When Clayton was inside, Eldon looked downhill, toward the patchwork of flooded fields, the stubble of orchard trees beyond, and finally the dark line of forest. "You remember how to go to Dobney's?"

Minn nodded.

Ian stared at the blood dripping down the side of Eldon's pants. "But, Pa, I don't want you to die."

Eldon reached into his pocket and put something in the boy's palm and then closed his fingers around it. He kissed his son's hand, then hugged him, pressing his grizzled cheek against Ian's chest, needing to hear that little heart beating, the breath going in and out of his lungs, the blood flowing through his veins, and all the promises of youth.

Ian looked at what was in his hand. The red carnelian stone shimmered in the rain. For a second Eldon felt the warmth of a campfire on his face as the stone seemed to brighten everything around him.

"I'll be right behind you," he said. Then he slapped the horse and watched them shoot down the hill.

It was the last lie he'd ever tell.

FORTY-ONE

CLAYTON POUNDED UP THE STAIRS, ROUNDED THE HALF landing, and hopped the last two steps to the second-floor hall. The pain of his bullet-smashed ribs had been erased by the anticipation that Eldon, Ian, and Minn would make it out, and that whatever spirit he possessed would live on with his brother and the family he would make.

As he headed for the pull-down ladder at the end of the hall, a clamor of footsteps turned his head. A snarling creature was charging from one of the dark bedrooms, big red nostrils flaring over a black rake of a mustache, the blink of a knife in the reddish light seeping through the stained glass.

Before Clayton could raise his rifle, a blade slid into his side, glancing off his ribs. He grimaced as steel scraped bone, but he managed to grab the imp's wrist and slammed the wiry man into the wall. The imp staggered back, but brandished the knife, feinting and lunging. This time Clayton grabbed him by the shirtfront and hurled him over the side of the railing. The imp bounced off the wall, then fell straight down on his back across the staircase. Instantly he was back on his feet, racing around the landing, his big bloody knife leading the way.

Clayton turned into the back bedroom. Light from the storm-beaten window streaked across the bed, across

Magdalena's wooden leg. The imp came low and fast through the door behind him. Clayton reached for the peg leg. He swung backhanded with as much force as he could muster. The peg leg connected with the imp's chin. His head slammed into the wall and he fell in a heap.

Clayton stood heaving. Then he used his boot to roll the little man onto his back. The imp's eyelids twitched and his nostrils bubbled with blood.

The air smelled faintly of orange blossom and rosewater, and Clayton could almost feel her fiery coils of hair settling against his chest, the mossy sweetness of her breath. He raised the heavy wooden prosthetic and swung with all he had left, crushing the imp's face. But the imp wheezed, still trying to bring oxygen through the pulpy strands of his lips. Clayton swung again and again, until the monsters painted on the wooden leg became a brilliant rainbow.

He lurched out of the bedroom holding the bloody prosthetic, and he collected his Winchester at the top of the stairs. Then he went to the end of the hall and pulled down the ladder. Stuffing the blood-slicked peg leg into the pocket of his coat, he climbed up, one arm hanging limp. When he pushed open the hatch, a bucket's worth of freezing water dumped over his hat. He stuck his head out, rain coming sideways into his eyes. His black bolero blew off. With his good arm he dragged himself onto the black rectangle and grabbed his hat just before it blew through the rails of the low white fence.

He crouched at the southwestern corner and set his hat on the ground, stepping on the brim to keep it from blowing away. Peering through the rails, he saw no one in the backyard.

A distant whinny, barely audible in the rain, dragged his attention down the hill. Minn and Ian were on the horse, swimming across the rushing creek. They were almost to the other side. As he searched for Eldon, there was a loud flump down below. He craned over the top railing. Two Indians carrying empty rum jugs staggered around the side of the house, followed by a white man carrying a torch.

Smoke billowed over the edge of the roof.

They were trying to burn him out.

Clayton fired at the white man twice. A third bullet killed him.

One Indian dropped his jug and ran while the other Indian fired back.

Clayton ducked, then heard two rifle shots. When he looked over the rail, the Indian was facedown in the mud. It must have been Eldon down there, but the wind had picked up and plumes of smoke burned his eyes.

He heard something and looked to his right. A man on horseback came loping around the western side of the house. For a moment he thought it was Eldon, but the man was a clumsy rider. With the barrel between the fence rails, Clayton tracked the hired gun as he turned down the hill and splashed into the fast-moving stream.

On the opposite bank, Minn and Ian were lurching out of the high water, their horse stumbling through the bunchgrass. She kicked the animal wildly toward the distant blockade of forest. Clayton had never seen a woman run a horse like that in his life.

It was all on him to keep them safe, to make certain that Ian was the first Quint to break the chain. It had never been on him to do anything before, but now that it was, he found his hands had never been so steady, and never had he breathed so calmly or been so assured in his own power. Not even Daddy could sway his resolve.

The shot blew out the rider's back.

He fell from the horse and was washed away in the current.

Clayton reached into his pouch of cartridges. The brass casings were slick with rainwater and blood. As he crammed rounds into the tube he looked south across the fields. Smoke whipped over the roof, blotting his view. He stood up, wiping soot from his eyes.

Minn and Ian were now in the middle of the field, galloping toward the orchard.

Clayton swung his rifle around to the front of the house.

The Major's stagecoach was stuck at the top of the roundabout, the flood rushing around it. Three or four Indians were off their mules, wading in chest-high muck, dodging big branches that rushed down from Commercial Avenue. The coachman stood on top of the coach, whipping the parade horses. Clayton rubbed the smoke from his eyes, then put the watery blot in the notch of his gunsight and fired.

Pieces of the coachman's head slid down the side of his gown.

Clayton turned back to the rain-beaten fields.

Minn and Ian had reached the orchards. He could hardly see them.

Flames licked over the roof and he stepped back, the fire shriveling the stubble on his face. He swung his rifle to the front of the house. The Indians were swimming against the current. Two of the mules had drowned and were caught up in the neighbor's trees. Waves swept down from Commercial Avenue, taking whole trees with them now. Clayton's eyes watered from the smoke. Everything seemed to be melting away.

Turning back to the fields, he squinted in the heat, trying to see Minn and Ian through the smoke and fire. A bullet hit the roof just below Clayton's foot. As he crouched, looking for its source, another shot snapped the railing in two. Smoke and heat blasted his face. Bullets sang past his ears.

He sprawled, covering his head, the waves of fire sweeping up the roof toward him. A bullet sliced down the side of his leg.

The smoke cleared with a gust of wind. Through a line of trees, he saw two men on the roof of the neighbor's porch, an Indian and a white man, crouched thirty yards away. The Indian let off a shot, splitting open Clayton's shoulder. Clayton shot back four times, so rapidly that it sounded like one long blast. The Indian's head opened like a rose. The white man pressed up. Three bullets blasted him in the gut and he rolled over the side of the roof and slapped facedown on the stone steps below.

Clayton turned on his belly to look for Minn and Ian. His body shook violently. He pushed up on an elbow and forced himself to squint through the rails. When he spotted them they were so small in the distance, he could no longer tell there were two riders on the horse.

Smoke clawed at his eyes, blistering waves of heat coming with each gust of wind. He found his hat and used it to shield his face. He kept his eyes on the tiny watery blot moving among crooked trees, so close to the forest, so close to being safe. When the smoke blocked his view, he reached for the top rail, and even though the paint was bubbling he dragged himself up and looked between the flames. Nothing moved in the orchard but the tops of the trees.

He dragged the buffalo coat over his body as the flames rushed in around him. He could hardly breathe, hardly see through his raw, dripping eyes, but for a moment it was warm and dark and damp under there. For a moment he could hear singing. For a moment Momma's heart was beating all around him.

FORTY-TWO

ELDON ONLY WANTED TO SIT DOWN, JUST FOR A MOMENT. Minn and Ian were almost across the creek and the porch steps were right there. He just needed a rest before he went to finish the Major. The rain felt so cool and cleansing. He fought the urge to close his eyes. Then he heard men on horseback coming for his child and fired both pistols at the passing shadows. He punched the ghost out of three or four of them. Clayton's rifle cracked from the top of the house and two more riders fell. But now the darkness was creeping over him again. Overhead, the roof crawled with flames, paint blistering. He tried to stand. His ribs felt as if they'd been chopped by an ax. Grabbing the railing, he pulled himself to his feet, stumbling into the backyard.

He looked for Clayton up on the widow's walk, but the roof was churned with black smoke. Maybe he'd gotten out.

Floodwater rushed around him, the current strong and cold against his thighs. Uprooted shrubs and pieces of broken timber whipped around the sides of the house, crashing into the raging stream down below.

A half-burned animal pelt floated past. It was Clayton's buffalo coat.

He watched it slide down the hill, swallowed into the churning crush of water and debris. Looking into the middle distance, he searched for his son and Minn. Waves of rain billowed across the fields. He thought he caught something moving in the orchards. All that was left for him to do was make certain the Major could never hurt them again.

He had one pistol on him and two cartridges left. Trudging along the back of the house, he came to the eastern corner. A dead mule floated by, vanishing down the hill. Water rushed around his waist. Bracing against the current, he looked up the side of the house, past his wagon. All three of his horses were dead.

The Major's stagecoach sat like a drowned beetle across the road, waves breaking around it. Perched on the top was a man with a rifle. Eldon steadied his shooting arm against the side of the house. He fired and the man fell into the water. The current took him and he floated past the house. Eldon could have finished him off, but he needed the last bullet for the Major.

Fighting the current, he started toward the coach, dodging branches and shattered pieces of lumber as they swept past. A wave hit his chest and he went under, inhaling a big gulp of brown water. He could almost hear the Major's heart beating inside that green coach. He surfaced, sputtering, trying to get his boots back on the bottom. Freeing himself from his coat, he swam with his one good arm, hardly making progress against the current.

There was something bobbing ahead and he reached desperately and felt bristly hair and feathers. It was one of the parade horses floating sideways. He dragged himself along the body, got hold of the harness, and rested for a moment. When he looked again at the stagecoach, the animal heads seemed to be daring him to keep coming.

Pulling himself along the traces, he worked his way down the sidewall until he reached the coach door. He grabbed the handle and swung open the door and looked into the big, cavernous interior. It was dark and smelled of ether. The walls were decorated with hideous orange felt.

Two small pops came from the blackness, like a child's fireworks. Eldon spun from the opening, a hand going to his side where one of the rounds had bitten him. He swung his good arm around the door frame to keep from being swept away, latched his boot to the stepladder, and raised his pistol.

The Major lunged from the murk. Eldon fired his one and only bullet, striking him in the chest. The giant toppled sideways, landing just before the open door like a slain dragon. He was facing away, but Eldon could see he was still breathing, raspy and labored, his back fluttering up and down.

A revolver lay on the floor near the Major's twitching pink hand. Slowly, Eldon reached for it, keeping his eyes on the green beast. He checked the cylinder. Four shots remained. He closed the cylinder and took aim at the Major's bell of gossamer hair.

"Think about it," came the Major's voice, hardly a whisper over the rain. His big head turned and his hard blue eyes flashed up. As he spoke, blood bubbled from his mouth. "With the bounty I put on your head—a bounty to be serviced whether I am dead or alive—you will spend the rest of your days looking over your shoulder. You will never be free, you or your boy. Only I can make you free." He rolled onto his belly and pressed up on his forearms.

Suddenly a giant pink hand shot forward. Eldon fired the steel revolver but couldn't stop the appendage. The huge hand clamped around his throat, and he fell backward off the footstool into the water.

He choked as water shot up his nose, thick and sandy. When he broke the surface, the Major's hands clamped around his neck. With his one good arm he tried to pry off the thick pink fingers, but the Major drove his head underwater.

As darkness surrounded him, he thought of his son. He could see him in his new school, making new friends, wearing ready-made clothes, getting his meat from the icebox instead of the wilderness. He thought of all that coming to an abrupt end the day the Major graced his doorstep. And all would be for naught. The line of hurt would continue, extending from the past through the present, poisoning the future.

His heart slammed madly into his chest. And with it came three decades of wrath, a surge of power so great that he pried the giant pink hand from his throat as if it belonged to a child. His head broke the surface, mud spraying from his mouth and nose.

The Major lay on his belly in the doorway. With a great cry, Eldon smashed his forehead into the Major's nose. He did it again. And again. Blow after blow he felt the wrath of all who had died under the Major's reign shooting from the top of his head. Taking a fistful of hair, he plunged the man's vile head under the water.

The giant thrashed like a hooked fish, throwing up great hazel waves. With one immovable arm, Eldon held him under, just as Daddy had once done to him. Now it was his ropy fingers around that bloated neck.

He was the judge now, delivering punishment and death.

Bubbles rumbled up around the Major's head, great exploding domes at first, then smaller ones, until there was nothing coming from his lips. Eldon dragged the big green body into the current and set it adrift, watching it bob face-down among the expanding circles made by the rain.

Wind cut through Eldon's clothes and he dragged himself into the coach. As he lay there, shivering and bleeding, his eyes roamed over the orange-walled interior. At the back was a curtained bed one might find in the compartment of a private railcar. The curtains were open. Suspended above the bed was a mobile of sorts. Twenty or so tintypes dangled from strings. The kind of thing one might hang over a baby's crib. He pulled himself up on the bed and yanked the mobile down. The images were silvery and dark, of young girls' faces and bodies, naked and afraid. Some were still being ravaged, crying or blank-eyed.

He was about to throw it into the raging waters when he saw a familiar face. Minn looked younger, but even then revolt was in her eyes. He lay down across the bed and reached in his pocket, praying it was still there. He felt the leather binds and pulpy edges, and the jagged hole in its center. He held the waterlogged journal to his chest along with the tintype, ready to let the darkness roll over him.

The coach began to tremble so violently that Eldon's teeth rattled. He lifted his head as a gust of wind blew through the door. The coach lurched. Then it was floating, turning counterclockwise in the current. Through the open door he saw the burning house, then trees, then the neighbor's house, then he was looking up the road toward Commercial Avenue.

There was a deep rumble, like a charging locomotive. He pushed up to his elbows and stared out the door. A dark wall of water raged out of Commercial Avenue and crashed down the road. Maybe a dam had broken. Or maybe God had finally decided to wipe him off the face of the earth.

But he never really believed in God, did he?

God was for Eldon Quint.

The wave crashed around the neighboring houses, rolling right for him. He smiled because the Major was dead and Ian was safe, and because he wouldn't die curious of what killed him.

CHICAGO

FORTY-THREE

WHEN THEY STEPPED FROM THEIR TENEMENT, THE CITY WAS still yawning. Long shadows streaked the paving blocks, a summer sun glaring between the tall buildings. It was a brilliant Saturday morning, the cool air coming off the lake tempered by a breeze blowing up from the plains.

They were happy to be out of their two-room basement apartment. "Quaint" was the word Miss Yancy used to describe it, but Ian figured it was her attempt to make the moldy, overheated tenement feel more like a home. As they breathed the morning air, church bells sent waves of pigeons flapping into the sky. The smell of popcorn and bubbling chocolate and fresh cigars filled their noses while the singsong of fruit vendors and newsboys rang out from the squares.

They had been there only a few months and he was still getting used to the city. Miss Yancy would point out that its renewal—the monoliths growing taller each year—mirrored their own. He wasn't quite sure what that meant, but school had let out a week before and he was just happy to be free again.

Their Saturday morning jaunt had become a ritual. They would walk east out of the canyons toward the lake, taking a different route each time, heads upturned like explorers treading an undiscovered chasm closed in by walls of brick and granite and limestone.

As they came out of the canyons, distant whistles began to sound—hot, brazen, unnatural—and the streets steamed with that smell, that Chicago smell: rotten, piney, with an acrid stab of turpentine. He'd never smelled anything like it.

They went to cross a drawbridge, but a tugboat beat them to it and they stood watching the bridge open like two unfurling hands. Ian studied the tug as it churned up the cloudy river. He quickly pulled out his small drawing pad and a pencil. In minutes he had completed a preliminary sketch, then stood cataloging the scene so he could fill in the details later. Before he put the drawing away, he surveyed it, then looked out, then put a small mark on a distant ledge where he would put Shane. His brother was always watching.

They continued east, passing cable cars that nosed along like grumpy hedgehogs toward vast, unfinished structures. Iron beams weighed down so many carts, straining the draft horses to their limit, carrying with them the promise of infinite skyward expansion.

Their path soon met the port. A warm breeze seesawed ships' masts. There the smells became intolerable; so putrid that he didn't have the words to describe them. Shane would have had the words, though. He tried to think of what he would write. Something like "a kaleidoscope of filth so horrific that the ladies on Lake Street passed with handkerchiefs over their noses."

Just beyond the fish-spoiled deckhouses, the port gave way to rolling green grass. They walked under the shade of trees, past the painted flowers and windswept elms. He was never more homesick than when he was here.

The city could be a splendid place when at sunset the riverfront was crowded with ships, the grass dotted with leisure-seekers, the great buildings translucent in the light. But the sun would fall, the sky would darken, and thoughts of Shane and Pa and Momma and Uncle Clayton would fill his head.

On those hot nights, Miss Yancy would do what she could to lift his spirits, reading to him or taking him for long walks to get peanuts or ice cream. He tried to fight the gloom, as much for her as for himself, but the harder he struggled, the tighter it twisted into him. On such days, the city's inhabitants, once jolly and industrious, turned queer and crooked, and the neighborhood where they had settled became a jumble of hot bricks and gas-vomiting chimneys, spiked railings, and hideous stretches of broken stone and cracked mortar. A far cry from the beauty of his old home. On those days he would reach for the carnelian ring that hung from a cord around his neck.

Miss Yancy had her bad days too. She tried to hide it, but he knew. When they first arrived, she hoped to be a teacher but was informed that she did not possess the proper certificates, and it would be a year or more of training to earn them. She could have easily subsisted on the money his father had given her, but she refused to spend any more than was absolutely necessary. That money, she told him, was meant for his education.

They ate soup six nights a week and shopped the bargain stores for secondhand clothing. Miss Yancy found work as a scrub girl in one of the tallest office buildings in the city, cleaning up after the one thousand souls who inhabited that colossal tower of marble and brass. She would come home beaten and weary, her head knotted with the pains of the day. Yet she would always read him a story, and he would always hug her and tell her how much he loved her.

A month into her tenure as a scrub girl, she caught the eye of an older man who ran a cold-storage business. He was dignified, and he had been kind to her without asking something in return. He'd seen her reading before her shift and they'd struck up a conversation about her book. A week later she traded backbreaking toil for the relaxed drudgery of record keeping. The pay was better, and she would come home half as tired as before, yet Ian could tell that she was not happy.

As they sat reading one night, he asked if she would ever marry. Self-consciously placing a hand on her belly, she said that she didn't want to. She didn't say anything else, but he knew she was thinking that she might have to.

During suppertime one evening, the nephew of Miss Yancy's employer called unannounced. In the doorway he sunk to a knee and proposed marriage. Ian watched from behind the bedroom door. The man was a big, blundering wag. With all his sweating and swaying, Ian figured he was drunk.

Minn spoke calmly. "I am going to confess something, Gordon," she said. "I hate to keep house, I despise cooking, and I'm an utter failure between the sheets. And, of course, there is this."

She pressed the loose fabric of her dress flat against her belly. His watery eyes ran down her body, but either he didn't care or was too drunk to realize she was five months pregnant. When he shuffled into the apartment, Minn ordered him to leave and threatened to cry for help and tell his uncle.

He was so drunk that he kept coming at her. Ian ran to the closet, took up the floorboard, and got Pa's Model 3. When he walked out of the bedroom, the oaf laughed at him. Ian put a bullet an inch from his boot. Then he pointed the barrel to the man's groin and promised he would not miss again.

That was the last they saw of Gordon. Miss Yancy's employer never spoke a word of the incident and she kept her job. But the fact remained that in a tower of one thousand dogs, there would be more Gordons to contend with. Though that wouldn't even matter in a month or two when she could no longer hide the pregnancy.

But on that fine Saturday morning, as they walked along the lake wall, they left their troubles behind. They strolled north to the sculpture park and folded in with the nameless multitudes, admiring the statues and heavy busts. After a lunch of mutton sandwiches, they were tired and headed home for a nap. Too drowsy to walk, they caught a crowded streetcar at Adams and Wabash and sat arm in arm on the bench, heads tilted inward, resting their eyes.

When they got back to the apartment, they washed off the city smell in the sink. Ian was still amazed that with the twist of a handle, all the water in the world was at their mercy. No thawing the pump or lugging buckets up from the well. Miss Yancy would always make him wait a few moments before putting his hands under the faucet. Something about watching out for minnows, though he had yet to see any.

Ian's sketches covered the walls. There was one of a truck laden with sheet iron; one of a junk cart; one of a pair of old hands grasping a pair of reins; one of a woman chasing her hat down Lake Shore Drive; one of a rabid cur snapping at a streetcar.

In each drawing, a skinny adolescent figure appeared in the background. Shane was with him everywhere he went.

In the wind and the sunlight and the grass. In some pictures, he drew his brother as a distant observer. In others, Shane was the subject, proudly hauling a deer through the gates of their farm or sitting at the table, curled over his journal.

After they washed up, they went to the back room for their nap. It was stuffy and the family of Germans who lived above them were stomping around as usual. There were nine of them in an apartment only slightly larger than their own.

It seemed like an hour had passed before Ian began to doze off. A distant clap sounded. He ignored it. But there it was again. A hard rapping sound. He sat up and hung his feet over the edge of the bed, then looked back.

Miss Yancy was sleeping peacefully and he couldn't stand to wake her. But what if it was Gordon again? He looked at the small closet at the foot of the bed, where under the floor-boards he kept the pistol. But it was only midafternoon and he figured it would be uncivilized to answer the door with a weapon. He pulled on a pair of stained pants and a cotton shirt and a pair of shoes, then crept into the front room, shutting the door behind him. He looked past the cast-iron stove and rusty icebox to the front door. The only window in the room, a transom above the frame, was too high to be of any use in revealing the identity of the caller.

There was another knock, not demanding or impatient, but insistent. The floor was rough and splintered. He pulled on his boots, then crossed to the door.

"Who is it?" he said.

A gruff voice replied. He thought he recognized it, but it was muddled by the street noise and the nine pairs of feet stomping overhead.

He slid the door chain into place, then wrenched the stubborn bolt until it clicked. He pulled the door open a crack, stopping just before the chain went taut.

Sunlight burned his eyes and he could only make out the man's silhouette.

With his left hand, the backlit man reached up and removed his wide-brimmed hat and wedged it between his right arm, which hung stiff and crooked against his body like a dead limb. He had a beard and tangled hair and wore a long coat. He straightened up as if to properly present himself, though his face was shadowed.

Ian's chest fluttered. He slid the chain loose, then opened the door and stepped back into the room, making space for the man to come fully into existence. Blinding light poured in as the man moved carefully through the doorway, hobbled by some dull, constant pain.

He smelled of roots and grass, and something sharper, like the stuff his uncle used to drink. His face was dark and dusted with a kind of dirt that had no business in Chicago. His eyes grew soft and he smiled behind the beard. It was the kind of smile his father made to show he was proud of him. Or was it the forced grin his uncle made when he was trying not to look sad?

The man's face was still lost in the glare. The boy reached for the carnelian ring around his neck, hoping a few strokes might bring him into focus. As his thumb brushed the gemstone, the man stepped closer, moving softly like his father, yet with an assuredness that belonged more to his uncle.

The man lifted his arm and placed a rough-knuckled hand on Ian's shoulder. He spoke the boy's name, his voice hoarse and clipped, yet with a hint of rakish singsong.

It shocked the boy that he couldn't tell which man it was. For a moment he wondered if there were really two of them, or if all along they had been one.

AUTHOR'S NOTE

WHEN I BEGAN WORK ON THIS STORY, I WAS APPROACH-
ing forty and my screenwriting career was going nowhere.
My wife and I were trying for our first child, and a sinking
feeling, that this could be my last chance to "make it" as a
writer, had taken hold.

One day my wife suggested I write my new story as a
book. I thought she was giving up on me; what did I know
about writing a book? It was a fool's errand. So I forged
stubbornly ahead with my screenplay. Then my wife became
pregnant, and that sinking feeling became blind terror. If I
didn't succeed now, I probably never would, and my child
would come to see me as a failure. I vowed to give myself one
last shot, then it would be time to move on.

Over the months that followed, I wrote and researched
and eventually caught the eye of a publisher. With the help
of talented editors, I had something that resembled a book,
though its heart had yet to beat. Then, two years into the
process, my son was born.

On his way out, Leon "Leo" Hyun-Soo Pletts aspirated
meconium—quite literally eating his own shit—and within
seconds a respiratory therapist was ramming tubes down
his throat, sucking vials of gray-brown liquid from his lungs.
Before my wife could even hold him, Leo was rushed to the
neonatal intensive care unit (the NICU). But he was strong.

And for three days we watched him grow stronger. They told us he would be home in a week. Then, abruptly, the doctors transferred him to the Children's Hospital Los Angeles (CHLA).

My wife rode in the ambulance with Leo while I drove our car. We were going from one end of Los Angeles to the other at five p.m. on a Friday, and the thirteen-mile trip would take over an hour. I just assumed the ambulance would turn on its sirens and cut that time in half, so I drove like I was in an ambulance too: flashing my headlights, riding up on the curb, standing on the horn. Thirty minutes later, I arrived at CHLA and called my wife to see what room they were in. She told me they hadn't used the sirens and were still ten miles away.

Over the next twenty-four hours, we learned that Leo had bleeding in his brain. After a battery of tests, the doctors still couldn't figure out why. He stabilized over the next week, then we got some hopeful news: after another round of antibiotics, we should be able to take our son home. But a few days before Leo was set to be discharged, his infectious disease doctor delivered some bad news: Leo had tested positive for bacterial meningitis.

The neurosurgeon then explained that because of the meningitis and the brain bleed, Leo had developed a serious condition called hydrocephalus. His head was rapidly swelling due to spinal fluid backing up inside his brain. To stop the swelling, the neurosurgeon wanted to insert a brain shunt (a valve that drains excess spinal fluid from the ventricles). We were assured this was a common procedure, though not without risks, and it was something Leo would have to live with for the rest of his life. We asked if there was a chance that the swelling would resolve itself. The neurosurgeon shook his head. He wouldn't allow us to wait more than the weekend to move forward with the surgery.

We were in shock. How had we gone from antibiotics to brain surgery? But we reminded ourselves that even though one bad thing kept leading to a worse thing, we had to remain hopeful. So we waited the weekend to see if Leo's brain would stop swelling on its own. On Monday morning, Leo went for his MRI. It took two long hours to get the results. When the doctors came to give us the prognosis, they were smiling—against all odds, Leo's brain had stopped swelling. His pediatrician still calls him "miracle baby."

Over the five weeks I spent in the NICU with Leo, I was never able to speak my deepest fear aloud: that I might lose him. Instead I worked obsessively on this book. Maybe it was a means of escape, maybe it was the only way I knew how to get through the scariest time of my life. In the end, I poured my fears into Eldon, and that allowed me to be hopeful for my son.

To Leo: You were with me every step of the way, from Dakota to Springfield. May we always be able to share our regrets, our fears, and our pain with each other. One day when you have children, I hope you will do the same with them.

ACKNOWLEDGMENTS

THIS BOOK WOULDN'T HAVE BEEN POSSIBLE WITHOUT THE support and encouragement of my wife—I love you.

I have four parents. Each one has taught me something invaluable along the way. They never stopped believing in me. For that I am eternally grateful.

My wife's parents, Andrew and Judy Kwon, presold more copies of this book than anyone. They wrangled friends, neighbors, golf buddies, distant family members, cruise ship passengers, and total strangers. It meant so much to me.

This book began as a screenplay, and that screenplay was nurtured by the generous and talented people at CineStory, as well as the dedicated writers and actors of Lab Twenty6.

To the 347 people who supported me and have waited nearly four years for this book—I hope I've done you proud.

Matt Harry and Barnaby Conrad: you made this a far better story, and you made me a far better writer.

Avalon Radys, thank you for your insight and your exceeding patience with this project.

Marjorie DeLuca and Christopher Huang, your notes on not one but two drafts of this manuscript were invaluable—cheers.

Kaitlin Severini, thank you for copyediting through tears.

Richard Bernstein, you came through in the clutch. Alex Rosen, you gave me a much needed boost of confidence. Christopher Adler graciously served as my twin consultant.

Phil Sciranka, George Pollack, and Terry Meginniss, thank you for one last kick in the behind.

Thank you to Dr. Michele L. Simms-Burton for teaching me the "one hundred books rule."

Thank you to fellow authors Noah Broyles, Benjamin Gray, and Evan Graham for your time and insight.

Finally, Adam, you pushed me to the edge and beyond, and became a true creative soul mate along the way—"Brilliant!"

GRAND PATRONS

Catherine Ballan
Elsie Choi
Gregory Herman
Kelli Shaughnessy
Kraig Amador
Peter Osei Mensah
Ryan Koo
Shoot Good Films Inc.

INKSHARES

INKSHARES is a reader-driven publisher and producer based in Oakland, California. Our books are selected not by a group of editors, but by readers worldwide.

While we've published books by established writers like *Big Fish* author Daniel Wallace and *Star Wars: Rogue One* scribe Gary Whitta, our aim remains surfacing and developing the new author voices of tomorrow.

Previously unknown Inkshares authors have received starred reviews and been featured in the *New York Times*. Their books are on the front tables of Barnes & Noble and hundreds of independents nationwide, and many have been licensed by publishers in other major markets. They are also being adapted by Oscar-winning screenwriters at the biggest studios and networks.

Interested in making your own story a reality? Visit Inkshares.com to start your own project or find other great books.